Shadow Beast

LUKE PHILLIPS

For my Catherine

ACKNOWLEDGMENTS

This book would not have been possible without the kind support and help of a great deal of people, all of whom I am going to try and mention. Firstly, my gratitude must be expressed to those who contributed to the contents of the book directly.

Major thanks must go to Richard and Dani of Valle Walkley, whose talent is displayed in the wonderful cover art of the book. It looks fantastic.

Pete and Liz Harwood, thank you for your advice on human anatomy and climbing, as well as the brain storming session that helped shape a great chapter.

Without the technical and helpful advice of Dr Rachel Bennett at the Royal Veterinary College in Cambridge, parts of this book would have never made sense and the same also goes for Professor Stephen J. O'Brien, who helped unravel Xenosmilus' DNA for me.

Thanks also to my first-time round editors Abigail, Maria and Robin. The story has come a long way with your guiding help at the beginning. To Lucy Ridout, my second-time round editor, I owe the greatest thanks for her patience, understanding and insight that helped bring Shadow Beast to the place I always wanted it to be.

There are those who took care of me in my time outs as well – my friend Rosie Marr for the many dips into her pocket for nights out, incredible curries and a hospitable shoulder to moan on.

To my family huge thanks must also go, who put up with late night proof reading and general disturbance, research trips at the drop of a hat, a general lack of money from me - and a huge amount of patience from them. For everything from saving Sunday lunch to use of the car, my heartfelt thanks.

Pretty much everyone in my group of friends have all at some point dipped into their pocket, encouraged, supported and generally helped me reach the end of Shadow Beast, and if I haven't mentioned you by name then please accept these last few words as genuine, albeit anonymous everlasting thanks to a lot of special people.

A WORD ON ANTHROPOMORPHISM

Anthropomorphism is the attribution of human form or other characteristics to anything other than a human being. There is a long tradition of using anthropomorphism as a literary device in storytelling and art, and most cultures include anthropomorphic fables in some way. Some of my favourite stories such as Watership Down, Tarka the Otter and the works of Jack London and Ernest Seton Thompson are unashamedly anthropomorphic.

I have spent a large portion of my life as a naturalist and studied as a zoologist. It is only very recently that we have begun to look inside the minds of the animals around us in any great detail, and what we are finding is stretching our understanding of their cognitive abilities beyond our imagination. In the case of many higher mammals such as whales, dolphins, great apes, elephants, dogs and cats, we have discovered they have similar pleasure centres to our own, and are therefore capable of enjoying all kinds of sensations from taste to simple play. We know they also have long term memory cells that are as good as ours, or even better in many ways. We have discovered that their sense of emotional bonding and social interaction is in some cases thousands of times stronger. Whales and dolphins have even developed an extra part of the brain to cope with this.

It is quite likely that the animal thought process is very

different from ours and based on far more powerful senses. Scent is the likely overwhelming factor for cats and dogs for instance, and visual reference and memory will almost certainly play a part. Language is almost certainly used by whales, dolphins and some of the great apes. This is a world we are just beginning to explore and whilst we do not know how an animal thinks or how it might experience emotion, it is becoming clear that they are certainly capable of doing so. Ravens, black bears and mountain lions have all proven themselves impressive problem solvers and capable of planning. This alone revolutionises how we should think about the animal mind. It is only human arrogance that concludes animals are not capable of cognitive processes or emotional responses.

In The Tiger: A True Story of Vengeance & Survival, John Vaillant tells of an Amur tiger that waited for three days outside a poacher's cabin, slowly disappearing beneath the falling snow as it anticipated the return of the man who had killed its mate and cubs. After killing him, his dogs and pulling apart the cabin, it tracked the man by scent back to a toilet he had used on a construction site and destroyed that too. If that isn't vengeance, I don't know what is. It is suspected that elephants that have witnessed the violent deaths of parents as calves can have these painful memories triggered by the loud noises and flashing images that accompany their performances in circuses, resulting in the death of at least one animal handler in the U.S. More happily, Christian, the famous lion from Harrods exhibited nothing but unbridled joy when reunited with his former owners in the wild. Shirley and Jenny were two Indian elephants that had been separated for over 25 years before being reunited in a Tennessee sanctuary, and were so desperate to get close again they bent the bars of the gate between them in order to touch.

The animals in Shadow Beast do experience emotions and to a certain extent, there is some poetic license taken in this, but it is based as much on science as it is on conjecture, and I hope you can forgive me for expressing in this way where I thought it necessary, and I hope you enjoy the story regardless of who's perspective is telling the tale!

"There is no fundamental difference between man and animals in their ability to feel pleasure and pain, happiness and misery."

Charles Darwin

CHAPTER ONE

The creature stopped in the last reach of the shadows of the tall pines and dropped to the ground. It watched the group of stags charge from the tree line a hundred yards down, driven in a state of panic and changing direction instinctively as they went. Their feet pounded the earth and sent trickles of stone and mud sliding down the steep slope as they moved across it. It felt the vibrations under its feet and sensed the urgency with which they moved. The deer kicked their feet high to avoid the strewn boulders and scrub of the mountainside. It watched as their eyes darted back to the darkness beneath the trees to search for their pursuer. Their nostrils frothed in exhaustion, but as they stopped to snatch a few life-giving breaths, the leader of the group let out a strained bellow as he expelled the air from his lungs and continued on. The creature licked its nose as the wind brought the sticky sweet must of the animals towards it. A wave of static energy rippled along its back and across its shoulders like wind on water. It had flanked them without being seen and now lay motionless, its black hide blending into the darkness behind the thick gorse bank where it had slunk down onto the earth. Dawn was approaching and the night was retreating to the west.

It watched still, taking deep slow breaths that inflated its lungs to full capacity, the oxygen rich mountain air the fuel for the coming charge. Its paws rested on soft, dew drenched earth and budding heather that would silence the heaviest of footfalls. It waited, panting soundlessly as its silver whiskers warned it of micro-changes to the direction of the wind and air pressure, as the distance between it and its prey narrowed. It allowed a twitch of frustration to flick through its tail as the deer changed course again and headed down the hill, instead of towards it and the tree line. It rose slightly and continued its journey along the knotted and twisted branches of the thickly entwined gorse. Not in flower yet, the bank provided a dark and dense veil of branches to hide behind. Its movement was snakelike, its head naturally rising and falling as it followed the cover and the deer, its pelvic and shoulder muscles pumping together as it accelerated and slowed to match the pace of its prey. At the end of the gorse bank it came to the welcome shadow of trees again and disappeared within their darkness. Here it moved more cautiously, walking on stones and roots or flicking away the dry branches that lay in its path. Then it paused.

The sweaty, ripening must of the deer was intoxicating now and it knew they were close, even though it could not yet see them. Ahead of the creature was a small earthy bank that marked the boundary of the wood it had entered. This led to a sparse, grassy knoll that bordered a long, straight river of stone along the valley. It knew that rather than cross the stone river, the deer were more likely to hesitate and turn back to the trees with the coming dawn. It crept towards an opening on the bank between an oak and a pine, their intertwined boughs locked in a centuries-old battle for the light that formed a natural arch. The bank was steep and the creature paused, calculating its approach. It slunk down onto its belly and used the exposed roots of the oak as a stairway up the bank. It hunkered down, coiling its hindquarters beneath it and stretching its neck and head forward. Its whiskers bristled as they sensed the changes in air pressure and the breeze moved round the animal coming towards it. From the shadows it watched as the stag approached closer and it once again licked its nose and muzzle in anticipation. It repositioned itself slightly forward for better purchase and inhaled one last time. Silence fell upon the wood. The stag was stung by the sudden quiet and snapped to attention as it peered towards the darkness. The creature saw its moment and burst from the shadows, barrelling forwards in a furious and fluid sprint that silently engulfed the ground between it and the leader of the herd. In its final bound, it launched into a headlong leap, claws outstretched for a murderous embrace as it let out the thunderous roar that had built in its chest.

In a microsecond, the creature knew its initial attack would fail. It had leapt too soon and too high to hit from the side as expected. It collided with the stag head on and gravity and the slope of the knoll did the rest, as both it and its prey tumbled backwards in roars and bellows of displeasure and panic. Instinct took over and it slashed upwards with its right paw as it slithered backwards in the wet grass, losing the poor purchase it had momentarily gained on the stag. It lunged forward again, hissing in anger as it glanced at the other stags that had bolted in fright back up the hillside, but now stood motionless, waiting for the great play yet to come.

The stag lowered its head, thrusting its antlers towards the creature. It kicked up the ground with its back legs and grunted through its nose in aggressive defiance. Its body began to shake as the deep cut on its chest began to seep. The creature uttered a purr-like, rumbling growl as it padded forward. The stag reared back in panic but then brought its antlers down towards its attacker again, but the creature was too swift for it. It batted the stag's head sideways with a clip of its paw and dashed forward to meet the exposed throat, opening its maw and biting down into the flesh. As it felt the taught skin puncture in its vice-like grip and its throat was stung by hot air and bubbling blood, the creature savagely snapped its head sideways, throwing the stag to the ground. Its claws raked downwards through the stag's neck and shoulder like iron pins. It calmly watched the other deer flee in panic towards the trees, never releasing its hold on the stag, even as it bucked in final futile spasms against death. It saw its own green eye reflected in the amber one beneath it and watched ever patient as the last life-spark went out. As the body beneath it slumped, the creature relaxed its hold and began to feed.

CHAPTER TWO

The sounds of a Scottish Highland morning were whispering against the dew-frosted windows of the house. On an ancient battleground to the east, fresh combatants gathered and sounded off to each other. Black cock grouse strutted out of the mist and onto their lekking mounds at the very first stirrings of dawn. They proved their worth to the watching grey hens in rumbling song and skirmish before departing back to the trees and mist from which they came. A singular lofty cry of a golden eagle carried on the wind as it descended upon a fresh deer carcass below. Further along the valley the warning bellows of a red stag sounded along the mountainside and the sharp, piercing cry of a vixen echoed through the woodland close to the house.

As the vixen cried again, Thomas's eyes opened and the lingering discomfort of a troubled sleep began to fade. The grey cotton t-shirt clung to his back in a cold glue of sweat. His head ached a little and he felt dizzy as he threw aside the bed covers and lumbered over to the window. The curtains were still half pulled as he had left them the night before, and he thrust them aside. He liked how the old glass seemed to stream downwards and thicken at the base of each pane. He caught his reflection and noticed how his thick, dark hair and pale blue eyes seemed more washed out than usual against the frosty background. The weathered grey and white paintwork of the casings surrounding the windows suited the house, and more often than not matched the weather too. The village of Cannich was situated five miles away and the nearest big town, Inverness was some twenty miles further. Here in the heart of the Highlands and nestled between the Mullardoch Mountains and Cannich Forest, Thomas had first appreciated the old farm for its remoteness. But now more than ever, he was drawn to its beauty.

From the bedroom window he looked straight down the valley. It was surrounded on three sides by Munros, the 3,000-feet-high peaks that Scotland was so famous for, and ten of which formed the walls of Mullardoch as they were locally known. He could see the snow-capped tops of six from where he stood. To the west and stretching nearly ten miles in the same direction was Cannich Forest, ancient Caledonian woodland. Thomas considered taking a morning stroll whilst he still had the chance. In the last few days he had heard the guttural clucking call of the horse of the woods, a rogue male capercallie that seemed to be without a mate and therefore happy to vent his testosterone on anything else coming into his territory. He knew it might give him an opportunity for some good quality photographs of the large rare grouse, but once the breeding season started, he would have to give it a wide berth for both its and his own protection.

To the east was Loch Mullardoch and he could make the shore from the house and even walk to work if he felt so inclined, although there was no official path and the terrain was hard going in places. Out of sight lay the great Mullardoch Dam, something for which he was glad, as the natural architecture surrounding him was much more to his preference. In fact, the house and its setting were perfect for him, which had led to him naming it Sàsadh, Gaelic for a place of comfort and contentment.

He had bought Sàsadh a little over eighteen months ago. Originally a deer farm, he had made taking the fences down his first priority. The animals were still culled annually, but he had never been a livestock farmer. He wondered if the forests would ever sound again to the call of predators long since gone such as the wolf, bear and lynx. As a conservationist it was one of the many things he was involved in the campaign for, to see the return of predators and the revival of a more balanced ecosystem. He had once heard a lecture at Yellowstone where a ranger had referred to the newly reintroduced wolves as the painters of mountains. The return of the wolf had seen the deer lose their dominance on the landscape. They became naturally more skittish and lost their boldness. They returned to a more natural lifestyle, feeding at dusk and dawn instead of all day, and retreating to high ground more often. In their absence, flower meadows returned, saplings began their skyward search for the sun and the landscape flourished. In the Highlands, no wolves roamed, and the mountains and moors were poorer for it in his opinion.

He had grown up not far from here in Drumnadrochit, a village on the shores of Loch Ness just over ten miles further to the east. Buying the dilapidated farmhouse had marked his return to Scotland, and the final chapter in a journey that had taken him half a world away. Working with the wood that became the new doors, windows and floors of Sàsadh had stirred fond memories of his childhood. His father's bespoke carpentry business and workshop had sat on the northern side of the bridge over the Enrick River. Although it was now a bed and breakfast enterprise, the nessie climbing frame his father had built for him and his sister still stood in the garden. The pirate ship he had pushed through the warm wood shavings on the workshop floor, as if they were waves, was now moored snugly in a porthole window in the bathroom. The wood burner in the living room was almost identical to the one his father had used to heat the cold shop.

Thomas had shared the renovation of Sàsadh in e-mails, pictures and videos with his father. The mutual acknowledgement and joy of their shared tastes and sense of perfection was left unspoken in the scattered mementos. A year had passed. It was now home. The warm cedar timber had mellowed and softened. The granite and slate exterior had weathered and lost its new-looking shine. It managed to feel refreshed and comfortably old at the same time, something he could identify with.

As these familiar sights and sounds that signified home to Thomas filled the voids left by the restlessness from the night before, he felt further awakened and soothed as the glow in the east brightened and the day dawned. He showered, made himself shave and dressed in dark brown corduroy jeans, a comfortable, tailored khaki shirt and a thick black woollen sweater. Last as always, he slipped on the leather strap of the Rolex Cosmograph Daytona watch and glanced at the slate coloured dial to check the time. He made his way down the staircase that led to the kitchen. On the other side of the door at the bottom, he heard the unmistakable sound of scrabbling feet on the stone floor beyond, and he grabbed the handle and swung the door open quickly. Meg froze in her tracks, knowing she had been caught red handed. The blanket from her bed was between her teeth. It had been the same for the last three nights. Each morning he had come down to find she had moved her bed from the back door to the far side of the kitchen. The first night it had happened, he had even heard her growl, which was something she never did. He had considered that she might have been asleep. He couldn't help but wonder if she too was tormented by nightmares.

Meg was a pedigree border collie, born from working stock. Thomas had picked her at first for her unusual yet beautiful chocolate, white and grey merle markings, but her bright personality, keen intelligence and uncanny ability to track had soon become virtues he wouldn't be parted with. Coming home to the Highlands had signalled their retirement from a life he no longer wanted, and she was no longer capable of. In his opinion, she had coped far better than he had since. He knelt down as he stroked her head, looking into her eyes

"We're gonna have to sort this out you know," he sighed.

Thomas smiled as Meg looked away sheepishly, then back up at him with an energetic thumping of her tail against the floor. They both needed the distraction of breakfast. Thomas opened the cream coloured door to the retro-style fridge and stared longingly in at the contents. Over some years, and through a lifestyle of normally waking early with the wisps of a hangover on an uncomfortable camp bed, Thomas had developed the need for a protein rich breakfast. He scrambled some eggs in a pan and dropped some mushrooms and two thick slices of bacon beside them. Most breakfasts in the Kenyan bush had also started with cold lager when available, but today orange juice would suffice. There were definitely aspects of that life he missed. Most of those aspects were the people and how they had made him feel. His smile faded as he considered it may have just been one person all along.

Meg was duly served a can of canine finest, but she looked longingly at Thomas's plate before accepting her loss and settling down to eat. Both of the kitchen's inhabitants finished their breakfast in silent satisfaction and contemplated each other.

"Come on then," declared Thomas.

He was answered by a short bark from Meg, who jumped to her feet. They went into the hall and Thomas sat down on the stairs. He pulled on his leather walking boots and grabbed the thick Barbour waxed jacket from the rack. The tartan and corduroy lining would protect him from the wind and the waxy outer would keep out the rain. As he opened the front door, he was greeted by an icy blast of wind. He looked towards the snow covered peak of Sgurr Na Lapaich from where it undoubtedly came. The frost coated air seemed to clasp at his exposed face and he shivered unexpectedly. It made him feel uneasy, and he turned away from the malevolent bite of the polar storm he sensed was gathering in the peaks.

There was no need to lock the door, being so remote. Not many knew how to find the tiny lane that led to Sàsadh and even fewer knew the way to it from there. Most of those who did, he was on first name terms with. He pocketed the keys and took a few steps towards the trail that led to the woods. Meg didn't move, and when he looked back to her, he noticed she was staring intently at the nearside brow of the hill in the direction of the road. He shielded his eyes from the low-hitting rays of the winter sun to find what was holding her attention. The small group of red stags moved in graceful bounds and as he focused on them, he picked up the rumble of hooves as they raced across the hillside and disappeared over the ridge. He could see the urgency and resolve in their movement as they swept upwards and rounded the hill, just like a flock of birds evading a hawk. His curiosity was aroused. The deer would usually be at rest by now, taking shelter in the trees further up the mountainside and out of sight of people. He idled for a moment, wondering what might have spooked them, but could see nothing else.

He turned and began to make his way towards the woods. The anxious whining from behind made him stop and turn. Part of him had hoped it wouldn't happen this morning as the weather had improved, but Meg was not budging. He knew he would not be able to get her to follow him into the trees, and it didn't seem fair to drag her along.

"Fine" he shrugged, "we'd have probably only ended up being late anyway".

As soon as he started walking towards the converted stable block that now served as a garage, Meg yelped in triumph and trotted alongside him, getting under his feet where she could and barking with pleasure. He clicked the remote in his pocket and the large wooden double-doors began to swing outward. From inside, the contrasting slate grey and metallic black Overfinch Defender short-wheelbase stared out at them. He had grown to love Land Rovers when he had worked in Kenya's Tsavo region and India's Sundarbans, where they were a way of life. Although he was now thousands of miles away, he didn't feel comfortable behind the wheel of anything else. He still needed something with all-wheel drive given his work and the location. Other cars made him feel claustrophobic and he could afford a little luxury and performance now, something he had always appreciated. He opened up the back and let Meg scramble up in the undignified manner only a three-legged dog could manage, with a slight helping hand as he lifted her back end up for her. She looked round at him as if to suggest she could have managed, and then gave a short bark of triumph as she sat down between the cherry and chocolate coloured leather-clad sports seats of the rear compartment. Thomas smiled at her and ruffled the fur on the top of her head, then climbed into the driver's seat.

It was still early and not much past 7:30. The sun still hadn't quite cleared the horizon and shone palely, slowly gathering intensity as it climbed skyward. He knew the hill farmers of Glen Cannich would have already been up for long hours before, as they attended the Highland sheep and cattle most of them specialised in. *Rather you than me* he thought smugly. The frost stung lanes seemed tight and closed in as he navigated his way through the twists and turns. The performance tuned diesel engine complained at the low revs and speed, and the hands of the old-fashioned analogue clock on the dashboard sat at 8'o'Clock by the time the familiar outline of the Highland Wildlife Research Centre appeared on the horizon. The whitewashed walls stood out against the stark background of Càrn Eige in the distance, and the centre represented the closest you could get to the vast mountain by road. Another six miles lay between there and the peak.

As he pulled into the small car park to the side of the

centre, he noticed the white van sporting the blue logo of the Scottish Society for the Prevention of Cruelty to Animals, parked in one of the bays. Thomas wondered what was waiting for him inside. He got out of the car and kept the door open for Meg to drop down to the ground. He walked straight up to the double doors of the entrance and opened them wide. Meg bounded through, barking excitedly as Catherine – the Centre's owner and Thomas's boss – leant down to greet her with a stroke of the head.

"Morning," she said, seeming in good spirits and smiling at Thomas.

"Morning it is," he replied, smiling himself whilst scrutinizing her for any clue as to what was lurking in the examination room she'd just come from.

Catherine always dressed more casually than he did, sporting jeans and a fleece top. She tended to wear green, which complimented her short, dark-red hair and unusually pale, almost turquoise eyes. Thomas repeatedly told her that jeans were awful clothes to wear if they ever went out in the field, which she always took as an opportunity to remind him that fieldwork was what she had hired him for. Thomas had found working with Catherine a surprising comfort, and their relationship had very quickly blossomed into friendship. It was a different pace from what he had been used to, and the past twelve months had helped him refocus on his work again. It was almost like being able to catch your breath, and Thomas was now more than happy to let the world rush on ahead for a few years without him.

Catherine stroked Meg's head and slipped her what looked like a chocolate drop.

"Don't spoil her," Thomas said mockingly. "Anyway,

what have we got this early from the SSPCA?"

Catherine smiled. "Something you'll like, a piece of mutton."

"I always did like an older woman," he laughed, playing to the joke. "Perhaps that's where the appeal came to work with you," he added smugly, always happy to remind her that she was actually older than him, albeit only by a few days.

"Oh bless, that joke probably seems funnier every time you say it, doesn't it?" she mocked.

He smiled, then took off his jacket and walked through into the examination room.

A uniformed SSPCA officer stood behind the high table where the remains of a sheep's carcass lay strewn across it. The man looked to be somewhere in his forties Thomas guessed. He had a ruddy face and was relatively short and round, and seemed very uncomfortable.

"Royston Macintyre, SSPCA" he said in a thick Scottish accent. "Bit of an odd one for yer. The McNash farm has been losing sheep for a wee while now. They put it down to the winter, but the lack of carcasses concerned me. I've been checking ravines, streams and even the loch, then this morning I found this." He pointed to the sheep.

Thomas slipped on a pair of rubber gloves and began his examination of the sheep, starting at the head. It had been almost ripped from the rest of the body, only still attached by a few stringy tendons. There was an enormous hole in the top of the skull, which went deep into the cranial cavity. No flesh remained on the face of the sheep or around the head, just a sticky pinkish residue left in its place. Whatever had made the hole would have undoubtedly followed through into the brain, and the sheep would have died instantly.

All of the meat and fat had been stripped from the carcass and every limb, as well as the spine, had been broken. Thomas could see great pressure had been put upon the skeleton at almost every point. The exposed rib bones had been sheared off in a neat line, leaving a uniform row of stumps in their place. It had also been on the mountainside for a few days, because he could readily identify the gnawing marks on the stumps from scavengers. A fox, a stoat and even a pine marten had left tell-tale bites around the fleshy sinews, all happy to take advantage of such windfall meat in winter. Buzzards and ravens had also left their mark, all the while helping to cover the signature of the actual killer. Thomas probed further.

"Where was it when you found it?" he asked, not looking up from the carcass. "Could it have fallen? Has it been damaged in any way during transport or since you found it?"

Thomas knew this wasn't the case, as he could already see it had obviously been killed and then devoured. But he wasn't dismissing anything as wild ideas started to float around his head.

"I found it in a clearing in Cannich Forest actually, nowhere near anything that it could have fallen from, unless it had taken to tree climbing. And it's in the same way I found it," Royston replied, a little defensively and looking more and more puzzled.

Thomas stuck two of his gloved fingers into the hole in the skull, somewhat surprised that there was ample room for him to do so. Finally Thomas stood back from the table and took off his gloves, taking time to consider the thoughts now forming in his head. He threw the gloves into a waste bin nearby. Catherine came back into the room and gave the sheep a quick glance before she turned her attention on Thomas.

"So what's the verdict, Doc?" she teased.

"It's dead," was Thomas's shrewd reply, although he couldn't quite hide his smile. "Actually, it was killed and eaten, but by what would be the mystery, or certainly mysterious," he explained. "If we weren't in the Scottish Highlands, I would be pointing my finger at a serious predator and something pretty large too." He looked up, seeing that he had the attention of them both and drew in a breath before he spoke again. "For instance, the kill marks on this carcass might indicate that it was attacked by a member of the big cat family."

Catherine and Royston looked at him in surprise. Catherine was the first to break the silence with a stifled giggle. Royston in turn suddenly seemed to want nothing to do with the carcass and took a few steps back from the table.

"There are reports of big cats right up and down the UK," Thomas continued. "It's maybe not as far-fetched as it seems, and nothing else kills in the way this sheep was killed."

"So is there a mountain lion or one of these so called panthers lurking round the glen then?" Catherine asked, almost veiling the disbelief in her voice.

"Possibly," answered Thomas, throwing her a slight scowl in the process. "If the hole in the top of the skull is the entry wound of a tooth, then it's a kill highly characteristic of a big cat. I've seen jaguars and leopards kill that way."

"But that hole is enormous," objected Catherine. "Surely

it couldn't be a tooth?"

Thomas shrugged. "I admit the size of the hole is a problem, the diameter would belong to a canine tooth even larger than an African lion."

"So, what then?" she asked, scrutinising him closely.

Thomas shrugged again. "Maybe the skull was already damaged, or gave in under pressure."

She smiled at him, shaking her head slightly, and then turned and walked out of the examination room.

"So," said Royston, shuffling his feet and looking impatient to leave. "What shall I put on the report as to cause of death?"

"Predation," replied Thomas quietly.

CHAPTER THREE

Catherine punched at the keyboard of the computer without taking her eyes off the huge screen. She didn't stir or look up as Thomas entered the office, and he peered over her shoulder to see what she was doing. Satellite mapping imagery was popping up on the screen showing Glen Cannich, Loch Mullardoch and the surrounding Munros. At its northern most border, the map showed Loch Beannacharan ,then went east to the River Glass, west to Sàsadh and as far south as Loch Affric, an area of nearly thirty square miles. Catherine was working her way through a list of ciphers, typing them into the control panel of the imaging software, and Thomas suddenly realised they were GPS tracking codes.

"I thought maybe a cat recognised as a resident species might be a better place to start," Catherine declared with mocking scorn, and without looking away from the screen. "Do you remember One-Eyed Tom from when we were doing the wildcat survey?"

"God yes!" Thomas exclaimed, "I've met tigers with less attitude."

"He was a serious piece of work and he was big too. Do you think he could pull down a sheep?"

"I think he could pull down the Loch Ness Monster if given the chance, but in all honesty I don't think he could do the kind of damage we've just seen. I was thinking of something much bigger."

"I knew you were going to say that," Catherine groaned playfully "but these guys have got my attention now, and at least we know they are officially recognised as living here," she added smugly.

"Not according to that map they aren't," Thomas exclaimed, pointing at the screen.

The pulse-like error code repeated again and again as the software cycled through each of the twelve GPS ciphers Catherine had punched in, tried to acquire a signal, failed, and tried again.

"Okay, not to worry. We're a wildlife agency that just lost five percent of the population of a critically endangered species," stated Catherine, the attempt at casual flippancy failing to completely conceal the underlying stress in her voice.

"Are the tower aerials all up and connected?" Thomas asked.

"According to this we're at full strength," Catherine replied, pointing at the aerial icon on the screen, but distracted by the blank and blinking map. "There's just no way all twelve collars could have stopped working. It's like they just disappeared."

"Thinking about it," asked Thomas, "when did you last see one?"

Catherine spun her chair round to face him. Now his eyes were glued to the screen as hers had been. The corner of her mouth rose into a smirk as she read in his eyes the same intrigue and need for investigation she had felt. She turned back to the screen again and called up the data.

"Well according to this, the last registered track was ten days ago. Before that it was whilst we were still monitoring them, which is almost two months now. It's a shame the Forestry Commission didn't want to keep funding the project."

"At least we were able to keep the equipment and kept track of them," offered Thomas, detecting the frustration in her voice.

"But we didn't, did we? Where could they go? We need to get out there and check the ground, make sure it's not a software glitch or something like that," Catherine snapped, agitated.

"We will," replied Thomas casually, staring past her at the screen still.

Catherine looked round and saw from his eyes that he meant it genuinely and reassuringly, rather than the carefree response she had taken it for. *Should have known better*, she thought. She knew Thomas would readily take to the field if given the opportunity. She studied his expression for a short while.

"So what do you mean by bigger, and realise that for the moment I am humouring you rather than believing you, because I have temporarily misplaced the more likely suspects," she smiled, knowing that her taunt would do nothing to provoke him.

Thomas turned to his desk and pulled his chair across to him, turning it round so that he could sit facing Catherine. Their desk areas were arranged so that normally they would sit back to back, and away from whatever each was working on at the time. This was not necessarily for secrecy, but more for a sense of privacy. They both enjoyed being able to immerse themselves in a project and feel like they were working on their own.

"Just think about it," smiled Thomas. "Every region in the UK, every county and even cities and towns like London and Guildford have had reported sightings of big cats. Eyewitnesses are now in their thousands, and there are a number of species that could readily adapt and survive in our climate." He took Catherine's silence as an invitation to continue. "In 1976 the dangerous animals act was passed. Up until then, you could keep exotic pets without any license or restriction. You've probably heard of the lion from Harrods?"

Catherine nodded. "Didn't it end up scaring potential thieves at a scrap metal yard?"

"Nope, that was a different one," smiled Thomas. "In addition to them though, tigers and what are popularly referred to as black panthers were incredibly fashionable. I've even seen archive news footage of a woman wearing a leopard skin fur coat, whilst out walking a slightly more alive one on a lead."

"I hope it ate her, or at least the coat," Catherine exclaimed in disgust. "I can't believe that only a few years before I was born, people were keeping endangered animals as pets, or worse, wearing them."

Thomas smiled. He loved how passionate she got about the mistreatment of animals.

"Luckily, the act was passed in any case," he continued, "suddenly if you wanted to keep your grizzly bear, Bengal tiger or black leopard at home, you couldn't just let it bed down in your living room. You needed a license, secure enclosures and so forth. Rather than suffer the expense, it's reported that a large number of people simply turned their pets loose in some of the more remote parts of the country. If even a few survived to breed, then the UK would be a virtual paradise. There's abundant food, no competition from other predators and plenty of habitat."

Catherine laughed and shook her head in disbelief. Then she turned back to meet his gaze.

"So, are you implying there could be a lion out there ripping our sheep to shreds and frightening off the neighbours?" She nodded towards the computer screen showing the absent wildcats.

"It's unlikely", Thomas laughed, trying to imagine how a hiker or farmer would react coming face to face with an African lion. "Things like lions and tigers would probably have a hard time in our climate, and they aren't adaptable enough. But leopards and pumas are two of the most adaptable species of cat on Earth, incredibly robust and far more likely to establish breeding populations if they got the chance. They also just happen to be the two species most often reported, if we assume the black panthers are in fact melanistic leopards."

Thomas could see Catherine was at least taking in what he was saying. The smirk had gone from her face, although a hint of suspicion flickered in her eyes.

"So why haven't we seen more evidence. Some of the eyewitness reports have been so sketchy they might as well have been about Bigfoot,"

"Wait a minute, you don't believe in Bigfoot?!" Thomas taunted with a smile.

"This is thin ice Walker," Catherine scolded with a withering look "and I won't be coming to the rescue should you fall through." She wasn't going to let him know that she was buying into the theory, not quite yet anyway.

"For every case that's questionable, there are cases that are undeniable," Thomas continued "Remember that gamekeeper we helped prosecute down by Comar Wood?"

"Yes. I remember. You mean what was found in his freezer don't you?"

"You don't think a full grown European lynx was a slightly odd thing to find amongst the poisoned sparrowhawks and Sunday roast? He said he shot it in the woods. There were no reported escapes and it's not the only incident. Other lynx have been trapped elsewhere in the country, and there have been plenty of reported signs of larger species setting up territories too. Things like scratch marks, scat and paw prints, all of which were too big to be attributed to be any native species of cat."

"And all summarily dismissed once examined," Catherine interjected. "Everything from the Stroud deer-eater to the Beast of Bodmin and Surrey Puma have all been investigated and chalked up to mere urban legends or worse, misidentification. If they're here, we would see them sooner or later, no matter how infrequently."

She picked up a biro from the desk and began to turn it over in her fingers in frustration.

Thomas paused and sighed. He could see she needed something a little more conclusive.

"You could walk right up to a big cat. You could be inches from it and you'd have no idea it was there. Every one of its senses would be focused on you, every muscle tuned for fight or flight whilst it made up its mind what to do with you. They are ambush hunters. You wouldn't know it was there until it wanted you to. I'm not saying it's likely, but for now it seems to me it's the only explanation that fits the evidence. Something tore that sheep apart, feasted on it and cracked the ribs open to suck out the marrow. It wasn't a fox. It wasn't a dog and it wasn't a wildcat, it was something big and powerful..."

"I get it," Catherine exclaimed, "I just don't like it."

She narrowed her eyes as she scanned Thomas's face for any trace of the smile she suspected, or at least hoped would follow. As he sat back in his chair she realised he was utterly serious. A shiver ran down her back as she contemplated the idea of a big cat concealed in the undergrowth, invisible and biding its time until just the right opportunity walked past.

"Okay," she sighed, "let's say for now that we do have ourselves some kind of big cat. The implications of tracking it, catching it and proving it's here are huge. What are we going to do about it?"

"Our first job should be one of elimination," replied Thomas. "We need to put in the research and make sure it couldn't be anything else. We'll have to check reports for escapes, do the usual rounds and so on. Why don't we start this afternoon?"

It was only then he realised what he was saying. He would be hunting big cats again.

CHAPTER FOUR

Joshua Felton sat in his highchair, lifting his beaker and smashing it down onto the chair's tray, managing to get his mother's attention in the process. Janet turned round and smiled at him with mock annoyance, recognising from his expression that he knew full well what he was doing.

"It will be ready in a minute Josh," she cooed "and you won't have any drink left at that rate."

Joshua chuckled with insane triumph and started drumming both arms against the tray. Janet poured out the mashed carrot and leek into his plastic bowl, took a rubber spoon from the drawer and carefully placed it in front of him. As expected, his first and rather exuberant attempt to cram the entire contents of the bowl onto his spoon resulted in a quick redecoration of the floor and walls. But he soon calmed down enough to feed himself, although still rather messily. Janet cleaned whilst he ate, and then got ready for the walk into the village to get to work.

The sun was streaming in through the window and she smiled as she put the clean plates on the rack to dry. From the kitchen sink she could look out into the woods that surrounded the cottage and see the stream that led to the river, which in turn led to the village. It was a very tranquil setting, but also lonely. She missed David. His current posting on a Canadian container ship meant he was missing the little things, like Joshua learning to feed himself and play jokes on her. But Joshua was more than good enough company she reminded herself as she cleaned his bowl and spoon, especially now she was seeing more of his personality and sense of humour. He reminded her very much of David in many ways as it was. She turned round to face him to find him squirming and arching his back in an attempt to get out of the chair. He knew it was time to go and she knew he was right. He was a far better time keeper than she was, something else he had in common with David.

Janet stuffed Joshua's arms into the heavily padded hooded jacket and tied up his boots. Like a miniature Michelin man, he toddled forward in a top-heavy stagger. When he reached the buggy in the hallway, he grabbed it eagerly for stability, looking round at her and grinning as he did so. She couldn't help laughing as she lifted him up and strapped him in. She opened the door and stepped out into the crisp morning air.

The cottage was just over a mile from the village and the walk in was along the one road into Cannich itself. There were no other houses on the road, but the dense pine forest soon gave way to pastures and meadows that had been given over to farmland. Walking into the village was easy due to the slight descent, but it made for a harder return journey. Janet didn't mind too much, and told herself it kept her fit and healthy as she stepped along the road.

Soon, she became aware of a very powerful and pungent smell. She looked around and spotted the unmistakable dark orange hide of a Highland cow in the field opposite. It was lying on the ground on its side, occasionally kicking its legs up awkwardly as it rolled back and forth gently in the mud. She presumed it was trying to take a mud bath, which would probably also explain the smell. She knew the long, dense hair often got matted and tangled with mud and debris. Up close, there was no mistaking the smell of the hardy breed.

"Whew, smelly huh Josh?" Janet exclaimed. She paid it no more attention and carried on along the road. The smell faded as she walked, and soon it had disappeared altogether.

~

What couldn't be seen from the road was that the cow was dead. Under the cover of the bracken and heather surrounding it, the creature tore the stomach free of the carcass and split it with its long and powerful canine teeth. The creature savoured the nutrient rich contents and licked the blood from its muzzle. Each time it tore at the dead cow, the carcass would roll forward slightly with the momentum, giving the impression of life. Not much was left of the carcass now in terms of actual meat. The two strange animals that had passed by the creature had startled it at first. It had seen animals like them before, but had never been so close. Now it had finished feeding, it became more curious and listened to them as they travelled along the stone river that bordered the field. They moved slowly, and at first it thought the larger one was injured in some way as it stopped and started erratically. Its nose was stung by strange chemical aromas, mixed in with the overpowering, oozing, honey-like scent of the animal itself.

The field was separated from the stone river by a dry rocky wall just over four feet high. The creature padded over to the natural barrier and began to creep along it, always careful to keep its muscular outline and the wisp of its long tail below the top stones. This allowed it to remain hidden whilst its hearing and sense of smell still focused on its new quarry. It wasn't particularly hungry, but it was curious at this animal that moved strangely and clumsily, despite being relatively small. Small prey was generally fast and difficult to catch, but this animal was different. It soon realised the animal had young, as it interpreted the different scent and sounds it caught, more delicate and again wrapped in other distasteful taints. Its movement became more deliberate and urgent. Each time they stopped, it paused and slunk back into the cover. It froze when it heard a distant humming growing louder and it instinctively crept back to the bracken.

~

Janet flinched a little as the car passed. She didn't like how fast some people travelled on the lanes, but she recognised the beaten up Renault as belonging to Jimmy, the caretaker at The Castle Retirement Home where she worked. She knew they were only a few minutes away and she would give him a gentle scolding when she got in.

~

As soon as the humming grew faint, the creature emerged again from the bracken. It knew the strange animals that travelled along the stone river. It had learnt to avoid them a long time ago. It snarled a silent grimace in disgust and cleared its head of the lingering fumes by lifting its nose high into the air. It picked up the sweeter scent again and began to shadow the strange upright animal from the other side of the wall. It caught up with it effortlessly as it gamboled along the rocky path before it with ease, still hunched and hidden in the shadows.

~

Soon, The Castle Retirement Home came into view and Janet smiled, glad to be at the end of their short walk. The road was quiet now and although she knew the route and surroundings well, she had been unable to shake a feeling of unease. Perhaps it had been the strange odour from the cow or the speeding car. The Castle Retirement Home was the first building on the road after the house, and she couldn't help a quick glance over her shoulder as she lingered under the large arched gate at the entrance. There was nothing behind her but the frost laden fields and woods she had passed along the way. She smiled to herself for feeling jumpy and waved to Jimmy, who was waiting for her on the steps to the lobby, smoking a cigarette as he did.

~

The creature crept to the edge of the boundary wall and waited. Its ears pricked up and its whiskers protruded forwards as a new group of scents flowed towards it. An acrid, burning smell came to it and stung its nostrils, making it shake its head in displeasure. It recognised the more pungent scent of the male and for the first time registered the strange animal it had followed as the same species. It knew of man and had kept a distance out of instinct, but now curiosity overrode that instinct as it raised its head clear of the bracken. The cry of the young animal and its struggled movements excited it. It licked its muzzle in recognition that this was meat and it was capable of taking it. It made for a part of the wall that had collapsed and pushed its head forwards. Its whiskers flattened and bristled as it tested the width, and the creature padded through the gap in silent ease. It dropped to its belly as it brushed against the strange animal on the other side that it had seen many times travelling along the stone river. It was cold to the touch and made an alien ticking noise, but did not flee or raise the alarm to the other animals like others it encountered. The creature's curiosity again suppressed its instinct to flee. It had never been so close before, and it brushed against the animal in a show of strength. It bent slightly to its touch but made no attempt to move, and again made no sound. It licked the surface and jumped back, alarmed at the metallic, tingling taste. Its whiskers brushed alongside and it registered the electromagnetic field coming from it. Its curiosity satisfied, it realised this was not an animal and dismissed it, now using it for cover as it crept forward.

~

Janet and Jimmy were deep in conversation, and Joshua realised the futility of trying to get out of the buggy whilst he did not have his mother's attention. He sat facing the archway and he soon saw the little black and white cat on the other side of the car park. It walked along the wall and dropped casually to the ground, trotting over towards them, past a row of cars along the back wall.

"Kat!" shouted Joshua, bending his head up to look for his mother.

Janet looked round. The little black and white cat had stopped on the far side of the gated archway. Suddenly, the fur along its back rose and it spat and hissed, looking at the boundary wall and then back to Janet, Jimmy and Joshua.

"That's right Joshua," Janet cooed, "Cat. Well done"

"Not a very friendly cat by the looks of it," exclaimed Jimmy.

Janet and Jimmy went back to their conversation. Joshua's arms rose up and he clucked with excitement as he watched the large dark form cross the gated archway in a fleeting bound. The black and white cat jumped backwards and skidded out of sight behind the cars along the back wall. Janet was just beginning to pull the buggy up the steps, when she froze as a chilling snarl echoed and reverberated around the courtyard-style car park. As her eyes met Jimmy's, she could see he too had heard it, and had snapped to attention. They stood in silence momentarily until Jimmy took a few quick steps past her. A loud cracking sound ricocheted around the car park, breaking the silence. Jimmy took a few more steps and Janet suddenly felt compelled to hold him back, a wave of fear sweeping over her. She opened her mouth, but no words came as Jimmy rounded the line of cars and crouched down, looking underneath as he went.

"Oh my God," he said, popping his head over the bonnet of a grey Mercedes, "Come and look at this!" He beckoned her over with a waving hand.

Janet sprang forward and soon joined him, her fear

quickly subsiding. She soon saw what Jimmy was looking at. A single piece of blood-smattered black and white fur lay against the tyre of the Mercedes. The soft hissing noise drew her attention to the deep slash in the tyre that was now venting air, and the small pool of blood beneath it.

"A fox must have grabbed it or something," exclaimed Jimmy, straightening up and dusting off his hands

"Poor thing," Janet said pityingly, slightly shocked by the gruesome scene.

They walked back to the steps, and by the time they had reached them she was laughing at one of Jimmy's jokes. Joshua watched in silent reverence as the black form seemed to rise up and slither over the back wall.

"Kat-Kat," he whispered, as his wide-eyed stare of fear and wonder followed it. Then it was gone, and he turned back to his mother in a maddened scream of excitement as they went inside.

~

The creature had killed the cat in one blow from its paw. It slunk back into the bracken, bristling with adrenaline. It settled amongst the backdrop and shadow of an exposed group of rocks and began to eat. It skinned the cat with one tug of its jaws. Its rasping tongue soon cleaned the bones of the flesh and it gulped down the few small mouthfuls they provided. It stood up and growled its intentions. It was still hungry.

CHAPTER FIVE

Thomas glossed over the YouTube videos and internet articles he had opened up as they flickered across the computer screen. He was writing down species names as he came across them. They ranged from the small jungle cats of South America and Asia to leopards, panthers and pumas. He had a small map of the UK on his desk. As he noted the location of each report, he marked it with a coloured sticker depending on the species.

Catherine looked up from her desk, twisting round to find Thomas deep in thought as he studied the map.

"What are you doing?" she asked.

Thomas did not move or reply, his eyes darting from the map to the screen and back again in deep concentration.

"Tom?" asked Catherine again, with questioning impatience.

"I'm sorry," he said, caught by surprise. "What did you say?"

Catherine laughed and leaned back in her chair. "What are you doing, it looks like you've invented a portable version of Risk."

Thomas laughed and relaxed a little. "I just noticed something, that's all."

"What?" Catherine enquired.

"There is a pattern emerging that makes sense to me. See the yellow stickers here? They represent alleged sightings of puma type animals. They tend to be in fens, or on moors where there's sparse, rocky habitat, basically exactly where you would expect to find them, and where they can hunt their typical prey such as rabbits, hares, game birds and small deer. As you can see, South Devon and Cornwall are real hotspots for them. The same is with the red ones that represent panthers and leopard type animals. They're more often reported in heavily forested areas, where they'd be able to hunt larger deer and their camouflage would be more effective. Notice anything?"

"We certainly have a good few here in the Highlands, allegedly as you say," she mused. "And it looks like Cannich has more than its fair share."

"Well spotted," Thomas agreed. "They were mainly between 1976 and 1981 – remember what I was saying about the dangerous animals act? There are reports of both a large black cat and a tan coloured animal, along with livestock attacks and the capture of a very tame cougar to back it up. Cannich would seem quite the hotspot, and there are still relatively regular reports as you can see."

"If you say so," she replied with a raised eyebrow and a mischievous grin. "What about those ones that have been reported in cities though?" She pointed to the red stickers that marked South London and Guildford.

"That still makes sense if you think about it," Thomas replied. "The Surrey Puma has been described both as the namesake puma and as a black cat. Reports go back nearly fifty years now, so we're clearly dealing with more than one animal. The animal seen in Guildford was black, so more likely to be a leopard or jaguar, and towns and cities are referred to as the urban jungle for a reason. They offer incredibly thick cover with parks, open areas and numerous food sources. In many ways it's perfect. The one in London was also a black cat, reported near Crystal Palace Park, 200 acres of prime leopard habitat if ever there was."

Thomas studied Catherine's expression as she studied the map. He knew that at least some of the sightings were questionable and he doubted all were genuine, but he wasn't going to let her know that.

Catherine sat silently for a couple of seconds, but eventually let the smile she'd been holding back creep out. She could tell he was excited, but was curious as to why he had such a strong conviction, although admittedly it was one of the things she liked about him. He was like a bloodhound once he had a whiff of a story that had got his attention. She decided not to press him on it for the moment. She couldn't decide if his background made him the perfect person to spot something like this, or made him more likely to see a crouching cat behind every livestock killing. But for the moment her gut told her to trust him. She had heard the stories about big cats in Britain, but had always dismissed them as an urban myth. As a naturalist and a scientist, she thought that if such animals were really roaming the countryside, there would simply be more evidence, especially if they had been running around since the seventies as Thomas was suggesting.

It was this quiet tenacity and confidence, as well as his passion and whole-hearted commitment that had made her hire him in the first place. He had been a true catch for the little research centre, giving it some much needed PR and credibility. She thought about the long climb it had taken to get where they were, and how long it had been before they had been taken seriously by the scientific community. She had originally trained as an RSPCA inspector after her A-levels. Her curiosity and love of wild animals in particular had taken her to night classes and eventually to Royal Holloway University's Zoology department, where she left with a first degree. Her Scottish mother had encouraged her to head north after a disastrous relationship, and she hadn't looked back. She had worked as a consultant with the SSPCA and their prosecution teams in a number of high profile cases, targeting the illegal poisoning and persecution of critically endangered hen harriers and golden eagles on some of the most famous game estates in Scotland. In doing so, she made a name for herself and plenty of enemies. Her real passion though was in conservation. When her father had died, he had left her a sum of money to go towards a crofter's cottage she was saving for. Instead, she bought a dilapidated SSPCA animal shelter and hospital at auction, plunging head first into her work. She had been the first to conduct a successful population survey of Highland pine martens, discovering that they had a particular fondness for peanut butter in the process. An interview in Nature magazine gained her some acclaim when she became involved with the successful reintroduction of the European beaver in a secret Highland location. Scientific American had also come calling when she took over an eradication programme of American mink from the Inner Hebrides. Her hands on approach had seen the unwelcome mustelid replaced by a healthier population of tourist friendly otters and water birds, including the reintroduced white tailed eagle. Now they were the go-to organisation for reintroduction and population management studies, for everyone from the government to Greenpeace. Announcing they were now genuinely looking into big cats could put that in jeopardy.

She knew that part of the problem was that it was Thomas's suggestion rather than someone more independent. He had shown up just at the right time, arriving just as it had dawned on her that she needed some help. She had of course known him by reputation and had read his papers on predator relationships in university. He was not only a highly practical field biologist, but also a well recognised name, often consulted and referred to in debates centring on wildlife and conservation. She had hired him instantly. Their equally competitive natures had suited the work perfectly and they had gone from strength to strength since. He had even encouraged her to write and publish a book on the UK's responsibility to reintroduce native species under EU law, and the possible positive affects it could have on the ecosystem. But there was a shadow that accompanied Thomas's brilliance and it was the shadow of his past. They had escaped it until now, but there was no doubt in her mind it would readily jump to the forefront of any investigation into big cats.

She let out a deep sigh that signalled her reluctant acceptance that for now, it wasn't a bad idea to at least keep their options open. She also knew that the scientific relevance of actually discovering and documenting such an animal in the UK would be significant and well worth their while.

"So, where are we going to start?" she asked, watching as Thomas stuck another sticker onto the map.

"We had better get up to Palaeo Park first. Eliminate the usual suspects and make sure there haven't been any escapes and so forth. It's unlikely, and I would have thought Hugh would have reported it straight away, but we need to check as a matter of course," he replied.

"Oh good!" exclaimed Catherine. "He might feed us too if we're lucky. I'll get my coat. Are you happy to head out straight away?"

"Yeah," Thomas chuckled. "No problem, let's go."

Thomas followed Catherine into the hall and grabbed his own coat as he passed on his way to the back door. As he opened it, he was greeted by Meg, who hung her head low. She whined sheepishly as Thomas caught the whiff of urine and saw the stain on the steps. He bent down and stroked her head reassuringly.

"Ah Meg, what are we going to do with you? At least you were outside this time," he said, gently caressing both sides of her muzzle with his thumbs as he held her head in his hands. "Not to worry, we're heading out."

Meg licked his nose and bounded off to the far end of the garden. Whatever had spooked her had passed. He watched her for a few minutes as she nosed through the leaves and took to stalking a robin that landed near her. She started to try and herd the busy bird as it hopped from branch to branch of a small bush. He told himself she was fine, but he knew that Meg was either scared or ill. If she was ill, she showed no other symptoms, and he knew in his heart she was just plain terrified of something. He had seen it in her eyes every time she had been discovered. More than that, her fear seemed to infiltrate and catch him unawares each time. He knew it mirrored his own. He called her to him.

"If you mess in the car, there really will be trouble," he scolded mockingly.

Meg happily wagged her tail and bolted past him towards Catherine. As he walked out of the front door to join them, he glanced up at the imposing peak of Càrn Eige, and for the first time wondered if something lurked unseen within its shadow.

CHAPTER SIX

The drive to Palaeo Park took the best part of an hour. As the grand home and estate of the Chisholm family, the park occupied over 250 acres of the uplands of Glen Moriston, the next valley to the south of Cannich. The River Moriston ran alongside the A887 that led to the park. Glad to have the freedom of the main roads, Thomas gunned the engine, gleefully sending the pools of standing water from the drizzling rain back to the churning torrent of the river. The large brown tourist signs indicated they were close, and Thomas eased off the accelerator. He rolled through the entrance and up to the ticket gate, where they were waved through by the attendant who had recognised the car.

Thomas loved coming here. The park had opened in 1976 and was managed and endorsed by the Scottish Wildlife Preservation Fund. Thomas and Catherine had worked alongside them on the wildcat project, and he knew that Catherine was nervous about discussing the apparent sudden disappearance of the animals with Hugh Chisholm, the family head who chaired both the charity and the park. Thomas had convinced her it wasn't necessary, at least until they had investigated further themselves. The park played an important role in conservation and endorsed several captive-release programmes, including red squirrels, wild cats, pine marten and capercallie. But it was still very much a zoological park at its core, and Thomas knew Hugh wouldn't be too interested if it didn't directly affect his bottom line.

As Thomas drove slowly through the main paddock, he was forced to slow as he found the road blocked by a large, shaggily haired animal. The bison looked up momentarily as it chewed slowly on the mouthful of grass it had just plucked from the verge. It lumbered off the tarmac and onto the hilly outcrop nearby, where it stood and watched the car move off, still chewing. As well as being home to some of Scotland's most iconic wildlife, Palaeo Park also represented animals that had long since disappeared from the British Isles, and it was these that were of the most interest to Thomas today. As they continued their cruise through the paddock, Thomas spotted the moose and wild horses that shared the open space with the bison. He was glad that February meant there were fewer tourists about, and he soon spotted the track that led to the main house and away from the main drive.

The large red-brick manor house sported impressive columns to the front and interwoven pink granite blocks along its foundation. It had once been the centre point of the estate, but now sat almost out of sight. They passed through the ornate pillars that had once held magnificent gates, and came to a stop on the deep gravel outside the house. A short, plump man wearing a smart tweed jacket came out of the house and walked down the entrance steps to greet them. Thomas had always had both a healthy respect and a quiet distrust of the man, from the point of view that he would never put anything past him. Hugh was very business-minded and made no bones about the fact that his priority was profit, and lots of it. This had been very clear when he had added big cats to the collection, and invited visitors to 'come meet Britain's beasts of the moors'.

They stepped out of the car and Hugh warmly shook Catherine's hand first, clasping hers with both of his.

"Hello," he beamed. "The gate called ahead and said you were on your way. It's so nice to see you, both of you, of course." With that, he let go of Catherine and shook Thomas's outstretched hand as well.

It had always amused Thomas that Hugh obviously had quite a thing for Catherine. It was more than understandable though. Catherine glowed with natural beauty. He had been somewhat taken back himself when he had first met her at the Centre. Her short, dark red hair and dazzling green eyes had been distracting enough, but her active choice of careers as an RSPCA Inspector had kept her toned, and her figure was nothing short of breathtaking. Luckily, he had never dwelt on it long enough for it to become a distraction, and now that he worked with her he managed to keep it from ever playing on his mind for too long. But there was a comfort he got from seeing the reaction in other people, especially men when they were out and about. It was nice to be regarded with such envy by the men and boys of the glen.

Hugh beckoned them into the house, and they walked along a short corridor to reach his office. Hugh sat down behind his large traditional looking desk, a green banker's lamp sitting to his right hand side. There were messy piles of papers all over the desk and almost none of the top of it could be seen because of them. A computer monitor sat to the other side, humming away to itself. Thomas got the impression that it was rarely used. Hugh seemed the type who was stereotypically against technology, as if it might suggest something else was in control other than him.

Thomas and Catherine made themselves comfortable in the two impressive dark red leather armchairs that were placed at opposing angles to the desk.

"So, not that it isn't always a pleasure to see you both, but what might I do for you?" Hugh enquired.

"There was a sheep carcass found early this morning that seemed to have been killed by something a little larger than we're used to," Thomas stated as matter of fact.

"And you wondered if we had had any wanderings off we'd forgot to mention?" Hugh replied with a sly smile. "I hope you know we'd inform the authorities straight away, but I realise you have to check."

Catherine smiled. "We just want to do a head count if that's okay? We'll try not to get in the way."

"Of course, I understand. You know it's no problem," Hugh beamed again. "I'll get William to go round with you and give you the full guided tour as it were."

Hugh smiled and picked up the telephone. A few moments later they were walking back out of the office, waiting for William the head keeper to join them.

It wasn't long before they heard the familiar crunch of boots on gravel as someone made their way up the track. The keepers had their own little row of cottages on the grounds, not far from the manor. William waved as he walked across the drive to meet them. Over the last year they had met many times, and Thomas was glad that someone he trusted would be their guide rather than Hugh. A keeper was much more likely to tell them if something was amiss. As they climbed back into the Overfinch, Meg showed her appreciation at the company by barking enthusiastically and performing a quick dash round the back seats. William in turn showed his appreciated of the luxurious surroundings with a silent nod to Thomas.

Thomas and Catherine weren't really interested in the animals housed in the main paddock, as they were all herbivores and unlikely suspects as sheep killers. But they took their time to drive through and listened as William talked about the animals on show. The paddock was shared by large herds of European bison, European elk also known as moose, Prezwalski's horse and red deer. Then there were also smaller animals like mountain goats and arctic hares. Although some were now extinct in Britain, they all had once been native animals. Thomas had often been saddened by the thought that some of the most beautiful creatures in Britain's zoological heritage had been killed off or driven from the land for no real reason. Although many of the animals would have been a likely food source, it was hard to believe that it would ever have been necessary to drive species after species into 'geographical' extinction. No one knew for sure when the elk and bison had eventually disappeared, but their bones were still relatively common finds in parts of the country.

William directed them towards a gate that wasn't used by the public and Thomas drove over to it slowly, making sure he wasn't spooking any of the animals unduly. William quickly got out of the car and unlocked it, swinging it open and waving them forward as he did. Once they were through, he opened a second inner gate that had been concealed by the brow of the hill, and again waved them forward. He closed it behind them and got back into the car.

"If you just creep forward a bit, we'll get a better view" said William.

"What of?" Catherine asked.

"The wolves," replied William. "That gate leads directly into their enclosure. We should be able to get a complete head count from here."

Thomas inched the car forward as directed, stopping as he came to the crest of the hill. They looked down another slope that led to the fenced off road for the tourists. Most of the wolves were standing together, collectively alerted to the car's presence as its silhouette broke the outline of their ridge. A large black wolf stepped forward and let out a long howl, at which the others all lifted their heads and joined the chorus one by one.

"They're letting us know it's their territory," said William. "I can see from here that they are all there, nine adults in total. We're hoping for litters next year," he added, beaming.

William directed them out of the enclosure whilst Catherine ticked away at the inventory sheet that Hugh had passed to her. She marked clearly that the wolves had been visually accounted for and looked up as the car came to a halt again.

After getting through another security gate, William directed Thomas towards a large grey concrete structure on the horizon. As they approached it, they could see that it was fenced off with high wire posts and spikes. One of the Park's pick-up trucks was parked awkwardly in front of it. When they drew close, William motioned them to stop.

"We can get out for these ones," he said.

Catherine recognised the buildings. They were the enclosures where the park's big cats were kept. William waved at another keeper that had come round the side of the building and beckoned him over.

"This is Jamie, our cat keeper," explained William. "Jamie, meet Thomas and Catherine from the wildlife research centre over in Cannich."

They were all going through the formality of shaking hands when Thomas was distracted by the appearance of a large fawn coloured cat close to the fence.

"Ah, right on time," exclaimed Jamie. "That's Boris, our male puma."

Thomas could see straight away that Boris was in his prime. He guessed that he was about five years old and weighed about 230lbs. He was big for a puma, nearly seven feet long. He could see by the shine of his handsome tawny coat that he was extremely well fed and in the peak of condition. Boris eyed them all silently, only emitting a quiet whistle occasionally when one of them moved or made a noise.

"He's just telling Doris to stay indoors whilst he checks us out, that's all" explained Jamie. "Never seen a better boy than our Boris, and I've been to zoos and parks all over the world."

Thomas was suitably impressed with Boris and didn't doubt he was probably one of the biggest in captivity. Even compared to his wild cousins Thomas had come across in Yellowstone and Wyoming, he knew Boris was still a heavyweight.

A quiet yowling noise brought their attention to another part of the enclosure, closed off from where Boris sat watching them.

"Of course, being a typical teenager, Doris is paying no attention," Jamie smirked.

A smaller, more golden skinned cat walked out onto a rocky ledge that helped the enclosure mimic their natural habitat.

"Why have they been separated?" Catherine asked.

"Like most predators, puma come into heat during the winter so that their young can be born in the later part of spring. It means that just when there is an abundance of fawns, rabbit kits, leverets and baby birds, puma kittens are born so that their parents can take advantage of the bounty. In Doris's case, she's only two years old and has really only just become sexually mature. We do want to breed from her eventually, but as it's not recommended for their first few seasons, we've decided to separate them for the time being. But we're hoping next year will be different."

Boris stepped right up to the fence and gently rubbed his jaws on the strong mesh. Doris responded by angrily slapping the fence between them and catching Boris by surprise, hissing her disapproval at his closeness on the other side of the structure.

"At least they're already acting like a married couple," Thomas smiled.

They all laughed, and then Jamie motioned for them to follow him as they walked round to the lynx enclosure on the other side.

Almost to Thomas' disappointment, both of the parks resident lynxes were sitting in their enclosure, lazily lying on top of their shelter for all to see. Catherine went through the now mandatory exercise of ticking the animals off her list and then put it away. They had reached the end of the short list of predators kept at the Park.

"Let's head back to the house then," suggested Thomas.

"No doubt we can squeeze Hugh for lunch," he added brightly.

William decided to stay with Jamie whilst Catherine and Thomas returned to the house, this time taking the more easily accessed tourist track that led round the Park. Once again, Hugh waited for them by the steps of the manor.

"So Hugh, everything's all accounted for," Catherine beamed as they got out of the car. "All that's left now is for you to invite us in for lunch and coffee"

"Oh, I see," replied Hugh, "and there I was thinking you came here on business." He chuckled and extended his arm towards the house, warmly inviting them in.

They enjoyed an impressive lunch of Highland beef sandwiches and huge chunks of a homemade tea loaf with Hugh, before returning to his office for coffee.

"So, where will your investigation take you next?" Hugh enquired.

Catherine looked at Thomas, realising that she had no idea what the next move would be. Thomas smiled at her, and then he turned back to Hugh.

"We'll go and have a look round Cannich Forest and the nature reserve. There were some reports of wild boar a little while ago which we need to look into anyway."

"Ah yes," said Hugh. "The rumour is we have quite a little population growing now."

Thomas let the coffee warm his hands a little, still feeling the cold from their morning out in the open.

"Another fine example of an alien species setting itself up quite comfortably in the UK," he stated finally, looking up at them both. "And handily providing another link in the food chain at the same time."

CHAPTER SEVEN

"It's been ages since we've been to the woods," Thomas said as he steered the Overfinch back up the valley towards Glen Cannich and the Forest. "I'm quite excited to see what's there."

"Me too," replied Catherine. "Do you think we might actually get close to the boars this time?"

"It depends. They must be quite a big pack by now, so we have a good chance I think. If McAllister wasn't exaggerating, they pretty much uprooted an entire field in the past few days. I feel sorry for him really. He was trying to get ahead after the wet summer and autumn by planting an early crop of Duke of York potatoes. The boars loved them apparently."

Catherine knew Jim McAllister. His farm was the nearest in the Glen to Cannich Forest, bordering the Campbell estate to the North. A few years ago, he had tried his hand at boar farming, when the luxury meat had been high in demand. Unfortunately for Jim, being so close to the estate and being a farmer that allowed the Campbell hunt onto his land, he had been targeted by a group of saboteurs and animal rights activists. His thirty boars had been released from their pen one night and that had been the last he had seen of them, despite extensive efforts to recover the animals. He had shot a large male the winter before, and had phoned Thomas a few days ago to let him know of their latest rampage. Occasional reports came in of a boar seen on a road or crossing a field, but they stuck to the thick cover of the forest for the most part.

There were a number of trails through Cannich Forest, especially to the north and towards Loch Mullardoch's south-eastern shoreline. Catherine knew two or three of the trails very well as she sometimes ran there, but she also knew Thomas would want to venture off the beaten path. Most of Cannich Forest was a nationally important nature reserve. Red squirrels, pine martens, red and sika deer, and their wildcats, all called the nature reserve home. Maybe something else did too. She wondered what Thomas's plan was.

"Are we going to try and track the boar, then?" Catherine asked. "I'm just a bit worried about getting close to them. Aren't they dangerous?"

"I think we need to go in and have a look around first," replied Thomas. "We're looking for anything that might be out of place, and the boars certainly are that. And the best way to find the kind of predator we're looking for is to find the prey, and the boars are certainly that too. But it's more about the dynamics of the forest changing. If there is a new predator in there, the other animals will be behaving differently. There might also be tracks, scat or other physical evidence like territory markings. That's what we're really looking for. The likelihood of us coming across either the boar or a big cat is very slim and if we do, they'll be running in the other direction, trust me."

"So will I, trust me," Catherine smirked.

A small gravel parking area on the very edge of the nature reserve provided a convenient place to stop the car. Thomas and Catherine changed into their heavy walking boots, which were always to hand just in case. Thomas patted Meg and slid out a metal bowl from beneath one of the seats. He poured some bottled water into it. He stroked her head and slipped her a few strips of dried beef jerky to make sure she was as comfortable as possible. Unfortunately her missing leg meant that although she was a gifted tracker, stealth was no longer an ability she possessed. Thomas was also concerned that if they did come across the boars, they might act aggressively if confronted by a dog, and they would be unpredictable enough as it was. Even though it was a cold day, he slid the passenger side window open a little just to be sure she had plenty of ventilation.

Thomas and Catherine began to make their way through the forest. Rainwater that had collected in the dense branches above them dripped from the pine sprigs. As a large part of the forest was made up of elderly Scots Pines, the canopy was mostly evergreen, even in winter. The bare and brittle branches of the oaks and beeches that also made up the forest seemed dull and dead comparatively, but their leaves had carpeted the forest floor in a mosaic of gold and amber some months before, and their own green hues would return soon enough. Catherine thought the water seemed to make the colours of the forest even more vivid than usual. The smell of the pines seeped into her, and she became momentarily enchanted by the life of the forest. Beneath her feet stirred millions of invertebrates, energised by the tremors sent through the earth by the rainfall, churning and regenerating the soil through which they ploughed. Soon, when the remaining snow turned to melt water and spring finally began, the seeds of the dogs-tail and sweet grasses would be provoked into sprouting, and meadows of bluebell, foxglove, primrose and wood sage would erupt throughout the forest. It was as if she could feel it all happening beneath her feet as they went.

She followed Thomas, who had already fallen silent and had his head tilted towards the ground, only occasionally looking up. In Wyoming and Colorado in the United States, she knew Thomas had depended on his tracking skills for a living. He had worked in the dense swampy jungles of India's Sundarbans and had called the Maasai Mara of Kenya home. To him, this was easy country and an equally easy task. She wasn't anywhere near as experienced at tracking, stalking or even just keeping quiet, but she tried to copy Thomas where she could. He in turn was always patient with her, always waiting as she caught up and never reprimanding her when a careless step broke their cover or a startled bird or animal bolted from the shadows, giving away their position.

She soon realised they had left the trails behind them, as Thomas steered them instinctively through the undergrowth and began to follow the more natural paths that for now only he could see. Every now and then he would stop and pick leaf litter from the ground, smelling and examining everything that came within his line of sight. He reminded her of a pointer dog, diligently following the trail with eyes and nose to the ground as it relentlessly and methodically closed in on its quarry. He moved in total silence and began to stoop lower and duck and weave between the branches. Catherine knew that he was instinctively trying to break his profile so that the wildlife around them wouldn't spot his upright human silhouette. She followed suit.

They had been walking for nearly an hour when Thomas

came to an abrupt halt, gently and silently dropping to his knee. He motioned with his hand for Catherine to do the same, turning his head round and pressing a finger to his lips as he winked at her. He stared directly ahead of them. Carefully raising his hand slowly, he pointed to an opening in the trees about a hundred yards ahead of them, where a small striped animal was pushing its snout through the leaf litter. It was very small, but Catherine soon realised it was a boar piglet. She watched as it crossed the opening and jumped into the brush on the other side, shortly followed by a number of adult boar and a few adolescents she hadn't even noticed.

Thomas waited a minute or so before he moved again, and then began to creep slowly forward. He looked up into the branches of the trees and noticed that the coal tit, whose warning cries had alerted him to the presence of the boar, was now flitting back and forth in more usual fashion. He started forward more confidently, eager to examine the point where the boars had appeared.

"Look here," he whispered to Catherine. "This looks like a well used game trail. You can see animals have been passing back and forth in both directions. That's why it seems so flat and worn here, and why the bushes are bent back like that."

Catherine took a moment to get her bearings. "That makes sense," she replied. "The river and loch would be to the north-east and guess whose farm would be roughly south-west?"

"Yep," smiled Thomas. "Food and water. Definitely a game trail, and where there's game, there are predators. We're on the right track for sure. Keep your eyes and ears open."

Thomas was about to carry on, when he noticed the thin brown hair stuck to the underside of the bracken where it had been parted. The sticky, hook-like barbs that were found on the underside of the leaves often caught the hairs of animals that passed by them, and when he examined them up close he recognised them as guard strands from a young boar. He slipped a specimen bag from his pocket and put them inside and sealed it.

Suddenly, the coal tit flew down to the brush and piped its alarm call again, flicking its tail in agitation. He looked into the trees ahead and peered through the undergrowth around them. He froze, trying to ascertain the danger and where it was coming from. With lightning reflexes he jumped up and took a few lengthy strides to reach Catherine, quickly pushing her to the ground and covering their faces with his dark green coat.

"Lie perfectly still," he whispered.

Catherine had no chance to ask why as the undergrowth ahead of them was suddenly flattened in a barrage of boar and all around them sounded shrill grunts and squeals of panic.

Through a small gap between the ground on which they lay and the coat that almost covered them, Thomas peered back down the path. He saw an estimated twenty boar crossing the same trail they had just identified and the smaller group had used earlier. But this time, a large tusked female guarded the others as they crossed. Thomas thought it safe to presume that it wasn't them that had spooked the boar into flight, but he wasn't going to invite a charge from an animal that was capable of killing him if he could help it.

Soon the boars had passed, and their squeaks and squeals began to fade. The female grunted loudly and began to turn to follow the others, when Catherine shivered in shock as a drop of water fell from the tree above and dripped down her neck. The slight rustle from the coat's waxed covering caught the boar's attention immediately. She grunted a loud, rasping snort, expelling her steamy breath into the air. She stood rooted to the spot, as if she'd been struck by a bolt of lightning. Thomas could see the ridge of hair along her back bristling. He knew she had heard them, but he wasn't sure she could see them. This was her challenge, inviting them to step into the ring as it were. He knew their best chance now was to remain perfectly still. He glanced at the coal tit in the bush beside him, a wild statue with black beady eyes trained on him, willing them into stillness. He could sense Catherine tensing beside him and saw her knuckles flex as she prepared to get up, presumably to run.

"You'll never make it," he whispered, placing his hand over hers whilst never taking his eyes from the boar. "Stay perfectly still. She can't see us, and she can't smell us downwind."

What seemed like an eternity passed before the boar lost interest at the noise, her poor eyesight unable to detect the source of the disturbance. She disappeared in the direction the others had gone. Thomas and Catherine dared not move until they could no longer hear her crashing through the undergrowth. Thomas stood up and brushed himself off, helping Catherine to her feet as he did.

"Well I think the question as to whether the boar are established here or not is something of a moot point now, don't you?" he grinned.

~

The creature woke, disturbed from its slumber in part by hunger and in part by the echoing bark of a roe buck off in the distance. Without stirring from its nest of grass it flicked its ears and whiskers forward and raised its nose slightly into the wind. Its eyes flashed wide as it sensed the failing light of the sun in the shadow that slowly descended the mountain. The wind brought the scent and sound of water from the river, and the pungent punch of pine from the forest. Enveloped within it was a veiled musk, sweet and honey like, and very faint. It flexed its muscles and arched its back as it uncoiled from where it lay. The forest was almost a mile further down the mountain. The honey scent tugged at it softly. It obliged its instinct and slipped from its bed of grass into the maze of rocks and heather towards the trees.

~

The damp soil fell untidily from Catherine's jacket as she dusted herself off, leaving tell-tale stains from where they had lain on the soft ground.

"Don't worry," chuckled Thomas, "it's great for camouflage and hides our scent a bit." He was smiling kindly. He could tell Catherine was upset and embarrassed. "It's completely natural to want to run, and many people would have done. Chances are nothing would have happened and she would have run off in the opposite direction. But she was pretty big, and the most dangerous boar you can ever come across is a female with piglets, and I didn't want to risk it. I also didn't want us to become the accidental target of whatever might have spooked them. But you didn't do anything wrong and you were very brave to trust me. You did fine," he explained reassuringly.

"It could have charged though couldn't it?" Catherine asked shakily.

"Yeah, it could have. But she didn't. And we now know without a shadow of a doubt that the boars in the forest are the escapees. She was nearly three feet high at the shoulder and had plenty of weight. Boar only get to that size if they've been well fed and looked after as domestic animals."

"Those tusks weren't small either," Catherine smiled, a little more reassured.

"Just imagine the males. They have two sets, upper and lower." He smiled back.

"Sorry," Catherine shrugged. "I feel stupid."

"Don't," Thomas shrugged back, and he put his arm around her warmly. "That's what happens sometimes when you track. You're never going to be as good at it as the animal you're on the trail of. I tripped over a leopard in Kenya once. Had no idea it was there, practically stood on its tail. It was so surprised by my sudden appearance it bolted, but at that range it could have killed me before I'd even raised the rifle. It scared the hell out of me and left me looking pretty stupid. It's why whisky was invented, and we'll have a large glass when we get back, okay?"

Catherine smiled and nodded. She appreciated Thomas the most in times like this. She'd met enough hunter-types to know that not everyone was so forgiving. The thought of him tripping over a leopard was funny and helped steady her nerves as she imagined the scene.

Thomas walked ahead again, eager to try and follow the boar.

"So how come you were following a leopard then?" enquired Catherine, a smile of relief creeping across her face now.

"It was a man-eater," Thomas replied, pausing. "It had killed a small boy in a local village and I had been asked to track it down. I was pretty damn lucky it ran."

Catherine was slightly taken back, as she had not expected Thomas to ever raise the subject of man-eaters, especially with such flippant honesty. After a short moment of silence, she ventured the question she had wanted to ask ever since they had first met.

"Was it the one that...?" She couldn't quite bring herself to say the words.

Thomas smiled, parting some ferns ahead of them. There seemed no discomfort in his voice or expression.

"No," he replied softly, although still concentrating on the undergrowth around him rather than looking at Catherine. "Amanda was killed by a lion, a lioness to be exact." He corrected himself and hesitated a second. "I never went after that particular lioness and I don't think anyone else killed her either, certainly not before I left Tsavo anyway. She's still out there somewhere in all likelihood." He tried to smile, but it didn't come across convincingly. His brow wrinkled, almost making him look angry.

Catherine was embarrassed and looked away. She was torn between prying further and dropping the subject altogether. Thomas looked directly into her eyes and smiled, as if reading her thoughts.

"It's alright," he said. "We never really talked about this did we?"

Catherine shook her head, not really knowing what to say.

"There's not much to add to be honest," he continued. "We were investigating a strange pride of lions in Kenya. Tsavo has a historical connection with man-eaters and even the word Tsavo translates as 'the place of slaughter', referring to a battle between the Maasai and Akamba tribes. Both think the place is cursed. Amanda and I had hunted man-eaters all over the word, and it was only a matter of time before somebody suggested we go to Tsavo. It was more than that though. We wanted it. This wasn't just a single lion. It was a whole pride. Now I look back, I don't know what we were trying to prove."

Thomas paused again. He seemed far away, and Catherine noticed the corner of his mouth twitch.

"Anyway," he continued, snapping back to Catherine, "we weren't exactly met with a fanfare. The locals thought the lions were controlled by a local witch doctor and that our presence might anger him. Things went downhill from there. The lions attacked seemingly at random and always at a village we were on the way to or had just come from. One day, I suggested we make camp in the bush rather than at a village. With the camera crew and our own people it wasn't a small affair, and it seemed no less safe than anywhere else. I pretty much passed out straight away. When I woke, it was still dark and Amanda was gone. The door to the tent was open. I thought she'd gone for water or to the toilet, otherwise the door would have been closed, so I went back to sleep. I was woken at dawn by the lions roaring in the distance and found the crew in a state of panic. I followed her footprints in the dust until we found what was left of her. She'd left the tent and walked away from camp. She'd been running, but there was no lion spoor near camp. The lion's trail came from beyond camp and fell in behind her. I don't know what happened next. I know I started to run in the direction of the roaring. I remember the wait-a-bit thorns tearing my arms and legs. Then everything went black. Next thing I knew, I woke up in a Nairobi hospital. I never went back."

Catherine saw Thomas's brow wrinkle. He looked distant again, but confused rather than angry. For a while they walked in silence, Catherine trailing Thomas by some yards even though he was still scrutinising each step he took. Soon, his mood seemed to brighten and his step seemed lighter. Catherine realised he was following a trail again. He stopped suddenly as something caught his attention. She could see the branches to the side of the trail were snapped and broken. She watched Thomas move across to examine them. He beckoned her over.

"Look, the bushes on this side have been flattened and pushed forward. Something has crossed the trail here, rather than turning and following it, which would have been easier. It must have been big too, in order to get through that gorse without any difficulty," he explained.

"Why wouldn't it follow the trail?" Catherine asked.

"Good question. Let's presume it was somewhat preoccupied. Whatever it was, it stood higher than the bushes, otherwise it wouldn't have got through them. I think we should follow it in," he suggested excitedly.

A few feet from the trail, he saw flecks of hair caught up

on the thorns. As he inched closer, he immediately recognised from its length and reddish grey hues as those of a red deer. The hair was caught on thorns almost four feet from the ground, which he knew would be roughly shoulder height for a stag, or maybe a large hind. He stooped to duck under some of the lower tree branches and found it slightly easier going. Catherine followed as he patiently held back the thorns and helped pull her through. From where they were crouched, Thomas could see that the undergrowth had been pushed flat.

"Look at this," he motioned to Catherine, pointing at the floor. "Whatever we're tracking came through the bushes here, but it looks like it tripped and fell. But it was up almost immediately and carried on through there." He pointed ahead of them, seemingly into a wall of gorse thorns.

"So, I take it we're not tracking the boar anymore then?" enquired Catherine.

"No," replied Thomas. "I think this is a deer, a stag. But he was in one hell of a hurry."

A little further on, the gorse began to break and wasn't so thick, although they both already had a good number of scratches.

"Look," said Thomas again, a little more excitedly, "there are specks of blood here."

Catherine could see the dried, dark-red blobs leading away from them into the trees. Thomas was staring at a young silver birch that had been smashed through about a foot high up. The remains of the sapling had toppled sideways and hung precariously against a much larger pine, only attached to its splintered stump by a few ribbons of bark. The sapling was just less than two inches thick and the stump seemed to mark where the blood trail began.

"What's up?" Catherine asked impatiently after a few moments.

"Well that birch sapling isn't anymore," exclaimed Thomas, not looking at her as he spoke. He examined the torn trunk where it lay suspended against the pine. He guessed it to be nearly twelve feet in total, making the sapling a good thirteen feet when it had been upright.

"The largest red deer stag I've come across was roughly 300lb, but even that weight hitting the trunk at full force wouldn't bring the tree down"

"So...?" said Catherine, now uncomfortable having crouched for so long. Thomas stood up, but still looked at the ground.

"It's a little crazy, but the signs on the ground seem to suggest that this deer was being chased, right?"

"How the hell would I know?" Catherine despaired, though smiling at him to show that she didn't really mind. "So what in this forest, other than a man would be hunting red deer? Even your panther is going to think twice about pulling down a stag."

"Not necessarily," Thomas replied. "Both pumas and leopards target deer as prey, but you're right that they would usually take on much smaller species. But it doesn't mean they're not capable. What's more unbelievable is what I'm seeing here. Let's say something is chasing this stag. It takes a swipe at the rear legs here and..."

"Cuts a tree down as it does so?" Catherine was fixing him with a stare he wasn't comfortable with, and all humour had gone from her expression. "Honestly Tom, what kind of cat could cut a tree in half?"

Thomas could see that the faith and trust Catherine had placed in him and his theory was evaporating fast. Having heard it from someone else, even he had to admit it sounded somewhat fantastical.

"I've seen a bear do it," he replied sheepishly, still looking down at the stump.

"Lions, tigers and bears? Oh my," Catherine retorted flippantly.

After a moment passed, she relaxed her stance a little.

"What about a shotgun?" She asked. "Could that do that kind of damage?"

"Absolutely," Thomas replied, "but where's the buckshot? Let's just keep going for the time being and see if we can find anything that sheds a little more light shall we?"

Catherine smiled and shook her head, but followed in Thomas's wake further into the gorse.

~

The creature slunk from the rocky maze and instinctively hugged the crest of a rock-strewn knoll, hunkering down onto its belly as it slipped past the mountain's resident hill sheep unnoticed. It reached the edge of the hillock and froze, sensing the change in wind direction through its whiskers. The sheep would soon know it was there. But the change in the wind also carried the sweet scent to it more strongly now. Dismissing the sheep, the creature padded out into the open, just as its own scent hit their nostrils. The group of ewes looked up instantly but did not move. The creature padded softly past them in a wide loop. Its tail flexed and bounced in a relaxed fashion as it moved. The ewes stayed alert but knew instinctively they were not in immediate danger. Even so, they bunched together and with a few short bleats of warning, began to move upwards. The creature slunk lower to the ground as the sloping sides of the mountain began to level out and it crept towards the welcome darkness of the trees.

~

Thomas pulled a final layer of gorse aside to find himself in a small clearing, surrounded by a thick perimeter of Scots Pines, only broken by the brush where he and Catherine had entered. On the other side, in the shadow of the overhanging trees, lay the remains of the stag. Thomas crouched near to the carcass, picking up a small branch from the ground. One of the stag's antlers had been snapped in half, possibly as it had fallen. The belly had been ripped open and had split onto the ground. Only the best and most succulent parts had been removed or eaten, leaving a hollow cavity of broken bones. A few strands of tattered flesh hung from the rear legs below the knee, but most of it had been stripped down to the bone.

"It hasn't been here too long," Thomas announced. "A day or so at best I'd say. It takes about that long for scavengers to feel comfortable to feed from the carcass. Birds have taken one eye but not the other, and they're usually the first things to go. The smell isn't too bad either." He could see from Catherine's face that she wasn't inclined to agree.

"It looks like it's been stripped clean," she said, holding her hand over her mouth and nose.

Suddenly she yelped and jumped backwards as she

kicked something over in the mud. The dismembered head of the wildcat rolled a little and then came to rest.

"Sorry," said Thomas with an apologetic chuckle. "That's what this is for," he motioned to the stick. He used it to turn the head over so he could see it more clearly. The gnarled face of one-eye glared back at them, the cat's jaws locked in a death snarl. Other than not being attached to a body, the head was untouched.

"So that's what happened to poor old one-eye and probably the rest of our wildcats," exclaimed Catherine in shock. "I think I'm beginning to believe you."

CHAPTER EIGHT

Archie Campbell had lived with the hunting ban as long as he could. He had become the youngest leader of the Mullardoch hunt at thirty-five years old, and enjoyed one glorious season at its head before the hunting act of 2004 came into effect. His accomplishment had not been easy or quick, and he heavily resented the unfair timing of the ban. The Campbell name in the Scottish Highlands still came with negative connotations that did not match the prestige of their wealth and land ownership. Older Highlanders still instinctively mistrusted the Campbell name and he had fought hard for the appointment.

Archie's father had always enjoyed telling him the family history, chequered as it was. Their support of Robert the Bruce saw the family rewarded with land, titles and marriages into the Royal family itself. Clan Campbell rose to become the controlling power of the Highlands, taking over weak districts with stealthy precision and gaining further titles as they spread west. They manipulated the clan system by joining forces with those with strength and power whilst exterminating the weak. In 1490, Clans Campbell and Drummond joined against Clan Murray at the Battle of Knockmary. It would become known as the Massacre of Monzievaird. The Campbells met the Murrays as they retreated from an overwhelming force of Clan Drummond, and hunted them down until only one man remained, who was saved by a family member. Duncan Campbell was hung for his involvement as an example, but the family gained allies in Clan Drummond and further land and titles in their name.

From there on in, history repeated itself. The Campbell family continued to support the Royal family and were rewarded for it. They fought beside King James IV of Scotland and Mary Queen of Scots, and there were many oil paintings and tapestries around the grand house depicting these historic alliances and battles. In the early 17th century, MacDonald lands were given over to the Campbell family in recognition of their loyalty. When the Clan Lamont tried to take these lands back, Clan Campbell fought them off. A year later, they hunted the Lamonts down and exacted their vengeance at the Dunoon Massacre. When death and debt allowed Clan Campbell to seize Sinclair lands, the remaining Sinclairs disputed the claim and tried to take back their birthright. The resulting Battle of Altimarlech gave rise to the legend that so many Sinclairs were killed, the Campbells could cross the river where the battle was fought without getting their feet wet.

Archie's 10th great grandfather, the 9th Earl of Argyll, was involved in the Monmouth rebellion and had tried to depose James II. Although they were not successful, his 9th great grandfather, Archibald Campbell 1st Duke of Argyll, was rewarded with the surrender of Clan Maclean, their lands and home - Duart Castle on the Isle of Mull.

There was no sacrifice a Campbell wasn't prepared to pay in return for power, and at no point in history did this become more evident than at the infamous Glencoe Massacre. When bad weather delayed clan leaders taking an oath of allegiance to the English King, an opportunity was seen by two Campbell cousins. With help of an accomplice, they coerced the King into signing an order to extirpate the MacDonalds of Glen Coe, whom they described as a den of livestock thieves. As the snows of February were on the mountain now, so were they then in 1692. Robert Campbell of Glenlyon and over a hundred men of his command were greeted with the traditional hospitality of the Highlands by his relation in marriage, Alexander MacDonald. For two weeks they enjoyed his protection, and dispelled the suspicions of the MacDonalds by suggesting they were collecting tax. One evening, orders were received and confirmed by Robert. He bid his hosts goodnight over cards and accepted an invitation to dine with the clan chief, Alasdair Maclain, the next day. Maclain was killed as he rose from his bed the next morning. Thirty eight others were slain in their homes or as they tried to flee. Their wives and children died of exposure as the village was burned. Nine of the commanding officers involved bore the Campbell name.

Clan Campbell were seen to be guilty of murder under trust, a heinous crime under Scots Law, and their name had been associated with the acts of traitors ever since. The centuries old feud between the Campbells and MacDonalds became glorified in popular films and works of fiction, helping the further staining of the Campbell name in modern times. Archie was aware that even now, the Clachaig Inn of Glencoe, a popular bar and hotel with climbers, bore a sign advertising 'No hawkers or Campbells'. Archie had been brought up to expect the malcontent, and had also been taught by his father that despite the scapegoating and occasional reprisals, the Campbells had gained lands and furthered Scotland's borders to their credit.

He viewed his family's villainy with shrewd scepticism, but not everyone had been quite so level-headed.

Archie had hosted cocktail parties and dinners for years before his approval in the hunt had been gained. His rise through the ranks had been uncharted, to the point where he had even provided the land for the new stables, along with kennels for the hounds. Slowly but surely he had brought them under his wing, until total control was inevitable. He gained it just in time to be threatened with being shut down completely.

Like some of his descendants before him, he was a gifted archer, and he had turned to hunting deer with a crossbow whilst the fate of the hunt had been decided. He took some satisfaction from this activity, and wondered how people who had never known the exhilaration that came from hunting and making a kill could make comment on it. Within a few months of the ban becoming effective, both he and the committee for the hunt had decided to focus on trail hunting. Bags of aniseed would be dragged before the dogs to scent and trail. Archie found it ironic that the very thing that so many protestors had used to sabotage hunts in the past was now being used to keep his going.

When the new season had started, things began well. The hunt would meet as usual and follow the trail. Almost every aspect of the previous hunts was the same, only their lack of quarry had changed. But Archie had noticed the apathy of the other riders from the very first day. There was no thrill of the chase when you were hunting a grubby brown sack. At the end of the trail, the pack hounds would look round in bewilderment. It pained Archie to have spent so much time and money on preparing events that were becoming more and more seemingly futile.

Then one day, quite unexpectedly, as they were following the pre-laid trail as usual, a fox had bolted out from the cover of some bracken in front of the pack. A large foxhound named Hamilton had let out a deep long howl that alerted the rest of the pack to the fox's presence, and suddenly the entire hunt was on the trail. As the hounds led off, Archie caught the wry smile of some of his fellow riders. He looked around him. The hunt was well within Campbell lands and there was no way anyone would know. He had slipped the small hunting trumpet from his waist and let out a quick burst of tally ho. The hunt was on, for the first time in months it had really been on.

Archie contemplated all of this as he walked towards the feed barn. His gamekeeper Bill Fowler had asked him to meet him somewhere they wouldn't be seen, and had suggested here. He was impatient to get the hunt underway and didn't like the idea, but Bill had pressed it was necessary. He glanced quickly behind him to check nobody had seen him slip off as he passed through the large double doors of the barn.

The sight he was met with wasn't anything he had expected. Sitting on the floor was a grubby young man with greasy looking hair. He looked somewhat dishevelled and was shaking slightly. His jeans and dark green anorak were torn and tattered, and then Archie noticed the blood on his right hand. Bill stood over him, his shotgun resting over his arm. He met Archie's gaze with a smug smile. Licking his muzzle and sitting a few feet from both of them was Bill's Dogue De Bordeaux, a rust-red coloured French mastiff named Rochefort.

"So I'm guessing this is the problem you wanted to talk to me about?" Archie asked, a look of smug disgust creeping over his features as he addressed Bill.

"Aye. Came across him trailing the back meadow as I made my rounds," Bill answered, his eyes darting to the torn sack of aniseed a few feet away.

"Unfortunately, he ran. Rochefort saw to that. Poor wee bugger dropped his phone though," Bill smiled smugly, handing over the smashed remains of a smart phone. Archie could see the battery and SIM card were missing.

"What a shame," he replied, this time smiling at the hunt saboteur directly. He let out a sigh. "In a way you're lucky. We used to have the power to deal with trespassers privately. All I'll do today is have you arrested. Its tomorrow you should be worried about. I don't know where you live or work, if indeed you have a job, but I will find out, and I'll do my best to have you removed from both. There aren't many landlords or employers around here I can't influence," he sneered. "And as you've done your best to ruin my afternoon, allow me to show you the same courtesy. We will be calling the police as I say, but I am not disrupting my schedule to do so, so you'll have to be patient." Archie nodded to Bill and began to walk out.

"I need medical attention!" the man blurted out. "I'll have that bloody dog destroyed too."

Archie stopped and turned back towards the man, his eyes narrowing with contempt.

"What's your name?" Archie asked with a whisper of a threat.

The man went silent.

"The dog was doing his job and if you hadn't trespassed,

he wouldn't have had to. Believe me, we will be making a very good case as to how we couldn't possibly know your intentions or what you were carrying. You may be a poacher. You might well be a terrorist. I haven't decided yet. You're lucky he's so well trained he didn't do anything but hang on to you. Frankly, I miss the old days."

With that, Archie beckoned Bill over.

"I'm not worried about this little fool, but I am worried he might not be alone," he whispered. "What do you think?"

"We can't use the back meadows now, the trails will be ruined," Bill replied. "If he's not alone though, they could only have come from the farm road. It would be a slight risk, but you could take the hunt towards the forest. You're miles from any trails, and with dark approaching you should be safe from prying eyes I'd say."

"That might make things interesting," smiled Archie, liking the idea. He looked back at the young man. "Call the police and give my solicitor a heads up about him will you. In the meantime, I'm going to enjoy myself," he snorted, and strode out of the feed barn.

~

The creature paused a few feet from the trees. It cocked its head ever so slightly to taste the scent on the breeze that teased and distracted it from its intended path. The strong yet sensitive leathery pads of its paws felt the distant vibrations in the ground, telling it of prey on the move. The rich honey sweet aroma was intermingled with two distinct and stronger smells, both of which it recognised. The creature turned and began to prowl the perimeter of the forest, each silent step taking it towards the prey it could sense but not yet see. It stopped to scent the air repeatedly as it went, flexing its muscles each time it did so in preparation, warming and stretching its body into readiness. It began to hunt.

~

Thomas and Catherine checked the rest of the clearing. They found a few more dismembered parts of the wild cat, as well as some hair and dried blood.

"What do you think happened?" asked Catherine, staring at the head on the forest floor.

"Territoriality," answered Thomas. "Whenever cats meet, regardless of species, there will be a fight to claim the territory. Big cats especially show a very low tolerance for other cats in their territory. I would guess that old one-eye found himself outsized for once"

"That's awful," exclaimed Catherine. "Do you think the same thing has happened to the rest of them?"

"It's hard to say, but the fact that you couldn't find any signatures from the radio collars hopefully means they have moved on, rather than anything else." He held up the broken radio collar he had found to show Catherine, just as the distinct blast of a hunting horn floated across the tops of the trees. "The Mullardoch hunt is out tonight," said Thomas, a look of total disgust forming on his face. Just as quickly though, a wry smile became visible. "Want to get a closer look?" he asked.

Catherine smiled in turn and patted the digital camera in her pocket. They had both long suspected the hunt was still fully active. They had found a number of dug out fox earths, but they had never been able to prove it was the hunt. Catherine realised this might just be the opportunity they needed.

Thomas was pretty sure he could creep up on Archie Campbell without him knowing. He had plenty of practice, tracking and ambushing the illegal bush and trophy hunters he had encountered in Kenya and Tanzania, and he doubted Archie would be much of a challenge. He especially hated sport and trophy hunters. He understood and recognised the skill, nobility and respect needed to make use of an animal for food and other practicalities, but to kill an animal just because it gave you pleasure was no different to how you identified serial killers as far as he was concerned. More than that though, trophy hunting had changed and become something very ugly in the 21st century. People hunted polar bears from helicopters and stalked tame lions in tiny enclosures and called it sport. There was no skill or risk in what they did. He had stared down charging man-eaters in the wild and taken out marauding elephants. There had been plenty of risk and certainly a very real elation in survival, but no pleasure there. In any case, it was simply now illegal to hunt with dogs for sport and he needed no further justification.

~

Archie sat upon Saracen, his 16-hand grey gelding thoroughbred/Belgian-draft cross, a fast and formidable jumper with strength and stamina to spare. He picked out Hamilton and watched the old dog expectantly. The large hound moved methodically from one side of the track to the other in a soft and lumbering gate, taking his time to check each and every scent he found. The hunt moved forward as one, almost silent in their anticipation to find their quarry. As if on cue, Hamilton suddenly lifted his head and let out a deep, long howl as the familiar musky scent hit his nostrils. Archie spurred Saracen on and quickly started moving up through the other hunters. He knew to stay close to Hamilton no matter what.

~

Thomas was lying flat on the ground. He and Catherine had reached the edge of the forest, and from their position could just see the hunt as it edged towards them. Thomas took out a small leather pouch from one of his jacket pockets and popped the button holding it shut. He removed the small pair of binoculars and held them up to his eyes.

"Are you sure you were never a spy?" Catherine whispered.

Thomas smiled without taking the binoculars away from his eyes. The Sony DEV50 digital binoculars had a 12x zoom and a 20.4 megapixel camera that was capable of full HD video. They were a relatively new purchase for Thomas, and he had been desperate for a chance to try them out.

"Archie Campbell is leading the pack," he told Catherine. "They're heading this way, so they could be heading towards any of the dens on this side of the forest," he continued, still looking through the binoculars. "Looks like they have a scent, they're changing direction slightly, moving towards that clump of gorse on the right." He pointed so Catherine could see where he meant. Sure enough the hunt was arching round and were beginning to pick up their pace. They could hear the hounds baying now, as they moved along the track.

~

Archie knew that any moment now the quarry would break from its cover. He could somehow always sense when the quarry was near, picking up on the dog's excitement instinctively before anyone else. The dogs were almost skipping now, as the slower hounds in front stopped the more eager and younger dogs at the back from surging forwards. Instinctively, Hamilton broke from the pack with three other hounds following him, heading to the left of a patch of gorse in front of them. As soon as he did, there was a blur of red-brown fur as a small fox bolted from its thorny refuge and sprinted across the open field towards the cover of the trees.

~

The creature accelerated forward. Its whiskers flicked back and forth and it moved with maximum alertness, ears pricked and eyes scanning forwards. It sensed the prey had turned and was moving towards it. It gambolled forward and left the ground silently in order to clear the chicken-wire fence in front of it. It used the thicker cover of the inner-forest trees to break its outline and shield its silhouette. The sweet honey-like scent was closer now, and it detected the underlying odours of the leather saddles and the hay the horses had lain in. The putrid, smoky scent of the dogs it knew and recognised, as well as the pungent, prickly equine musk. It followed its instinct and crept closer.

~

"Right," declared Thomas. "Let's see if we can keep up with them. I need to try and get as much of this on video as possible."

Catherine hesitated, a slight sense of anguish becoming clear on her face.

"Tom," she asked softly. "Are we going to let them make the kill?"

"Not if I can help it," he replied quickly, glancing back at her and registering the anxiety in her voice. He put his arm round her. "We're in the conservation business, I do remember you know?" He smiled kindly.

Catherine returned the smile and felt better. In her time as an RSPCA officer, she had once nursed and raised a fox cub, which she named Bold after a popular children's novel. She had always been fond of them and knew she wouldn't be able to watch one get killed, even if it meant securing a conviction against Archie Campbell. Thomas turned and started making his way through the undergrowth again, and Catherine followed.

~

The fox was streaking away over the brush, nature making it far better adapted for cross-country dashes than the heavy hounds and horses that followed it. Archie had been pleased that they had found the fox out in the open, as entering the trees was always risky, albeit necessary to hide a kill effectively. Killing a fox in the nature reserve meant there was always a risk that some naturalist could be in there at just the wrong time, and they would be discovered. Even if they claimed they were trail hunting, they definitely didn't have permission to enter the forest and they would be in serious breach of the agreement that still allowed them to hunt.

Archie had already seen by the bulge in her stomach that she was a vixen carrying cubs. This was good, as it meant the extra weight would slow her down. It also meant she was much more likely to rest up or go to ground sooner, her exploits exhausting her far quicker than a younger or less burdened animal. Archie followed Hamilton as the hound instinctively broke away from the other dogs, his three loyal followers sticking with him. Archie smiled as he saw the hound's cunning at play. Whilst the younger dogs dashed across the field, enjoying the run as much as the pursuit, Hamilton was cutting across the field to intercept the fox at the forest's edge, where a chicken-wire fence with a stile marked the far boundary of the Campbell estate. He spurred Saracen on, hoping the vixen wouldn't make the trees. As Hamilton banked towards the fox he broke into a gallop, but Archie could already see the vixen was just enough ahead of them. With a final burst of speed she squeezed under the fence and Archie caught the white wisp of her tail as it disappeared from sight.

Hamilton stood with his forefeet on the stile and he bayed with the forlorn voice of his kind.

"Go on Hamilton," yelled Archie, thundering towards

him on Saracen.

The dog needed no further persuasion and bounded over the fence. His three companions skidded after him and moments later, Saracen cleared the fence and thundered into the forest. Hamilton and his followers pushed past the thick brush quicker and easier than Archie did, but their furious barks and baying howls let him know exactly which path to take through the trees. The branches were thickly entwined, which he was glad for, as it meant they were far from any of the forest paths and were less likely to be discovered. He was keen to make the kill soon though, as the sun was beginning to dip below the trees and in about fifteen minutes there wouldn't be enough light to see. The less experienced and more hesitant riders soon got left far behind in the maze of tree trunks, thorny gorse and brush. Hamilton led his small band and Archie further and further ahead into the darkening trees.

~

The creature crouched in anticipation. It could hear and feel the approach of hooves and sensed the dogs getting closer in their reckless charge through the brush. It had killed dogs in self defence before, as well as hunted and eaten them with ease. It wasn't concerned by their presence. The muscles in its shoulders coiled like wound springs and its eyes widened in anticipation. It licked its muzzle, wetting its nose to help intercept the exact direction and strength of the scents. As a gorse bush shivered, it twitched slightly, but let the fox bolt past as instinct held it in position. It knew that better prey followed.

Damn, thought Thomas. Even though he could hear the dogs and thought he had seen the flash of a red hunting jacket, he wasn't close enough to catch any of it on film or clearly prove they were hunting in the nature reserve. He had though managed to get one very clear shot as the fox had sprinted towards them, obviously pursued by the hunt in the background. Now what he wanted to do was surprise the hunt, make them aware of his presence and hope that they would withdraw. He knew that there might be a confrontation, but he doubted they would recognise the binoculars as a camera, and they would probably presume he was out bird watching. Thomas could easily justify his presence, which he knew the hunt could not. He had always told Catherine that lying was a matter of confidence, and he had plenty at the moment.

~

Archie gunned Saracen over a bank of gorse and found himself in a small clearing. The horse came to a lurching halt and bellowed a fearful whinny, stamping its front feet and trying to turn away. Archie hung to the reigns as Saracen bucked and stamped in fright. The hounds were whimpering in terror and desperately turned back to the thorny gorse, finding their way blocked by branches they had passed through just moments ago. Archie glanced to the trees but saw nothing. Saracen dashed sideways and bucked again as he clung on for dear life. Even the dogs were backing away from the horse that was now whinnying in what could only be madness or terror.

The deafening roar that filled Archie's ears made him turn and face the trees in front of him. He tried to scream as something immense burst from the shadows and leapt towards him, but no sound came from his throat. He felt the molten touch of outstretched claws, as they swiped downwards across his face and chest and reached for their target on the far side of the horse's neck. He was flung backwards as he slipped from the saddle and both he and Saracen crumpled to the ground. His eyes glazed, the brain not yet giving in to death as the overpowered horse fell on top of his body. The creature that had killed both of them gutted the three dogs with casual flicks of its claws, as they leapt upon it in a futile attempt to protect their master. He watched as it padded over, its great head blocking out the last of the light as it paused above him. The last thing he saw, although his body no longer registered the pain, was the gleaming flash of its teeth as the creature bit down into his chest and tore his rib cage open.

The creature lapped at the hot blood, enjoying the slightly metallic and salty taste. The skin was easy to puncture and it yowled quietly as it sucked and tore at the body beneath it. There was little taste of fat on the meat, but it was soft and tender and smelt clean. The organs spilled freely from the cavity it had made and it enjoyed these the most, finding their taste and smell unusually rich. It had found the animal easy to kill and it savoured the meal. It had learnt to trust its instincts from its earlier experiences and now knew that the strange scent was that of prey, and no longer had to be avoided. It had feasted on man flesh for the

87

first time and it would remember the satisfying taste from now on.

CHAPTER NINE

Thomas ran as fast as he could in the direction the roar had come from, his chest heaving as he crashed through the heavy bushes and branches on all sides. The sound had seemed to engulf the forest, echoing from all directions. But his sharp hearing had pinpointed the true direction. His feet had worked faster than his mind at first, but his thoughts were catching up with him quickly. It had been too loud and savage a sound to be one of the smaller cats. The simple fact that it had roared meant that whatever this animal was, it was a true big cat. It had sounded like a lion, but somehow more guttural and wrathful like a tiger. It didn't have the savage anger of the leopard and lacked the cough like bark of the jaguar, but it could only be one of those four. The sheer volume of the roar made him consider the possibility he was running straight into the path of a very angry African lion and he slowed, suddenly wary and more conscious of his approach.

Catherine was following him but finding it difficult to keep up. Thomas didn't want her with him now. When they had walked into the forest earlier, he could never have imagined he would be putting Catherine in danger. The smaller cats he considered an acceptable risk – they were much more likely to flee than attack. But a lion was a capable killing machine and their size simply made them much less afraid of man. An adult male could be up to eleven feet long and weigh as much as 700 lbs. It wouldn't think twice about attacking a six-foot man who weighed 160 lbs.

He gingerly pulled back the thick gorse, his nose telling him what he was about to find on the other side. He came to an abrupt stop, gulping air as he fought the rising vomit in his throat. He suddenly felt the cold sweat of the night before on his back and neck, as flashes of his nightmares and memories were violently torn from their deep slumber, triggered by the scene before him. He took a deep breath and clenched his fists as he fought to get a grip over the panic threatening to engulf him. He let his breath out slowly and took another deep gasp before opening his eyes again. He scanned the clearing, shutting out the conflict he felt by keeping his right hand clenched, the fingernails digging into his palm as he made his observations, the concentration distracting him enough to stall the despairing cry he wanted to scream.

A little over six feet from where he stood lay the large horse he had seen galloping across the field just a few minutes ago. Deep long slashes had torn through its neck and flank, and he could see it had bled out almost instantly. The strewn and mangled carcasses of three foxhounds adorned the surrounding bushes like macabre Christmas tree decorations, each lying where they had landed after receiving a single eviscerating blow to subdue them. A fourth foxhound lay on the other side of the horse, its bloodied head crushed. Most of its muzzle and lower jaw were missing. Thomas thought he could see where it had been bitten right through and took a step closer.

The silent scene of slaughter was suddenly engulfed by noise and frantic movement as three hunters burst from the brush to the right of him. The youngest of the men was unable to control himself as well as the others, and lent over the side of his horse to vomit. The horses began to buck as they smelt the blood, and their riders were forced to dismount quickly. Catherine emerged from the trees behind Thomas and for a few seconds both parties just stared at each other in disbelief, unsure what the next move should be. The largest of the three hunters, a broad, red-faced man, took off his riding cap and fixed his eyes on the dead horse in front of them.

"Where's Archie?" he whispered in dismay.

It was then that it dawned on Thomas that the horse was missing its rider. Close to where the horse lay and half buried in the mud, he spotted part of a torn riding tunic. As his eyes scanned further he saw a boot lying on the far side of the clearing and a trail of blood leading away from the horse into the dark trees. Thomas instinctively stepped towards them. He knew the cat would be taking the body of the man somewhere more sheltered, so it could feed without being disturbed. He was very aware that he didn't have his rifle with him, but he knew if he didn't follow the trail now, the body might never be found. His only chance was to hope the cat was disturbed enough by being followed, and would abandon its kill in order to escape. It was a huge risk to take, especially if the cat decided to defend its kill instead, which was a very real possibility.

The huntsman suddenly stepped forward and grabbed him by the arm. "Good God, man, stay where you are!" he bellowed.

Thomas recognised the fear in his eyes. He looked past him to the other two hunters and could hear shouting as the rest of the hunt approached.

"You all need to stop and dismount before you destroy whatever evidence there is here," Thomas shouted to them. "The horses will just panic and they may be thrown. And try to keep the hounds under control, we don't want them rushing after whatever did this."

"Why the hell not?" retorted the large huntsman, now shaking with anger as the situation impacted him.

Thomas fixed him with a cold scare.

"Because they'll be gutted and killed one by one, just like these were. I haven't got time to explain myself, but I suspect this was an attack by a big cat. What's more, I think it has encountered dogs before."

Catherine stepped in. "Why do you say that?" she asked.

Thomas let out a sigh. "A cat that hasn't encountered dogs before will normally tree or flee. This one not only decided to face them, but knew how to kill them quickly and effectively, and did so effortlessly."

"Still," said the hunter, "no bloody cat can take out an entire pack of hounds."

"On the contrary, I've seen much smaller cats than what I suspect did this do just that. They ambush a small group of dogs, then race ahead and do it again and again. And these would be dogs that are used to hunting cats. Yours aren't."

The huntsman tried to stammer a reply then thought better of it.

"Now, if one of you has a phone we need to get hold of the emergency services," Thomas continued. "I'm going to see if I can find your man."

He looked round to Catherine who smiled weakly at him. "You stay here," he said to her quietly. "I won't be long. Stay with the others." Then he stepped into the trees and began to follow the trail.

~

The creature bounded through the dense gorse and brush with the torso of the man it had just killed in its jaws. It leapt effortlessly upwards onto the trunk of a towering Scots Pine, its hooked claws digging deep into its woody flesh as it hoisted itself high into the branches. On one of the larger supporting limbs, the creature hunched down and began to eat again. It pricked its ears forward as it caught the distant sound of the hounds and horses that had already disturbed it once. It growled protectively of its kill. It waited a few seconds, listening intently and tensing slightly as it readied to move again. But as the sounds remained distant, it relaxed and turned its attention back to its meal. It licked the skin from the flesh with delicate brushes from its rasping tongue. It took a firmer grip of the carcass within its paws and turned its head, using the side of its mouth to gnaw the flesh from the rib bones. When it had finished there, it cracked them open between its teeth and sucked at the soft marrow. Finally it tore into the remaining limbs, pulling large shreds of muscle and fat from the bones. Satiated, it let the remains drop from the branch and onto the forest floor below. It began to lick the blood from its muzzle and paws in long, precise strokes.

~

Thomas walked carefully through the trees. He could sense

the light failing quickly now and his instinct and fear began to kick in, telling him to turn back and return to the others. Each step he took was a controlled and considered movement. One mistake or sound would give away his position to the cat and encourage it to escape or even attack. On a gorse bush ahead of him he stopped to examine the thick thorny branches. A small tuft of fine black hair hung impaled on a woody barb. The tops of the branches were snapped forward, but the rest of the bush seemed intact, suggesting the animal had cleared it in a leap. Thomas estimated the bush to be a little over five feet high. He examined the ground on either side for pug marks where the cat had leapt or landed. He found none, but it was clear the animal had easily cleared the bush whilst carrying a man who could have weighed anything up to 150lbs. Thomas couldn't help the trembling in his hands as he made his way further in.

~

Concealed and content in the branches of the pine, the creature heard the man approach. The sweet tasting flesh had sated its hunger momentarily and it watched from the branches, taking in the man's scent. It lay outstretched on the tree limb, its head to one side with one eye lazily open. It watched motionless as the man came into view, cautiously approaching the tree. Nearly thirty feet from the ground, it felt concealed and protected from his advance. Even so, it bunched its hind feet together, preparing to spring at the man if it became necessary.

~

Thomas could feel the stillness of the trees around him as he moved silently and steadily through them. He stopped motionless as his eyes came to rest on the ground in front of a large pine tree. The white bones and tattered flesh stood out against the dark forest floor. He felt his knees threaten to buckle and he clenched his right hand again. The silence gnawed at his self control. He knew that the forest was quiet for a reason. It was how nature let you know you were in the presence of a predator. Each and every creature reacted instinctively to its presence. The birds were the first to stop calling, their high vantage points normally allowing them to spot the threat before others. Small animals in turn would freeze in their burrows and runways, fearful of an attack from an unseen hawk or the stealthy strike of stoat or weasel. Even insects and invertebrates would stop their stirrings and join in the silence, the whole ecosystem on alert.

Thomas changed his focus and clung to the silence, carefully checking his surroundings and calming himself by taking longer and deeper breaths. He was aware that he could very well be the predator that had brought the natural silence to the clearing, but he also knew that the creature he was tracking had either passed through not long before, or was still nearby. He silently cursed his foolishness as he realised there was nothing he could do with the remains. He would have to go back to the others and lead the emergency services to the clearing.

He was about to turn back when he noticed the scarred bark of the Scots Pine in front of him. His curiosity got the better of him and he stepped forward until his face was a few inches from the trunk itself. He could easily identify the scratch marks on the tree - four long grooves where thick sharp claws had torn into the bark and punctured the soft wood beneath. Thomas stretched his fingers out wide but still couldn't cover all four of the slashes. It was obvious that the paw that contained the claws had been far bigger than his hand. *This cat is enormous*, thought Thomas.

Suddenly, he felt totally out of his depth and overwhelmed by the crushing silence of the forest. He backed away from the tree, not turning round until he found himself back in the thick brush. Then he ran back to the clearing where the others waited for him.

~

The creature relaxed and yawned loudly, disturbing a tiny crested tit that shot away from the branches above in trills of panic and alarm. The branch shook violently as the creature stood up and braced itself for the leap down to the ground. It landed in a perfect pounce-like movement in total silence, not even disturbing the dry matter of the forest floor. Darkness was now moving across the forest quickly, and the creature felt the slight pull of hunger again. It had planned to return for the dead horse, having marked its prey where it lay with claw slashes and urine. But it could already pick out the distant shouts and other alien sounds back towards the clearing. For a few seconds it contemplated going after the man after all, but then hesitated. It sniffed the air tentatively, and the rich, sweet honey-smell came to it. There was prey to be had elsewhere in the forest.

~

By the time Thomas reached the others back at the clearing, the mountain rescue had arrived. He realised no normal ambulance would have been able to reach the forest's perimeter. With members of the hunt following him and the mountain rescue team carrying a stretcher and black body bag, he retraced his steps back to the remains of Archie Campbell. It turned out he needn't have worried about the dogs following the trail. They refused to venture past the carcass of the horse, and had whimpered and howled in fear as the men moved away. He knew what was bothering them, as he too had smelt the strong odour of the cat's markings on the horse.

He was bothered by the scratch marks he had found on the tree. He had discounted the leopard because of its relative small size, but he had personally witnessed the strength and stamina of a man-eating member of that clan, and knew of their incredible adaptability and ingenuity. He also knew that contrary to popular belief, both lions and tigers could climb trees - but it was still unlikely to be either species. That left the jaguar. The jaguar was bigger and heavier set than the leopard, but shared some aspects of its behaviour. He hoped the hair sample would shed more light on what they were really dealing with. He smiled weakly at Catherine, and they began the long walk back to the car park.

~

The creature stared through the glass at the sleeping dog. It saw its reflection in the glass and the flash of its own green eyes as it moved its head. As it expelled a snort of breath, the glass frosted and its reflection was lost. It growled with longing as it listened to the dog whimper in its sleep, then it moved off past the car and into the growing darkness of the night.

CHAPTER TEN

Sergeant Matthew Hooper checked the SA-80 rifle he was holding, as one of his men went about lighting a fire. The yellow blank firing adaptor annoyed him slightly. He had served in both Gulf wars, and had patrolled in Northern Ireland as well as Afghanistan. He saw the gun as pointless without ammunition, and there was always that slight worry at the back of his mind about not being prepared for something.

"Carter, if you don't start that bloody fire soon, you'll be eating this shit raw," he threatened matter-of-factly to the private, who was now rummaging through his pockets for his kerosene and waterproof matches.

A number of good size trout sat inside one of the meal tins. They had caught them earlier in one of the forest streams and it had been the only excitement the day had contained so far.

It was only the first day, and Hooper already knew that the men were as bored as he was of the survival exercise. There weren't any rookies on his squad and they could all do this kind of thing in their sleep. *If I'd wanted to go camping, I could have taken one of my delinquent kids* he thought. Then he smiled. There was little point in complaining, he just had to get stuck in like the rest of them. That eerie thought came back to him about not being armed and he stroked the sheathed hunting knife on his belt out of habit. *Not totally ill equipped*, he smiled. He watched as Carter dug a hole in the fire and half buried the meal tin containing the fish. There was a little stream-water poured over them and they would soon poach in the heat once it got going.

"Well done Carter," he said sarcastically, "it only took you twenty minutes."

The rest of the squad grinned and laughed quietly.

"Right after grub I want three two-hour watches. Carter and Hawkins, you're up first. Ginster, Curtis, you're up afterwards, and from there on you can work it out yourselves."

Ginster was actually Private Harris, but had acquired the nickname from his fondness of pies. The seven soldiers got ready to eat and settle down for the night.

~

The creature had followed the sweet scent on the breeze. It was close enough now to see the flickers of flame from the fire and it paused. The smoky aroma of the cooked fish and the salty sweat of the men wafted towards the creature as the breeze ruffled its fur. It had taken the high ground, circling above the group of men, and was now within thirty feet of them. It stared directly ahead, panting to take as much air into its lungs as possible before it attacked. It edged closer. It extended its left forepaw with deliberate care, holding it slightly off the ground before it took a step. It brushed the soft leaf litter from the ground by turning its paw, enabling it to continue forward in silent confidence. As its front paws left the ground, it moved its back feet forward to take their place. It did this by instinct, knowing that the ground it had cleared or tested with its front paws held no obstacles that would give its position away. It could feel the warmth of the fire and it enjoyed the sensation. It licked its muzzle in anticipation.

~

The soldiers had chosen a small gully for their camp that night. The rocky walls on either side protected them from the cold wind that came through the valley, and also helped prevent the warmth of the fire from spreading, keeping it relatively contained. Carter stood on watch, looking out into the darkness of the forest. He heard the shriek of an owl from somewhere in its depths. A fox answered from out of the blackness. Then the silence returned. He looked over at Hawkins on the other side of the camp who was doing exactly the same, peering out into the darkness. Both were already bored and they were only half way through their watch.

~

The creature had slowly edged to within fifteen feet of the nearest man. It crept along an outcrop that narrowed into a ledge and set its gaze on the man four feet below it. It crouched ready for the spring, its back straight and rear legs bunched under its body, ready to hurl its bulk from the outcrop. Its claws were unsheathed, spiking into the ground and ready to reach out for the prey below. It lowered its head, now holding its breath in the ultimate act of concealment. It waited until the man turned and exposed part of his back. Then it leapt.

~

Hawkins wasn't sure what came first – the movement above Carter, or the ear-splitting roar that suddenly filled the forest. In what seemed silent slow motion, he watched a monstrous shape engulf his squad mate. Without realising it, he found himself raising his gun. As his face twisted in horror and he registered what he was seeing, he squeezed the trigger.

Carter was smashed to the ground, not having time to register four of his ribs breaking, or the pain from the claws that ripped through his legs and shoulders. A canine tooth drove through the soft bone that formed the top of his skull whilst the other slashed through the vertebrae at the back of his neck. His struggle was over. The creature roared again, startled by the noise and flashes of light coming from the gun in Hawkins' hand, but within seconds it realised that it was unharmed and it sprang upon the man with furious speed. The only word that went through Hawkins' mind was *blanks*. The creature savagely bit through his neck, and as it noticed movement from the ground to its side, twisted its head in that direction and neatly decapitated the man. It let the head in its jaws drop to the ground. The excitement that flowed through it as it saw the men twisting and moving in front of it spurred it again into action. The nearest man was still in his sleeping bag, and the creature pounced, its heavy front paws driving the scythe-like claws with crushing force through the soft down and into the man's chest, puncturing the heart, liver and lungs. The man spluttered as blood pooled in his mouth and then lay still.

Hooper sprang to his feet, for a second under the impression that he was still asleep and dreaming. He watched as a dark and darting shadow engulfed the two men left standing, only to leave them disembowelled and crumpled on the ground. He picked up the SA-80, intending to use it as a club as the shadow took shape and stepped toward him, growling softly. It didn't seem to be a threatening sound, in fact Hooper got the distinct impression the beast was letting him know how much it was enjoying itself. If thunder could laugh, it would sound like that he decided. He yelled at the monster as it took a step forwards, curved black claws extended and readying to reach for him. Hooper swung the SA-80 rifle against the monster with all his might. It was like hitting concrete. As the casing hit the cheek of the animal, it cracked under the impact. Parts of the plastic splintered away and fell to the ground. Hooper dropped the gun in disbelief.

The creature stopped dead in its tracks and then sat on its haunches, as if contemplating the new attack. Hooper took the moment to unsheathe the hunting knife. He held it toward the animal.

"Come on you bastard," he yelled, "I'm gonna cut you three ways, slow, wide and deep."

The moon broke from behind a cloud. In the eerie light, Hooper could have sworn the animal was grinning at him. The creature tilted its head slightly, then sprinted forward and sunk its teeth into Hooper's side. In a last effort, although he already knew he had only seconds to live, Hooper swung the knife downwards, slicing through one of the toes on the creature's paw. The creature screamed in pain, momentarily dropping the man from its jaws as it sprung backwards. It spun on its heels until it faced the man again and then with renewed vigour, it picked up the now limp body and shook it violently.

When it was certain the man was truly dead, the creature lay down in the darkness of the gully. The embers in the fire still glowed and it enjoyed the warmth. It licked at its wound until the blood stopped flowing. It began to clean itself all over, deliberately and carefully smoothing its fine coat of fur. When it was content, it lifted its head and began to feast on the nearest corpse. It moved from body to body until it had eaten its fill. Then in the silence of the watching forest, it slunk off towards the mountainside and disappeared back into the darkness.

CHAPTER ELEVEN

Thomas stirred as he heard the sound of tyres crunching over the gravel of the drive. He blinked and rubbed his eyes in an effort to shake off the cold and tiredness he felt as the images and memories of the night before flooded back to him. He rolled off the large fawn coloured sofa and sat up, suddenly feeling light headed as he did so. He caught sight of the bottle of 30-year old Lagavulin, the contents of which had been greatly reduced since fetching it the night before. A small amount still sat in the crystal glass tumbler on the coffee table where he'd left it. He picked it up, only to spot Meg lying in the doorway that led to the hall, watching him closely.

"Hair of the dog, hey Meg?" Thomas croaked.

Meg raised her head and cocked it to one side as he raised the glass to his lips and downed the dark tawny liquid.

"Sorry, bad joke. Too good and too expensive to waste though," he continued, as if in explanation.

Meg whined slightly, then yawned and placed her head back on her paws.

"Not that I don't enjoy our little chats Meg, but make yourself useful and get the door will you?" Thomas scoffed, attempting to laugh off the shakes and tremors he felt in his arms. He glanced at his watch and was surprised how early it was, 6.34am. He stood up and lumbered towards the hallway, stepping over Meg as he did so. He stopped and glanced back at her.

"You stayed up and watched me all night didn't you?" he

stated in realisation. Meg didn't look round but her tail thumped the floor a few times.

Thomas walked over to the large oak door and swung it open, expecting Catherine to be walking over the drive. Instead, he found himself face to face with two men, a policeman and an Army officer. He recognised Major-General Fitzwilliam, the barracks commander of Fort George in Inverness. Thomas had been on a number of local shoots with him and had seen him in the Dam & Dram bar and restaurant on the outskirts of Cannich. He didn't know the policeman, but recognised the three emblems on his shoulder as the uniform of a Chief Inspector. Both looked incredibly serious.

"Mr. Walker?" the Chief Inspector asked.

"Yes, what's left of him at least," replied Thomas, beginning to predict what the visit was about, although he was surprised at the Army already being involved.

"We'd like to talk to you about some animal attacks that happened yesterday," the Chief Inspector continued.

It took a moment for the simple effect of the plural to register.

"Attacks?" asked Thomas surprised.

"Yes," replied the Chief Inspector, "there was a second attack during the night."

Thomas beckoned them both inside and they followed him through to the living room. Both men took a seat opposite him on the large sofa, whilst he settled into a tan leather armchair opposite.

"My name is Chief Inspector Roberts Mr. Walker and this is Major-General Fitzwilliam of the Highland Brigade in Inverness. I understand you were present at the first attack?"

"Yes" said Thomas, "but I know nothing about the second?"

"A number of soldiers on an exercise were attacked and killed last night, we found their remains this morning," the Major-General explained solemnly.

"This morning?" said Thomas in surprise, "that's unusual."

"How do you mean, Mr. Walker?" asked the Major-General

"The animal had already fed," explained Thomas. "Normally, large carnivorous mammals will only kill every couple of days."

"This animal killed seven soldiers in one sitting," continued the Major-General.

"And as far as we can tell, it ate from the remains of each corpse," the Chief Constable added.

Thomas sat back in the armchair and frowned. *This isn't making any sense*, thought Thomas. *What animal would feed like that?*

"I see that you are as perplexed as we are, Mr. Walker," said the Chief Constable. "We spoke to your director. She said that you had some experience in this area?"

"Yes, you could say that," replied Thomas distantly, re-joining the conversation.

"What on earth do you think it could be?" asked the Major-General.

"I think that we are dealing with a member of the big cat family, possibly a jaguar," Thomas answered. "And it's big, although I can't be sure as I haven't found any pug marks yet."

The Chief Constable and the Major-General looked at

each other with grim expressions. Rather than dismissing the theory, Thomas thought they looked quite worried and had readily believed him.

"When you say big?" The Chief Inspector asked.

"I mean bigger than anything I've come across," Thomas answered quickly. "I found claw markings larger than my hand on a tree near the hunter who was killed. I also found indications that the cat carried the body for over half a mile. That on its own reduces the list of suspect animals dramatically."

The Major-General looked incredibly grave and he addressed Thomas with a serious tone that he wasn't accustomed to. It made him feel very uneasy.

"Mr. Walker, we were told that you had specific experience dealing with man-eaters, is that true?"

"Yes," said Thomas hesitantly. He felt panicked, that he was somehow being pushed towards a situation he wasn't ready for.

"Has there been anything you've seen in the last couple of months that would lead you to believe that a large predator was in the area?"

"Actually, yes we have" replied Thomas. "There have apparently been a number of livestock killings, one of which I examined yesterday morning. And our local population of wild cats seems to have vanished. Both would indicate the presence of a large, territorial carnivore. Most of the evidence I've only seen in the last twenty-four hours though, suggesting this cat is a new arrival."

"Mr. Walker" said the Chief Constable, "would you mind coming down to the village with us, we've set up a temporary headquarters there. There are a few people I think you should meet."

"Well I think I'll need a shower first if you don't mind," Thomas shrugged.

Major-General Fitzwilliam glanced at the bottle of Lagavulin on the table. He smiled knowingly and seemed to relax.

"Expensive night," he stated.

"In more ways than one by the sounds of it," sighed Thomas as he headed towards the stairs.

Thomas emptied a large quantity of dry dog food into Meg's stainless steel bowl. She padded through from the hall at the sound and began to eat, slowly. He patted her head softly and left her to it, knowing that she needed the rest. As he pretended to busy himself in the kitchen, he slipped his phone from his pocket and hit Catherine's number on the speed dial. She answered instantly.

"Sorry I couldn't give you a heads up you were getting visitors," she explained in hushed tones. She sounded anxious.

"It's alright. I doubt it would have been much help anyway. You okay?" he asked.

"Not really. Are you coming to the village hall?"

"Yup, full police escort it would seem. Why, what's wrong?"

"You'll see when you get here," she whispered, then hung up.

~

The drive to Cannich seemed fast and frantic as he followed in the wake of the Volvo XC70 police car. There were no lights or sirens to accompany them, but the urgency was clear. The hillsides gave way to patches of woodland and then they were among the fields closer to the village, passing the sign that marked Cannich's outer limits. He followed the police Volvo into the village hall car park, noticing it was surprisingly full. There were several other police cars, Army vehicles and a large, navy blue Jaguar XJ saloon that seemed out of place amongst the others.

The Chief Constable and the Major-General stood waiting for him. Thomas stepped out of his own car and followed the men through a side entrance into the building. Inside, the hall was just as crowded as the car park. Army and police officials hovered over tables and were posted at every entrance. SSPCA personnel also dotted the room, as well as plenty of people Thomas presumed were civilians from their lack of uniform. Then he saw him. Towards the back, facing the square formation of tables and chairs lining the hall sat David Fairbanks. Black beady eyes scanned the room occasionally from behind dark square-rimmed glasses, held on a stern and intelligent face. His silver hair was dashed with black wisps, which had not gone unnoticed by his detractors when his department had tried to roll out a controversial badger cull. He was deep in conversation with two smartly suited men on either side of him, and Thomas didn't think he had seen him yet.

As secretary of state for the environment, Fairbanks' presence meant that the Department for Environment, Food and Rural Affairs were already involved. Matters of wildlife and the countryside did come under their jurisdiction, but again Thomas was surprised at their involvement so quickly. DEFRA had always fiercely denied and rejected the reports of big cats. *I wonder how this will go* Thomas thought, suspicious as to how they would now handle such a high profile attack.

Everyone seemed to be taking a seat at the tables, so Thomas followed suit. The Major-General and the Chief Inspector sat on either side of him.

"If you're asked anything, just stick to the facts and try not to speculate too much," whispered the Chief Inspector into his ear. "Shortly after this brief there will be a press conference. One thing out of context and we'll either have a panic or worse, a rush of spectators. Just keep it in mind."

Thomas drummed his fingers on the table without replying. He was already nervous about being unprepared, and the mention of a press conference was close to sending him over the edge into blind panic. David Fairbanks leant forward and the room quietened as he addressed them.

"Ladies and gentleman, now that we are all here, let's get started shall we. First of all, I'd like to introduce you to Mrs. Molly Roberts, a member of Cannich's neighbourhood watch."

An elderly woman in a floral blouse and cream cardigan stood up from the table, holding some notes in her hand. She wore a pair of half-moon spectacles, which she adjusted nervously as she began to speak.

"I have been asked to speak to you today on a number of matters that have come to our attention in the last twelve months, and that have subsequently been reported to the police. Firstly, the matter of raided and damaged waste bins behind the pizza restaurant on Inverness Road. Just over a year ago, nightly damage occurred to the disposal bins of the Roma Pizzeria. Almost every night the bins would be raided, eventually ending in the actual destruction of the bins. In the end, the owners of the pizzeria invested in a large sealed disposal unit that seemed to stop the problem."

She paused, looked up, and then hurriedly continued. "The other matter that I have been asked to speak on, is the number of missing pets that have been brought to our attention in the last twelve months. This includes seven cats, three dogs and a pony. I am led to believe there has also been an unusually high level of livestock killings in the area including poultry and cattle. At the time, these disappearances and deaths were attributed to wild predators such as foxes, or the result of dog attacks." With that, Molly Roberts sat back down at the table.

Thomas, the Chief Constable and the Major-General all glanced at each other knowingly.

David Fairbanks eyed the crowd coolly.

"Thank you Mrs. Roberts. Now, Inspector Gerald of the SSPCA will give us some more details on the livestock attacks." Fairbanks made the introduction without even looking up this time.

Thomas listened carefully as the SSPCA Inspector detailed a number of livestock killings in the area, including a prize-winning bull, horses, sheep, deer and goats. Thomas began to consider the possibility that more than one cat was operating in the area, as it seemed almost unthinkable that one animal was responsible for so many acts of slaughter.

Following the SSPCA Inspector, the Chief Constable spoke. He shared the grisly details surrounding the deaths of Archie Campbell and Sergeant Hooper's squad. A number of photographs that had been taken at each scene were distributed amongst those sitting at the tables. A few gasps were exclaimed as the graphic images circled. Thomas studied each picture diligently and expertly. He clenched his right hand again under the table, out of sight. He passed over the gore and carnage, only seeing the path of the creature. The pattern was very clear. Each photograph more or less showed a body with a hole punched in the chest where the stomach and organs had been removed, then presumably devoured. Where the men had put up more of a fight, there were more exaggerated wounds from where the animal had engaged more tenaciously. Each picture exhibited the traits and tell-tale kill marks of a member of the big cat family. Thomas now knew it beyond a doubt.

The Chief Constable finished his address and sat back down at the table. David Fairbanks again sat forward and checked his notes. He smiled and looked up, scanning the room again. Thomas hadn't been sure if Fairbanks would remember him, but as he met the piercing stare filled with ambivalent menace, it was obvious from the predatory smile forming on Fairbanks' lips that his recollection was as vivid as Thomas'.

"Mr. Walker, what a pleasant surprise. And might I add, how fortunate for us to find you given such unfortunate circumstances," he cooed coyly, raising a ripple of murmured laughter and whispers from the room. "I'm sure we'll all be very interested in what you have to say as an expert not only on man-eaters, but non-native animals making themselves at home in the British countryside. I'm sure your opinion will prove valuable."

Thomas hid the flinch he felt as Fairbanks addressed him. It was clear that he was going to be held responsible for everything he said in the next few minutes. He had no doubt that Fairbanks would seize on any errors in his judgement with utter delight. He decided to stick to the facts, but still, he didn't like feeling intimidated.

"I'd certainly recommend the wild boar sausages at the Dam & Dram minister," Thomas replied casually, almost under his breath. There was another ripple of laughter around the room and this time it was Fairbanks who flinched.

"I'm sure as many of you are by now suspecting, it would appear that we are dealing with a large non-native carnivore, most likely in my opinion to be a member of the big cat family." Thomas paused, checking and steadying himself. "All of the kills so far have been carried out in a method that is highly representative of big cats. Exactly what species we are dealing with is unclear, but all the evidence we've seen suggests that we are dealing with a very large animal and as far as I can tell, one in perfect health. It's strong, athletic, and capable of killing normal prey such as the missing livestock."

At the mention of big cats, hurried whispers echoed around the hall and Thomas could see questioning and worried faces all around him. Fairbanks held up his hand to bring quiet and order back to the room.

"Major-General, what security measures are being taken?" he asked.

"We are stationing armed response units at every car park, gate and trail that leads into the forest, and cutting off access to all civilians. Sniper teams will be sent on a search and destroy mission once the area is secure, and we are consulting with a number of experts in order to track the animal," Major-General Fitzwilliam explained.

Fairbanks looked across to Thomas again.

"You have at least one expert sitting next to you Major-General, so I suggest at least for the time being you make use of him. In the meantime, this building will be our operations centre and a press conference will be held here at 2PM. Until then, there is an absolute media blackout." Fairbanks declared.

The meeting ended there and Fairbanks was whisked away and out of the hall by the men on either side of him. Thomas, the Chief Constable and the Major-General were the only ones who remained seated as people filed out of the hall. Thomas caught the flash of red hair as Catherine paused in the doorway. She smiled and winked at him before walking over.

"Hi," she chuckled, seeing that Thomas couldn't quite hide how relieved he was to see her. "I looked at those hair samples you gave me. They're definitely feline and definitely black."

"Wonderful," declared Thomas sarcastically, "I gave you some black cat hair and you've told me that it's black cat hair."

He introduced Catherine to Chief Inspector Roberts and Major-General Fitzwilliam.

"Where would you like to start Mr. Walker?" asked the Major-General. "Obviously we have no real protocol for dealing with this kind of thing."

"We could do with a team of beaters," Thomas suggested, still slightly uncomfortable with the sudden attention. "If we send them in ahead of the snipers, we might be able to drive the animal towards the guns, just like on a pheasant shoot."

"That's easy enough to organise," replied the Major-General. "Anything else?"

"Dogs could help achieve the same result. We could send in small groups of dogs and handlers to see if we can find a scent trail. If we kept them on the lead and they can be relied on to work, they might be able to flush the cat out. I have some experience, as does my dog Meg. We might be able to help."

"I'll get it organised," said the Major-General "and your help would be greatly appreciated. I'll let Chief Inspector Roberts fill you in as I need to make arrangements for the press conference," he explained, getting up and dismissing himself from their company as he did.

"Sorry," offered Chief Inspector Roberts, "we've had little time to explain ourselves and it appears Mr. Fairbanks is happy to have you both consulting with us."

"For now," interjected Catherine coyly.

The Chief Inspector nodded and smiled. "I'll escort you to the forest after the press conference. For the time being, it is going to be a simple statement with some already vetted and invited questions. Nobody will be required to comment further for now," he explained. "I'll leave you both to it, I'm sure you want to get back to collect your dog and things for this afternoon, I'll see you both later." He smiled and walked away, heading for the door.

Catherine slid one of the cups of coffee she was holding over to Thomas. "Black with two sugars," she grinned. "You sounded like you needed it earlier."

"Thanks," Thomas replied, "I get the feeling it's going to be a very long day."

"The press conference will definitely get us a lot of

attention," she sighed. "But it could be good for us. The press, TV, radio. We can't say no to that kind of exposure," she explained.

"I know," admitted Thomas.

"Now we're alone, what was that thing about the boar sausages?" Catherine asked.

Thomas smiled. "I'll tell you later. Needless to say, we aren't exactly friends as I'm sure you knew from your warning. We clashed a few times whilst he was a junior minister, and I've written anti fox-hunting and badger-cull articles that I'm sure only endeared me to him further."

"He seems like pure slime, but still, do try not to piss off the head of the government body that gives us work, including this work," Catherine jested.

"No promises," replied Thomas flippantly with a mischievous smile.

~

The press conference caused a much bigger stir than anyone had first thought. For years, various groups around the UK had collected information on the various sightings and reports of big cats in the country. Two Scottish groups were at the conference, and they were more than keen to make up for the lack of information being given. Various conspiracy theories about DEFRA cover ups were offered. The grim nature of the discovery and the attacks secured the attention of every newspaper and television network in the country. Thomas contemplated the possible repercussions as he and Catherine drove back to Sàsadh. He knew there was always going to be the chance some idiot with a camera would go in search of a picture, thinking they were immune to the normal forces of nature. Nature never failed to prove them wrong given the opportunity.

Catherine followed Thomas into the house. Meg barked a greeting and wagged her tail enthusiastically, now rested and much more energetic for it.

"Has Meg done any trailing since the accident?" Catherine asked, suddenly curious.

"Not really," replied Thomas, frowning slightly. "I don't know how I'll be, let alone her if I'm being honest."

Catherine smiled gently and ruffled the fur on Meg's head. "She's got a good nose on her still, and I trust yours," she replied kindly.

Thomas smiled in appreciation. "It's not like I'm expecting her to corner the thing, but she's pretty much the only dog I know that can definitely do the job. She'll get us to it, and that's all that matters. The Army can clean up from there as far as I'm concerned."

He walked through to the kitchen. He passed through and went down three stone steps into what he called the boot room. The stone-floored utility area had a low sink with an overhead washer for muddy boots, dogs and people as needed. There was a large boot rack and bench to the rear that ran along the back wall and held a collection of outdoor footwear and gear. Until recently, it had also been where Meg usually slept. He took a small key from his pocket and headed to the pastel green metal door at the back. He turned the key and stepped into his gun safe. He ignored the fly-fishing gear in the corner and cast his eye over the collection of shotguns and rifles on the rack. He knew he needed something powerful and precise to bring down a big cat. His eye fell to the Holland & Holland .465 calibre bolt action rifle. He lifted it from the rack, pausing as he caught the glint of the small gold plaque bearing his stamped initials in the strong artificial light. He twisted the Leica 3-12x50 scope onto its custom, quick release mounts, and grabbed a box of the H&H .465 magnum cartridges. He slipped both them and the rifle into the aluminium carry case, designed to fit into the tailor-made lock-box in the boot of the Overfinch. He turned off the light and locked the door behind him.

Catherine glanced at the case as he carried it back out with them to the car. Thomas didn't speak to or look at her as he opened up the back, helped Meg up and secured the case. His mind was already miles away, back in the forest and hunting a killer cat. He knew better than to go back unarmed. He also knew that once a cat had accustomed itself to killing and eating human beings, it would never stop.

CHAPTER TWELVE

Louise Walsh looked out over the playground from her classroom window. The afternoon play break was nearly over, and she watched as the children finished up their games of chase and hopscotch. A small group of them huddled in one corner, no doubt playing on their portable games machines. *At least they're out in the fresh air,* she thought. The small primary school in Cannich was a beautiful stone building that had originally been a church. The traditional layout had been put to good use, with the three rooms that came off of the main hall now serving as the classrooms for the different age groups the children were separated into.

Louise had the eldest group - the nine to eleven year olds. Her elder colleagues, Mrs. Jones and Mrs. Henderson, took the younger groups of the fives and the sevens. Amongst other things, Louise was also the acting Headmistress. With such a low intake of children and small classes anyway, there was no need to appoint someone separately in a permanent position. They had run the school like this for two years and it worked well enough.

Being the youngest of the three women, Louise had at first encountered a great deal of subversive hostility, and a two-faced attitude from the older women she found herself working with. The fresh ideas she had brought with her from the London inner-city schools had received a warm welcome on the surface, but had been constantly stalled when she had tried to put them into action. On more than one occasion, she had returned from a difficult day to her small one-bed roomed cottage and burst into tears with thoughts of returning home to the south. But sticking to her guns on her good days had seen her through, and she now wouldn't change Cannich for anywhere else in the world.

She picked up her whistle, and walked out of the classroom through the big double doors of the empty hall into the playground. It was a crisp winter's afternoon and the sun was beginning to burst through a cloudbank. She looked up onto the mountains surrounding the village. *If the weather holds, I'll go for a walk and clear my head*, she thought. There was only another forty-five minutes of school left. The overdue marking and reports on her desk could wait. She had all weekend after all. She looked up again to the ridge of the nearest mountain, lifting her hand to shield the glare of the sun from her eyes. She could now see that there was a lot of activity up on the mountainside, and whole parts of the forest seemed to be moving although she couldn't make out any individual people. *I wonder what's going on*, she thought as she heard the buzzing of a helicopter in the distance.

~

Thomas opened up the back of the Overfinch and helped Meg jump down onto the ground. The forest car park, which had been empty yesterday, was now almost full with Army and police cars, some of which sported large radio antennas. The Jaguar saloon had also rolled in behind them. No one had got out of the car though. The Major-General came over to Thomas.

"I've asked some of the Army dog handlers to follow in behind you," he said. "They'll follow your lead, and will be under your command. This is new territory for them, so we're all looking to you really."

Great, thought Thomas with some concern, although he managed a weak smile anyway. He could see four men with German shepherd dogs standing near one of the trucks. A young soldier in a beret ran up to them and saluted the Major-General.

"Major-General Sir, we've finished the first sweep and found nothing so far. The snipers are on hold and it's safe for the dog team to move in."

"Thank you Corporal," replied the Major-General. "So Mr. Walker, it looks like you have your leave. I'll introduce you to the dog team."

Thomas followed the Major-General across the car park. The dog-handlers were all wearing the red berets of the British Military Police. As he looked around, he noticed the green berets of the Royal Marine Commandos gathered around a Land Rover with a large radio mast. The other soldiers were from the 3rd Battalion Royal Regiment of Scotland, based at Fort George. It didn't escape Thomas that they had been well known for their involvement in operation PANTHER'S CLAW in Afghanistan. He wasn't sure if it was irony, fate or just some marketing officer who was laughing at him right now.

Major-General Fitzwilliam returned the salutes he received as they neared.

"Sergeant Brodie, this is Thomas Walker. He'll be leading your team and giving you some insight into your quarry. He has experience with this kind of dangerous animal, so take his advice seriously."

"Yes sir." Brodie answered.

The sergeant's smile seemed genuine, and there didn't seem to be any question or mistrust in his expression. He looked down to see Meg earnestly leaning in to the sergeant's German shepherd dog, her tail wagging as she licked at its nose in an exuberant fashion. The big dog looked to his handler in confusion, completely unsure how to react to the friendly newcomer.

"Meg has been trained to follow trails and has plenty of experience tracking cats. She'll let us know if she's onto something. Keep your dogs on the lead. We know it's a dog killer and it's not my intention to put any of them, or us for that matter in harm's way. We've just got to find it," Thomas explained to the group of soldiers. He noticed the rifles slung over their shoulders and winced as he realised his was still in the car.

"Sergeant Brodie, do you mind holding Meg for a second. I've been given permission to bring my rifle and I need to get it from the car."

The sergeant nodded, his smile suggesting he recognised Thomas's nervousness. Thomas trotted back to the Overfinch, trying to stifle his urge to run. He felt like he was back at school, trying to impress the older boys on the rugby field. When he returned, he found Sergeant Brodie down on one knee, both he and the big German shepherd making a fuss over Meg. He smiled and felt his walk slow a little as he relaxed. She had always been better with people than him, cutting through any formalities with a confident wag of the tail.

"Nice gun," nodded the sergeant.

"Thanks," replied Thomas with a little pride. "Let's hope I won't need it."

~

The creature had dozed lazily for some time in the sunlight. It had found a fallen tree that had become hollow, offering warm, dry shelter after it had fed, as well as a comfortable place to sleep. It licked its muzzle as it raised its head. It stood up, arching its back and stretching its stiff muscles as it spread its paws against the ground. It turned its attention to the log and left deep, long scratch marks in the damp, dead bark. As it exerted a little more pressure, part of it splintered and broke away. The creature swatted playfully at the log now, rolling it back and forth with its paws and smashing it carelessly with its own weight as it clambered on top. The soft shards of rotten bark would still make a comfortable bed. The creature rubbed the ground with the sides of its face. As it trotted forward, it lifted its tail and squatted, spraying the area with a potent blend of urine and a secretion from its scent glands.

Satisfied the new extension to its territory had been marked, it became aware of its thirst and disappeared into the bracken. Its tail flicked casually above the greenery as its head emerged through a hole in the brush to drink from the mountain stream. It drank steadily and enjoyed the rejuvenating taste of the fresh water. It suddenly lifted its head, completely alert. Its ears pricked forward and it scanned the ridge and tree line behind it. Strange sounds echoed through the woods, the same noises that had driven it to this side of the mountain earlier. As it picked up the barks of the dogs, it slunk back into the bracken. It bounded with silent ease out of the trees and foliage. It looked towards Glen Cannich, the loch and nearest of all, the village itself. It listened intently to the sounds floating up the hillside. Having slaked its thirst, it began to heed its body's next need and padded forward, heading towards the farms and buildings below.

~

Meg was enjoying herself. She strained on the lead and was pulling Thomas along like a locomotive. Her occasional yelps of excitement were met with the same response from the army dogs behind. Thomas and the soldiers encouraged them further into bouts of barking, and he was glad they understood their role as both noise makers and trackers. He hoped to drive the cat from cover, especially if it was lying up as most of its kind would during the day. They had left the pathways of the forest behind, and were now working their way up a steep ridgeline with a thick cover of bracken and overhanging trees that formed a narrow, natural track to the west. Meg stopped at the crest of the ridge and barked in triumph at the edge of the bracken. Thomas had suspected she'd had something on the nose as they steamed up the hill, and now he was certain of it. A dog searching for a scent would have zigzagged to find it.

Meg stared intently over the bracken. She stood, balancing precariously as she stretched her muzzle out over the brush. Her ears lifted and she let out a whine of unease. Thomas knew she couldn't see over the bracken and was less sure of herself now. She flattened herself against the ground and looked up at him. He knew this meant that she wanted to be carried and was afraid of something. Slightly more alert, Thomas carefully peered down the mountainside. Nothing stirred or seemed out of place. He tugged at Meg's lead gently and she took the hint, getting to her feet again. After a quick glance behind her to check the German shepherds were still close, she gambolled forward, this time sticking to Thomas's side on a slack lead as they headed down the ridge.

~

Louise blew hard on the whistle and slowly the sounds echoing around the playground began to soften and fade. Games drew to a halt and the children began to look in her direction.

"Okay children," she shouted, "form three lines please."

They separated into their three classes, some slowly packing away their things with exaggerated displeasure that playtime had ended so soon. Out of the corner of her eye, Louise could see Mrs. Jones and Mrs. Henderson making their way across the playground. *Hurry up* she thought, *it's cold*.

~

The creature had edged its way down the mountain, drawing closer to the warm sounds coming from the village. It slunk along the verge and crept up to the stone river that separated Cannich from the mountainside. It paused, hesitating to enter the new environment. It watched and waited, making sure there was no danger here. Its unease lifting, the creature bounded effortlessly across the warm dry surface and over a wall on the other side. It found that the hard ground naturally silenced its footfalls, and it slipped from shadow to shadow as it followed a tree-lined hedgerow. It heard the two female animals chattering on the other side of the hedge and stalked closer. It could sense their frailty in their laboured breathing and padded nearer. They were sitting on a flat piece of dead wood, and had not heard the creature's approach. Just as it began to flank them, its nostrils were stung by the strong opium scent that hung about them like a cloud. Its lips wrinkled in distaste and it changed course back along the hedgerow. As it rounded a bend, it picked up the sounds that had first roused its curiosity. It padded silently between two stone columns and froze as it saw movement ahead. It had found its prey.

~

Thomas worked his way down the ridge with the Army dog team close behind. As they dipped below the tree line, they found themselves on a gentle slope covered with bracken. Snowdrops and wood crocus had begun to break free from the earth but were not quite yet in flower. It was beautiful and silent, except for the babble of a stream further down. Meg gave three short barks. Her attention was focused on the other side of the bracken and Thomas knew she had found something. He turned and signalled to the soldiers. They all raised their rifles in readiness and began to creep forward.

~

Aaron Meeks had taken his rucksack off and was putting his games machine into it, when a movement near the gate made him look up. He started to tremble as he watched the hulking creature strut into the playground. He began to shake with fear as he looked around to see if anyone else was watching. He went to call out but found his voice frozen in his throat. He glanced back again to the creature. It had stopped, and was looking straight at him. Its green eyes were fixed on his. As Aaron stared back, he realised the only thing it could be was a monster. He dropped his rucksack and began to stumble backwards towards the other children. The monster lurched forward with a terrible roar that almost knocked Aaron over. This time, the scream came freely as he ran in terror towards his teacher, Miss Walsh.

~

Thomas and the soldiers spread out over the area where they'd found the smashed trunk and flattened bracken. Thomas could see the clear outline of the bed the creature had used. It reminded him of the grass nests he had seen tigers make in the Sundarbans of India. Meg and the other dogs would not walk onto the bracken or approach the trunk shards, whining uneasily in the presence of the strong territory marking they all could smell. Meg pulled gently on the lead, her nose pointing down the slope.

"Let's not waste any time," Thomas declared, "call the helicopter and let them know where we are, and that it might be heading towards more open terrain to the west."

Their position was relayed to the camp at the car park to pass on to the helicopter, and they began their descent. The village lay below them as the forest swept to the north over the mountainside and into Glen Cannich towards the loch. He paused for a second as he tried to anticipate the route the cat would take. The forest path seemed the most likely. He was about to tug Meg back that way, when what sounded like a scream floated thinly up the mountainside. As a second wail met them, the real route the cat had taken became painfully clear to him.

"Oh my God," exclaimed Thomas in disbelief as the reality struck him.

He slipped Meg's leash as did the soldiers with the German shepherds behind. They all began to run down the slope towards the screams.

~

The creature was startled by the sound and movement that suddenly erupted around it. It roared in angry warning as the young animals bolted back towards the older females and the stone dwelling behind them. It pounced instinctively towards the movement in front of it, cuffing the small thing with a swipe of its paw.

Louise watched in horror as something from a nightmare played out before her. She watched as the gruesome, rippling shape sent little Aaron Meeks flying across the playground. He landed in a heap and did not move once he had crumpled to the floor. Before she had time to think, she found herself running, screaming as she streaked towards the boy. Crying out in terror as tears formed in her eyes, she gasped for air and checked Aaron for signs of life. He was still breathing but looked incredibly pale. She turned his head carefully and as she went to pick him up, felt the blood under his clothes. She glanced towards the open doors of the hall, but instinct spun her back round. She stopped dead as she came face to face with something monstrous, and stared into the green flashing eyes of the creature as it stepped towards her, its face distorting into an angry snarl.

Louise and the creature stared at each other. She felt rooted to the spot, as if she couldn't move. Instinct tried to pull her away from the hypnotic gaze of the monster. Somewhere in her subconscious, genetic memory of something sinister stirred. It triggered her body, resuscitating movement to her limbs as she took a step backwards and glanced again at the doors behind. Mrs. Henderson ushered in the last of the children, sobbing as they went. She looked desperately towards Louise, but she too was frozen in fear. Louise looked back to the creature. It snarled. The implied menace was clear and guttural this time. It had not come across an open challenge to a meal before, and the snarl was meant as a warning. Louise instinctively knew this and could see the creature's intent in its eyes. It wasn't going to let them leave the playground alive.

Holding the boy tightly with one arm, she fumbled with the whistle that hung round her neck. Taking a deep intake of breath, she blew as hard as she could on it. It had the effect she was hoping for. The creature leapt back in surprise, roaring again at the unwelcome sound, but putting a little distance between them. She began to edge backwards, the whistle still in her mouth. The creature flattened its ears and lowered its body to the ground as it began to creep towards her. She blew the whistle again as hard as she could. The beast shook its shaggy head in displeasure, spitting a roar at her as she edged back further. Its anger seemed to seep from it and threatened to root her to the spot again. She felt nauseous and dizzy, but fought her fear as she continued to step back. She blew on the whistle again, but this time the creature closed the distance between them, coming within several feet. It now knew the sound wasn't going to hurt it. Shaking with fear, she almost tripped when her heel hit the concrete step of the entrance. She blew the whistle one more time, the sound lost to the answering roar of the creature as she turned and fell through the door. Mrs. Henderson slammed it shut instantly from inside.

"Take him!" Louise screamed as the older teacher scooped up the unconscious boy in her arms.

She picked herself up and flattened herself against the full width of the double doors. The hall was now empty, and she was sure that Mrs. Jones and Mrs. Henderson had closed the outer doors on the other side of the hall. She hoped they had made it to the classrooms. She wanted as many doors closed between them and the thing in the playground. Even now, she couldn't quite place what it was. All she could think of was the deep green eyes, and the intelligence and emotion she had read in them. Only then did she notice the sudden silence. She had time for one sharp intake of breath before she was knocked to the floor in a violent explosion of wood and metal, as the creature forced its way through the doors.

The wood beneath the creature broke into shards just like the log had done and it raked its claws down and through. Louise screamed in agony as if red hot pokers had been steadily drawn across her back. The creature yowled with pleasure as it discovered the soft, wriggling flesh beneath it. It nosed through the shards and bit down. Louise felt the hot breath of the thing and cried out as teeth sliced through her ribs and the top of her shoulder. She sobbed, paralysed and helpless as it dragged her out from beneath what remained of the door. It paused momentarily as it bit down again for better purchase. She choked as blood flooded into her throat from her punctured liver and lung. She used the last of her strength to kick out with her arms and legs, her hands scraping against the right eye and nose of the beast. The creature ignored the mild scratch and calmly lifted its head, carrying her forward in its jaws. It stepped proudly through the smashed doorframe and walked the length of the playground with deliberate caution, never taking its eyes from the far wall as it ignored the screams and cries that met is macabre parade past the windows of the classrooms. When it reached the wall, it hesitated only for a second before leaping. Louise never felt the impact as they hit the ground on the other side.

Now within the darkness of the forest trees again, the creature dropped Louise to the floor. It towered over her. She knew all her strength was gone and that life was leaving her. A last breath moved to her lips. The creature bit down into her skull, killing her momentarily before her body gave up naturally. Satisfied that its kill would resist no more, the creature picked up Louise's corpse in its jaws and began making its way through the thick cover of the trees.

~

Less than a minute passed before Thomas and Meg entered

the playground. He had been pointed in the direction of the school by two terrified old woman at a bus stop on the edge of the village. Thomas looked over the empty playground. He saw the fearful and tear stained faces looking out at him from the windows. But it was the blood trail leading away from the smashed remains of the heavy oak double doors that he couldn't take his eyes away from. He read the scene like a map, from the bashed and broken doorframe, to the shredded door parts, twisted bolts and battered hinges littered over the ground. Finally his eyes were drawn to the trail of crimson dotted blobs that led to the wall, where they stopped. He had no doubt they would continue on the other side and into the dark shade of the forest. He heard the buzz of the Army lynx helicopter as it rumbled into view and began to circle overhead. He looked up and saw the faces of the soldiers as they returned his gaze, the barrel of the 7.62mm general purpose machine gun silhouetted in outline against the sky. But Thomas already knew they were all too late.

CHAPTER THIRTEEN

Thomas studied the ground intently and followed the blood trail that led from the doorway. It told the tale of what had taken place with brutal honesty. Here and there he dropped to a knee, turning the shards of wood over and examining them as he went. He had once encountered a leopard in India that had learnt to break through the flimsy coverings of the huts in the small villages it claimed as its hunting ground, but a secured door of English oak would have presented far more of a challenge. He picked up a twisted hinge and its shredded bolt and wondered if he would have been able to break through it, figuring he probably could with enough of a run up. Maybe then, it wouldn't be so difficult for a cat that might weigh twice as much as he did. He followed the blood trail back towards the wall. It wasn't a drag mark. The cat had carried its meal. The trail ended abruptly some twenty feet from the wall.

The soldiers had taken up positions at every entrance to the school and a quick thinking child had already called the emergency services. The sirens and blue flashing lights bounced and reflected off the walls and windows of the surrounding buildings. His right hand was shaking violently, and he was unable to stop it as the cries and wails of the children echoed around the empty playground. There was too much distracting him here and too many questions flooding into his head. He dropped to one knee again, feeling giddy and overwhelmed. His eyes fixed on the wall. There was only one place to go where he might find answers and peace. He stood up, took a moment to quiet himself and walked over to Sergeant Brodie, who was holding Meg's lead and stroking her reassuringly.

"I'm going to need you to wait here," Thomas explained to Brodie. "If it's feeding on its kill, I have a good chance to end this. We can't be stealthy as a group, but I can move faster and quieter on my own. I might be able to catch up with it."

Brodie raised an eyebrow. "Rather you than me sir," he replied. He glanced at Thomas's rifle then around the empty playground. "Kill this thing, get it done."

"I intend to," Thomas replied gravely as he turned away.

"Sir, one more thing," Brodie asked broodingly. "Why is it killing so often?"

"I don't know," Thomas replied, his frustration showing. "It's unprecedented to say the least. I can't help wondering if there's more than one of them. Maybe it has cubs."

"Maybe it just likes it?" Brodie offered.

Thomas nodded in silence and then turned and walked across the playground with quick strides. He used a bench against the wall to step up onto the top. He pulled himself over with a little effort and then gently and silently dropped to the ground on the other side.

At his feet was a splash of blood, quickly becoming dry. A studious glance told him the direction the animal had taken, and that it had been in a hurry. He crouched there in the shadows, pulling the collar of his jacket up to mask his face. He slipped a woollen hat from his pocket and pulled it snugly to his head, darkening his outline further. He fitted a magazine of cartridges into the rifle and slipped the safety off. He parted the brush ahead and began to edge forward.

~

Catherine normally enjoyed driving the Overfinch if she got the chance, but not today. She had grabbed the spare keys from her bag as soon as the news had come through about the attack on the school. She raced through the narrow lanes in a panic that kept her thoughts and emotions from overwhelming her. But she was unable to stop the tears from flowing as she screeched to a halt beside an ambulance and saw the young boy being loaded into it. She glanced into the rear view mirror and saw Fairbanks' Jaguar creeping into the maze of cars at the school entrance. She wiped the tears away quickly. She stepped out of the car and headed for Sergeant Brody, who was still holding Meg and comforting her.

"You just missed Mr. Walker," Brody explained as she approached.

Meg whined and held her head against Catherine. She stroked the dog without looking down as she gazed over the empty playground. The doorway in one corner was taped off, and she could see the damage and debris scattered across the concrete. Through the entrance to the main hall she could see the children huddled together and being looked after by two teachers. She smiled meekly at Brody and began to walk towards the open doors. As she entered the hall she saw that many of the children were wrapped in blankets. They sobbed to themselves, ignoring the comfort they were being offered by the adults.

As Catherine looked around the hall, she realised what she had feared most had indeed been the case. Louise Walsh had been the teacher killed. She had waved to her on the way to work just that morning. They had been there for each other through thick and thin. They had shared glasses of red wine and good whisky together. She remembered telling Louise why she had really left the RSPCA - the horrid affair with a married colleague who had manipulated her, and its aftermath. Louise had never judged her or mentioned it again. She was just one of those genuinely loving human beings, full of compassion and warmth. Catherine choked a little as she corrected herself. She had been. She was gone. She would never see her again.

Catherine helped the police with statements, throwing herself into trying to find out what had happened. She listened into the conversations around her and began to piece together what they had seen and heard. She paid intent attention to each child she spoke to, and the two teachers. She blocked everything else out but knew she wouldn't be able to stand it much longer. All too soon, the sound of screeching tyres, followed by the shouts and screams of parents, began to flood into the hall. Catherine was sitting with two little girls and they were drawing for her with paper and crayons she had found them. As they saw their parents, they jumped up. Before running off, one handed her the picture she had drawn. Catherine felt her hand move upwards and touch the girl's shoulder as she went. Although she had always wanted children, she was suddenly glad that this sort of pain wasn't something she was going to experience, at least not here and now. She thought of Aaron and his unconscious body being loaded into the ambulance, and what his parents would be going through on the journey to the hospital in Inverness. She put the picture the girl had given her into her bag without looking at it again.

~

Thomas squatted on the ground next to a large pine tree. The blood trail was becoming less easy to follow now. It was the only trace he could find of the animal's journey through the forest. It was choosing its path very well. *You know you're being followed*, thought Thomas. He looked around, tracking carefully from left to right and back again, scanning every part of the foliage in front of him. In the quiet and stillness, it crept over him inch by inch. The unmistakable feeling that he was being watched seeped into him. He had felt it before, in many different forests around the world. It wasn't one he ever got used to. Somewhere in front of him, a man-eating big cat was watching him, probably angry at being followed and fully prepared to protect its kill and territory.

Thomas sat crouched for twenty minutes, barely breathing, and still as a statue. Even when the cramp in his legs had built up to an almost unbearable pain, he dared not move. As the wind changed, he relaxed slightly as his scent was taken in the opposite direction. Slowly, he shrugged off the feeling of uneasiness and he stood up carefully, stretching his legs as he did so. He was sure the cat had moved further away or had slunk off, his hunter's intuition a little rusty but still working.

He decided to find higher ground. He turned to the large pine tree he had stopped beside and began to climb. Hugging the trunk and digging his heels into the dark, crumbly bark, he slowly made his way up the tree. Once he was in reach of the first few branches his going became a little easier, and he used them for purchase, pulling himself higher into the canopy.

From the top of the tree he had a better view of the ground, despite it still being partly obscured by smaller trees below. He scanned from north to south and back again, moving his head as little as possible. His eyes came to rest on a patch of disturbed blackthorn bushes. Looking back up at him were the lifeless eyes of Louise Walsh. She lay in a crumpled heap. Most of her body was hidden under the bushes, but her head leaned back towards him and her right arm and hand seemed to twist up at him in accusation. He couldn't quell the surge of emotion he was gripped with. For a moment, he thought he saw the dead, fear-frozen face of Amanda looking back up at him. He trembled, tears welling in his eyes and then streaming down his face. He looked aside, wiping them away. With resolute anger he forced himself to look back at the corpse. He could see the cat had feasted on her. He listened to the chitchat of the birds around him. Wherever the predator was now, it was long gone from the area. He began his descent of the tree.

At the base of the trunk, Thomas slipped off his rucksack and took out a flare he had been given by the sergeant. Aiming it straight into the air and towards the open sky, he pulled the pin and turned away as a bright burst of green light erupted from its end and shot up into the darkening sky. A few moments later, it was answered by three shots from a rifle. The soldiers were coming to him. Thomas sat down on the exposed roots of an oak and listened to the twilight sounds of the forest for a while. Somewhere ahead, crows returning to their roost were calling and bickering amongst themselves. He closed his eyes and focused on the bird calls. He picked out the hurried chatter of siskin above him. The shrill, vibrating call of a treecreeper came from somewhere to his left. Then the forest came to a hush as a female tawny owl made her presence known with a call of 'kivvik'. He shivered, suddenly realising how cold he was, and pulled his coat around him as he waited for the soldiers.

~

Catherine walked away from the school building in a daze. As she walked past the Jaguar saloon, the rear window slid down.

"A word if I may Miss Tyler," cooed David Fairbanks, greeting her with a cold grin. "I was wondering where I might be able to find Mr. Walker."

"He's in the forest as I'm sure you've aware Mr. Fairbanks," Catherine replied questioningly. "He's trying to track the cat and find Louise...the teacher who was killed." She was all too aware of the tremble in her voice.

"I see," Fairbanks added, somewhat in thought. "Not having a great deal of luck is he?"

"He's making more progress than those criticising from the sidelines Mr. Fairbanks. Warm in there is it?" she snapped frostily.

Fairbanks flashed a predatory, satisfied grin. "I'll be frank. I welcome your continued involvement Miss Tyler, but Mr. Walker seems to think this is 1930's India or something, casually waiting like any good sahib for the animal to take down a native before strolling off into the jungle to finish it off. Mr. Walker has known about this animal for two days, without any mention to the authorities

I might add. I expected it to be dead this afternoon, not increasing its tally of victims."

"I hardly think that's the case Mr. Fairbanks," Catherine snapped back angrily. "All of Thomas's advice has been valid and standard practice with man-eaters. We've never had to contemplate dealing with something like this before. Is DEFRA suddenly scared of the backlash and humiliation from having to admit it has ignored hundreds of eye-witness reports before now Mr. Fairbanks?"

Fairbanks flashed his crocodile smile again. "I have a statement to make to the press Miss Tyler. You can tell Mr. Walker his services are no longer required, I have called in some professionals to take over."

The window slid upwards and the car moved off. Catherine was shaking with anger as Thomas and two soldiers rounded the corner, awkwardly carrying a small black bag. She burst into tears.

~

Almost two hours later, Thomas was sat on Catherine's sofa, cradling a cup of coffee in both hands and allowing the warmth to spread through his palms. He was pretending not to pay too much attention, but his eyes were glued to the television whilst Catherine was in the kitchen. He smiled appreciatively as she brought out the bowls of steaming hot chicken noodle soup and warmed bread she had put together. Thomas sat up, put down the coffee and took a bowl from the tray, cradling it again in his hands for a while.

"You're meant to eat it duffus," she mocked.

Thomas gave her a knowing smirk, but snapped back to

the television as David Fairbanks appeared on the screen. Catherine beat him to the remote control and turned up the volume. They had been too tired to listen to the rest of the world's woes, but they hadn't had to wait long. A man-eating big cat on the rampage in the UK was big news, and only the second story of the night. *Here we go* thought Thomas, letting out a sigh and bracing for the official disgracing to come. Catherine had told him in private, but now he wondered just how public it was going to be. *How badly do they need a scapegoat?*

Fairbanks looked serious and resolute. "At three o'clock this afternoon, a wild animal attack in the Scottish village of Cannich resulted in the tragic death of a school teacher and the serious mauling of at least one child. We also believe the same animal is responsible for the deaths of at least eight other people. The animal is reported to be a large black cat, but we have not been able to verify this information as yet. We are currently urging people in the area and in the Highlands generally to show absolute caution when going out, and not to enter wooded areas or venture onto the nearby mountains. Specialists have been called in to track down the animal and kill it as soon as possible, and we expect a quick result with the co-operation of the public."

Fairbanks was suddenly drowned out by the uproar from the reporters, all wanting to get their questions in first. He held up his hands to ask for quiet and then began taking questions from a select few.

"Why have the specialists been called in so late if there were known previous attacks?" shouted a suited reporter to the front.

Fairbanks remained stern in his reply. "Up until today,

the investigation had been led by a local specialist who had some experience with such animal attacks. However, it has become clear that this needs a quicker and more direct approach in order to be dealt with effectively. We now believe there were personal reasons for the man involved as to why the animal was not approached or killed earlier."

Thomas flicked the television off and met Catherine's look of concern with a clumsy smile.

"It's quite clever really," he shrugged. "He'll send some of the heat over to me whilst they try and deal with the cat as quietly as possible. I'm not used to having to contend with politics in these things – maybe I should have spent less time in 1930's India," he laughed, a little too wildly to be casual.

Catherine put her hand on his and stroked his knuckles with her thumb. He smiled at her, appreciating the softness.

"It's okay, nothing I can't handle. I feel like such a shit. I haven't even asked how you are. I'm acting like this is only happening to me."

Catherine smiled kindly. "I've had a good cry and there'll probably be a few more tears to come. What's happening is horrible, but I know it's not your fault and I know you're the man for the job, whatever Fairbanks says."

The phone rang and Catherine jumped up to answer it, the sound taking them both a little by surprise. Catherine looked at Thomas and smiled again as she listened, her eyes flashing a little triumphantly as she did.

"Thank you Major-General, I'll tell him," she said as she put down the receiver. She shrugged her shoulders, clearly pleased by whatever had been said. "That was the Major-General, basically agreeing with me. He wants you to know he is on your side and that he'd still appreciate your advice, even if it has to come through me for the time being."

She tried to smile sympathetically, but she could see Thomas looked troubled. Then the door bell went. Catherine peeked out of the window.

"Crap. Reporters," she sighed, looking concernedly at Thomas. Strangely though, he suddenly looked more settled and a flash of colour had returned to his cheeks. He stood up, straightened his jumper, and smiled at her.

"I'll deal with them. Hopefully they'll lay off if I give them some time now," he suggested hopefully.

He walked to the door and reached out for the latch. He paused momentarily as he took a deep breath and then pulled the door open. A flashgun going off immediately stunned him, but he didn't let it falter him.

"Please don't do that again," he grumbled. "I have spent considerable time training my eyes for night vision and that won't help it much. Ladies and gentleman, it is very late and I was wondering if I gave you some time now you would then agree to lay off until the morning? I'm sure we've all had a very long day."

He looked out into the small group of reporters standing on the drive, and saw some of them were nodding. He knew reporters well enough that they would keep each other in line once a deal was made. None of them would risk letting another lose a story for them. He glanced at the dark sky as a flash of light streaked across an invisible cloud line in the distance.

"I'm sure you don't want to be here when that rain arrives either, so we might as well have the first question."

A bald man in the middle of the group raised his hand

and Thomas nodded to him.

"Mr. Walker, what was your reaction to the press conference? Did you know you were being removed from the investigation?"

"I did know yes," Thomas nodded. "My reaction is that of disappointment, although I don't believe Mr. Fairbanks is in a clear enough position to make any judgement on my performance. But I'm sure DEFRA, along with everyone else is under considerable pressure to bring an end to this animal's activities."

Catherine sat inside the cottage, listening to Thomas as he handled the reporters, going over the descriptions of the animal and the attacks in as much detail as he could. She shook her head in amazement. She knew that Thomas was rather skilfully not only gaining the trust of the reporters, but also turning the accusations of Fairbanks right back at DEFRA, and subtly building a defence.

A female voice sounded above the others this time.

"Mr. Walker, forgive me, but dropping you from the investigation seemed a rather deliberate act, almost as if there was some history between you and Mr. Fairbanks, do you have any comment to make on that?"

Thomas looked over his shoulder at Catherine and smiled knowingly. She shot him a playful look as she rested her chin on her hands. She was as eager as any of the reporters to hear the response.

"It sounds to me like you probably already know the answer to that one," Thomas laughed, joined by a few of the reporters. "David Fairbanks and I have come into contact before, both professionally and personally. I was responsible for compiling a report on wild boar in the UK a few years ago, at the time of his first appointment with DEFRA. The year after that, we met again in Kenya. I think it's fair to say that on both occasions we failed to appreciate each other's point of view. I'm not aware of any open hostility towards me, but I certainly wouldn't say we were friends."

As Thomas finished speaking, the first drops of rain began to fall noisily onto the drive, forcing everyone to look up.

"Ladies and gentlemen, I think nature is suggesting we bring things to a close for now. As this is a private residence, I would only ask that as of tomorrow, any questions and visits are directed to the Highland Wildlife Research Centre, where I promise to be available as much as possible. I also ask though that you allow my colleague Miss Tyler the space she needs to continue helping with the investigation - now get some cover!"

He smiled as he closed the door, and Catherine thought she even heard one of the reporters say thank you. She shook her head, laughing in astonishment.

"Okay, from now on you're doing all of our press work. Where on earth did you learn to work reporters like that?"

Thomas grinned. "Actually, it was Amanda who taught me. Some of our exploits would occasionally get the attention of the media. She seemed to always know how to get people to do what we wanted or needed them to, whether it was back off, leave us alone, or follow us into a jungle. She knew what made a good story, knew how best to present it, and never failed to credit what a little charm and good manners could do for you."

~

He was still smiling when he left a few moments later, warmed by the memory. As he drove off, he didn't spot the fair-haired woman helping a large man with some camera equipment into a van parked in the lane. Kelly Keelson stared after the taillights of the car as they disappeared into the darkness.

"There was something very familiar about him," she stated, almost to herself.

She had been the one to ask about Fairbanks and had been surprised at how helpful Walker had been. It had been a long time since anyone had shown courtesy to the press like that. *Especially in this country* she thought. The man, her camera assistant and driver, shrugged his shoulders as he put a case down.

"He did that thing on TV a few years ago, you know, where he and his wife went out catching killer animals," he reminded her.

Oh yeah," she said, her head snapping round in realisation. "Didn't something happen, to the wife I mean?"

"Yup," he replied, climbing out of the van and closing the rear doors. "She got killed by something just at the start of a new season. They were in Kenya I think. His luck didn't get much better, as I heard his dog got mauled doing the same thing. Makes sense he's up here in the middle of nowhere."

"Now there's a story I can get my teeth into," she smiled, pleased. "How come you know so much about him?"

"I used to know the cameraman who worked with them," he shrugged.

"Still got his number?" she asked as they got into the van, a smile beginning to creep across her face. *It was worth coming up here after all*, she thought.

CHAPTER FOURTEEN

The creature sniffed the air tentatively. The sky continued to blacken as it sensed the build of the electrical storm high above. The dark consumed the remaining light in a quiet purge, as a threatening and distant rumble from the belly of the tempest echoed across the mountain. The creature roared again, drowned out by thunder as the storm moved nearer. Jagged pillars of cloud were building high in the sky and the wind that had brought them to the glen was laced with a scent that pulled at the creature. It was like hot, thick blood, but with a musky, alluring sweetness. There was a warmth to the scent that enticed and tugged at the creature. It sneezed, half-trying to remove the sting from its nostrils, half trying to fill them with it. It spun in circles and growled threateningly at the open air, hissing and thrashing its tail. Its playful movements betrayed the building excitement it felt in every muscle, its eyes and nostrils opening wide as it leaned into the wind searching for the scent. It paused only momentarily, roaring as it launched into a gallop. Its paws pounded the ground as it gathered speed and tore down a treeless hillside into the glen. It covered the ground in fast, shimmering leaps and bounds. It roared eagerly again as the scent came stronger and it calculated the direction and distance to its quarry.

~

Jamie Tindall checked the padlock on the outer gate, making sure the enclosure was secure for the night. He smiled as

Boris the male puma rested his head against the wire and he scratched the cat between the ears, although he knew it was against the rules.

"Good night Boris," he cooed, whistling as he spoke.

Boris returned the goodbye with a whistle of his own, similar to the noise a person would make if they blew air against their teeth whilst opening their mouth. Jamie checked the padlock again and patted the key as he put it into his jacket pocket. It was a little ritual he went through every night to make sure everything was safe and sound. Like most big parks and zoos, Palaeo Park had suffered escapes and Jamie was determined that at the very least, it would never be his charges that one day found themselves wandering down the Inverness Road. He knew that it was unlikely that the pumas would ever go anywhere, even if they did somehow get out. If they did, they would have to cross the wolf enclosure. In the wild, pumas and wolves were natural enemies. Packs that came across a cat in the open would kill it out of instinct, and a puma that found itself with the upper hand against a lone wolf or a small band would happily return the favour. He doubted Boris or Doris would want to take the chance.

Boris had been the park's first big cat and Doris had been donated as a cub a little later, as part of a captive breeding programme. Now, they were both star attractions. Big cats always drew a crowd at any zoo. The lynx had come to the park when they had been discovered preying on the livestock of a few remote Highland farms. Their capture and move to the park had been handled in secrecy. Who had approached the park, or overseen the capture and transportation was still a mystery to Jamie. Then he thought about the new predator reported to be stalking the Highlands. Logically, if the animal was captured it could also end up at the park and would be under his charge. He couldn't quite help the tinge of excitement he felt when he considered this. The description had sounded like so many others he'd heard before, a large and mysterious black cat. Until recently, he'd always dismissed the reports, but now his imagination was running wild. *What if it's a black puma?* He thought. Such animals had never been recognised, but wherever the mountain lion roamed, reports of jet-black animals often turned up sooner or later. If it was indeed a black puma, it would be the first ever officially recorded. It would make Palaeo Park an instant zoological hot spot for worldwide visitors. *Wishful thinking* he reminded himself. He knew that if it was black, it was probably a leopard or jaguar, as they had said on the news. *It'd still make for a great attraction though* he thought.

Jamie got back into the Suzuki jeep that sported a large picture of Boris along the side, with paw prints and large graphics of the park's logo covering the rest of the bodywork. When your attractions were based in one of the coldest parts of the country, you needed as much publicity and advertising as you could get. He started the engine and steered the jeep down the track leading back onto the service road of the estate. It would eventually take him to the small cottage he was provided with, separated from the other keepers cottages so he could be nearer the animals in case of an emergency. As head of the carnivorous mammals, his charges were the most important in the collection and would also be the most dangerous if they ever got out.

When the park had first opened, farmers and locals

would phone every few days with stories of escaped wolves they had seen roaming the countryside. They always turned out to be stray dogs, foxes or as in one famous case that caught the news, a large ginger tabby cat that had been christened by the media 'the Turnberry Tiger,' after golfers reported seeing a giant cat stalking the greens. The only time an animal had actually gotten out was when an anti-captivity protestor had cut the wire fence to the wolf pen. A young female had dashed through the hole, bitten the activist for his trouble and returned to the enclosure. By then, he and the other keepers had arrived and the incident was over.

Jamie's mind was now set on two of a possible three things, a hot shower and a hot meal. The hot woman would have to wait, as his wife was a senior nurse at the Raigmore Hospital in Inverness. She was working nights this week and he wouldn't be seeing her much. He parked the jeep directly outside the cottage, knowing that nobody else would use that stretch of road for the rest of the night. He spent a few moments rummaging through his pockets for his house keys, which unlike the set to the animal enclosures, he seemed to constantly lose track of. He found them and opened the front door, swinging it inwards as he stepped into the hallway. He flipped on the light switch and draped his wax-lined jacket over the banister. The walls of the cottage showed signs of water damage and some of the paint was peeling, but it didn't feel unwelcoming. It was plenty cosy enough for him and he was happy to call it home. He shot a glance at the four small TV screens mounted on an old pine table, sitting against the wall at the foot of the stairs. They showed CCTV views of all the enclosures. Everyone was tucked up safe and probably asleep, except for Doris who was standing on a ledge in the enclosure. There was no sound, but he could see she was clearly calling out into the night. *Teenagers* he thought as he climbed the stairs.

~

Thomas drove slowly down the lanes as the rain became heavier, not wanting to take any risks on the narrow roads. His mood had improved so much that he switched on the radio, which he had turned off in case there were any further attacks on his integrity. Soothing classical music filled his ears and he smiled again. His thoughts were being taken far away by the melody. It was a piece he loved, the adagio from Bruch's violin concerto No.1 in G minor, and it began to lift him as he realised how long it had been since he'd been swept away by its soaring theme. He had forgotten how much he had loved this music. When he had first met Amanda, they were constantly trying to go to concerts whenever they could. He decided to start finding the time for it again. The talk with the press had stirred something within him. Somehow it had released feelings, memories, even the person he had been just a few short years ago. *Fairbanks be damned* he thought, feeling the tension in his muscles beginning to dissipate. He rolled his shoulders and stretched his neck, still feeling tired but more relaxed. He knew Catherine was going to be letting him be involved as much as possible, and the phone call from the Major-General had been a welcome surprise and boost to his bruised ego. He also couldn't help the smug feeling he felt from how well the press had responded. Deep down, he knew more serious questions might come later, but for now he was content.

He yawned and caught sight of Meg in the rear view mirror. *It must be late if even you're feeling sleepy* he thought, catching her eyes as she looked up at him, her head tucked neatly over her paws and her tail falling across her lower jaw. She thumped it slowly against the metal floor when she noticed Thomas's gaze.

He glanced out of the side window. Just for a split second, a monstrous silhouette appeared out of the darkness, only to melt away again into the night. He slammed the brakes on, coming to a juddering halt. He threw the door open and stood on its frame as he searched the field to the right. *Did I see that?* He reached back into the cab and flicked on the switch for the top rig of fog lights. The heavy rain drenched him within a few seconds and his eyes strained against the darkness, desperately trying to stare beyond the reach of the xenon lamps. After a few moments he realised how futile it was and more disturbingly, that it was he who was lit up in the darkness rather than anything in the shadows. He climbed back down into the cab and ruffled the excess water from his hair with his hand. *I really am tired* he thought, and criticised himself for driving whilst so fatigued. He considered turning round and staying with Catherine, and knew he really was exhausted when he lingered on the thought a little too long. *It was too big* he told himself as his thoughts returned to the moment. *There are probably cattle in the field.* He looked into the darkness again, shook his head and smiled. *A big black cat Thomas, even your limited imagination can do better than that,* he scoffed silently. He closed the window and started off down the lane again.

~

The creature raced down the ridgeline, watching the car approach along the stone river below. It was still cautious, but it knew there was nothing to fear. Though it looked and sounded alive, it now recognised the vehicle for what it was. It accelerated into a tremendous reaching leap as it cleared the car and landed in the field on the other side of the stone river. It slowed and stopped, instinct muffling the roar that had built in its throat as it heard the tyres bite into the tarmac and come to a shuddering stop. A muted growl instead was lost into the wind and rain. It looked back, a twitch of anticipation showing in the tip of its tail. It watched the man for a moment, decided there was no threat and moved off, only leaving a shadow in its wake before it disappeared into the darkness.

~

Thomas turned into the drive and was more than a little pleased to see Sàsadh come into view as he rounded the corner. He parked the Overfinch right in front of the house, not bothering with the garage and the dash through the storm it would involve. Meg jumped through to the passenger seat and he scooped her up under his arm. He opened the door, kicked it shut with the back of his boot, and ran to the shelter of the porch. He carried Meg through to the boot room and began to towel her down, making sure her paws were clean. When he was satisfied she was warm and contented enough in her basket, he headed up the stairs towards the snugness of his own bed.

~

The creature paused opposite the entrance to Palaeo Park. Its senses were exploding. Strange calls echoed into the night and a multitude of scents pricked at its nostrils. Laced thinly over everything though, was the sweet, musty taint it had followed. It cleared the twin five-bar gates and loped silently over a knoll. At the top, it saw a large wooden structure directly ahead. It could sense the animals inside moving and calling to each other. It dropped to its belly and crawled a little closer, its curiosity distracting it once more. The size and proximity of the animals intrigued it. Here was prey, but unlike any it had encountered before. The creature trotted over the ground and soon reached a small open doorway, which it squeezed through silently. It slipped past some stairs and rounded a corner and came to a halt. It licked its muzzle as twenty bison looked back at it in bewilderment.

The bison snorted and stamped in fear, pressing into the furthest corner of their enclosure. The creature became excited, realising their confinement. It lifted off the ground in a lazy leap and cleared the wooden fence between it and the bison. It stepped forward, a growl of intent reverberating around the barn. Some of the animals bolted at the sound, running in a circle around the pen that until now they had always come to for shelter. The creature sprung forward, leaping upon the hindquarters of a female as she rushed past. Its claws slashed at the moving flesh beneath, bringing the bison crashing to the floor under the weight of the beast upon its back. The creature lurched forward again, opening its jaws wide to engulf the bison's throat. Its curved canines slashed and severed the jugular vein and crushed the windpipe instantaneously. The warm blood flowing over its tongue excited it further, and it bit down harder, killing the animal quickly. The creature wrenched its head backwards instinctively, ripping out the throat of the bison with ease. It growled with pleasure. The action had come to it naturally, a matter of instinct that had lain dormant in its genetic makeup until now.

The remaining bison huddled in the corner, nervously calling to one another. The dominant bull snorted and took a few steps toward the creature. It stamped the straw covered floor and bellowed a warning, but it hesitated to draw closer. Its fear and nervousness were all too obvious to the creature as it emitted an equally cautionary growl. The bull lowered its head, exposing its small but lethally sharp and twisted horns. Another bellow followed. The creature snarled angrily and swiped at the bull, leaving deep slash marks on the side of its head. The bull charged instinctively, carrying enough force and momentum over the short distance to knock the creature to the ground, winding and surprising it. But in its defiance the bull drew too close, and as the creature twisted onto its back, it lunged upwards with open maw, meeting the bull's throat and finding purchase. The bull fell to its knees, a despairing moan escaping its throat as it slumped on top of the creature that had killed it. Squirming underneath the body of the bull, the creature kicked out with its hind legs and flung the carcass to one side. It stood up and tore a huge chunk of flesh from one of the bull's rear legs. It cleaned itself and slipped out of the building, back on the trail of the scent.

The first fence it came to it cleared with a powerful jump, only to find itself penned in by a second and higher wire barrier. It tested it first by pressing its weight against the mesh, feeling the buckle. It threw itself at the wire and again felt it give a little. It barrelled into the obstacle one last time, feeling it tear and give way under its bulk. It trotted up the brow of a hill beyond the fence and froze. Nine pairs of eyes glistened at it in the darkness. An ominous howl lifted into the night, causing the creature to flatten its ears and snarl a warning. It sank to the ground, coiled and ready to spring as it listened to the wolves approach.

The first rushed in, too eager and without caution. With a hiss, the creature landed a lightning quick strike with its paw and sent the young adult flying. The wolf did not get up again. Another dashed in, striking under the creature's head as it tried to snatch at the throat. The creature bore down on the wolf, trapping it against its chest with its weight as it bit down into its head. Enraged and fuelled by the scent of the blood, the creature leapt forward into the pack. Its claws slashed with deadly precision at the flashing flanks surrounding it, whilst its paws rained skull crushing blows onto the head of any wolf that ventured too close. It saw the pack leader dash past to try and get behind it, and readied itself. As the large black wolf leapt towards its back, the creature spun and rose up onto its haunches, closing its jaws over the dark, shaggy canine. It shook the pack leader violently and threw it to the ground. It roared at the carnage surrounding it and made a few vengeful swipes at the limp corpse of the nearest wolf. It licked its wounds and then stopped, sniffing the air purposefully. Its goal was close now. It trotted forward, purring as it approached the structure silhouetted against the night sky.

~

Jamie made his way down the stairs in a care-free manner, rubbing his hair with a towel and shaking off the remainder of a hard day's work. His mind was set on a bottle of beer that had been sat in the fridge for a while and maybe a film, if there was one on TV. He stretched his neck slowly and methodically until he heard the satisfying crack. He glanced at the monitors and dropped the towel in shock. He could make out Boris and Doris pacing in their pen. It was unusual for them to be outside at night, but that hadn't been what had startled him. The light was poor in the wolf enclosure, but he could still make out the lifeless bodies as they lay in the grass. The one nearest the camera was clearly dead, its broken back distorting its normally svelte shape.

Jamie dashed back up the stairs and quickly pulled his work clothes back on. He returned to the hallway and unlocked the large cupboard at the foot of the stairs. He took out the dart rifle along with a box of drugs and darts. He glanced at the alarm switch and the row of red bulbs below it, each of which designated an area of the park. He reached out towards the switch, but the bells started ringing before he got there, making him jump so badly that he almost dropped the gun. One by one, each of the bulbs began to flash. *What the hell?* Jamie thought, then opened the door and ran out into the night.

~

Boris growled menacingly at the creature as it approached. He turned and snarled at Doris in warning, and she bolted into her concrete bunker without hesitating. The creature stopped and lowered its head, staring intently at Boris. Its green eyes flashed and the purring noise stopped. In its place, came a low, penetrating growl filled with menace. Boris stamped his paws close to the fence, spitting and hissing at the creature as he did so. The creature panted loudly as it watched Boris begin to pace back and forth along the enclosure.

The creature sprang forward without warning, only to find the tough mesh before it less forgiving than those it had encountered earlier. Now it too began to pace, looking for an easier point of entry. Finding none, it sprang again, testing different sections as it went. On its fifth attempt, it felt the buckle and strain of the mesh. The worn screws holding that section of fence in place were no match to its fury as it charged. Boris didn't hesitate and threw himself onto the back of the intruder. Nature had equipped Boris with the largest teeth of the small cats, and he put the two-inch canines to savage use, tearing at the ruff of the creature's neck and drawing blood. The creature roared in pain, spinning round in order to try and dislodge its attacker. Boris used his agility over his larger adversary to his advantage, balancing precariously on its back and extending his claws into the taught muscular flesh, all the while refusing to release the folds of skin between his jaws.

The creature lashed out in frustration, then fury, but to no avail as Boris clung to its back, omitting a low growl through his teeth. In desperation, the creature bucked and reared up momentarily onto its hind legs. This was enough for Boris's rear end to slip. As he slid backwards, he was forced to release his grip, but not before he left deep gashes in the creature's flank with a rake of his claws. The creature spun round with a savage roar as it met its attacker face to face. The two combatants began to circle each other, Boris's hissing and snarls drowned out by the monstrous roars and guttural growls of the creature. Boris launched the first attack, serving a well aimed bite to the chest. But before he could jump away again, the creature dealt a deep slash with the strike of a tooth against his shoulder. Boris scuttled backwards, screaming with pain. Again they circled, snarling together as they slowly worked closer and closer to each other.

Boris relied on his agility. Not daring to risk another bite, he pounced forward and swiped at the creature like a boxer, with quick repetitive jabs and slashes from his claws. With a frustrated and angry roar the creature rocketed forward, taking a swipe at Boris with a paw that came down like a cudgel and knocked the big cat to the ground, stunning him senseless for a moment. It was all the creature needed. It stepped over Boris and took his head in his jaws, biting down with the merest of effort. Boris died sprawled on his ledge, his neck broken, windpipe crushed and his hot blood gushing from his severed jugular. He gargled his last breath watching the creature bring down the fence that had always separated him from Doris.

The creature towered over the female cat momentarily, growling softly as it lowered its head towards her. Doris playfully clung to the floor, her long tail swishing in the air carelessly. As the creature bore down upon her, she began to purr softly and rolled onto her back, taking a playful swipe at the looming face above her. The creature growled and she rolled again, shifting her body. She lifted her tail and presented herself to the creature, purring softly. For a moment the creature lamented its growling and returned her call with its own soft growl, gently burying its muzzle into her soft fur. It took her neck in its jaws and growled fiercely as it straddled her and they began to mate. Several times their bodies broke away from each other and several more times they repeated their ritual of growls and joined again. Doris screamed with pain each time but did not rebuke her suitor. It was only as it saw the glowing headlights of the car approaching that the creature turned and growled threateningly, stepping outside the now destroyed enclosure and calling to Doris to follow.

~

Jamie brought the jeep to a halt, staring in disbelief at the scene before him. It looked like a bomb had hit the puma cage. His eyes came to rest on Boris's carcass, where it lay strewn over the ledge. He peered out into the darkness and just caught sight of Doris disappearing over the ridge into the wolf paddock. His arms were shaking as he prepared the darts and picked up the rifle. He edged the jeep forward and over the ridge, letting it roll down the slope on the other side as he slid down the window. He brought the rifle up and rested it on the sill. Doris was ahead of him, trotting down the slope. He cleared his throat and called to her softly. She came to a halt and looked over her shoulder at him.

"Doris girl, come on," he whispered as he looked down the barrel of the rifle.

A shadow took shape next to Doris, dwarfing her as it nuzzled her softly. The creature lifted its head, its green eyes looking directly up the slope at Jamie. A heavy rumble that sounded like thunder resonated out of the darkness and engulfed him. Jamie found himself shaking. A wave of nausea washed over him and he felt light-headed. He struggled to breath, frozen as he watched the creature take a step towards him. In his confusion, he couldn't contemplate what his eyes were seeing, but he knew well enough what he was experiencing. He recalled an article he had read suggesting tigers used infrasound, a penetrating sub-wave of pressure emitted in their roar that could subdue and disorientate their prey. It was almost by accident that his trembling finger tightened over the trigger. The creature's roar brought him out of his frozen state and he quickly began to load a second dart. He looked back down the slope and saw that Doris was still staring back at him. He took careful aim and squeezed the trigger again. He watched the dart impact and puncture Doris's flank. She jumped as she felt the impact, and trotted a few feet before she quizzically looked back at him again and slumped to the ground. Jamie let out a sigh of nervous elation and wiped the sweat from his brow. It was then that he heard the growl again, much nearer this time and behind him.

The impact came a few seconds after. He was showered with shattered glass as the jeep rocked violently with the force. As a second blow came, the jeep began to overbalance and slid onto its side as the momentum pushed it over. Jamie felt something rip into his leg and then he was being lifted and dragged from the jeep. He tried to get his arms up over his head, knowing that most cats attacked from behind and looked to deliver the fatal blow at the neck. He felt no pain, only mild surprise as something punctured his back and seconds later sliced through into his lungs. He slipped into an unconscious euphoria induced by his brain as it began to shut down his nervous system.

The creature nuzzled at the sleeping Doris, softly growling at her as it encouraged her to get up and follow. It placed a paw on her shoulder and tried to roll her upright. It turned in frustration at the sounds and lights coming up the slope towards it. It roared one last time at the approaching figures and bounded up the hill, taking the body of Jamie Tindall in its jaws and disappearing into the black night.

CHAPTER FIFTEEN

Thomas woke as a slither of sunlight crept over the bedcovers towards him. He stretched and smiled in relief. No bad dreams, no sweat soaked sheets. He felt rested. The combination of exhaustion and the talk with the press had given him a good night's sleep. It was also the weekend, although he knew that Catherine would almost certainly be calling at some point. It wasn't like the cat was just going to go away. Regardless, he decided to start the day as if he had it to himself. It was early and the sun was still trying to find its place in the sky. He threw off the bed covers and lumbered downstairs.

A little while later he was sat in a cedar recliner on the matching decking at the back of Sàsadh. He closed his eyes and lingered a few moments as he enjoyed the touch of the warming sunshine on his feet. He could smell the aroma of the coffee on the table beside him, and he considered leaning down for it. The oily residue of the espresso glistened in the soft light, and he watched contentedly as steam wisped out of the cup into the cool morning air. He found the temperature refreshing rather than chilly, and he wasn't the only one who thought it was warm enough to be outside. As soon as he had opened the cantilever doors, he had noticed the visitor sitting between two ornamental boulders just a few feet off the decking.

The adder hadn't stirred since he had stepped outside and now he was in a private contest to see which of them would move first. Like many animals thought to truly hibernate in winter, adders were prone to occasionally wake and seek out warmth, or new lodgings if their holes became too wet or frozen. As Scotland's only snake, they also were the most versatile and adaptive of their kind, coping easily with a climate other reptiles struggled in. Eventually the viper lifted its head and tasted the air with its tongue. It seemed to look at Thomas and size him up before slithering off towards the undergrowth slowly, no doubt back to a hole or rotting log, where it would spend a few more weeks dozing before spring, sunlight and sex would tempt it back into the light.

Thomas looked back through the glass to Meg on the other side of the closed doors. He hadn't wanted to risk her disturbing the snake and getting bitten. The venom was rarely fatal to a human unless they happened to be allergic, but they certainly had the potential to deliver a deathly bite to a dog. Thomas had judged by the size of the snake that it was a female, being larger and sporting a rusty brown diamond pattern, instead of vivid black and silver like the smaller males. He had thought about fetching his camera, but decided he was happy enough knowing she was around and that come the spring, he might have an opportunity to see her being a little more active. He decided to leave it a few more minutes before letting Meg out. He picked up his coffee and went back inside to finish washing and dressing.

When he returned downstairs he duly let Meg out and flicked on the television in the kitchen, as he loaded the dishwasher with two days worth of dirty dishes and utensils. He listened to the news in the background, but when he heard the reporter mention Palaeo Park he froze. He turned to the TV and watched the unfolding story of what had happened during the night. Just then, his mobile rang. He didn't need to look at it in order to know it was Catherine calling.

"Hi, sorry to call so early," Catherine apologised.

"It's okay, I'm watching it," Thomas replied, slumping against the counter. He could sense how edgy she was, and by the noise in the background he could tell she was at the park. He flipped the TV off with the remote.

"You at the park already? What happened?" he asked softly.

"Our cat decided to do some sight-seeing. We have two dead bison, the whole pack of wolves was taken out, the male puma and," she paused for a second, "Jamie Tindall was killed too."

"Jesus!" Thomas reeled at the thought of another victim so soon after the school attack. "I don't suppose there is any way I could come down there?"

"Absolutely there is!" Catherine almost yelped, "I'm out of my league here, I need you."

"I'll be there as soon as I can," he replied grimly. Then he thought of something. "Cath, have a look around anywhere the ground might be soft. It rained last night, there might be tracks."

"I'll get on it, but we might have even more that. We think we've got its blood and if so, we'll have its DNA."

"That would be a result," exclaimed Thomas, "make sure you seal it quickly if so, blood spoils easily and we need to make a positive ID on this thing."

"Already done, this is the bit I'm good at remember?" Catherine replied defensively. "Sorry," she added after a pause. "I'm cold and I'm upset, but I am on top of it. I'm preparing it for transport, then it's going straight to the

Zoological Society in London. I don't think we can risk sending it anywhere else."

"I'll bring some coffee with me for the cold," Thomas reassured her gently, "and you're right about London. Nobody else has a better record of species. I didn't mean to question you. It's a shitty thing about Jamie."

"Just get over here," Catherine sighed. "Have you noticed how I'm always at work before you?"

Thomas smiled, appreciating her softer tone. He knew she was trying to smile too. "Lay off will you, Thunderbird 1. You may always be the first to arrive on scene but it's Thunderbird 2 that does all the heavy lifting and comes to the rescue."

"Whatever Gerry Atric-son. And don't forget that coffee now you've said you'll bring it!" Catherine retorted back, sounding a little more upbeat.

Thomas ended the call. He took out the green and silver Thermos flask from a cupboard and poured in the remaining coffee from the jug on the machine. As he went to grab his coat, Meg appeared at the back door and barked in anticipation, thumping her tail against the floor. He closed the door and stroked her head.

"I don't think so, you stay home today."

Meg tilted her head as if puzzled for a moment, then walked to her basket and slumped down, knowing her fate for the day. Thomas ruffled her fur lovingly as he stood up, giving her a quick glance as he left. *She'll be okay* he reassured himself.

He gunned the Overfinch furiously through the lanes, somewhat in anticipation of what awaited him at Palaeo Park. His thoughts turned to Hugh Chisholm and the keeper's family. It had only been a few days since he and Catherine had met Jamie. He wondered what he would say to the family if they were there. Would he be able to say he knew how they felt? He tried to imagine how empty those words would have sounded to him four years ago. He felt guilty at the small squirm of excitement he felt in his gut. He had never heard of anything like the rampage this creature seemed to be on. The more he thought about it, the more things weren't adding up. They were missing something. *Please let the blood be good* he thought as the gates of the park loomed into view through the windscreen, surrounded by police and Army vehicles on either side.

He was beckoned through immediately. He passed without stopping and saw Catherine up ahead talking to one of the policemen. He rolled the Overfinch onto the verge and parked up. He grabbed his bag from the passenger seat and jumped out of the car. Catherine watched him approach and gave him a weak smile, but didn't stop her conversation with the policeman. By the time Thomas had reached her, the officer was on his way to carry out whatever orders Catherine had given him.

"You look cold," Thomas observed with kindness in his voice as he handed her the flask.

"Don't be nice to me, I've managed not to cry yet but it won't take much," she snapped.

"Okay, give me the coffee back then," he replied, with an understanding shrug.

Catherine walked back with him to the Overfinch. She leant against it and poured coffee from the flask into its metal lid cup. She clutched it with both hands and seemed to relax as they stood together in silence.

"So, found anything?" Thomas asked.

"Too much by far," she said with a sigh. "It's the stuff of nightmares. Let me show you what this thing can do in one night if it really feels like it."

Thomas followed Catherine as they walked up the road. The great barn came into view and he could see keepers forking hay out onto the ground by the entrance. The huge double doors were open and he could see the bison inside, huddled together in a corner. Their snorts and bellows clung to the cold air in wisps of vapour. Thomas noticed the gates were open but the animals still remained inside.

"It's not just the cold keeping them there," Catherine explained, noticing his gaze. "They haven't been able to budge them. They moved the two dead ones to the other side of the barn, but they still won't leave. They're terrified."

As they walked in, Thomas could immediately feel the state of panic gripping the herd. They tossed their heads back and forth and flicked their ears forward as they watched the two humans. They rolled to and fro on their feet, and the whites of their eyes showed when they raised their heads to look at them.

"So strange," Thomas exclaimed. "I'd have expected them to bolt at the first opportunity."

"That's what the keepers said," replied Catherine. "Plus you'd think the smell of the blood and the dead ones would panic them further."

Thomas frowned. He would have expected that too. Catherine opened up a barred metal gate in the barn that led into a separate stable. The two dead bison lay inside, still easily visible to the others in the pen. Butchered and shredded as they were, the carcasses barely resembled the large and majestic animals sheltering next door.

The large bull lay closest to them. Thomas knelt down beside it and Catherine handed him some latex gloves. He slipped them on and began to examine the deep puncture wounds on either side of the throat. Further down the body were long, penetrating slashes into the bison's flank. Thomas knew immediately what had caused the wounds. He had watched lions in the Maasai Mara do the same thing, as they leapt upon the back of some unfortunate animal. Their mass and momentum would bowl them over, putting them on their back and into a vulnerable position underneath their prey. Claws would reach up for anything that would give them purchase, such as the neck or flank, and then teeth would rocket towards the exposed throat. It was a quick death. But Thomas could already tell that the wounds here were different. The claws had struck ribbon like gashes through the tough hide, and the teeth had crushed and opened the throat, leaving a burst mass of tissue and skin.

The cow bison was much different. The hindquarters had been stripped of their flesh in haphazard bites that left tattered globules of fat and sinew clinging to the hide. The throat had been torn out completely, along with the lower jaw. The claw marks were aligned, showing where the animal had been pinned down as the creature that attacked it ate. *You were in a* hurry, Thomas thought. He examined what was left of the head and neck. The violence here was something unprecedented and new. Many cats killed with strangling bites to the throat, but he'd never seen one ripped out before. There was something desperate and raw in the savagery of the attack, as if it had been a show of defiant strength.

The noise of a car engine made Thomas look up, and he saw Hugh Chisholm stepping out of a park jeep. He looked like a man who hadn't slept, and he carried none of his normal charm and swagger. Usually perfectly presented, Hugh's clothes looked misshapen and creased. His face was pale and the night's events had beaten his charismatic smile into a twisted frown. Catherine walked over to greet him, reaching out to touch him on the arm in comfort.

"How are you Hugh?" Catherine asked.

"Oh it's just horrible my dear," replied Hugh solemnly. "Not once in our twenty years have we had a keeper fatality. I know it wasn't one of our beasties, but still."

"Do we know that for sure?" Thomas asked, walking over to them.

"Aye, we have CCTV cameras all over the park. At least some of what happened last night was recorded."

Thomas felt a knot of excitement in his gut. DNA was great, but a picture or video footage would make it almost unnecessary. He suppressed his curiosity, hoping not to seem impatient or uncaring.

"I am truly sorry Hugh," Thomas gestured quietly. "What will the impact be on the park with so many animals being killed?"

"In practical terms, we're insured of course," Hugh sighed, "and a number of institutes have already been in touch to offer the loan of animals. We'll be bumped up the list in terms of priority for any breeding animals too. New attractions should mean new visitors, hopefully."

Hugh seemed to trail off and Thomas noticed that he wasn't really looking at him or Catherine. The words were intended to reassure himself rather than them. He seemed to notice the silence and looked up.

"Sorry. The wolves and bison are one thing, but the puma is a real blow. He was one of our star attractions. It's the least of our worries at the moment though with this thing still on the loose."

"What's happening with Jamie's body and the family?" Thomas asked.

"He was pronounced dead when the ambulance arrived. They've taken the body to Inverness for now. They said he would have died almost instantly from the wounds. I doubt that will be much comfort to poor Lizzy though."

"His wife?" Catherine asked. "She's not thinking of suing or anything is she Hugh?"

"No, the poor lass," Hugh replied. "She's been very brave. We spoke on the phone this morning. I don't think it's in her nature to be like that and Jamie was insured. We look after our own here. She'll be fine."

For a moment Thomas considered that Hugh was trying to reassure himself again, but he turned his attention back to the bull bison. He fumbled in his bag and found the metal depressor and mini Maglite torch he was looking for. He knelt down and began to examine the puncture wounds on the neck more closely. The flat shaped depressor was six inches long and easily passed into the openings on either side of the throat, to the point that his thumb and forefinger touched the surface of the void. He withdrew it and wiped it clean on the straw strewn ground.

"Has anyone measured the bite radiance of this animal?" Thomas asked, looking up.

"No," Hugh replied. "Our vet was here earlier, but his priority has been the other animals. You're the first people to

172

look at them."

"I know it's a lot to ask Hugh, but could we have one of the carcasses sent up to the centre? DEFRA may want one, but I can't see them needing both," Thomas explained.

Hugh paused for a moment. "As long as they're happy, I am," he replied.

"To be honest, that's why I'm asking you first," Thomas continued. "As the owner of the animal, you can release custody of its examination and disposal to whomever you wish. I want to try and make a model based on the wounds here. It could really help with the identification."

"If it's up to me, then yes. Of course yes," Hugh replied, beaming his brilliant smile for a moment.

"Thanks," said Thomas, "but if anyone asks, Catherine made the request. I'm on the backseat for the moment."

Hugh smiled weakly and nodded his head.

"I'll make all of the arrangements Hugh, you've got enough on your plate," Catherine offered.

"Thank you," said Hugh, taking Catherine's hand in his and giving it a squeeze of appreciation. "I think you should both see the CCTV footage, I don't feel like I'm being much help."

"Nonsense, we'd be lost without you," Catherine replied kindly, squeezing his hand back.

"We appreciate it Hugh, your input saves us valuable time and it's nice for us to know we still have some friends," Thomas added. "Can we walk? I want to go over the ground myself, just in case the police missed anything."

They began walking along the road, Thomas making a wide sweep of the grass areas on either side. He let Hugh and Catherine get ahead as he slowed his pace, scanning the ground methodically with each step. He steadily climbed the slope that led to the wolf enclosure, joining Hugh and Catherine at the top where they were waiting for him.

The destruction of the inner gate had bent and twisted the fence on either side. The once taut wires now hung loose and drooped towards the ground. Thomas tried to imagine the force needed to break through the impressive gates he had passed through only a few days before. He was about to take another step forward when he froze. His foot hovered over the depression in the mud. Some ground water had filled it and at first glance it just looked like an earthy slash in the hillside, but something told him to look closer. He knelt down and washed some of the water away carefully with his hand. Although still filled with muddy residue, the four toed track was much clearer now. He glanced back up at Catherine who was fixing him with a quizzical gaze. As soon as she realised what he was looking at, she dashed over to him.

Thomas held his hand over the deep impression of the pugmark. The palm of his hand could easily have fitted into the depression the cat's heel pad had left. His fingers couldn't stretch wide enough to cover the indentations of the four toes. The whole print had to be over eight inches long and seven inches wide. The rounded imprints could only be that of a cat, and its very size meant it could only be the one he had tracked in Cannich Forest.

"He was running," Thomas exclaimed. "This is the impact from a bound, that's why the impression is so deep."

"He?" Catherine asked.

"Definitely," Thomas replied. "He killed the male puma in a territory fight or for a mate maybe. Remember Jamie said Doris was in season?"

"That's why he came here isn't it?" Catherine asked in realisation.

"What else is worth the risk?" Thomas replied. "We're going to need to dry this and make a cast. Are any of your Army boys around?"

Catherine shot him a sarcastic glance, but pulled a small Kenwood radio from her pocket.

"Corporal Jensen, are you receiving? Over," she enquired with an air of authority.

Thomas raised his eyebrows, slightly surprised and a little amused. The glance she shot him in warning showed she wasn't in the mood.

"Loud and clear Miss Tyler, over," came the crackled reply.

"It's Ms actually. We're at the entrance to the wolf enclosure and we've found a print. We're going to need to cut it out, remove it to be dried and make a cast. Can you get your team up here right away, over."

"On our way Ms Tyler, over" came the polite reply.

Catherine put the radio away and took a few steps down the slope, so it was clear to the soldiers where they were.

"Somewhat fervid, isn't she?" Hugh exclaimed to Thomas.

"You have no idea," Thomas replied shrewdly, patting him on the shoulder.

Three soldiers soon joined them, led by Corporal Jensen. Catherine supervised them as they put a large card border round the print, and began to make deep cuts into the ground around it with their spades. As soon as she was reassured the soldiers knew what they were doing, the three of them moved on. Thomas continued to scan the ground as they went. He found a number of other prints, but none of them were in as good condition as the first. Each bound had been massive. He noted the distance between the prints. Kinematics was a method that explained how the gait and movement of an animal affected the shape, size and distance between sets of prints. Using these measurements, the size of an animal could be estimated, but Thomas didn't need to do the maths. The cat was enormous.

"What's on your mind?" Catherine asked quietly as they walked.

"Those prints back there are larger than a male Amur tiger's, and they're the biggest cats in the world. Then there's the speed and power it showed climbing this slope. Big cats normally run out of steam very quickly, but this thing kept going. It has incredible confidence, not to mention stamina. It's very unusual," Thomas explained, his eyes still scanning the ground.

"What does that mean we might be dealing with?"

"Given the size and the apparent lack of fear around man and other animals, maybe we're dealing with a captive bred animal. Perhaps the only way a cat could get this big is if somebody was feeding it. Or it could be a cross-breed of some kind, again suggesting it was bred in captivity. Gigantism and dwarfism are common in cat crosses. But honestly, all I know is that whatever we're dealing with, it isn't something I've come across before," Thomas exclaimed, coming to a stop.

"Is that as scary as it sounds?" Catherine asked.

"Pretty much," shrugged Thomas.

Although the prints had now disappeared, the trail of the

marauding cat was undeniable. The inner gates to the wolf enclosure sat in sad ruin, hanging precariously from their battered hinges.

They walked silently through the empty pen. Thomas could make out the stained ground where the wolves had fallen. He was in awe of the cat, at its bloody mindedness. To battle its way through the fences and take on the wolves was one thing, but to face the male puma afterwards was even more brazen. Unlike dogs, cats didn't easily back away from a fight, and a confrontation carried the real risk of death or serious injury. Generally, cats avoided each other unless it was absolutely necessary. If they broke a tooth or ripped a claw, it could mean starving or becoming crippled. Thomas had come across several tigers in the Sundarbans of India that had switched to the easy prey of local villagers after sustaining such wounds. People had softer skin and flesh to break through if you had damaged teeth, or they were slower and easier to catch than wild pigs and deer if you couldn't run.

He read the ground like a book. The wolves had not lasted long. His thoughts returned to the man-eaters he had encountered before. The cat they were tracking was clearly strong and as the bison and wolves proved, more than capable of taking down adequate prey for itself. It hadn't turned to humans as a food source due to an injury or disability. He thought about the more opportunistic species. Pumas in the United States had gone a century without killing a person, but attacks were on the rise since the 1990's. Leopards were natural born primate killers and regularly extended their repertoire to people throughout their range, and he knew only too well the formidable power of an angry

177

jaguar from his time in the Mato Grosso. And then there were lions. The pride that killed Amanda had been in their prime. As the three of them approached the puma enclosure, he realised that a cat already had everything it needed to become a man-eater, save the opportunity.

The puma enclosure was in ruins. The mesh wall had been ripped away and lay in a tattered coil on the floor. The supports were buckled and broken at both ends. A deep, rust coloured stain showed where Boris had fallen on his rocky ledge. The blood had dripped downwards and saturated the vegetation and straw on the ground. The smell was rank and penetrating, hanging heavy in the air. Thomas looked at Catherine but he had no words. It was a scene of slaughter.

Hugh walked them down a side track that led away from the puma enclosure. It took them down the other side of the hill and rounded a bend. A little further along, a large two storey wooden barn came into view. The side door was open and Thomas could see a 4x4 buggy inside. As they entered, Thomas saw the ground floor was made up of a number of enclosures, some of which had outside areas. The barn had a curious hospital-like smell and feel. It was then that he noticed the female puma in one of the largest cages. She seemed to be sleeping and her breathing was slow and deliberate.

"This is our medical and security centre," Hugh explained.

"What did you use to sedate her?" Thomas queried.

"Jamie darted her, we found the rifle on the ground near his jeep," Hugh replied, pointing to a rack of firearms on the wall.

Thomas stepped over to examine the weapons. It wasn't hard to spot which one Jamie had used. The contorted and twisted barrel made it sit uneasily within the rack. Thomas recognised it as a DAN-INJECT IM rifle, a high-powered model that was fired using a pressurised cylinder of carbon dioxide. It had been developed by the manufacturer with extreme field conditions in mind. He had used them himself and had always been impressed by their accuracy.

"We use a standard Etorphine based anaesthetic dart, normally knocking an animal out within five minutes," Hugh added.

Thomas and Catherine followed Hugh through a set of steel-enforced double doors into a large office. Three large screens were mounted on the far wall. The two outer screens showed live CCTV footage from around the park. In front of the central screen sat a short and skinny young man. He was wearing headphones and his scraggy red hair came down to his shoulders. He wore a short sleeved black shirt with the collar and sleeve ends finished in the ancient Macleod green tartan. Hugh walked over to the metal table that was covered with computers and equipment. He knocked on it gently to get the youth's attention, who took off his earphones and turned round.

"This is Stuart," Hugh gestured, "the sum total of our IT department, and something of a genius with these things, at least compared to me."

Stuart turned round to greet them and nodded to Hugh in acknowledgment.

"Okay Stuart, can you show us what you've got?" Catherine asked.

Stuart swivelled back to the keyboard and began typing

fast as Thomas and Catherine stood either side of him, their eyes glued to the monitor.

"Most of it is pretty blurred," explained Stuart, "but there's still enough good stuff to make a pretty decent found-footage monster movie if you wanted."

Most of the cameras were focused on the tracks and paths leading round the park. There were none in the interior of the barn, so the attack on the bison had not been recorded. But the large black animal that moved past the camera at the front gate was enough to make Catherine feel a shiver down her spine.

"What's that?" Thomas asked, pointing at two glowing dots on the screen.

"This is where it gets a little interesting," explained Stuart. "This is at the entrance to the wolf enclosure. And I think those are eyes."

"What's it doing?" Catherine asked.

Thomas thought for a moment, but then remembered something he had read in Scientific American.

"He can sense the electromagnetic field of the camera," Thomas explained.

"That certainly explains what it does next," Stuart remarked.

Sure enough as they watched, the glowing green dots seemed to fade and disappear. The animal had apparently backed away.

"It's a growing problem researchers are experiencing with camera traps," Thomas explained. "Cats are very sensitive to micro changes in their environment. Studies on everything from pumas to tigers are struggling to record the presence of subject animals more than once, even in established territories. It's now thought they can sense the magnetic field generated by the cameras or can see the infrared beams that some of them use as triggers. Once they know a camera is there, they basically avoid it."

"Our system isn't especially high-tec," Stuart added. "It could have also heard the servo's as the camera moved or even seen the light blinking."

"Either way, it's a little spooky," Catherine exclaimed.

There was no sound to accompany the images, so they watched in eerie silence as the wolves were slaughtered, an especially large wolf falling close to the camera and obscuring most of the view a few seconds in. Thomas could feel his frustration growing.

They moved on to the puma enclosure. The cameras here were put in place to help monitor the animals, rather than for security. They were positioned close to the dens and night shelters of the animals. Thomas watched as the female puma called out, her face pushed right up against the mesh. The male puma was pacing his part of the cage in the background, almost out of shot, but not quite.

A massive black paw the size of the puma's face appeared in the corner of the screen. It disappeared, but soon the entire image was filled with a blur of raging darkness. As it moved off, the damage to the enclosure became clear. They continued to watch, catching glimpses of movement in the background as the terrible fight played out beyond the scope of the camera and behind the rocky ledge in the puma cage. Then, just for a second, something loomed into view at the back of the female's den.

"Can you freeze that?" Thomas asked.

"Can do," retorted Stuart. He turned a dial on the

system's control pad a few clicks anticlockwise in order to take the footage back a few frames. Then he paused it.

The image was far from clear, but it was good enough. The hulking outline of the cat as it stood behind the den was immense. The top of its head and shoulders cleared the roof of the shelter by a few inches. They caught a flash of the green eyes again before it stooped down, presumably towards the female. It disappeared from sight.

"That's pretty much all we have. The cameras flick from one to the other every five minutes to save disc space." Stuart explained.

"Can you send me a copy of everything you have?" Catherine asked, handing Stuart a card.

"No problem."

Thomas and Catherine walked out of the office led by Hugh.

"Jamie's jeep is out the back, you should look at that too," Hugh offered sheepishly. Seeing the footage had clearly shaken him. He led them round the side of the barn to a canvas awning behind it.

Thomas walked round the little Suzuki Grand Vitara in quiet disbelief. The driver's door hung from busted hinges and the window glass had been smashed and broken. The force of the impact had ricocheted down the entire side of the car, completely crushing it inwardly along the chassis. It seemed to be slouching as it drooped over to the driver's side, where the suspension had buckled under the pressure.

"They found Jamie's body near the perimeter fence," Catherine explained.

"No signs of feeding?" Thomas queried.

Catherine shook her head in silence, her eyes darting

towards Hugh. He looked ashen and pale. Thomas felt a great swell of pity for the man and what he was facing today.

"Hugh, why don't you head back?" Thomas offered. "Cath and I won't be long and we'll catch up with you once we're done."

"I think that might be best," Hugh smiled weakly. "You'll make those arrangements for the bison?

"Of course," Catherine smiled reassuringly.

As Hugh walked off down the track, Thomas noticed the casings of the two empty syringe darts on the seat. He picked one up.

"He'd only need one dart for the female puma right?" Thomas asked.

"I'd have thought so, Etorphine is pretty powerful stuff," Catherine replied.

"So where did the second dart go?" He held up the syringe casing.

"The female is still out," Catherine exclaimed. "You don't think..?"

"I think Jamie shot our cat," Thomas replied, "and it could be out there somewhere in the same condition."

.

CHAPTER SIXTEEN

The creature had approached the fence with the body of Jamie still in its jaws. The barrier was no higher than any of the others it had already cleared that night, but it sensed the weakening of its body as it readied itself. As the lights and noise drew nearer, the creature reluctantly let its meal drop to the floor. It tensed momentarily and then leapt high into the air, clearing the fence but landing clumsily and losing its footing as it did so. It tripped and rolled on the slight slope, yowling with displeasure. It had never felt weak before, but now it was overwhelmed as waves of dizziness washed over it. The creature slumped to the ground, panting for air. As its heart rate slowed, its vision began to blur and the creature could feel the gentle pull of the need to sleep. Startled by the sensation, it leapt to its feet in panic and roared, shaking its head in blind fury. The blurred vision melted away and it surged forward, driving itself away from the park in fast and powerful bounds.

~

Bill Drayton woke with a start, the cold air of the early morning creeping into the car even with the windows fully wound up. He had been surprised the old Volvo estate had even made it past the border, let alone up into the Highlands. He stretched his stiff muscles and yawned as he looked back through the still-frosted glass at the caravan, now pitched and set up several feet behind the car. He could see that the lights were on inside from the gentle glow reflecting off the dulled paintwork of the car.

He opened the driver's side door to step out, and was hit by the blast of frosty air that suddenly invaded the interior. He stood up and stretched as an involuntary shiver quivered down his spine. He could see his own breath in the air as he exhaled. He had always enjoyed seeing that, remembering cold winter mornings when he and his sister would run to school blowing puffs of smoke at each other, pretending to be dragons.

He approached the door of the caravan, pausing a second to listen to the noises within. Through the thin fibreglass, he could hear Sarah talking to Alex in his cot. It had been Alex's crying that had forced him to leave the comparative warmth and comfort of the caravan in the middle of the night. The long drive had been so tiring, and he knew the long weekend would have been ruined if he hadn't caught a little shut eye. He also knew Sarah had been disappointed when he had told her he was going to sleep in the car, but she hadn't said anything. He added it to the long list of reasons why he loved her. *I'll make it up to her with breakfast* he thought as he turned the handle and opened the door.

~

Thomas looked out at the distant Munro peaks and then down at the empty syringe dart he held in his hand.

"I didn't know they used Etorphine here," he commented to Catherine. "We used to use it to sedate elephants in Kenya. It's a very powerful opioid. In its most concentrated form it can be nearly 80,000 times more powerful in effect than morphine."

185

"A lot of safari parks use it now instead of Ketamine, but it's really still for emergencies," she answered.

"Because they want a faster reaction?" he queried.

"I guess so. Ketamine can have a delay of up to twenty minutes and not every animal takes kindly to being darted. If you're working with big predators, it makes sense you'd want to knock them out sooner rather than later."

Thomas smiled. The first time he had used a Ketamine dart, the leopard he had expected to fall gently from a tree as it drifted into painless sleep, had instead roared and sprung at him in fury, missing him by inches before disappearing into the night. It had taken another thirty minutes for the drugs to kick in before he could track it down in safety.

"I'm a little surprised Jamie used it on the female puma though, she seems a little small to me," he added.

"I guess he felt he didn't have much of a choice," shrugged Catherine. "It can have a serious effect on cardiovascular and respiratory activity though, and Jamie would have known that. She seems fine, so I'm guessing he got the dose right."

"You've got more experience than I do with these kinds of things," he acknowledged. "What do you think the effect would be on our cat? We know he's much bigger than even the male puma, so let's say over 400lbs."

"Like any powerful opioid it's going to bind to opioid receptors, which are mainly found in the central nervous system and gastrointestinal tract. If the dart wasn't enough to knock it out, it would have difficulty in moving and breathing, as well as feel disorientated and sick," she explained.

Thomas knew that Catherine's previous work with

DEFRA on reintroduction programmes and species monitoring surveys had meant she had regularly sedated animals. He on the other hand had only used them a few times, with most of his past work being animal control rather than conservation. He liked that they knew each other well enough to fill in the knowledge gaps like this, but he could also tell she was holding something back.

"What is it?" He asked.

"The antidote to Etorphine is Revivon. It is made up of adrenal receptors and a catalyst to boost the natural production of adrenaline, as well as an increase in cardiovascular activity."

"So?"

"Okay Mr. big game hunter, how have the animals you have darted reacted to being shot with a large needle?"

"They either panic and try to bolt or they get angry and try to fight," Thomas replied with a smile.

"Exactly," Catherine exclaimed. "Adrenaline is the flight or fight hormone. My concern is that the cat was darted with a dose calibrated for the much smaller female puma like you've said. If it didn't knock it out and it got scared or angry, its body would be pumping out the adrenaline. If it produces enough, it could act as a natural antidote to the Etorphine."

"Great," Thomas sighed, "I'm beginning to think this cat can do anything."

"It gets worse. It's still a very powerful drug, so despite the animal's size, it 's definitely going to have an effect. At best our cat is going to have one hell of a headache, at worst it could go into cardiac arrest. But if it's still awake, it is going to be virtually unstoppable with that kind of adrenaline surge. It will be the proverbial bear with a sore head."

"I don't doubt it," Thomas replied in hushed realisation as he stared at the wrecked jeep.

~

Bill let the mug of milky tea warm his hands. It had been bitterly cold in the car, but with one good night's sleep behind him he silently vowed he would spend the remaining evenings of the weekend within the confines of the caravan. The little kitchen was steaming up quickly as the bacon, sausage, eggs and mushrooms all bubbled away in the pan together. Bill reached up and gave the small rectangular window above the stove a shove, pushing it open to let out the smell of the sizzling fat, and to stop the windows misting up completely.

The caravan was small but quite well fitted out. The kitchen sat to one side of the galley, opposite a small dining table with a wrap-around sofa. Behind and to his left were the bedroom and en suite bathroom. At the opposite end of the caravan was a sitting area with another large wrap-around sofa, and a television and stereo system built into a cheap looking unit in one corner. Bill looked round and saw Sarah sitting on the sofa, feeding Alex his bottle. They were watching television with the sound turned down. It looked like the morning news from what he could see.

"Do you mind turning that up a bit?" he asked, humming quietly to the theme tune as he cooked.

Sarah turned to him about to answer, but instead laughed when she spotted the colourful floral apron he was wearing.

She picked up the remote and turned the sound up. Her expression changed to one of concern as she watched the unfolding story.

"Bill, come and look at this," she beckoned.

He walked over and sat down next to her, one eye still looking over the frying pan on the hob. The reporter started giving details of the events at Palaeo Park. Sarah looked round in alarm.

"Isn't that near here?" she asked.

"I guess it's not too far," he admitted, "I think it's in the next glen."

"But I thought you said this cat thing was miles away from where we were staying?" she accused.

"It was at the time darling," he sighed. "To be honest, I didn't really pay it too much attention. I thought it was tabloid rubbish. Looks like I was wrong."

He could see the concern in her face as her eyes became glued to the screen. He looked out of the large window in the side of the caravan. He hadn't noticed when they had arrived last night, but they were the only people on the small campsite, which was really no more than a gravel car park and a small field cut into the side of the mountain. He had spoken with someone on the phone. They had told him to pitch anywhere and that someone would be along in the morning to collect the cash for the electricity, as well as show him where the chemical waste for the toilet was. He looked over the empty field and further out onto the mountainside beyond. He felt a shiver go down his spine and he couldn't help the uncomfortable feeling of insecurity creeping over him. He moved back to the frying pan in the kitchen.

"I think we should move on after breakfast and find

somewhere a little more popular anyway," he smiled.

~

The creature lost its footing again, snarling savagely as it slipped a few feet further down the mountainside. It stood up again and yowled with fear and frustration as it swayed unsteadily, its legs threatening to give way any second. It padded a few feet forward before it stopped and began to retch and cough violently. It panted hard, closing its eyes as it became overwhelmed by the nausea it felt. It vomited and tilted over, verging on collapsing into the bracken that surrounded it. Then it caught the salty, smoky scent on the breeze. Instinct kicked in. Its nostrils flared as it sought the direction the lingering smell was coming from. It crouched and crept forward, close to the ground. Its tail flicked back and forth in anticipation as it edged towards a rocky outcrop of boulders ahead of it.

~

Bill handed Sarah a plate of breakfast and then returned to the kitchen for his own, picking up the two small glasses of orange juice precariously with his free hand. He placed them on the small table in the living area and smiled at Sarah reassuringly. He had opened all the windows now in order to get rid of the smell of the hot fat and cooking meat, which would otherwise soak into the walls of the old caravan and cling to them for days. He took his fork and dug into the scrambled eggs, savouring the soft texture and salty taste as he ate them down heartily. He looked out onto the field, taking in the breathtaking Scottish scenery.

They had pitched the caravan so that they faced away from the entrance of the little campsite and the road. The view was straight out onto the back field, which then gave way to a large rocky outcrop that jutted out from the mountainside. Several peaks were visible from where they were. Closer to where they had pitched, Bill could see the first green shoots of Scottish Bluebells and snowdrops. He could see the rocks were covered in heather plants and wood anemones too. Come the spring, the outcrop would look like a waterfall of cascading wild flowers, but in the thawing grip of winter their frost-bitten buds lay dormant and verdantly uniform. Bill began to relax again. He looked up as he heard the melancholy croak of a raven as it circled the campsite. His eyes drifted back down to the outcrop, as the sun bathed the moss-blanketed rocks with lingering warm rays that peeked from behind the cloud cover. He thought he saw a flash of green deep within the rocks as something reflected in the sunlight, but it was gone in an instant. He rubbed some of the tiredness from his eyes and looked again. The outcrop was still and solemn, just as it had been throughout the morning. He looked away and sipped his orange juice.

~

The creature chose its footing carefully as it made a precarious descent of the outcrop, hugging the ground and lying in cover where it could. When its bulk had loosened the slick of mud and gravel beneath its hind quarters, it had slipped momentarily, forcing it to dig in with its claws and scramble quickly to more solid ground. It froze as it locked eyes with the man, fearing its prey had been alerted to its presence and would flee. But it was learning that man had neither the instincts nor the senses of its usual prey. It watched carefully and patiently before moving again, resisting the grease tainted scent beckoning it closer. Eventually satisfied, it slunk forward and dropped to the ground from a small ledge, hunkering down into the green heather and bracken within a few bounds of the peculiar structure the man was inside of.

The descent of the outcrop and the brief climb to reach it had been more of a strain than usual for the creature. It lay completely still under the umbrella-like canopy of the bracken, listening to its unusually fast heart beat pounding in its chest. It used the time to survey the strange thing before it, which seemed familiar. It sat up slightly, raising its head just above the bracken, torn between curiosity and its natural instinct to remain hidden. It had approached the broad side of the structure. Its whiskers twitched, picking up the slight charge of electricity from the thin metal walls. It could sense the flexing of the floor as the man inside moved, and the slight judder made the doorframe twinge. It tensed its legs for the spring but delayed its charge as a buried memory fought its way from its subconscious to the surface.

It had been very young, and its mother was calling it across the broad flat surface of the stone river she had just crossed. Hesitantly and full of fear, it had mewed loudly for her, tapping at the surface with its paw. She returned the call with a reassuring yet warning growl. It had trotted out onto the surface and had almost reached its mother, when two lights had appeared in the darkness and a roar like that of its mother drew closer and closer. The creature froze in fear, finally flattening its ears and arching its back defensively as the terrifying animal had approached. It remembered seeing the ghostly form of its mother drifting across the stone river towards it, blocking the path of the marauding monster. That second was all it took for the creature to be spurred into action, and it bolted across the winding black surface. It tripped over its feet and tumbled into the ditch on the other side in its panic. It cowered there in the darkness. Its mother lay sprawled, the great beast illuminating her from behind. It could smell the blood in the air, but it dared not move as two silhouetted figures climbed out of the monster and began examining her. They made loud, harsh noises that the creature had wanted to snarl at, but instinct and fear had frozen its voice as well as its limbs. After some time, another glowing eyed beast approached. The men had walked back and forth along the stone river, finally picking up the creature's mother and placing her inside something behind the monster. The creature growled as the memory faded. It had always remembered what travelled the stone rivers, but it had forgotten about the cylindrical capsule that had swallowed up its mother until now. It focused on the similarly shaped structure ahead of it with renewed intensity.

~

Bill sat up and looked out of the window.

"Did you hear something?" he asked Sarah, looking round at her.

She shook her head, frowning as she did so. There was a

moment of silence before the caravan pitched upwards in a violent judder, sending ornaments, CDs and anything loose crashing to the floor. The windows buckled in their frame then smashed as the momentum of whatever had hit the caravan rolled it over onto its roof. Bill flailed wildly for a second on his back, snatching a look at Sarah who was on her knees and huddled over Alex. He looked up at what moments ago had been the floor. There was a creaking groan as it buckled in towards them. The weakened fibreglass and twisted metal wailed once more before it splintered into daggers that exploded towards them, and they were showered with droplets of fuel and chemicals from the undercarriage. There was a deafening roar and then an enormous dark shape engulfed the interior of the caravan.

Bill was up in an instant and he stared in disbelief as the creature took a step towards Sarah, who still clutched Alex and was screaming in terror as she scrambled backwards. Bill picked up a can of beans that had been strewn from the cupboards and without thinking, threw it with all his might at the creature. It whipped round instantly, growling a menaced warning as it shifted its attention to him. Bill glanced at the upside down doorframe behind him and the busted door, and knew what he had to do. He picked up a second can and took a step backwards. He raised his arm and then as he moved back again, tripped over what would have been the top of the door. Before he was fully on his feet again, the outer wall of the caravan exploded as the creature erupted from the wreckage and the structure collapsed completely. Bill turned and ran, throwing a glance over his shoulder to make sure the creature was following him as he sprinted across the field towards the outcrop.

He raced upwards, following the worn path where he could and scrambling when it disappeared. The creature stopped as it watched the man disappear into the rocks. It backed up and snarled in anger as it bounded forward with incredible speed. It roared as it sprang upwards and landed on the path several feet ahead of Bill. The creature's muzzle crumpled into a savage snarl as it took a purposeful step towards him.

Bill glanced down and saw Sarah dashing to the car, clutching Alex close to her. She looked up at him, but he had already brought his finger to his lips to silence her scream.

"Just drive," he mouthed at her, "don't stop."

She looked at him for an agonising second, then flung the door of the car open and jumped inside. The creature roared again and took a few steps towards the ledge, looking down at the car.

"I'm right here," Bill bellowed, "an easy meal right here."

The creature turned its head and faced Bill again. They were now only a few feet from each other and it seemed to relax as it realised he was unable to escape any charge it made. Bill looked into the huge green eyes as they met his. Time stood still for a moment as he became lost in the depth and beauty of the intense stare. He hardly felt the impact as the creature swiped at him and brought him to the ground. He watched from the corner of his eye as the Volvo estate tore out of the car park and out of sight. He closed his eyes, thinking of the man Alex would grow up to be. The creature took Bill's head in its jaws and buried its teeth through the side of his skull and into his neck.

The creature licked the flesh from the skull and ate some of the tender parts along the back and legs, but vomited each time it tried to swallow. It felt its heartbeat race uncontrollably, then suddenly slow and violently stall before starting again, sending a wave of agonising pain across its chest each time. Frustrated, it got up and walked slowly down the ledge, making its way back to the ground. It slipped through the field and passed the destroyed caravan before it headed back into the bracken and towards the far side of the mountain. In a small gully it stopped, staggered and finally fell to the ground, as another bolt of pain shot through its chest and down its front legs. It curled into a ball as it began to drift into unconsciousness, its back legs caught in a violent spasm as its tongue lolled from its mouth and it collapsed into dark and dreamless sleep.

CHAPTER SEVENTEEN

Gary Harwood looked back down the rock face he had slowly been ascending over the last hour, letting out a long exhale of breath as he rested for a moment. He had cleared another hundred feet and was making good progress for his first climb of the year. From his position on the Fiadh crag he couldn't yet see the summit of Càrn Eige, or that of its parent peak Ben Nevis, to which it was only a close second in height in the whole of the British Isles. It was his favourite route and he had tackled it many times before. He was in no rush today and wasn't out to beat his personal best. He was enjoying the sensation of being out on the rocks again and he knew there was nowhere else he wanted to be. The air was cold, chilled by winter snows on the hidden plateau that led to the pyramid shaped peak at an elevation of 3,881 feet. It hit him in refreshing icy blasts that cooled the sweat on his brow.

When he had signed in for the climb at the youth hostel close to the boat ramp on Loch Mullardoch, Samantha had been a little surprised to see him in all his gear so early in the season. He had been quick to reassure the cute twenty-something brunette he knew what he was doing, and that the weather was holding. He had allowed a generous time in the log book just in case, even though he knew he would probably be much quicker. In fact, he hoped to be back before Samantha finished up in order to invite her to the Dam & Dram for a celebratory first climb drink. He always logged his climbs, however mundane he thought they would be, and there was nothing easy about the ascent of the

Eige. His mobile phone was also in one of the pockets of the North Face climbing trousers he was wearing, although he was more worried about someone calling and spoiling the tranquillity than the need to make an emergency call.

He stood on a narrow ledge and let go of the rock, balancing precariously for a moment or two as he dusted his hands with chalk from the bag on his belt. He reached up and felt out the position above him with his fingertips, eventually finding a small crevice just big enough for him to squeeze his hand through. Once he had done so, he made a fist, creating a tight plug that would hold him in place whilst he levered himself up with his free hand and used his feet to scramble higher. His free hand was now resting on another small ledge that would be big enough for him to sit on and catch his breath properly.

He carefully looked over the slab of rock he was clinging to, searching out the hand and footholds before he moved. He let his fist hold him in place whilst he turned his hips so that they were at a right angle to the crag face. This made it easier for him to use the sides of his feet, and for him to take a higher step. His right foot found a hold on a smooth and sloping outcrop, on which he instinctively flexed his ankle so that the sole of his climbing boot was as flat to the surface of the rock as possible. As he did this, he relaxed his fist and shot it upwards in search of the ledge above him, whilst his left foot swung sideways and found a crease to cling to. The manoeuvre he was making was called a mantelshelf. He used his hands to push and pull himself upwards, enabling him to swing his right leg up onto the ledge. By turning his left hand outwards he then effectively locked his arm in position as he pulled himself up with the right, bringing his other leg up so that he was now on the ledge. He wiped the sweat away from his forehead and looked out onto the glen below.

He wasn't quite beyond the tree line yet. The tallest bows of the Scots Pines still reached a few feet above the ledge where he rested. He looked through the branches of the nearest trees and noticed a small troop of native crossbills flitting from branch to branch. The flock was made up of a mixture of lemon coloured females and berry red males, all chirping loudly. Gary knew they were early breeders and this was a pre-mating ritual of kiss-chase. If they had been feeding, they would have been moving through the pines in silence and more guardedly. Their noise brought a red squirrel out from its winter dray, to where it swiftly returned when it noticed the human spectator.

Gary looked down towards the ground. A small stream trickled at the base of the crag and just through the trees he could see the alien blue of a lake, stained turquoise by the copper from an old mine nearby. The landscape was scarred by many such mines and marks of industry long gone, but nature was reclaiming them back piece by piece. He thought he caught a glimpse of movement in the direction of the water, but it was too far to make out. He turned back to the crag and began to climb again.

~

Thomas walked with Catherine back along the main drive of Palaeo Park.

"I've asked Fairbanks to arrange for a transport to take the blood sample and track cast to London," she explained.

"It will be in Army hands all the way to the Institute of Zoology."

Thomas knew from his own experience that the research division of the Zoological Society of London had one of the most complete DNA databases in existence, collected over forty years from leading scientists across the world as well as from the collection in London Zoo itself. Since DNA testing and correlation had begun, a multitude of different species had called the famous zoological gardens in Regents Park home. As and when the animals required veterinary attention, blood and tissue samples would be taken as a matter of course, making the building of the database a little easier for the society in a certain sense.

As Thomas opened the door of the Overfinch he saw the large Jaguar saloon pull out of the front gates. *Nice of Fairbanks to say hi*, he thought. As he watched the car slip from sight, his eye was drawn to the same female reporter he had spoken to the night before. A group of policemen and soldiers were in heated conversation with a woman holding a baby, who was trying to get past the blockade. The reporter though seemed to be looking straight at him. He turned back to Catherine.

"I think I should go and check if our cat has left a trail we can follow," he suggested.

"There's probably not much more you can do here," Catherine agreed, "but we'll meet back at the centre in a couple of hours to see if either of us has made any progress, okay?"

Thomas smiled. "That's fine, although it looks like you'll have your hands full here for a while." He nodded towards the huddle of people at the gates. "I'll put some coffee on if I get there first."

"Just be careful," Catherine warned. "Official or otherwise, take your rifle."

"I intend to," he replied assuredly, "it's already in the car."

Catherine smiled weakly as he climbed in through the open door and started the engine. He gave her a quick casual wave to try and brush away her concerns. He could see he wasn't fooling her. As he turned out of the drive, he caught a glimpse of the reporter hurriedly climbing into her van in the rear view mirror. He suspected she intended to follow him. *Not far to go* he thought, smiling.

He knew that a little way down the winding road was a track that led into the forest, an old service road to a mine long forgotten. It was some distance from the more popular walking areas and few people ventured there now, as access was difficult. He knew the Overfinch could cope with it easily, but he doubted the van would get very far. He also knew that if he could keep the van out of sight for long enough, there was a good chance she would miss the track altogether, hidden and obscured by overgrown pines as it was. He pressed the accelerator down with some satisfaction. The engine roared throatily and began to pull away instantly. The supercharger whined and spat as it engaged, its pitch building in intensity as it wound and whirred with the acceleration. The anti-roll springs fitted to the suspension allowed him to corner flat with vicious speed, the four wheel drive pulling him through the bends and racing into the straights. The van was soon lost from sight. He almost missed the small opening, braking hard and turning harder onto the dirt track in a cloud of chalky dust.

Pine boughs swiped at the sides of the car as he dropped down a gear and roared along the rocky road as fast as he dared.

~

The creature lifted its head from its heavy slumber. It tried to stand, but its front legs crumpled under its own weight. It let out a yowl of frustration as it tried again, only to crash back to the floor after a few seconds. Two black and silver hooded crows lifted into the air at the disturbance, their alarm calls echoing against the mountainside. On the third attempt it managed to stand and it slowly began to feel some of its strength return, only to become aware of the pulsing pain in its head. It growled grumpily as it walked slowly, shaking its head continuously as if to dislodge the surging, spiking bolts of agony. It panted hard, taking huge gulps of air. It needed water. It instinctively headed down the mountain path.

~

Thomas steered the Overfinch along the trail through thick patches of bracken, dislodging dry coarse rocks and pebbles that had once made up the road. He shifted the car's four-wheel drive system into a lower ratio to suit the unstable terrain. As the trail became more of a slope he felt the car fighting harder for grip as stones and small rocks became dislodged under the tyres. In the far distance he could see the bulbous outline of Càrn Eige, its summit seeming to dwarf the peaks on either side and below.

The rusted corrugated roof of an old shed signalled the end of the road. He pulled the car over to one side and got out. He reached behind the two front seats and opened the steel lock box to take out his rifle, slinging it casually over his shoulder. As he straightened up, a sound caught his attention. It was the noise of a hard-revving engine and spinning wheels spraying gravel. He realised the reporter must have seen the dust cloud he'd left when he had pulled in, following him as far as she could before getting stuck. He looked to the trees and smiled. He was pretty sure he could lose anyone who tried to follow him into a forest. Quickly and silently he slipped into the shadows of the towering pines.

~

Gary stood with his hands on his hips, catching his breath at the top of the crag. What he saw before him was something he hadn't expected, but it added an extra challenge to the day. The muddy bank of rock and scree lying across what should have been the path was the result of a minor landslide. Two uprooted conifers stuck out from the mound of rubble at an unusual angle, and between them a small piece of metal glinted in the light. The abseil loop had been bent over by the momentum of the slide, but it seemed to have held fast. He placed his pack on the ground and took out the static rope he always carried just in case. He began to feed it through the looped piece of steel in a figure of eight as he prepared to abseil back down the face of the crag.

~

The creature slowly made its way towards the turquoise coloured water it could see through the trees. Even the smallest movement caused the pain in its head to pulse quicker, and it only kept going in order to quench the burning thirst in its throat. It instinctively found the deepest cover between the trees and used it to approach the water's edge. Being an unnatural and manmade lake it had no real shoreline, but on the far side nearest the rock face there was a narrow corridor of shale and loose stone. The creature walked along this, its fur lined paw-pads smothering any sound as it approached the water. It paused briefly to look over the lake before wading a short way into the cool, turquoise lake.

Slowly and deliberately it lowered its head to drink. It took long, deep draws from the water, ignoring the slight metallic taste it could detect. As it lapped and gulped, it felt the pain in its head begin to dull and fade. It pushed its muzzle deeper into the water and quenched the burning in its throat. It lolled in the shallow water for some time, occasionally dipping its face beneath the surface and blowing bubbles through its nostrils with a wistful and playful deliberateness. Finally, it stood up and shook the residual water from its body. It lifted its head to the sky and roared with defiant pleasure as the last few residual pulses of pain dulled away into nothing.

~

Over a mile apart in their two separate locations, Thomas and Gary froze as the roar echoed off the face of the crag and thundered along the corridor of interlocking lakes, rocky outcrops and the enclosing walls of the gully they were all contained within. Gary looked down towards the ground, but his position did not allow him to see all the way to the bottom. But he could distinctly hear the sound of something moving at the base of the crag.

Thomas stood motionless as he leaned against a large Scots Pine. He flinched as he caught a glimmer of movement from the corner of his eye, his heart rate suddenly soaring as he was swept with a momentary panic. The timberman beetle continued its slow ascent of the trunk whilst Thomas caught his breath. He watched as the invertebrate stopped and its perfect camouflage markings hid it against the bark again. The panic over, and with his heartbeat returning to normal, he suddenly remembered the reporter and began to make his way back through the trees, occasionally shooting a cautious glance over his shoulder. His experience with the forest tigers of the Sundarbans was that man-eaters would use the densely packed trees to attack from behind.

~

Kelly Keelson stood next to Thomas Walker's car waiting for her cameraman to catch up. It was a pleasant enough day for the time of year, but the darkness underneath the close knit pines had prevented her from even seeing which way Walker had gone. She took a cigarette from the green and gold St Moritz labelled box in her bag and placed it between her lips, lighting it with a Zippo she'd had since she turned sixteen. She shook her head in disappointment. *We'll go when I finish this* she thought. *Maybe there will be some more news from the park*. Her mind raced, desperate to find a new angle, new blood for the story. With everyone working from the same DEFRA press releases and covering the same locations, the story was going to get stale quickly. She needed something to stir things up a bit. Her cameraman had made the arrangements with his contact, and she was counting on that paying off, literally. She had paid for the airfare with her own credit card, but Channel 6 had never refused to pick up expenses yet. Then again, she usually gave them good reason, in the shape of a well-moulded and exclusive report. She bit her lip quietly, hoping everything would come together as planned.

Thomas emerged from the trees, breathless. She turned in surprise as he approached her at a run.

"You need to get out of here," he commanded, "the cat is somewhere in the gully behind us and it isn't safe for you to be here."

"Surely we'll be safe with you," she cooed, signalling to her cameraman. He was still struggling his way up the track, but lifted the camera to his shoulder instantly.

"I don't even know what species we're dealing with or what it's capable of," Thomas gasped. "Please don't take offence Miss?"

"Keelson, Kelly Keelson, Channel 6 News," she replied, with a hint of a flirtatious smile.

Thomas hadn't noticed before, but she was very attractive, if typically so for a TV news reporter. Her soft hazel eyes gazed fixedly at him and her nut brown hair was sun kissed and golden in the light. Her perfectly white teeth gleamed at him behind soft pink lips. He wasn't immune to her charms, but he knew she was fishing for a story.

"As I was saying, please don't take offence Miss Keelson, but I have no chance of getting either a shot off or even a glimpse of this animal if you're with me, so you need to get out of here and do as I say, but you could do me a favour?" It was his turn to be charming.

"What's that?"

"It's when you do something for someone else out of the kindness of your heart," Thomas grinned. He realised that the cameraman was now recording them, although he wasn't sure how long he had been doing so. "You could go back to Palaeo Park and alert the authorities. I haven't been able to get through."

"I can play the Good Samaritan, but not out of the kindness of my heart," Keelson replied, "I'll do it in exchange for an exclusive interview. I'll be at the Dam & Dram later on. Perhaps I'll see you there?"

"Perhaps," smiled Thomas, "but only if you leave right now."

"The van's only a few hundred yards round the bend. Happy hunting Mr. Walker," she added.

Thomas watched them walk back until they were out of view, then turned back towards the darkness of the trees.

~

The creature paced the water's edge, slowly becoming aware that its body demanded further sustenance now that its thirst had been quenched. It checked the breeze for a scent, but nothing indicated the presence of nearby prey. It reared up onto its hind legs and scratched deep long gashes into the wood of the nearest Scots Pine. Returning to all fours, it circled the tree and lifted its thickset tail, spraying the ground with liberal quantities of urine. It finished the territory marking by leaving a powerful and musky scent on the bushes at the water's edge, using the scent glands underneath each eye. It lifted its head and froze, rippling to the ground as the movement on the rock face above caught its eye.

~

Gary's heart was pounding. He could feel its strong beat against his chest and the sound flooded his ears. He couldn't tell if he was excited or terrified. The roar had been deafening, to the point that it had hurt his ears - and he had definitely seen something moving. It was just outside of his field of vision now, obviously quite close to the cliff face. *Perhaps it's getting water* he thought. The stream at the bottom of the cliff passed quite close to the crag on its run down to the lake. He tried to lean over as far as he could, gripping the rock precariously with his fingertips. For a second he thought he saw something big and black, but it had moved even closer to the rock face now and he couldn't see it anymore.

He fumbled in his pocket for his mobile phone. He was excited now and he quickly flicked the camera on. He held the rope steady in his hand and with a push from his knees he jumped away from the rock. He passed the lip of the ledge that had been obscuring his view of the ground and flexed his ankles as his feet touched rock again. He swivelled out from the crag face and pointed his phone down towards the ground, his finger poised over the red button to take a picture. He was over sixty feet up and felt safe enough. The blurred black mass that shot up towards him surprised and frightened him so much that he momentarily let go of the rope. He shot down another twelve feet before he grabbed it, checking his fall. Black, razor-sharp claws slashed at empty air then fell back towards the ground. Fierce green eyes met his as a savage snarl greeted him from below. Now gripped with sheer terror, Gary punched 999 into his mobile phone and pressed the green dial button.

The creature looked up at the man dangling above its head. It licked its muzzle in anticipation. It stretched its neck muscles upwards, its eyes fixed on the man. Every muscle in its rear haunches tensed for the spring. It shot up into the air again, but this time it bunched its hind feet almost immediately after it left the ground, kicking them out in mid-air to find the rock face. The rock acted like a springboard, propelling the creature further up into the air as it angrily slashed upwards with its claws. They easily ripped through the soft material of the climbing jacket, just scraping the skin underneath.

The jolt of pain took Gary by surprise. He didn't feel himself let go of the rope as he began to slip downwards in what seemed like slow motion. His hand shot upwards in an arc to grab the rope again. He dangled dazedly for a moment, staring at the rock beside him. His senses suddenly returned and he thrust his hand into a crack to make a fist jam. The sudden jolt caused the mobile phone to slip between his fingers and he watched it tumble towards the ground. It landed on a small mound of moss and bracken that had pushed itself up through the shale and gravel close to the water's edge.

He looked at the rope with its vibrant bright red colouring, flecked with blue and yellow spots. He suddenly realised how much it would stand out against the rock face. *Are cats colour-blind like dogs?* he wondered. He seemed to recall reading that somewhere. The violent tug on the rope ripped him away from his thoughts. He almost toppled over, but instinctively plunged his free hand into the crevice and made a second fist jam that held him fast. His feet scrambled against the rock, sending a shower of smaller stones and loose gravel to the ground.

He had seen the news about the attacks, but it had been over ten miles away in Cannich and he had figured he would be safe enough on the crag. As he felt the pull on the rope for a second time, he realised he had figured wrong. He took hold of the double-upped rope in his hands and pulled on it with all his might, bracing himself firmly in position.

The creature watched the bright snake-like vine press tight against the rock and then go slack again. The swipe with its paw had brought down a small number of rocks and as it looked up, it realised that somehow the man and it were somehow attached. With its head to one side it carefully took the trailing material in its mouth and began to pull. It tugged gently at first, stepping backwards as it did so and avoiding the new shower of rocks and gravel brought down by its efforts. Pulling harder, it now saw the man high above it looking down.

Gary watched in horror as the animal came into view. It was enormous and he couldn't recall ever seeing anything like it in a zoo. If not for the pitch-black fur, the closest thing it resembled was a tiger, but it was much bulkier still. The broad, deep face turned to meet his gaze and glistening dagger-like teeth bared at him, whilst the deep green eyes gazed into his in an unblinking stare. He couldn't believe what he was looking at, momentarily holding his breath in a combined moment of awe and terror. The creature began to tug again, meeting the resistance that Gary was forcing on the rope by pulling against it like a counterweight. The creature growled, still with the rope between its teeth. It took a single, powerful step backwards that took up all the slack left in the rope. Then it took another, almost as effortless as the first.

Gary cried out in pain as he braced against the rock. He could feel blood trickling over his fingers as his fist held fast in the crevice. Far above his head, he could feel the abseil loop now taking the brunt of the strain as the monstrous creature paced and pulled below him. He closed his eyes as he felt the minute vibrations running along the rope, telling him the metal ring at the top was buckling with the tremendous pressure being forced upon it. Already weakened by the landslide, it began to inch out of the ground.

Gary could feel the slack increasing in the rope and he knew it was only moments away from giving out altogether. His strength too was ebbing away, and the blood covering his hand was acting as a lubricant, causing him to slip. With a single metallic ping, the damaged loop sheered in half and shot up into the air in a graceful arc, tumbling over the edge of the crag and down towards the stream below. The sudden pull on the line was all that was needed to wrench him away from the rock face. He let out an involuntary scream as he lost his footing and his hands were torn from the crevice.

~

Thomas could see the turquoise water through the trees now and stopped running. He stood with his back to a tree to mask his silhouette and listened carefully. He heard something plop into the water not far away and stood on tiptoe to cast his eye over the lake. The surface was still and quiet. He took a deep breath and held it, crouching down and edging closer to the water. He had only got a few feet when he saw the head of an otter breach the surface. It held a small fish between its paws and he could hear the crunching sounds of the teeth as they made short work of the fish's head. He knew that if the otter was happy to be in sight then there was no obvious danger that it could see or smell. Thomas stood up and began to make his way to the far side of the lake, where he knew a narrow path would take him along a stream and Fiadh Crag.

~

Gary flailed helplessly as he fell, and his neck craned backwards as the great cat coiled beneath him. It was looking straight up, its eyes and ears trained on him with unbroken attention. Its shoulder muscles rippled as it flattened itself against the ground, its back legs tucked beneath it and its tail held out straight behind. It leapt straight up in a vertical leap towards him, its open jaws revealing the pale ivory teeth against the black and red throat before they closed around Gary's left leg and groin. He screamed in agony, the hot blood seeping into his clothes as he and the cat fell back towards the ground.

The cat hoisted Gary into the air and shook him violently, thrashing him repeatedly against the rock face. It released him, and he fell to the floor in a bloodied daze. He tried to lift his arm to his head, as blood trickled down his cheek and neck. He attempted to pull himself away, but the final shots of adrenaline were coursing through his bloodstream and his limbs were shaking violently. The creature padded forward and placed a weighty paw on his back, pinning him to the ground helplessly. It casually leant down towards its meal and Gary could feel its hot, foul breath on the back of his neck. The creature moved its head to one side and bit down into Gary's skull and neck, killing him instantly. The last thing he saw was his mobile phone lying open, the screen illuminated in mid-call. His eye flickered across the word on the screen, END? But he no longer registered the meaning or recognised the irony as he slipped into darkness.

The creature ate quickly, gorging itself only on the parts it could immediately get to, and those that held the most nutrients or fats. Its eyes registered the distant movement on the opposite side of the lake from where it lay feeding. Its keen vision enabled it to pick out and recognise the silhouette of the man stepping through the trees, as well as the gun slung across his shoulder. It growled angrily at the memory of the pain that had pounded in its head, and the fear it had felt as its strength had drained from its body. The creature looked over its shoulder to the trail leading back up the mountainside, before looking out over the body of water behind it, and away from the man and the thing he carried. The creature entered the loch silently, quickly leaving the crag behind it. Powerful strokes of its paws took it into deeper water and out of sight as it rounded the curve of the unnatural shoreline.

~

The small wake the creature left was swallowed in the
expanse of water only a moment before Thomas stepped
from the trees and into the sun again. He could see the blood
stained rocks ahead. He stepped over them and silently
appraised the remains of the body before him. He felt
nothing now, as if he were watching someone else from afar.
He had hardened himself against the cat's onslaught and
more so the animal itself. He saw the open phone in the
vegetation and could hear the tinny, hysterical voice of the
operator on the line. It brought him back to the here and
now. He took his own mobile from his jacket pocket and
dialled Catherine's number.

CHAPTER EIGHTEEN

Catherine told Thomas about the attack at the campsite over the phone. Thomas in turn informed her about the climber he had discovered at the bottom of the crag. An ambulance had already been called to the campsite, which was easily accessed from the road. With the climber it wasn't going to be so straight forward, and the mountain rescue service was going to have to be directed in to the location. As he hung up the phone, Thomas began to look around him to try and gauge what had happened. Sitting in the bed of the stream that ran past the crag was a bent piece of metal. He picked it up to take a closer look, a thin layer of sediment crumbling off it as he retrieved it from the water.

He knew that the Highlands of Scotland, like any exposed mountain range in the world, were subject to the dangerous effects of erosion. But the twisted, broken loop in his hand had sheered with brute force, not with years of weathering. He thought about the strength needed to rip it from a secure anchoring in the rock face. He was having trouble believing it was possible. He shook his head and put it down close to the body of the climber.

The head of the otter broke the surface of the water again, but this time it spotted Thomas's outline against the pale granite slabs behind him and dived immediately. It appeared again on the far side of the lake, where it clambered out of the water and disappeared into the undergrowth. Thomas stared after it for a few moments, before picking up the sound of the labouring diesel engine of the mountain rescue vehicle making its way up the track.

A little while later, Thomas watched the men pack up the body and place it carefully in the back of the ambulance-bodied Land Rover. The climber had followed all the rules, even logging his climb with a local youth hostel, but before there had even been time to report him missing, the cat had claimed its tenth victim. Thomas couldn't help compare the cat's activity to the legendary man-eaters that he had read about and come across in his own time.

He had originally been sceptical of the stories passed down to him about Assassino, the enormous man-eating jaguar that had terrorised farms in the Xarayes swamp area of Brazil. The area took its name from a large lake called Laguna de los Xararies, christened after the endemic tribe known as the 'masters of the river', long since vanished. In their place had come farmers, livestock and Assassino. The cat had only killed a handful of people, mainly preying on the beef cattle rather than the rancheros, but his size, boldness and cunning had made him something of a legend. His ability to dispatch any hounds set on his trail also made him a formidable foe. The most famous and feared tigreros - men who hunted jaguars for a living and protected the farms of the marshland, refused to hunt Assassino in fear of losing their valuable dogs. Even Assassino's killer, Alexander Sasha Siemel, only reluctantly went after him when his own dog got loose and took to the trail. Siemel had cornered the great cat and provoked a charge, allowing him to drive his zagaya spear into Assassino's chest at close quarters.

Such a spear hung on the wall of Thomas's living room. An elderly tigrero, one of the last of his kind amongst the Guato Indians, had taught Thomas how to hunt jaguars with the traditional weapon, in the same area of swamp that

Assassino once crept. It had been his first port of call after Amanda's death and he had spent nearly a year in the isolation of the Brazilian jungle. Sometimes he drank himself into unconscious sleep with the 'Maria Louca', or Crazy Mary moonshine the natives made. At other times he violently and illegally hunted any big cat that ventured into the area, which was secretly appreciated by the local farmers. He had been accompanied then by Padre, a faithful and fearless pure white Dogo Argentino, who had been a present from the elderly Guato on the completion of his training. Local legends told that Assassino's offspring still roamed the swamps, which was no surprise given the reports of giant 400lb cats that still came out of the area.

He had investigated the reports diligently. Although he never came across anything larger than 350lbs, he did notice that the majority of the jaguars he stalked were black or melanistic in colour, and also featured shorter, stumpier tails than others he'd encountered. It had roused his scientific curiosity and he had written a paper on the benefits of these genetic traits. A black cat in a thick, dark jungle undoubtedly had an advantage over spotted variants, and as ambush hunters they didn't need the acrobatic stability of a long tail, which might get caught up in the brush. He had later also suggested that the dark colouring was genetically linked to a heightened immune system, meaning melanistic animals were possibly more resilient to disease.

The publishing of his paper and the peaceful death of Padre had shaken Thomas loose of his destructive cycle, and he had ventured north into the United States. There he had sobered up and joined a team of cougar hunters. The mountain lion was known by many names across America, including catamount, panther and puma. The big cat had started to reclaim much of its territory after centuries of persecution, but some animals were still shot and killed. Hunting was a national pastime and some states still had bounties payable on the pelt of a cat. In other areas they had been welcomed back with open arms. Families fed them in their back yards and rallied to their defence when they became labelled as so-called problem animals. The first human fatality attributed to a cougar in over a century occurred in 1991 and since then, encounters, attacks and fatalities had been on the increase. Attitudes towards the cougar seemed to always be at opposite extremes, which meant there was never any balance to the argument.

Thomas smiled. It had all been worthwhile though. After helping an Iowa beef rancher, who had been struggling with a puma preying on his prize herd and crippling his finances in the process, Thomas had taken a sheepdog pup as payment instead. He and Meg had been inseparable since. Meg had run alongside the other dogs on the team with every hunt, learning fast and eagerly. But one day her youthful exuberance had got the better of her. Cornering an old tom in a gully, Meg and the other dogs had kept the cat at bay with their barking. Rather than stay treed as usual, the big cat had leapt amongst the dogs and taken them on. By the time Thomas had reached the gully, one dog had been killed and Meg had been savagely wounded. He hadn't hesitated to send a bullet into the puma's spine, but Meg's rear right leg had to be amputated and it signified the end of her short career as a hunting dog. That was when he had decided to return to Scotland and start things anew, putting to bed the bloody work of his past for good, or so he had thought. But that had changed now. He had to kill this cat.

He looked out onto the mountains that towered above him on every side. He still found peace and beauty in their soft hues of rust and pine. That at least, was still untainted by the events of the last week. He considered things from the landscape's perspective. The mountains had been there for millions of years before him and they would still be standing many more after he was gone. Everything that had seemed so huge and overwhelming a moment ago was now small and only momentarily significant. The landscape was indifferent to the rampage of the cat, to the dead and to him. His thoughts returned to the present and he realised the mountain rescue team had left. He hadn't been able to find any trail left by the cat and he decided to head to the campsite.

As he drove, he watched the sides of the road, scanning for any sign of the predator he knew was out there. He also checked for stray members of the public and kept an eye on the rear view mirror for Kelly Keelson's van. The roads remained deserted of dangerous shadows, tourists and reporters alike, until he had followed them to the other side of the mountain, where the campsite loomed into view. It was surrounded by the now synonymous emergency vehicles he was beginning to expect to see everywhere he went.

Thomas stood in silence as he watched the splintered remains of the caravan be moved onto a DEFRA trailer. The body of Bill Drayton had been recovered from the rocks and taken away. He saw Catherine walking back through the field towards him and he went to meet her. She smiled weakly at him as he approached. A gust of wind ruffled her hair and she patted it down quickly. It did nothing to help her dishevelled and shaken appearance.

"I'm really beginning to miss the wild cats," she sighed.

He smiled understandingly. He felt a wave of comfort having her close by again after the morning's gruesome discoveries.

"Can you see that ledge up above the path on the rock face?" Catherine asked. "How high up would you say it was?"

His eyes darted to where she pointed. "Is that where you found the body? I'd say about eleven feet maybe?"

"The victim's wife says she saw the cat leap up there from the ground to cut him off."

Thomas considered this for a second. "It's possible, but unlikely. Some cats are very agile and could easily make the jump, especially a smaller species like the caracal. But big cats tend not to be as capable, and we know this cat is definitely oversized."

He looked up at the rocks again. Sometimes it was easy to forget how agile even the big cats could be. There were numerous accounts of unfortunate people taking to trees believing that lions weren't especially good climbers, only to hear sharp claws digging into the bark below them in the darkness. Like any predator, he knew cats didn't expend their energy unless they really needed to, and he had learnt from years of surprises whilst studying big cats that even if you didn't see them exhibiting a specific behaviour, it was dangerous to assume they weren't capable. And more and more, Thomas was becoming less surprised at this cat's abilities.

He looked around the campsite but he could see that

Catherine had everything in hand. Army and police units were busy documenting the scene.

"You've got everything under control boss," he told her reassuringly. "Do you mind if I head back to the centre? I feel a bit like a fifth wheel here and I couldn't find any track of the cat."

Catherine could see he was restless, reading the frustration in his face as he fidgeted in the cold.

"Go on then," she smiled. "I've only got to finish putting the reports and statements together from here and then I'll be heading back too."

He knew she was putting on a show of strength for him and probably would have preferred him to stay. He hesitated for a second, but knew there was little for him to do.

"What would I do without you?" He smiled, offering her a friendly wink.

"Starve, or drink yourself to death? Maybe burn the office down?" She quipped.

"Good thing you won't be too far behind me then," he smirked, heading back to the car.

The drive back to Glen Cannich and up to the research centre took over an hour. His stomach rumbled as he opened the door and he realised that he hadn't eaten. One of the good things about not keeping regular hours was it meant there was usually something in the fridge that either he or Catherine had stocked up on, when they had the foresight to do so. Thomas prided himself on being a decent cook and Catherine was too, although he always teased her and suggested otherwise. But he secretly loved every mouthful and had become quite expert at sneaking platefuls when

Catherine wasn't looking. He walked through to the kitchen and opened the fridge, hoping Catherine had done her usual thing of bringing surplus food to work. He grinned at what greeted him from inside. A short while later Thomas was sitting at his desk tucking into a slice of homemade game pie. He fired up the computer just in case he needed it later and put the half-finished plate of food down before heading to the examination room.

He looked over the hulking carcass as he washed his hands and put on a protective gown. Usually the largest animal the centre had to deal with was a deer, and the bison was about twice the size and three times the weight of a decent stag. It took up the entire table and both of its fold-out extensions. He got the impression the stainless steel was straining under the bison's weight. He put together a small tray of instruments he thought he would probably need, put on some latex gloves and began his examination.

He used a small torch to go over the deep cavities on the neck. As he peered closer he could see that the flesh around the top of the puncture had begun to close around the wound. It was an obvious penetration caused by something smooth, conical and pointed. The bottom of the depression was torn and ragged though, as if it had been cut through much more violently by something serrated. The seemingly contradictory aspects of the wound formed a puzzle that Thomas couldn't find a satisfactory conclusion to.

He continued the examination, measuring the distance between the gashes on the neck, where he presumed the cat's teeth had delivered their killing blow. He placed the gauge back on the tray, looking back to make sure he hadn't misread the measurement. The aperture read eleven inches exactly. Instead of providing answers, the bison's wounds were adding more questions about what exactly they were dealing with. He started taking the rest of the readings he needed. He catalogued the vertical distance between the claw marks on the bull's flank. He then measured the reach from there to the similar scratch marks on the neck and shoulders, where the cat had completed its deadly embrace. With these he hoped he could guess the rough size of the animal. He continued to go over the carcass in minute detail, checking and re-checking every aspect he could think of. He had all he needed, and had written everything down in his Moleskine notebook. The examination was over.

The smell of the bison was all around him, and being in an enclosed room with a dead animal had made him feel somehow contaminated by it. He texted Catherine to let her know that it could now be collected and removed by DEFRA, then headed straight for the shower. He stepped in and let the water pound on him for a bit. Over the sound of the running water he heard the front door slam and the sound of Catherine's light step along the corridor.

"Yell when you're out," she shouted through the door.

Thomas smiled to himself as he listened to her make her way down to the kitchen. He knew she would be opening the fridge door just like he did. He washed quickly, knowing she was in much more need of a warming shower than he was. He towelled himself down and opened his locker opposite. He put on some jeans, took out a red, heavy-feeling cotton shirt and a black jumper, slipping them on quickly.

"All yours," he yelled towards the kitchen as he crossed over to the office.

He took a seat at his desk, noticing the plate of pie had gone. Rather than cut herself a new slice, she'd finished his. He couldn't help smiling, especially as it had been replaced by a steaming hot cup of black coffee. He glanced at the machine that sat on a sideboard in the office. It was bubbling and hissing as it kept the fresh pot she had made steaming hot. He opened his notebook with the intention of trying to put some of the pieces of the puzzle together. He was still flipping back and forth through the pages when Catherine walked back through to the office. She walked up behind him and leant over his shoulder. He could feel the warmth of her body on his back and he could detect the delicate hint of spice in her soft and citrusy perfume.

"You smell nice," he murmured without thinking. "Well, at least compared to a dead bison anyway," he added quickly.

She nudged him playfully with her elbow. "They'll pick it up tonight," she explained. "They already have keys to the examination suite entrance. You'll be glad to know Fairbanks is pissed we got to it first."

She put down a cardboard box she had been carrying onto the desk. Thomas looked at her expectantly as she began to take things out of it and place them on the desk. He was glad to see the plaster cast of the pugmark, as well as some hair samples and dossiers containing enlarged photographs.

"I'm shattered," Catherine exclaimed, slumping into her own chair and picking up her own cup of coffee. She smiled, clearly glad to be back inside and warming up. "Any luck?"

"Not really," Thomas sighed. "The measurements make no sense whatsoever. The bite radius alone is huge."

"How huge exactly?

"I could tell you it was bitten by a great white shark and make a good case with them, that huge. The distance between the carnassials is eleven inches at least, which is almost twice that of a lion," he explained.

"I see your bite radius and raise you my plaster cast," she smirked. "A very deep impact into the soil and an impressive distance apart as you know. I haven't made an exact calculation yet, but the animal that made them was almost certainly over 1,000lbs in weight and was probably clocking something like 50mph when it made its way up that slope."

"That's pretty much impossible," Thomas sighed. "There's simply no species of cat that fits that kind of description. There's never been anything like it."

"I know," Catherine agreed, tilting her head and smiling at him in understanding.

He sat up, a thought suddenly occurring to him. "Have you ever heard of a tigon or a liger? What if it's some kind of hybrid?

"That would make a lot more sense. Gigantism could be a possible effect of hybridisation."

"It would also follow that as these animals aren't natives, there'd be no guarantee they'd always be able to partner with the same species," he added.

"What if it's worse than that?" Catherine asked. "What if someone bred this thing and released it?"

"Nothing would surprise me," admitted Thomas. "But this cat knows how to take down prey and he's only recently adapted to people. If he was kicked out of someone's home, I'd guess it happened a long time ago. But there's something about how this cat moves, the confidence and ease with how it kills and the distances it roams. It all tells me he's as wild as they come. I think he's a rogue, a vagabond if you will, and it was just our bad luck that the shit hit the fan whilst he was in our neighbourhood."

"Maybe the DNA results will shed a little more light," Catherine suggested kindly.

"We'll see," Thomas smiled, a little defeated. He glanced at the clock. "I think our day is done and my brain is going to mush. I left a message for Stubbs a few days ago and I'm hoping he'll show up tonight. Want to come?"

"Throw in dinner and it's a deal," she smiled sweetly.

They closed up the centre together, grabbed their coats and were soon headed to the Dam & Dram. Above them, the first flakes of snow from the arctic storm cloud overhead began to fall on Glen Cannich.

CHAPTER NINETEEN

The Dam & Dram had once been a comfortable hunting lodge within the boundaries of the Mullardoch estate. The eastern shore of Loch Sealbhanach and the views across to the Affric Mountains provided an idyllic setting for the stone and oak beamed building. Its white painted upper parts and warmly lit windows lured the cold, weary and hungry from miles around. It also still provided lushly furnished rooms with roaring open fires to affluent sportsmen and other guests at certain times of year. The mountains and moorland were home to deer, pheasant and grouse, and the cold waters of the lochs and rivers provided excellent trout and salmon fishing. It also served Cannich as a public bar and restaurant. The remote, but beautiful location meant it was rarely overcrowded, something Thomas appreciated.

The dark-stained cherry wood booths helped those seeking solitude find privacy for their thoughts, and suited the intimate setting. It had also been where Catherine had first met him to talk about working at the centre. The heavy oak shelves behind the bar holding two hundred of Scotland's best single malt whiskies had been the first indication that it was his kind of place. There was even a small sign letting patrons know that anybody asking for blended, Irish or otherwise would be asked to leave. This was something he had no trouble believing after an American had asked for a bottle of Perrier, only to be told in no uncertain terms that Scotland had some of the finest mineral water in the world and that they should probably rethink their request. Alistair Burns, who owned the Dam &

Dram, believed in local, seasonal food and was a proud Scot to say the least. He nodded Thomas and Catherine a silent but friendly hello as they walked in.

"Don't let me drink too much seeing as I'm driving," Thomas warned. "Stubbs has a dangerous thirst when he comes down from the mountain."

"To be honest, I always thought alcohol improved your driving," Catherine chirped smugly.

Thomas looked around the large, L-shaped room. He quickly spotted Kelly Keelson sitting in one of the booths. She was deep in conversation with a man who sat opposite her, just out of sight. There were a few locals at the bar, and then his eyes darted to the furthest corner booth instinctively. There sat Stubbs. Thomas guessed he was in his late sixties, but nobody knew for sure. Grey stubble and whiskers peppered his chin and he had a thin, pointed nose. His skin was leathery and tight, the result of years of exposure to the Highland winds and rain. He wore a dark green Harris Tweed deerstalker cap that Thomas had never seen him take off. Long strands of silver hair fell from underneath it and cascaded down to his shoulders. He wore an immaculate dark coloured drovers coat with a hood and underneath was an aged but well kept jacket that matched the deerstalker, plus a warm shirt. His black woollen trousers and moleskin boots looked a little odd, but made him practically silent when he moved, ideal for his illegal habit of poaching. At first glance, Stubbs looked like a peaceful old man. He even feigned a limp in public to exaggerate his perceived lethargy. But Thomas had seen him out in the open at night, moving amongst the trees almost too quickly to be believed. He had only bumped into him by mistake on the evening they had first met, outside a hide as he waited for a glimpse of a pine marten.

Stubbs had been impressed with Thomas's own tracking abilities and had shown him where to watch. Their shared love of wildlife became clearly evident to Thomas. Rather than turn him in, Thomas had the foresight that Stubbs' unique knowledge of the area would be a useful resource. In return, Stubbs provided Thomas not only with valuable information on real threats to the local wildlife, but also with the odd bird, hare or slab of venison. Thomas had no real loyalty to authority anyway and he considered himself a good judge of character. The local gamekeepers accepted and respected Stubbs on the same grounds, and most of the local ghillies knew to use his exquisite hand-tied flies if they and their customers wanted the best fish.

Thomas smiled as Stubbs lit his handmade, cherry wood bull-moose pipe, ignoring the law as was his way. He liked the man and respected him. He was an old-school poacher who lived off the land and never took more than he needed, guarding his territory fiercely out of a love of the wild. His small and simple shack carved into the side of the mountain was sparsely furnished by his own creations. His water came from the hillside springs and he used oil-burning lamps to light his way. A wood burning stove was his source of warmth. The cold mountain air was his refrigerator, and he had fashioned a simple smokery from whisky barrels to help preserve his food stores. In many ways, Thomas was a little jealous of the simple lifestyle Stubbs enjoyed. The old poacher had no telephone, but Thomas had known to leave a message for him at the post office in Cannich. The reply had come through a day earlier as Stubbs had dropped off some of his offerings into town.

Stubbs carefully put away his tobacco whilst Thomas and Catherine ordered their food at the bar. Thomas eyed over the menu and went for the poached pike quenelle with brown shrimps and river oyster sauce, served with samphire. Catherine picked out the red curried pheasant with saffron rice, her favourite as Thomas knew. Catherine let Thomas choose the wine, knowing him a better judge. He selected a bottle of Beaune Premier Cru pinot noir. The floral notes would complement the delicate sauce of his fish and the bitter cherry tones would go well with the curry, he hoped. He also hoped it would prevent Stubbs coercing him into joining him as he sampled the whisky selection. They walked over and sat down opposite him in the booth.

"Hello Stubbs," nodded Thomas, "how are you?"

"Iy'm well lad, Iy'm well," he replied, beaming at them both.

"If you want anything to eat, we'll get the tab," hinted Thomas.

"Och no need lad. Alistair and I look after each other well enough," Stubbs grinned.

"I can imagine," Thomas smiled back.

"And how are yer lass?" Stubbs asked Catherine.

"I'm okay Stubbs," she replied. "Just a bit tired with this investigation. We don't seem to be getting anywhere very fast."

Stubbs leaned back against the booth interior and took a thoughtful suck on his pipe. "Aye, can't say I was surprised you wanted to see me."

"Anything you can tell us might help," Thomas explained, leaning across to Stubbs. "We figured if anyone knew anything more about it, it would be you." He was deliberately stroking Stubbs' ego.

Stubbs plucked at his whiskers and smiled. "Course, I only found out about the killings when I last came into the village, otherwise I'd have said something before lad," he explained. "His kind has been here before and weren't treated too well if you take my meaning?"

"You mean the sightings in the late seventies and early eighties?" Catherine asked.

"Aye lass, that's right. They did nee harm then, but that did nee stop the Army laying waste to the wee critters. It was nee som'in I wanted to see again." Stubbs took a sup of his whisky.

"This one seems different," Thomas stated quietly.

"Aye lad," Stubbs nodded. "Big beastie isn't he?"

"You've seen it?!" Catherine exclaimed.

Stubbs took another long draw on his pipe. "In a way lass, aye. I got a glimpse from behind. Do you know the big badger sett not far from the loch? The entrances are all among the roots of the oak trees there?"

Thomas nodded.

"I was there close to dusk. It's about the time the big boar comes out and I was resting up against some roots myself on the ridge above."

Thomas smiled, suspecting Stubbs was doing anything but resting at dusk. He also knew the boughs above would have been filled with plump estate pheasants. If you stayed quiet and still, and used something noiseless like a slingshot, you could fill a bag with birds without them even being disturbed.

Stubbs grinned, acknowledging Thomas's knowing look.

"As it got dark, I noticed the slightest movement. It was the beastie's tail. The body was so large I thought it was a bear. Then I saw what it was after. Old Brock was just nosing his way out of the entrance of the sett. Quick as a flash, this thing hooked him out of the hole with a paw and caught him in its jaws. Never seen anything like it lad, I can tell ye."

Stubbs sighed. A hush fell over the table as Alastair brought over the three plates of food, including a suspiciously fresh looking piece of pink salmon for Stubbs. The old poacher winked at Thomas as he stabbed it gently with his fork and shovelled a quick few mouthfuls before he continued his story.

"I found badger bones all over the woods for the next few days. They forage during the day now, but there's only a few left. Glen's been cleared of wild cats too. I don't go to the lower ground too much these days. I've found kills from squirrels to stags, it's not so picky yer know?"

"We know," Thomas sighed.

Stubbs continued to eat. "Whatever this beastie is, every animal in the glen knows it's here. The deer are moving differently. The hares and birds don't sleep long now. It's done me a tasty favour to be honest, everything's moving to lower ground and too ragged to worry about little old me." Stubbs glanced to the windows. "If you're desperate to get close to it lad, it'll snow the next couple of nights. That black hide might stand out a wee bit, and tracks are easier to follow aye?"

Thomas and Catherine glanced out of the windows too, realising he was right. They began to eat, deep in thought.

~

A few booths down, Kelly Keelson sat opposite the man she had paid to meet. Danny Reeves was a wildlife cameraman who had travelled the world, working for the BBC and National Geographic amongst others. A great deal of his reputation had been gained as he worked with Thomas and Amanda Walker on a successful television series called 'Hunter Hunted'.

Kelly knew she had to be careful. So far, Danny hadn't shown any disloyalty towards Walker.

"So Mr. Reeves, considering your close relationship with the Walkers, would you say Mr. Walker was ever reckless in his attempts to get close to his quarry?" she asked.

"No I would not," Danny replied defensively. "In fact, I would say it was just the opposite. Thomas was always careful, calculated. Amanda was the risk taker."

"Really?" exclaimed Kelly in surprise, "what makes you say that?"

"Thomas had a passion for the animals. He understood them. He could distance himself from what they were doing, but Amanda was different. Every day that went by was another where a person might be killed. She didn't like that. If you ever saw the show, she would often put herself up as human bait. It was quite a big part of the set up. Thomas would design some ingenious trap, only for Amanda to put herself at the centre of it. There'd be arguments and nerve wracking moments, but she usually got her way. And we got the viewing figures." He looked down, turning his drink round on the coaster nervously.

"So, were you with the Walkers when Amanda was killed?" she asked.

"Yeah, it happened just after we had started filming a new series," he replied with a sigh. "We had moved from the Sundarbans and tigers to Tsavo in Kenya and lions. We had filmed in Africa before, but that had been Zimbabwe with leopards."

"What exactly happened?"

"It was as if the lions knew we were there for them. It felt like we were being taunted," Danny explained. "We could hear them roaring defiantly in the distance most evenings. One morning, Thomas found pugmarks of a big lioness that had walked all the way round the tents and out of the camp again. After that, we moved to a camp where there were huts. Thomas and Amanda stuck to their tent though. We did all the usual things like introducing a curfew for the local villagers. We built barriers and lit fires. It all looked good for the cameras."

Danny paused for a moment and took a sip of his drink. Kelly noticed the slight trembling of his hands as he did so.

"During the day, Thomas tracked," Danny continued. "Amanda focused on the people and community, whilst Thomas was the 'big white hunter'. He roamed miles every day and eventually tracked the lions to some hills on the edge of the territory. The lions were travelling a great distance to get to us, and the villagers believed they were evil spirits being controlled by a local witch doctor, which made getting their co-operation harder. One day, Thomas returned to camp very late. He'd walked nearly twenty miles, but had finally scoped out the cave he thought they called home. We set about planning the hunt and the shoot for the following day. We were patting ourselves on the back as to how easy it was going to be."

Danny paused again and looked down at his drink. Kelly had no trouble reading the sadness in his face. She kept still and quiet, waiting patiently and expectantly for him to continue the story. He let out a long sigh.

"It must have been the early hours of the morning when we heard the lions. They were close and calling to each other, at least a dozen of them. The sound was terrifying. Every single one of us was up, switching on lights, panicking basically. Someone ran to get Thomas. That's when we discovered Amanda was gone." He stopped, his eyes gleaming with tears he was trying to hold back.

"Sorry," he coughed, "it's just been a long time since I thought about it."

"It's okay Mr. Reeves, really. Take your time," Kelly replied reassuringly.

Danny cleared his throat and took a big swig of his drink to steady himself again. "There was no sign of a struggle at the tent, just an open flap. Thomas was in a deep sleep, but when we roused him, he tracked Amanda straight from the tent by torchlight. We continually called her name and at first we were hopeful, as she seemed to head straight towards the huts. But then she had turned. She went way beyond the camp into the long grass. That's when Thomas found the pugmarks falling in behind her. Thomas thought it was the big lioness that had been through camp, but it was hard to tell in the dark. We eventually found where the kill had taken place, but they had dragged her body into the shelter of the thorns. We went to get axes, but Thomas just ran head long into them. He was torn up pretty bad by the time we got to him. We found him cradling Amanda's head in his lap. He had run into the thorns because he had seen a hyena feeding on her. He was completely delirious by then."

Danny winced. "She was beautiful you know?"

"Amanda Walker?" asked Kelly.

Danny nodded, seeming calmer now.

"Why did she leave the tent?"

"We didn't realise at the time, but Thomas was actually in the early stages of rift valley fever. Tsavo is a river valley and there are plenty of swamps and even more mosquitoes. He'd been bitten whilst out tracking. It's quite mild as things go, but Amanda was probably going for water."

"So, you don't know for sure?" Kelly queried. Her tone was deliberately a little more accusing now.

"You don't get out of your tent during the night in man-eater country. Especially when you know they know you're there. Amanda would have known she was taking a risk, so why do it?" Danny replied, a little defensively.

Kelly could see a little fire in his eyes now and knew she was getting somewhere. She relaxed a little.

"If she was going for water, why did she move away from camp and into the grass then?"

Danny sighed. "It doesn't make any sense. There's no conceivable reason we could come up with. The local guides were terrified. They could only presume she had been cursed by some spell of the witch doctor they all feared. Thomas on the other hand was pretty sure she was following the trail of something or even someone. But as you pointed out, no, we don't know for sure."

Danny slumped in his seat. Kelly could tell he was done, at least with this part of the story. She tried to move things on.

"So what happened after that?"

"Amanda was buried in Kenya," he replied. "Thomas had to fly down to South Africa to hold a press conference in Johannesburg shortly afterwards. He came under a lot of fire. Soon afterwards he just disappeared. A few years later I got a letter from him saying he was in the States and was thinking of heading home."

Kelly sat forward, leaning in a little closer over the table. "Danny, do you know where the hostility between Walker and Fairbanks comes from?"

Danny almost choked on his drink as he put it back down on the table. "I'm amazed as a journalist you don't know that?" he exclaimed. "Fairbanks was on safari in Kenya when Amanda was killed. He couldn't get in front of the cameras fast enough to tell everyone how irresponsible the show was and that it was practically an inevitable outcome. He used it as a platform to talk about how green his party was. As you can imagine, a Conservative talking about the wrongs of hunting and the rights of conservation got him considerable press."

"I can see how that would ruffle Walker's feathers," admitted Kelly. She felt a little flame of anger ignite in her gut. She understood ambition fine, but injustice always got to her.

"Well it didn't quite end there," smirked Danny. "When Thomas returned to the UK, the research institute he freelanced for was commissioned to look into the reports of wild boar. Thomas identified populations in Kent, the forest of Dean and up here in Scotland. Fairbanks called the report inflammatory and biased. DEFRA's official line was that they were just escapees and far fewer in number than Thomas was suggesting."

"Why would he refute the report?" Kelly asked, curious.

"The government at the time were trying to bring in tougher laws and sentencing against illegal activism and protest. They wanted the focus to be on what they called eco-terrorism and the vandalism of property by groups who had released the boar, not the animals."

"So what happened when the report was published?"

"Thomas made a case that wild boar had once been a native species and this was effectively a reintroduction. The populations were viable enough to be sustainable and there were too many to hunt down and eradicate. Instead of having the boar labelled as an alien invader with no legal protection, Thomas was making a case for conservation. There were even EU initiatives and policies that encouraged doing so. It was going in the opposite direction to the one the government had wanted."

"I think I need to give Walker more credit than I have," smirked Kelly.

"It gets a little better than that," Danny replied with a smile. "Fairbanks made a statement that he was confident that the boars had already been dealt with by DEFRA, and again played down the report. Thomas promptly spent a day in the woods near Bedgebury in Kent, which just happened to be within Fairbanks' own constituency of Tunbridge Wells. He shot a boar and had a local butcher prepare it, before offering it up as a hog roast to a group of protestors who had been moved off of parliament square. He also took pictures of boars with piglets to really prove his point. He's very practical is Thomas, doesn't really have time for red tape when he knows he's right."

Kelly clicked off the dictation machine in her pocket and

straightened up in her seat. She beamed at Danny. "Thank you Mr. Reeves that was the full story I was after. I'm happy to keep you anonymous if..."

"No need," said Thomas quietly.

They both turned in surprise to look at him as he stood motionless and silent in front of their table.

"The one thing I can trust Danny with is getting the facts right," he added just as softly, his eyes fixed on Danny Reeves. Catherine stood behind him with a look of frozen shock and apprehension on her face. Her eyes flashed from Keelson to Thomas and then back to the man the reporter was sitting with.

"Enjoy your visit to the Highlands Danny," Thomas offered scornfully, unable to maintain his demeanour any longer.

The glance he shot Kelly was full of silent venom, but it was the pain behind the anger that made Kelly squirm in her seat a little as she felt a pang of guilt in her gut, something she thought she had got rid of a long time ago. She and Danny stared silently at their drinks as Thomas and Catherine walked out of the door into the cold night. She wasn't entirely convinced it was the chilling blast from outside that sent the icy shiver down her spine.

CHAPTER TWENTY

Thomas walked to the Overfinch, silent and sullen. He blipped the remote and climbed into the driver's side. Catherine clambered into the passenger seat, pulling the fingers on her gloves tight as they sat in silence for a few moments. Thomas let out a deep sigh as he rested both hands on the steering wheel.

"That was unfortunate," she stated, offering a sympathetic smile, her eyes open wide in enquiry.

"I guess I should have expected it," Thomas replied, shaking his head. "I knew there was going to be some digging sooner or later. To be honest, I could have handled it better. Amanda would have been disappointed with that performance."

He didn't look at Catherine. Instead he stared out through the windscreen, his eyes far away and vacant. At last he straightened up in the seat and sniffed slightly as he offered a weak smile to Catherine.

"Just what I need," he shrugged. "I think I'm getting a cold."

"Oh dear," Catherine replied. "With you being a man you could be dead before the night is out," she grinned.

Thomas shot her a sarcastic smile but found himself staring back out through the windscreen.

"Stubbs was right," he exclaimed as he watched the small white flakes fall and begin to settle on the ground. He swivelled round towards Catherine. "I'm going to take his advice," he said softly. "I'll drop you home, but then I'm going into the forest. It's too good an opportunity."

"Maybe you are ill then," Catherine muttered angrily, staring at him in disbelief. "That's egotistical nonsense and stupidity if ever I heard it. It's going to be cold and dark and you won't see anything."

"I'll see its tracks," Thomas challenged. "By the time I've dropped you off, there'll be a good covering. I can just find a nice tree and wait if I'm lucky."

"Well that's one way to go," she retorted icily. "And may I be the first to remind you that you're NOT that lucky."

"That's what I'm trying to change," he shrugged.

She turned away from him, deep in thought. She looked out of the window and noticed the snow was coming down more thickly now. She glanced back at him, feeling the anger leave her as she noticed how completely focused on her he was. There was just a hint of pleading in his eyes as he met her questioning gaze.

"Oh fine," she exclaimed with some surrender. "But you go on my say so, you take a radio, you take your gun and if I call you back in, you do it immediately and without question. Is that understood?

"But..."

"No buts!" she snapped. "I'm responsible for you, and this investigation in case you're forgetting. If you don't agree to my terms then one phone call sees you spending the night in a cell in Cannich. You'll be seeing bars, not stars, understood?"

"Yes ma'am," Thomas smiled, a little surprised. "I'll grab a radio from your place then."

"Where are you thinking of heading?"

"I think our cat's likely to be back in the forest. We know it's part of his territory, and he was coming down from the

241

mountain, not heading back up it. There's plenty of prey and no people to get in his way right now. It's a logical place to start," Thomas explained.

"Trust me, there's nothing logical about what you're suggesting," replied Catherine, shaking her head as they drove off.

~

Danny Reeves sat in his room in the Dam & Dram. He emptied what remained of the quarter bottle of 12-year old Cragganmore he had ordered from the bar. It and the room were all on Keelson's tab, and he was far from caring now. He sat and watched a log on the fire as it glowed a final radiant red, dulled and then died. He kept going over what he had said to the reporter, but couldn't shake the image in his head of Thomas in that hospital in Nairobi, his arms and face torn and bloodied by the wait-a-bit thorns. He had stayed silent whilst Fairbanks had made his statements, all the while knowing Thomas was unconscious from the rift valley fever and his treatment. He had thought his explanation of events to Keelson would have helped Thomas, but now he wasn't so sure. He couldn't help questioning why if it had been the right thing to do, he had decided not to let Thomas know he was coming up. He supped down the rest of the whisky, and then picked up his camera and keys as he left the room.

Kelly Keelson watched him walk through the bar from the booth she still occupied. Her eyes darted to her own keys on the table. She knew she should be running to the van and following him, but she felt something in the pit of her stomach stopping her. Her gut instinct had never been wrong yet and she decided not to ignore it now.

~

As Thomas pulled up outside the cottage, Catherine jumped out and ran to the house, leaving the passenger door open. Thomas shivered involuntarily as a sharp blast of icy air suddenly hit him. He dismissed the doubts that suddenly crept into his thoughts as he watched the snow fall. It was coming down quite thickly now, and he knew that by the time he reached the forest the covering on the ground would be thick enough to show the tracks and trails of anything passing through. The noise of an animal walking across snow also carried further. *All I have to do is keep quiet and still,* he thought.

Catherine stepped out of the house and scurried back to the car. In her hand she brandished a radio with a connecting ear piece, which she passed to him. It was a Center One Baofeng. She fished a matching one from her coat pocket.

"You keep it on at all times. I've given you an earpiece, as I imagine you want to keep thinks quiet out there, but if I say come in, you come in. No pretending you didn't hear me okay?"

"I promise!" Thomas exclaimed, holding his hands up.

She closed the door and was shaking her head at him as he drove off, but not before he gave her a little wave that was meant to be reassuring. He could see straight away that it hadn't been successful.

~

Danny Reeves pulled into the quiet car park he had seen earlier in the day, on the way to the Dam & Dram. He had noticed it because there had been no Army guard posted at the entrance. As an experienced cameraman he had developed a keen eye for opportunities to get into places he shouldn't. He opened the door, the blast of cold air taking him a little by surprise as it invaded the car. The warmth of the fire and the whisky had still been keeping him warm until then. He took out the camera from the back seat and buttoned up the thick coat he was wearing. The trees creaked and groaned in the wind. Trickles of snow rained from their branches as they swayed back and forth in unison with the storm. He hesitated only for a second before heading towards the comparative shelter they offered.

His eyes grew accustomed to the dark quickly and the snow was so white it acted as a source of light in itself. Each step he took was followed by the crunch of the soft impact on the frozen ground underfoot. He knew he was making too much noise. He had to try and find some cover and get out of sight as soon as possible.

~

Thomas pulled up to the Army Land Rover sitting across the entrance to the nature reserve's car park. He lowered the window, prepared to explain himself to the bored private in the driver's seat, but he was waved through. He smiled, knowing Catherine was clearly planning to be in charge for the night. He was glad the forest would be deserted too, especially as he was going in armed. It was just him and the cat tonight.

He brought the car to a stop close to the trees. He opened up the back and took his rifle out of the lock box. He unscrewed the scope and took out a small leather bag from the case. He unsheathed the Pulsar Apex XD50 thermal scope and put the smaller Leica eye-piece in the bag. He checked the sights and battery to make sure they were set and charged before attaching it to his rifle. He looked down the scope. The world around him was illuminated in hot white warmth and cold grey darkness.

He took the scope down from his eye and pointed the barrel of the gun down towards the ground. He stood motionless and closed his eyes. The sounds of the forest night flooded his ears. His sensitive hearing caught the near silent wings of an owl. As he heard the bird call out in alarm, he opened his eyes to momentarily catch a glimpse of the male tawny as it passed over him and disappeared into the gloom behind. He edged forward, using the wide spread of his walking boots to cushion the noise of his steps.

~

The creature awoke as cold night air crept in through the broken bark of the tree trunk it had chosen as a cosy resting spot. It raised itself up into a standing position, shaking off the soft covering of snow that had settled over its thick coat of fur as it slept. It leant forward into the breeze, taking deep inquiring sniffs as the wind blew across its face. It was hungry, and it preferred to hunt under the blanket of night. It savoured the scents that wisped through the woods. It recognised the boar and deer far off in the fields. It licked its muzzle, dismissing the closer roe buck. It took a step forward on the stirring of a pair of pheasants a few trees away, but then it stopped in its tracks. It considered its approach before moving off through the trees. It was now free of any effect of the drugs that had been in its system, and it moved with skilful stealth amongst the rocks and heather. The sweet, honey-like scent beckoned it deeper into the forest.

~

Danny's boot caught something hidden underfoot and he tumbled heavily to the ground. The snow lay two inches thick and for a few moments he just lay there, letting his head clear. The icy blanket stunned him out of the drunken dizziness he had been feeling, and he watched the thickening fall of the frozen flakes as they settled around him. The silence of the forest was eerie and haunting. More alert, he sat up and brushed off some of the sludge and snow from his coat. He looked around and realised the falling snow had covered his tracks. He couldn't pick out the direction he had come from, each path into the trees looking equally dark and deserted. For the first time in years, he felt a little wave of fear and paranoia flutter in his gut. He shook it off with a smirk, and dusted himself off as he stood up and trudged off into the trees.

~

Thomas stopped every fifty feet or so as he made his way

through the forest. With each pause he would check his surroundings thoroughly and listen to the soundless night for a lengthy period before moving on again. A familiar feeling that he had encountered in forests and jungles all over the world crept over him now, amplified by the silent cold of the night. He was being watched. Most hunters had stories about the unique sixth sense they all seemed to possess. The defining moment when they knew that the tables had been turned and the hunter had become the hunted. It was a feeling that struck the senses like no other. Thomas's eyes grew large as they drank in all the available light and his hearing became acute as it sought the silent approach of a predator.

Thomas dropped to his knee and took a deep breath, his eyes fixed ahead of him. He carefully and deliberately brought up his rifle and settled his eye on the scope. With his back to a tree, he trusted his gut that the animal was somewhere in front of him. He knew that at the subconscious level his senses were much more likely to have picked up something ahead rather than behind. He had probably come across the animal unexpectedly, maybe while it was sleeping or feeding.

The forest seemed motionless and he became a statue against the towering pine he rested on. He began to imagine the unseen cat creeping towards him in the dark, its razor sharp claws unsheathed and ready for the spring, its eyes set on him and its teeth revealed in a grinning snarl as it savoured his scent and hungered for a taste of his flesh. A bead of sweat formed on his brow and he shivered unexpectedly as it ran down the back of his neck. He froze again, knowing he had just given his position away. His eyes darted to a fern that shuddered as if some unseen body had just passed it by.

As a slither of moonlight broke through the snow clouds, Thomas was able to see the area ahead of him a little better, and the snow was now only falling as inconsistent flurries. The large black form skipped silently from the undergrowth and stood a moment as it surveyed the man before it. Thomas stared into the beautiful green eyes as the cat's ears flattened and a dreadful hiss emanated from deep within its throat. Held between its jaws was the limp body of a rabbit. As Thomas momentarily shuddered in fear, his senses quickly kicked in and he began to realise the cat he was looking at could not be the animal that had attacked Palaeo Park. It was only a little over three feet long, including its thick bushy tail. It was jet black in colour with a stocky and muscular body, and it suddenly dawned on Thomas what he was looking at.

There had been stories about black wild cat hybrids in the Highlands going back thirty years. They had first been reported near the small village of Kellas, to the north-east of Dundee. Since then, they had been reported spreading further and further throughout Scotland. They were suspected to be crossings between the native wild cat and feral and domestic types, and their existence had crossed from mythology to reality when the BBC and a local zoologist had caught a specimen in the early 80's. Since then, the debate over their origins had continued and many considered them a separate species to wild cats altogether. Thomas wondered if with everything that was going on, people would maybe have to come to terms with something much larger and dangerous, equally thought to be myth but now very much reality.

As Thomas and the Kellas cat looked at each other he was able to pick out the beautiful markings in its dark coat. It was flecked with white, and a shimmer of faded stripes could be seen along its flanks as it stretched its muscles. There was a small concentration of white guard hairs on its chin and another patch of white on its chest. Thomas had seen the stuffed specimen that ordained the lobby of the Aberdeen University's zoology building, but there was no comparison to the rippling, hissing and very live specimen before him now in the snow.

Despite the arguments over its origins, Thomas suspected the Kellas cat was in fact a great deal older and more of a native than people realised. The Scottish legend of the 'Cait Sith' had been around for centuries. The Cait Sith was a mystical cat of the fairy realm and was always described as being a beautiful animal, black in colour, with flecks of white. He suspected the resemblance was far more than coincidence. Whatever the Kellas cat was, it had been in the Highlands for centuries and although there almost certainly had been a pollution of the bloodlines, Thomas still suspected it had once been a pure and separate species.

As the cat turned and bounded off through the snow, Thomas could see the long powerful legs that many eyewitnesses had described in the past. Some natural historians had concluded this aspect of their physiology meant that the Kellas cat was more likely to be built for running than tree climbing. As it made off in fluid bounds, Thomas suspected that was probably true. His curiosity was aroused and he took a few steps forward, following the cat a little way. Hearing the man behind it approach, the cat stopped and turned to hiss at him again. He stopped, deciding to give the cat its space, but was surprised as a second black head popped up from among the ferns in front of him. He smiled. Kellas cats had also been reported as unusually hunting in pairs, and it seemed another aspect of their behaviour had just been confirmed. He watched them disappear into the darkness together.

~

Danny Reeves began to realise how futile and foolish the task he had set himself was. The drink too was slowing his pace and dulling his senses. He dropped to his knees, took a handful of snow and rubbed it into his face. He had wanted to give Thomas something tangible, something that he could come back at Fairbanks with. He had hoped to find a trail, a den or even a glimpse of the animal itself, but he now knew that had been the drink inflating his ego. What he was attempting would usually take weeks, if not months. He sighed, disappointed with himself. He stood and faced into the wind, deciding there was logic in turning round and heading back. Giving up all attempts to hide his presence, he began to trudge through the snow, now simply determined to just get back to the car and his warm room.

~

Thomas stopped. The high gorse bushes surrounding him felt familiar. A small covering of snow now rested on the smashed trunk of the birch sapling he had found a few days earlier. As he pushed it aside, he could see what remained of the stag carcass on the forest floor. Many of the forest's scavengers had taken advantage of the bounty the carrion had afforded them. Most of the bones had been stripped of their remaining flesh, but there was still some meat on the back and bottom parts of the hindquarters. He knew it was unlikely, but there was a small possibility that the cat would remember its kill and come back for the few morsels that remained, especially given the conditions. This is what he had been looking for.

Not far beyond where the stag carcass lay was a tall oak tree. Its leafless boughs offered a good view of the ground below, and he soon spotted a small cross-section near the top of the canopy where he'd be able to sit comfortably against the main trunk. He'd be hidden against the tree, and he was confident the branches wouldn't support the weight of the cat if it decided to try climbing up for him. It was also too high for it to jump. It was perfect. He slung the rifle over his shoulder and began to climb.

~

The creature moved slowly through the snow towards the man. It had to be much more cautious with its footing in order to conceal its presence, moving slowly and in silence. Several times the man had changed direction, confusing the creature and making it hesitant. But now the man seemed to be following a more obvious route. The creature watched carefully, concealed and separated from the man by a bank of trees that skirted the path he was taking. As it licked its muzzle, its paw came down to rest carelessly on a soft dome of snow, which gave way with a muffled thump, collapsing into the exposed hollow beneath.

Danny froze mid-step at the sound, which rang as clear and loud to him as if it had been a gunshot. He turned his neck slightly, trying to look behind him without moving his head too obviously. Just for a moment, he thought he caught the sound of something panting softly in the undergrowth. Panic began to build up inside him, overwhelming him as he lurched forwards into the heavy drifts of snow. The ear-splitting roar shook him to his core. He fought for breath as he plunged forward, fighting the nausea he felt and overriding his body's urge to be still. He then heard the thuds in the snow as the animal fell in behind him and began to draw closer. The thick blanket of powder made it all seem like it was happening in slow motion, but it was gaining on him.

~

Thomas listened intently, not moving a muscle. The roar had echoed through the forest and seemingly through him as well. He estimated the cat was no more than half a mile away. He slowly brought the rifle up and trained his eye down the scope. The thermal imager registered no movement or heat signatures that he could pick up on. Like most hunters, he had learnt to keep both eyes open in order to better gauge distance and conditions that might affect the shot. The forest was quiet, but something in the pit of his stomach told him that was about to change.

~

Danny felt the powerful swipe lift him up into the air as the creature tried to end the tiring pursuit in the snow. In a last ditch effort, Danny crawled forward again, his eyes now resting on his camera where it had fallen a few feet from him. He quickly reached out and grabbed it as he heard the nearing footfalls of the cat and a shadow fell across him from behind. He turned the camera on and squirmed onto his back as he tried to get into a better position. *You need to see this Thomas* he thought.

Nothing he had imagined prepared him for what now bore down on him with icy breath and savage glowing green eyes. Its sheer proximity flooded his senses, turning his blood cold with fright. He whimpered involuntarily as it loomed closer. He pressed the record button on the camera unexpectedly, a blinding flash of sudden illumination taking him by surprise and startling the creature. The guttural growl in response seemed to stun Danny, making him drop the camera in confusion. The light fizzled out as it hit the ground. The creature lunged forward and opened its maw wide, slicing its fangs through Danny's thighs on both sides. He screamed in pain, trying to place his hands over the gushing wounds as the creature used its purchase to lift him off the ground. It shook him vigorously back and forth, smashing him to the floor several times in unbridled fury. The sickening crack that echoed in the still night air was the sound of Danny's neck breaking as it was thrashed against the frozen ground. As his body went limp, the creature let Danny drop to the floor. It sniffed the corpse with satisfaction before it began to feed.

~

Thomas's hand was trembling as he fumbled for the radio in his pocket. He knew the scream he'd heard had been human. *It must have been a soldier* he told himself as he flicked the radio on.

"Catherine?" He whispered, his voice catching in his throat. "Come in, over." He shut his eyes, waiting for the crackle that would signal a reply. It came almost immediately.

"Receiving, finally! Which bit of keep it on at all times was difficult..."

"Cath," Thomas interrupted, "sorry, but listen. I think I've just heard this cat killing somebody out here in the forest. I'm in a big oak tree near where we found the stag carcass the other day. You need to send everyone you've got into the forest now if you want to catch this thing."

"But nobody should be out there!" Catherine replied.

"Someone was, I know it," Thomas stammered. He suddenly felt very cold and alone.

"Stay put. I'll get through to headquarters straight away."

The radio went dead and the wind and the darkness whispered to him in the absence of Catherine's voice. He heard a large crack echo through the trees and realised with grim horror it was the sound of the cat feeding. He could hear its grumbling snarls at the edge of his hearing. As another crack ricocheted into the forest, he was certain he was listening to human bones being broken as it feasted. He again looked through the scope of the rifle, hoping for a glimpse of heat that would allow him even half a shot. There was nothing but the cold and unchanged snow-covered forest. He knew he couldn't risk moving and there was nothing he could do for whoever it was out there. Their troubles were over. His were escalating. His resolve became icy as he distanced himself from his frantic state.

The radio crackled into life again.

"Tom?" She sounded shaky and hesitant.

"I'm here," Thomas replied, preparing himself for the bad news.

"We've checked. Everyone is accounted for at their stations. Fairbanks thinks you're jumping to conclusions. He isn't willing to risk sending anyone into the forest. My authority has been overridden.

Thomas glanced at his watch. It was ten minutes past midnight. That meant there were at least seven hours to go until he could leave the tree in relative safety.

"Things have changed Cath. The cat is too close, I can't move in safety. I'm stuck here," he sighed.

"I told Fairbanks that. He says there's no proof. You haven't seen anything," Catherine explained. He could hear the strain in her voice.

"I understand," he said quietly. "As soon as it's light enough I'll be able to move."

"I'm so sorry Tom, I shouldn't have let you go," Catherine stammered.

"It's okay. It's definitely too cold for me to fall asleep," he replied with a smile. He knew she was fighting tears now. He softened, wanting to reach out to her.

"If the idea of walking into a cold, dark forest that contained a killer cat couldn't stop me, what chance do you think you faired?"

"You're right," she sniffed, "you deserve it." They both

laughed sorrowfully.

"Look at my shelves in the office. You'll see books about Jim Corbett, Colonel Patterson, C. H. Strigand and Karamojo Bell. There isn't one hunter who took on a man-eater that didn't spend at least one night in a tree. I'm in good company."

"Well so am I," Catherine replied, "and I'm not going anywhere."

Thomas lay across the branch, trying to make himself as comfortable as possible. The cold was going to be a problem, but he wasn't going to let Catherine know that. He buttoned up his thick coat as far as possible and tucked his trousers into his woollen walking socks. He brought his knees up to his chest and settled himself. It was going to be a long seven hours. He closed his eyes and tried to centre his thoughts on the soft music Catherine had started playing for him, and not on the sounds of the cat as it fed less than half a mile from where he sat.

CHAPTER TWENTY-ONE

Dr Rebecca Stephenson wheeled her Marin Juniper Trail mountain bike round to the secure storage that just happened to be opposite the new reindeer paddock of London Zoo. She smiled as a heavily antlered female eyed her steadily through the ranch-style fencing. She made her way round to the front of the Nuffield building, the headquarters of the Institute of Zoology, and walked through the double doors. She smiled briefly at the receptionist, whom she didn't recognise today. She walked briskly through the large revolving doors into the maze of corridors, that in turn led to the laboratories and offices split over several levels. Hers was on the third floor, the highest in the building. She clutched her Cambridge Expedition Satchel close as she rode the lift up, wondering if she was early enough this morning. As the lift doors opened and she spotted the soldier outside her office, her shoulders slumped. He had beaten her in again.

She nodded to the soldier as she passed him and walked into the office. She had to suppress the wave of anger that swept over her as she found the man from DEFRA already inside, sitting at her desk and reading her notes. Rupert Pettigrew was a rat of a man, thin, sharp nosed and sharp faced. His grey hair was combed back and he peered out at the world through a pair of thick, black-framed glasses. He was an underling of the Minister of the Environment, a man named Fairbanks. He was nosy, rude and a pain. She disliked him intensely.

"You don't seem to have signed the official secrets act

declaration I gave you yesterday Miss Stephenson," declared Pettigrew with a crocodile-like smile.

"And you don't seem to have learnt to knock Mr. Pettigrew, or to have picked up from yesterday that you should address me as Dr," she snapped.

She was the senior research fellow for the institute's mammalian genetic research laboratory. Her work centred on cataloguing and securing data and records of some of the world's most endangered species. In a way, she and the institute were assembling a modern-day ark. She examined bloodlines that increased diversity in a species, helping channel research and funding where it was needed and would do the most good. It was important work and Pettigrew and DEFRA had interrupted it.

"I'm having the declaration examined by our legal department Mr. Pettigrew," Rebecca continued. "You know full well I don't have to sign it, and you are overstepping your authority by rooting through my office."

"I can only presume that you don't want to sign it because you wish to speak to the press," Pettigrew replied. "That makes me very uncomfortable."

"Then by all means take the sample somewhere else," she challenged. Her anger threatened to flare violently.

She had been aware of the animal attacks in Scotland from the media eruption surrounding it, but she had been surprised by the DEFRA directive that had come through to her directly. A sample of blood had been flown down for immediate analysis. Pettigrew and the soldier were waiting to take the results back as soon as they were available. Their overbearing presence throughout the day before had been the major contributing factor to her current bad mood, and the migraine she had suffered for most of the night with. It normally took up to two weeks to break down a sample of DNA, and she was being expected to produce results in two days. She didn't want to waste any more time than she had to.

She fired up her Dell desktop computer and glanced quickly at the mainframe units, housed in their protective air-cooled chamber of safety glass that made up the wall behind her desk. The little green neon lights that were flashing on the sides of each unit told her everything was up and running. As she waited for the computer to check through its start-up procedures, she looked through the streams of data that she had printed out in relation to the sample.

"Where have we got to Dr. Stephenson?" enquired Pettigrew with an impatient tone.

"We've identified the blood type at least," she answered, too distracted by the data to respond to his rudeness. "It shares all the common blood markers associated with the Felidae or cat family. Unfortunately, the preliminary tests didn't draw any direct matches, so now we're looking at the DNA contained within the blood itself."

"How do you do that exactly?" Pettigrew asked, more curious now.

Dr. Stephenson sighed. It was going to be a long day she realised, but she knew she had to at least try to play nice for a while, even though it was very unlikely to last. "We've taken six identical samples from the blood you gave us. These are then made up into slides. The mainframe uses cutting edge Israeli-made software to break down the sample into genetic code. It generates a computer model of base compounds made up of groups called mega-bases. Almost three thousand mega-bases are needed to code for a single gene, so it's going to take a little longer to analyse than us having a quick chat over a cup of coffee I'm afraid."

"I see," Pettigrew said acceptingly, although he seemed to frown.

"There are some results though," Dr. Stephenson offered, softening a little. She realised he was probably under extreme pressure, just as she was. "For instance, we've identified the MC1R gene."

"Oh, and what is that exactly?" Pettigrew asked.

"It's the gene for melanism. It's what gives some wild cat species a black fur colour."

"Like a panther?" Pettigrew offered.

"Yes, what is commonly called a black panther is in fact a melanistic leopard or other cat. There are actually eleven species in which it commonly occurs, and at least statistically speaking it could happen in others. Roughly, one in every ten thousand or so individuals of any cat species could be melanistic, if the right genes were combined."

"So are they basically just freaks of nature? Mutants I suppose?

"Far from it," Dr. Stephenson exclaimed. "We now know that melanism occurred in at least four separate instances during the evolution of the cat family. That means rather than being a sporadic abnormality, there were times when it was a significant advantage to have a black colouration. It's just a remnant of their genetic history that pops up from time to time, often I suspect in the same ideal conditions."

"Fascinating," Pettigrew stated dryly. "However Dr. Stephenson, we know it's a black cat simply from the witness statements. I need something we don't know."

"I imagine there are whole libraries full of things you don't know Mr. Pettigrew," Rebecca snapped aggressively.

Pettigrew's face fell. She could see he didn't really know how to react. It clearly was not the manner he was used to being addressed in, but she wasn't going to stand for it today. His pretence aristocratic arrogance was revealed as ignorance every time he pressed her for details.

"My apologies Dr. Stephenson," Pettigrew muttered. "Please continue."

"I can tell you a little bit about the animal's parentage," Rebecca offered, her glare letting him know in no uncertain terms that he was trying her patience. "We were able to correlate matches to records we already had for a melanistic jaguar at Chester Zoo, and that of an Asiatic lion held at the collection here in London. The jaguar element matched 43% of the sample. There is no doubt in my mind that at least one of the animal's parents was a melanistic jaguar, most likely its mother from the direct correlation of the genetic material."

"What about the lion?"

"That came in at a 17% match," Rebecca explained. "But that's where we've run into difficulties."

"It sounds fairly conclusive to me," Pettigrew stated, glancing down at the reports on the desk as if to glean information from the thickly bound bundles. "You seem to be saying it's a cross between a jaguar and a lion."

"That's definitely not what I'm saying," Rebecca scolded. "At 17%, it would indicate the other parent was a lion hybrid itself, but that doesn't seem to be the case. Unfortunately, other genes from other species have also been identified."

"Such as?" Pettigrew enquired. He seemed alert and nervous now.

Rebecca picked up one of the reports from her desk and flipped forward a few pages to the content she wanted.

"*Panthera pardus* – that's a leopard. *Panthera tigris* – tiger. *Uncia uncia* – snow leopard. But there are trace elements of smaller cats like the lynx, caracal and even the fishing cat here. Despite the large percentage of lion in its genetic makeup, the real clue is here with this other genetic material. Whatever the other parent was, it was a species of cat that evolved alongside these other species, indicating it originated in Asia. But whatever it is, it's older than they are in species terms and it's not something we have on record."

"But you said it was 17% lion. Aren't they African?" Pettigrew frowned.

"These are Asiatic lions Mr. Pettigrew," Rebecca explained with a little vented frustration. "They are a sub-species and although they look similar, unfortunately we now know that they are distinctly different in terms of their evolutionary genetics. A well meaning programme was started when numbers of Asiatic lions dipped below three hundred. They crossed Asiatic with African, but the results were disastrous. The animals had weakened immune systems that made them vulnerable to disease. Most could barely walk due to brittle bones in the hind quarters. They had to be separated from their pure counterparts in the end, as they were being torn apart."

"Well you seem to be the right person to talk to in any case," Pettigrew offered weakly.

"That's my work Mr. Pettigrew," Rebecca sighed with a

scolding tone. "If I hadn't been distracted by you and your sample, that's what I'd be doing right now, identifying the right captive breeding stock that may end up saving the Asiatic lion as a species."

"The British government is very grateful Dr. Stephenson and I'll make sure you're compensated for your time," Pettigrew mumbled. "But you still haven't told me what it all means?"

Rebecca sighed. "All of these genetic codes, each species it shares something with - these are all just little pieces of the puzzle. You'll just have to be patient until we can figure out how they fit together."

She picked up a bundle of reports from the desk and walked through a pair of double doors to the laboratory, shaking her head as she went. Pettigrew glimpsed the rest of Dr. Stephenson's team had only just started to trickle in. He too realised it was going to be another long day.

~

Thomas awoke with a start. The cold stung him as he tried to move. His arm dangled dangerously over the branch he was draped over. He looked behind him and breathed a sigh of relief. During the night he had taken the strap from his rifle and tied it tightly around his body, securing himself to the tree. He shivered violently, shaking a deluge of partially frozen dew from his jacket and arms. He tried to push himself up from the branch but found his icy muscles sapped of all their strength. He felt the tiny spasms that were jerking his muscles awake as his body fought the cold and stiffness. A thin layer of slush coated his back and legs where the morning dew had frozen and then melted in the morning sun. He was soaked through.

For how long he had been there, wet, cold and unconscious, he could only guess at. He tried to lift his arm to look at his watch, but the instant pain that shot through his shoulder thwarted him. He felt almost nothing as his arm fell back against the branch with a thud, and he realised he had almost no feeling in his fingers. *That can't be good* he thought. As he trembled uncontrollably, he remembered his backpack. He tried to crane his neck back to see if it was behind him, but could only glimpse so far. He managed to shuffle forward slightly along the branch. He gained a clearer view of the ground and his gaze hazily fastened on the roots of the tree below. There he saw his backpack, rifle and radio scattered around the base of the tree.

Just as a feeling of hopelessness was about to overwhelm him, he heard the crunch of boots on snow some way off. He suddenly remembered that it had been the sound of a car that had shaken him awake. He opened his mouth to call out, but found he could only manage a bare whisper. His second rasp was a little louder, but he quickly began to panic at the thought of not being heard.

As Catherine stepped from the far tree line, his heart leapt. He croaked her name, but knew she was too far away to have heard him.

"Over here!" She yelled, spying the backpack and rifle.

Catherine kicked her way through the snow, followed by two soldiers and four other men clad in mountain rescue gear. She turned the pack over and started looking around wildly in panic. Thomas managed a raspy cough to get her attention and as their eyes met, he suddenly felt a wave of warmth sweep over him. He had never been so glad to see her. He hadn't quite expected the cry of laughter she gave as she sank to her knees, shaking her head. He tried a weak smile as the mountain rescue team set about scaling the tree to reach him. With their spiked boots and the use of a rope for leverage around the trunk, it was only a few moments before one of them was beside him.

"Can't move," Thomas whispered coarsely, trying to lift himself up again to no avail.

"Don't try to then," the mountain rescue leader replied smugly. "My name is Lyle Ruskin and I'll get you down, don't worry."

Lyle secured the rope he had used to scale the tree, and Thomas suddenly felt the thick press of the man's grip on his wrists as he was hoisted into a fireman's lift. Thomas watched the ground and Catherine come ever closer as they gently abseiled back down the trunk. The colour of Catherine's bright red jacket jolted him awake as she smiled at him. He could see tears staining her cheeks, which she wiped away quickly now that he was on the ground.

"We're taking you straight to the mountain rescue ambulance," Catherine explained. "It's not far and I'm going to be right here to make sure you stay awake. I can't have you saying I bored you into unconsciousness before we get back, okay?"

Thomas smiled as well as he could. He was already wrapped in a foil blanket and was being laid out on a stretcher, but he shivered violently and uncontrollably, creating a rattle that annoyed and panicked him at the same time. He knew Catherine was talking to him to prevent a hypothermic coma taking over, something he could only guess he was dangerously close to as the rustling intensified.

Catherine turned away for a moment to pick up his rifle and bag. She let out a tiny gasp as she got closer. The hard brown scat that sat in a pile over the rifle had frozen in clumps over the casing. Her eyes scanned over the deep and heavy prints that had been left in the snow. They circled the tree many times over. She held her foot over the nearest, realising it could easily fit the void beneath. She knew there was only one thing in the forest that could have made them. She hesitated only for a moment before picking up the rifle in her gloved hands and brushing off the frozen faeces into a specimen bag. As she made her way back to Thomas and the team carrying him on the stretcher, she couldn't help an occasional glance back towards the tree and the dark forest beyond.

Catherine averted her gaze as the mountain rescue team stripped Thomas of the wet and half-frozen clothes that clung to his skin. He was quickly wrapped back up in the foil sheet, with towels and thick blankets folded round his feet and head. He winced as they hastily connected him to a drip that began to feed his body some much needed fluids. As they began to pump through his system, he felt a little warmth and his head didn't seem so foggy.

"We were going to take you to Raigmore Hospital in Inverness," explained Lyle, who sat beside him in the specially modified Land Rover ambulance. "Ms Tyler though has suggested you might prefer being released into her care, which I'm happy to do. Given that it's a lot closer, and with the promise of some hot home-cooked food, I presume that's preferable?"

"Kill me," Thomas croaked, cracking a smile.

"Yeah, he's fine," Catherine chipped in with mock scorn.

"It's more than preferable," Thomas nodded. "And I'm very grateful for your efforts."

"To be honest Mr. Walker, it was all worth it to see you up in that tree," Lyle smiled. "We're going to take you back to the research centre where Ms. Tyler says you'll be comfortable. Under no circumstances are you to go outside and you're to drink plenty of fluids. I also want you to keep extremely warm, even uncomfortably so. You're only mildly hypothermic, but it could quickly escalate, do you understand?"

"Yes sir," Thomas croaked as he heard the engine rumble into life. He was in no position to argue anyway. Ten minutes into the journey, Thomas was already feeling more comfortable and lucid, although he was still shaking under the blanket from the cold. As they passed through the village, Thomas glimpsed a large black American-looking pick-up truck, parked alongside the Army land rovers and police cars at the village hall. Catherine noticed him lift his head.

"An American team of trappers," she stated. "They are going to come up to the centre a bit later. I'm sure they'll want to talk to you if you're up to it by then." She could see even now he was still desperate to be involved in the investigation. It was why she had offered to take him in at the research centre, as well as it being somewhere she could keep a close eye on him.

"Tom," she said softly, getting his attention again. "I think you should know Danny Reeves is missing, He left the Dam & Dram some time after we did, but never returned. Police found his rental car in an unused timber yard this morning. It probably looked like a car park from the road, but nobody had thought to put a guard there."

Thomas looked at her, his eyes distant and confused for a moment. His gaze fell to the floor as he slumped in the stretcher. They didn't speak for the rest of the journey.

When they arrived at the research centre, Lyle and Catherine helped Thomas through to the office. Catherine pulled out his chair for him and reclined it as far as it would go, but kept it close enough to the desk so that he could reach out for it if he needed to. Thomas slumped into it, slipping his arm from Lyle's supporting shoulder.

"One of the best things you could do Mr. Walker is get yourself into a piping hot shower," Lyle suggested.

"That's a good idea," agreed Catherine, carrying a set of blankets over to the chair. "I'll get one running for you."

She disappeared again in a flurry, Thomas staring after her in a bewildered daze. He felt too weak to argue. He offered a trembling hand to Lyle and gave a heartfelt nod of thanks.

"It looks like you're in good hands Mr. Walker," Lyle laughed, shaking his hand firmly.

Thomas closed his eyes for a moment as he heard the sound of the shower in the background whilst Catherine showed Lyle out. She walked back into the office purposefully, and when Thomas opened his eyes again he noticed she was fixing him with a mischievous grin.

"Time for that shower Mr. Walker," she smirked.

"I think I can manage," Thomas replied sarcastically.

As he stood up, his legs threatened to buckle and he felt light headed. He clutched the blankets he was wrapped in with his right hand and reached out for the desk with his left. He staggered forward a few steps, steadying himself before attempting the gap between the desk and the door.

"You're the epitome of grace," Catherine stated, shaking her head with a smile. "Look, sooner or later you're going to have to drop the blankets. You're wearing every single one we have and you're going to need them dry."

She marched across the hall and opened the bathroom door, grabbing a towel from the rack.

"Wrap that round your waist. That you can get wet and I'll turn my back, promise."

Thomas gave up all effort to cling to his dignity as she promptly turned around. He let the blankets fall to the floor and he wrapped the towel round his waist. He trudged to the shower cubicle and gingerly stepped inside as Catherine turned back round.

The water was incredibly hot, the controls set almost to maximum. For a moment the heat didn't register against his hard muscles and aching joints, but slowly it began to seep through as he cracked his neck and began to relax. He tried to turn around to expose as much of his body as possible to the hot pounding water. He still needed to hold his hands against the wall in order to steady himself and he couldn't lift his hands to his head. Catherine seemed to sense his weakness.

"It's completely up to you Tom, but I can help you wash if you like?" She asked gingerly, no sense of playfulness this time.

He turned to her and nodded silently. He didn't want her to, but he could still feel the dirt and grit in his hair and the cold clinging to his skin. More than anything, he wanted that feeling gone.

Catherine opened the shower door, turning his shoulders away from her as she reached up for the shower head. She titled his head to one side and began to lather shampoo in her hands. As she gently massaged and tugged at his matted hair, he wondered who else he could have called on to help him like this. He realised there was nobody, and he suddenly felt very grateful to her, much preferring that it was somebody he knew and trusted seeing him so vulnerable.

"How do you feel?" Catherine asked as she turned off the tap.

"So much better," Thomas exclaimed, the steam still rising from his shoulders and from the soaked towel still wrapped around his waist.

"Think you can dress on your own?" She asked, flashing her mischievous smile again.

"Yeah, I think so," he laughed.

As Catherine closed the door behind her, Thomas sat down on the wooden bench against the wall of the bathroom and slowly began to dab himself dry, enjoying the warmth from the steam that still hung in the room.

~

Dr. Rebecca Stephenson took the latest printout of data from the reams on her desk, taking a large bite out of a chicken salad sandwich as she did so. She knew she couldn't put it off any longer. She picked it up and went to find Rupert Pettigrew. The little dweeb and DEFRA weren't going to like this.

CHAPTER TWENTY-TWO

Thomas woke with a jump, startled by Catherine as she placed a mug of hot chocolate and a bowl of steaming sticky toffee pudding down beside him. Her shadow falling across him had been enough to wake him from his light sleep. He opened his eyes wide, shaking off the sleepiness he felt. Something pressed against his knee and he looked down to find Meg resting her chin on his lap. He realised Catherine had gone to pick her up from the house whilst he slept. He felt relieved and extremely thankful. He stroked Meg's head and ruffled her fur gently between his fingers.

"You were lucky last night you know," Catherine stated sternly. "They found Danny Reeves. There wasn't much left, even some of the bones had been broken apart and chewed on. I don't think it was happy with one victim either. I didn't tell you when we found you, but you had company. Its paw prints were all around the tree. And..."

"What?" Thomas asked.

"You might want to clean your rifle really well before you use it again. I think it was sending you a message."

"Only people think like that," Thomas smiled. "It may well have recognised the gun. After all we know it's been shot at. It's probably almost certainly familiar with my scent now too. It won't have liked me following it or getting close to its kills, so maybe it was sending me a message as you say."

Catherine seemed to frown at his reply. "You get dessert first," she said, motioning him toward the bowl of pudding. "I'm told you need the calories. Then its mum's chicken soup," she beamed.

"Remind me to be poorly more often," Thomas smiled.

Catherine's mother lived in Drumnadrochit and had been the one to suggest her daughter move north to start things afresh. From her smallholding kitchen she sold a range of soups, stocks, jams and chutneys as well as farm-fresh eggs, cakes and cured meats. They were of the highest calibre as far as Thomas was concerned.

"She did give me a loaf too, in case you were wondering," Catherine added with a smile.

Thomas grinned as she took the hint and left the office to make them both lunch.

~

David Fairbanks took a deep breath before stepping out onto the platform. The hall was filled with reporters and a large number of bright lights and cameras were pointed in his direction. This was his moment in the spotlight, and it was all thanks to Walker and the animal. He wouldn't even have to thank them for it, in fact he was planning to do quite the opposite. He stepped up to the microphone array and placed his notes on the wooden stand below it.

"Please be seated ladies and gentlemen," he beckoned with a thin commanding smile. "I have called this press conference to update you on some recent escalations in the case." His gaze was constant and he shifted his stance slightly to face the cameras of the larger networks. "I regret to inform you that early this morning we found the remains of Daniel Reeves, the animal's twelfth victim. Whilst our utmost sympathy goes out to Mr. Reeves' family, he ignored safety advice issued regarding entering the forest areas, and once again we appeal to members of the public not to go looking for the animal, or to venture into the countryside at present."

Fairbanks took a quick draw of breath, wanting to continue quickly before anyone was able to interrupt with a question.

"I can also confirm that Thomas Walker was rescued from the forest alive and is recovering from a state of mild hypothermia. His actions were not condoned and I state again that he is no longer an active part of the investigation. Further lives were put at risk in order to mount a rescue and I am deeply disturbed by Mr. Walker's actions. I have already commented that I believe Mr. Walker's personal history makes him a liability, which is why he was removed from the investigation in the first place. I have no further comment on the matter and will allow you to draw your own conclusions."

As he finished speaking, there was an eruption of noise in the hall as zealous reporters started calling his name and fired off questions to his remarks. He revelled in the moment for a second before raising his hands, appealing that he had not yet finished.

"We have now called for professional assistance in hunting the animal and an American team have been flown in via the direct assistance of the United States Air Force. They will begin operations immediately, using well-trained dogs and state-of-the-art trapping technology. We expect quick results from these professional hunters and will update you accordingly."

As flash-guns blazed and cameras fired, another flurry of

unanswered questions rose from the crowd of reporters. Fairbanks again raised his hands and waited for silence. He was in complete control of the room now.

"I will not be taking any questions at this time, but I can offer you a further update in regards to the animal's identity. It appears that it is a hybrid of the jaguar species. Its origins are still unclear, but the hybridisation strongly suggests the animal is an escapee from a private collection."

He had added the last bit. He didn't want people thinking this could be a wild animal. With a smug smile, he closed his notes and turned quickly away as the reporters surged forward, their raised voices echoing off the high ceiling as he disappeared through a side door.

~

Thomas put down the second helping of sticky toffee pudding that had followed the chicken soup. A heavy rumble made the whole building shake slightly. It was the noise of a large diesel V8 engine. He could tell it had turned into the small car park to the side of the centre and he was in no doubt the Americans had arrived. He quickly threw off his blankets and headed for the front door. Catherine got there before him and opened it.

A tall man stepped out of the front cab of the pick-up truck, and Thomas found himself raising his hand in greeting in disbelief. As Thomas walked over to him, Lee Logan tipped his black cattleman hat with his thumb and forefinger to return the hello.

"Looking good Logan," Thomas smiled. "There's no mistaking the arrival of the beast," he added, looking at the huge black truck behind Logan.

"This one's new," Logan replied, shaking Thomas's outstretched hand firmly. "She's Black Ops, just like me."

Thomas smiled, noting the Special Forces insignia on the side of the truck. Lee had been an Army Ranger, and always joked about the supposed clandestine operations he had been involved in. Thomas never really knew if he was kidding or not. The grin spreading across Logan's face suggested the former.

Thomas knew enough about American cars to identify it as a Ford F450, but it had been heavily modified. Everything from the bull bars to the headlight surrounds and custom wheels had been blacked out for a start. The twin ram air vents on the hood and the super duty grill gave it a purposeful and aggressive stance. Thomas had a secret love of pick-up trucks and this was the best he'd ever seen.

"What's it got under the hood?" Thomas asked, intrigued.

"6.7 litre V8. 800ft of torque. 400 horse power. It has a lot to live up to if it wants to earn the name beast," Logan smirked, his weathered features still holding the warmth of his smile.

Thomas had fond memories of riding out in Logan's Chevrolet Silverado 3500HD, with its dual rear wheels and heavily modified engine and suspension, courtesy of Logan's son.

"Mr. Logan?" Catherine asked. She was a little taken back that Thomas seemed to know the man.

"Yes ma'am," answered Logan in his broad western United States accent. He winked at Thomas. "It's good to see you son but now I know why you stayed away so long," he nodded towards Catherine. She blushed.

"Cath, meet Lee Logan and the hole in the wall gang," Thomas gestured, as three other cowboys climbed out of the truck.

All three were younger than Logan, and probably Thomas too Catherine guessed.

"Ryan Jackson, Ethan Miller and Brandon King," Thomas continued, introducing the men one by one.

Ryan Jackson was a tall, thin man with dark hair and features that hid an extraordinary strength. Thomas knew he had once pulled a straying cow from a flooded river by himself. Ethan Miller was the youngest of the team, in his mid twenties. Catherine guessed he looked up to Logan as something of a father figure by the similar hat he wore, and the way he watched Logan for a signal to step forward. Brandon King was a huge man, nearly six foot six. Logan had once told Thomas he was a born mountain man, having lived in a cabin in the Rockies with his father until he was a young man. His strength was legendary, and there wasn't anything Logan had needed to teach him about trapping or hunting.

It made sense to Thomas that it was Logan who had been called. He had a large ranch in Johnson County, Wyoming, not too far from the famous hole in the wall canyon that had once harboured the notorious Butch Cassidy and Sundance Kid. Logan had returned to the family ranch after his Army service, but he had quickly gained a formidable reputation as a trapper. He had also soon become something of a cougar specialist. Although there were still bears in the state's famous Yellowstone Park, the cougar was the only considerable natural threat that faced Wyoming ranchers.

The state of Wyoming was excellent cougar territory. The rolling Great Plains meeting the Rocky Mountains made ideal habitat, and it was filled with wild game and some of the finest livestock in the whole of the U.S. The cats were now relatively scarce and easily controlled, so Logan and his team now travelled across the entire states to trap and often kill problem cougars.

"Hear you've got a cat problem?" Ryan remarked with a smug grin.

"Like nothing you've ever seen!" Thomas smiled. "Were you able to bring the dogs?"

"Yup," smiled Logan. "Weren't gonna make the trip without em'. They've been classed as bona fide members of the military jus' for the occasion. They're gonna need a run."

Just like Army sniffer and patrol dogs working overseas, Catherine knew they must have been issued military permits and passports for a quick deployment. She suspected that all the requirements such as rabies vaccinations and tapeworm treatments were probably already more than up to date, given they were working hunting dogs.

"There's a strip of land behind," Catherine explained. "They'll be fine there and one thing we're never short of is dog food. I'll open the side gate and you can let them straight out."

"Very kind of you ma'am," Logan smiled, tipping his hat again.

The flatbed of the pick-up truck had also been modified to house four dog crates, two on the bottom with the other two on top. Ryan lowered the customised tailgate that acted as a ramp down to the ground, and opened the four mesh gates to the crates. A dog emerged from each one, then jumped onto the ramp and trotted round to the front of the truck, as if waiting for orders. They were the best trained dogs Thomas had ever come across, Meg coming from the same school. He eyed each of them as they lined up.

First out as always was Lobo, Logan's fearsome brindle coloured Fila brasileiro. He looked like a cross between a bloodhound and a bullmastiff, which Thomas strongly suspected was where the origins of the breed lay. They were well known for holding large prey at bay rather than attacking, making them perfect cougar dogs. Next was Ryan's blue-grey cane corso, an ancient breed of Italian 'coursing' mastiff used for hunting deer and boar. His name was Arturo. Boomer, Brandon's black and tan coonhound was next. He got his name from his mournful baying howl. Last was Ethan's Carolina dog, Cody. The lithe form and golden colour of the breed often earned them the nickname of American dingo.

Everyone turned round at the sudden, excited bark that came from Meg, as she stood in the door of the research centre. She surged forward, wagging her tail as she ran straight up to the enormous Lobo. The dogs seemed delighted to see each other, rubbing noses and pawing at each other playfully. The others soon joined in. As Catherine unbolted the back gate, Meg streaked through the pack, leading the other four dogs into the little strip of trees and grass at the back of the centre.

"I see Meg hasn't lost her touch," smiled Ryan.

Thomas was glad to see Ryan was in good spirits. It had been Ryan's dog that had been killed in the pit with the old tom cougar when it had injured Meg. At first, he had been anxious there might be some resentment to that regard, but he could now see that Ryan had the same soft-natured, common-sense wisdom he had encountered in so many ranchers. His attachment to his animals was close, probably closer than between most pets and owners, but at the same time a totally different relationship. The animals often worked as hard as the men, sometimes harder, but they served their purpose. Ryan clearly wasn't looking to lose another dog, and the cane corso was a significantly weightier replacement, although he'd been just a pup when Thomas left. As the dogs chased each other round the trees and through the brush, the men followed Thomas and Catherine into the research centre.

Thomas caught Logan's glance as they passed through the narrow corridor into the office. American homes and in particular Logan's 3,000 acre ranch, were huge in comparison, and Thomas knew the cosy little centre was smaller than most of Logan's outbuildings. He couldn't help grinning. Logan and his men sat down on a corner sofa against the far wall of the office whilst Thomas and Catherine sat on a smaller two-seater opposite. They both often jokingly referred to it as the conference room. Catherine had been quick to fill up six mugs of coffee from the machine and the Americans helped themselves to cream and sugar.

"That politician doesn't like you too much does he?" Logan smiled. "Heard the press conference he just gave?"

Thomas shook his head and shrugged his shoulders. He had slept most of the day and hadn't known there had been a press conference.

"He didn't go quite so far as to say so, but he pretty much fingered you for the death of the other guy last night."

Thomas glanced at Catherine. He could see she was just as surprised as he was. She had been too busy taking care of him to have caught the news.

"I'm guessing Fairbanks didn't know you and I had worked together," Thomas smiled, "otherwise I doubt you'd have got the job."

"Guessed as much," Logan grinned back.

"We'll dig you out of that hole," added Brandon. "We'll make sure folks know that it was your information and help that bagged us the critter."

"Thanks guys," Thomas smiled appreciatively. "What do you want to know?"

"Have you gotten a look at it, do you know what we're dealing with?" Ryan asked.

"Not yet," Thomas shook his head. "Everything I've seen suggests it's a very big animal, bigger than anything we ever came across for sure. At first I thought it was a jaguar, but we're waiting to hear on that from samples taken."

"What Fairbanks said in the press conference backed that up, part ways at least," Ryan chimed in.

"When are you heading out?" Catherine asked.

"We're going straight from here ma'am," Logan replied. "We'll need some time to set the traps and it's gonna start to get dark in about an hour. I want the dogs on the trail before the light goes entirely and then we'll follow them up."

"This animal has killed a dozen people now and shown amazing strength and agility in doing so. Just don't treat this like a usual cougar hunt, or let your guard down for a moment."

"It's okay Tom, we're covered even if the boogie-man shows up," Ryan laughed.

"Could have done with you coming out with us son," Logan smiled kindly as he stood up and placed a hand on Thomas's shoulder. "You take it easy now and we'll see you in the morning."

Thomas and Catherine saw them out. The dogs came instantly to heel and were put back into the truck. Thomas stepped up to the driver's window as Logan pulled round.

"You know, this rig doesn't seem like you Logan?" Thomas queried.

"It's more comfortable and roomy than the old Chevy," smiled Logan. "The amount your politician is paying us, we were encouraged to travel in style. The air force even flew us in. Nice to have friends in high places."

"I mean it, be careful," Thomas warned, stepping back.

"I mean it too," Logan assured him with a tip of the hat, "we will be."

Thomas and Catherine watched the big black truck pull out of the driveway and head towards the forest. Thomas turned back towards the research centre as he heard the phone in the office start ringing. He walked in slowly, dropping the pretence all was well now Logan and the team had left. He still felt stiffer and weaker than usual. He picked up the receiver gingerly.

"Mr. Walker?"

He instantly recognised Kelly Keelson's voice.

"What can I do for you Ms. Keelson? Thomas asked coldly.

"I...I just want you to know how sorry I am about Danny Reeves."

Thomas didn't know what to say. He could hear the strained and genuine emotion in her voice.

"Well that's an unusual move for a reporter," Thomas stated, softening slightly. "I appreciate it though. Danny was a risk taker and he probably had been drinking. He didn't know what he was up against. It wasn't your fault." He didn't know why he had said that, but he guessed it was something she needed to hear.

"Look, I want to make this up to you. I want to use you in a piece where I'll portray you as the underdog, victimised by DEFRA and slandered," Keelson continued.

"Why would you do that? Thomas asked.

"Because in this case, I think it's true," she said humbly.

"Okay. Can you come up to the research centre? I can't really go anywhere and I guess I did promise you that interview."

"I can be there in an hour if that suits?"

"That's fine. I'll see you then Ms. Keelson." He put the phone down as Catherine walked back into the room.

"I'm going down to the town hall to get the details from this press conference. It looks like we might have the blood tests back," Catherine explained.

"That's good timing, Kelly Keelson wants to come up and set things straight. It could do some good if she's telling the truth. Feel free to punch Fairbanks though if you want, I won't hold you back," Thomas grinned.

"You never have," smirked Catherine. "Anyway, I won't be too long. Don't trust her too much though, she's still a reporter."

"I'll be fine, and on my guard," Thomas reassured her. More than that though, he was determined to repay the favour to Fairbanks and was already thinking about what he was going to say. No more holding back. Keelson was going to get her story.

CHAPTER TWENTY-THREE

The creature stirred, dazedly casting a glance back at its own tail that swung back and forth with lazy malevolence. It raised itself to its feet and yawned, opening its jaws wide and tasting the air as it did so. It arched its back and stretched its front paws out in front of it, shaking off the remnants of its nap.

The sun was beginning to set, casting a pale yellow glow on the forest below that reached up towards the glistening mountain tops. The creature bathed itself in the failing light, its senses alerted to the oncoming dusk. It was overwhelmed by the hunger it felt. It took a few silent steps forward, its nose pointing down the mountainside. It poised motionless on a jut of rock as it picked up the faint echo of dogs barking, no louder than an intake of breath on the wind. It licked its muzzle and bounded to the ground. It began to trot casually down the mountainside towards the forest.

~

Logan and Ryan started unloading the gear from the truck. They had driven some way into the forest, only stopping when it became impossible for them to go any further. Ethan and Brandon hauled a 30lb chunk of horsemeat around a small clearing close to where they had stopped. The sticky, sweet smell of the thawing, naturally marinating flesh wafted in waves into the forest. Every now and then Ethan would cut a small strip from it and throw it into the trees. They left the rest of the meat in the centre of the clearing and turned their attention to cutting off most of the paths that led to it with brush and piles of snow. When only three clear paths remained, they returned to the clearing where Logan and Ryan were laying out a number of wire snares and heavy-duty steel enforced coil-spring traps.

Logan started setting snares around the perimeter of the clearing. Some he covered, carefully and with skill. Others he left out in the open. He knew the cat would see them and avoid them, only to be channelled towards the hidden snares on either side. As he looked up, he saw the others were carefully anchoring and setting the spring traps along the paths they'd left open. They used the surrounding snow and bracken to cover each.

Happy with their preparation of the clearing, Logan called the men together. The dogs sat nearby, waiting patiently for the hunt to begin. He lifted up the rear bench seat in the truck's cab to reveal the gun locker and passed out the Browning BPS 10-gauge Stalker shotguns to each of them. He also handed out a mixture of slugs and shells as ammo, providing a mix of knock-down and killing power as might be required. Logan picked up his Smith & Wesson S&W500 revolver and put it in his shoulder holster. He also patted his Cold Steel Marauder bowie knife to check it was there. Ryan smiled as he leaned in and passed out the other handguns. He picked up his own Smith & Wesson 1911 pro pistol, then handed Brandon his Sig Sauer P220 elite stainless. With a smirk, he also passed him his carbon steel tomahawk. Brandon grinned as he fastened it to his belt. Finally, he gave Ethan his Taurus 444 Ultralite. Its small and stocky appearance hid the powerful punch of a .44 Magnum load.

"Okay men, you know what to do," Logan commanded. "The dogs are already showing interest, so I'm guessing they've got something on the nose. The idea is to let them take the trail so we can get an idea of where this cat's at. Once we know that, we push him back towards here and the traps."

The rest of the men nodded in agreement.

"Lobo and Boomer will lead until they're sure of the trail as normal. After that, it's a free for all as much as I care, but as for us, we stick together, no exceptions." Logan continued.

As the last of the light began to filter through the lower branches of the trees, Logan and Brandon walked over to their dogs. With a simple nod of the heads, the two big dogs raced off into the forest, Lobo letting loose a blood-chilling bay that Boomer answered with his own mournful howl. A few seconds later, Ryan and Ethan gave the signal to Arturo and Cody to follow up. They scampered off on the heels of the others, Arturo's thunderous bark drowning out the excited Cody as they disappeared into the trees. The men set off in silent pursuit.

~

Thomas sat with his chair fully reclined, warm and comfortable again under the blankets. Catherine had lit the fire in the office and Meg was sprawled out in front of it. He didn't normally let her in the room, but she had been very quiet after the other dogs had left, and he knew she was missing their company. He admitted to himself he also wanted her close for comfort whilst Catherine was out. He thought about making some tea, but as he got up a shiver of cold swept over him almost immediately, and he sank back down into the chair. Meg raised her head and whined. He knew she needed to be let out too and a glance at the fire told him it needed another log. There was nothing for it. He threw off the blanket again and stood up more surely this time, before slowly making his way to the kitchen.

~

Catherine was barely unable to contain her conceit as the meeting ended. She packed away the horrendous press release and the other documents she and the other attendees had been provided with, dumping it into her slightly ragged canvas messenger bag. Out of the corner of her eye she saw David Fairbanks slithering his way through the crowd towards her. She gave him one venom filled glance and headed for the door. *No thank you Mr. Fairbanks, I'm not interested in anymore excuses* she growled to herself.

As she climbed into her Mitsubishi L200 Barbarian pick-up, she noticed the splashes of mud now almost matched the faded brown paintwork. She banged the door violently against Fairbanks' Jaguar saloon that happened to be parked next to her. She smiled smugly, only to realise with horror that the driver was sitting in the car. As his head whipped round, Catherine had already started the engine and was gunning her way out of the village hall's car park. She even got a squeal from the tyres as she headed into the narrow lanes beyond Cannich, which made her smile.

As the sun dipped behind Càrn Eige and the glen began to slip into shadow, she set her eyes on the distant light visible on the hillside that was the research centre. It seemed to glow brighter as dusk fell and darkness consumed the valley in its relentless westward march. The four-cylinder diesel engine moaned momentarily as it fought for grip and power against the slush and mud. Some of the lower passes were slick with thawing snow and she slowed her pace. No burning headlights from the Jaguar saloon or any other car were behind her, and she began to relax. As she rounded a sweeping curve and the road began to climb, she could now see the lights of the village slightly below her. She hoped Thomas had kept the fire going as she waited for the truck to warm up. As she rounded the next bend, she had just enough time to spot the thick torrent of mud and water that had pooled across the road, and the collapsed bank that had strewn chunks of earth and stone into her path. She brought the truck to a grinding stop and flicked on her high beam lights. With a sigh she opened the door and stepped out into the cool night air, a slight shiver rippling down her spine.

~

The creature lay perfectly still, unconcerned by the approach of the car on the road a little way down the hillside. The world around it was becoming brighter and more sepia in tone with every passing moment, its irises enlarging proportionately to the fading light. Its vision was saturated by the blue and brownish tones of the darkness, allowing it to look out across the landscape as if it were cast in a permanent dusk. It saw everything. Movement was also easier to pick out against the sedentary silhouette of night too. It was the perfect time to hunt.

As the car stopped, the creature raised its head. It let out a quiet yowl of displeasure as the headlights momentarily scalded its eyes. It watched the female get out of the car and instantly froze, except for a twitch of anticipation that snaked through its tail. It pricked its ears forward and rose to a crouch. It took a silent step forward, and then another.

~

Catherine walked up to the stream of mud and carefully placed the toe of her boot into the sludge. It parted and revealed the terra firma of the tarmac less than an inch below. It wasn't too deep at least. Her eyes darted to the earth and rocks that lay over the road. It was a little tight, but she was fairly sure she'd be able to get the truck through if she stayed to the right hand side.

She suddenly felt another shiver pass over her, and the hairs on the back of her neck stood on end as she glanced up the hillside. The wind dropped and nothing moved in the unnerving, silent dark. She took a step back towards the car, and then another.

~

The creature worked its way down the hillside, heading towards a gap in the brush further down that would allow it to slip through onto the road and approach from behind. It crept, almost slithered over the rocky hillside towards the gap. It gingerly extended a testing paw and slunk down onto its haunches to pass through. It cleared the brush and stepped out onto the road. It turned to look at the car, which it was now some distance behind.

Catherine threw the door open and jumped into the driver's seat. She turned the key in a slight panic and hit the accelerator. She struggled with the steering wheel as the tyres slipped and squealed in the greasy mix of mud and silt. The truck veered from right to left, but suddenly found purchase and lurched forward in an ungraceful bounce as it suddenly found dry road beneath it again. She worked the gears aggressively to get the truck back up to speed.

The creature roared angrily, bounding forward as the truck began to edge further and further away. It stopped to watch the vehicle as it followed the road in a long and winding ascent of the hill. The creature purred as it tracked and anticipated its route. It loped forward and then broke into a series of elongated bounds, driving its bulk straight up the slope. It left the road in a single spring, cutting up the hillside and joining the road again further up. It quickly began to gain on the vehicle and its occupant.

Catherine was gripped by a terror-fuelled panic as she tore along the road. Even above the noise of the engine and the radio, she had heard the roar. She turned sharply into the car park of the research centre, sending a small spray of gravel against the boundary wall as she ground to a halt. She snatched the messenger bag from the passenger seat and threw the driver's door open. She peered into the night only for a moment before she ran to the front door. Her hand shook as she placed the key in the lock. She felt an enormous wave of relief sweep over her as the door swung open and she almost tumbled through. She slammed it shut and trembled as she held it against the frame and put her ear to its surface. There was nothing but the light breath of the wind on the other side. She sighed and straightened up. *You're imagining things and jumping at shadows* she told herself with a shake of her head. She stood in the hall for a moment as she let the tremble in her hands dissipate, before turning and walking into the office.

~

The creature paused at the edge of the driveway. The female had disappeared inside the dwelling. It panted, recovering from its fast ascent of the hill. As it took a step forward, it was blinded by a sudden blaze of light that seemed to come from the top of the stone wall in front of it. It recoiled instantly, slipping backwards into a drainage ditch along the side of the road. An unnerved and suspicious growl rumbled in its throat as the light disappeared. It tried once more, only to again be met by the dazzling flash at the perimeter of the dwelling. It retreated to the ditch once more, this time in silence. It flicked its ears forward as it caught the sound of the dog barking behind the dwelling. It paced along the stone wall of the perimeter, looping wide and a little way back down the hill, skirting round towards the prey it could sense beyond the reach of the light.

~

Thomas stood at the office window, looking out onto the trees and the peak of Càrn Eige. With the lights low in the office as they were, he could just about make out the mist forming on the lower slopes. The slight thaw meant the ground was wet and as the cold wind passed over it and travelled up the steep sides of the mountain, it rapidly cooled. The resulting bank of freezing fog rolled back towards the glen and the forest. There was also still plenty of snow on the ground to help cool the air further. He couldn't help thinking Logan and the others were in for a very cold night, but he knew they'd faced worse. Winter in Wyoming was anything but mild. He stood motionless even as Catherine walked in, still listening as he had been. Finally he turned to her and offered her a tired smile.

"Sorry, I thought I heard something a few minutes before you arrived," he explained. He walked back to his chair and sat down opposite her.

She smiled as she noticed the fierce fire in the hearth as a large dry log crackled within it. Then she frowned.

"You heard the roar too?" She queried. "I just got through telling myself it was the wind."

Thomas suddenly noticed that she looked tired. Colour was returning to her face and at first he had thought it had just been the weather, but now he realised something had shaken her.

"Okay, maybe it's just the cold. Acuity check, what letter comes after S?"

"T. And yes, I'd love some," she smiled.

Thomas laughed and headed towards the kitchen, but paused in the doorway.

"If we both heard it, you know that means it's on the mountain somewhere don't you?"

Catherine nodded in silence, her gaze lost in the fire.

~

The creature stood at the edge of the trees on the far side of the dwelling. Its ears flicked constantly, now picking up the muffled human voices inside. Every now and then it turned its head back towards the trees. It sensed other prey moving far off, but getting closer. The fine hairs within its ears fluffed outwardly, naturally amplifying its hearing and enabling it to catch the whispers of barking dogs coming from the forest. It stood against the wind, judging distance and direction before returning its gaze towards the rowan tree, and its bent trunk that extended over the wall. The creature dismissed the far off sounds for now and gently began hauling itself upwards, digging its extended claws into the ribbon like bark as it went.

~

Thomas returned, carrying a tray adorned with a polka dot teapot and two cups with saucers. Catherine smiled, appreciating the effort of using her favourite set. She had quite the collection at home. She noticed matching plates held two slices of heavily buttered tea loaf as he set the tray down on the desk.

"Should we let Logan know it's close by?" Catherine asked.

"Trust me, he knows better than we do where the cat is. We just have to hope they get the job done. For all we know, it could all be over already," he shrugged. He had meant it reassuringly, but he could see she didn't seem so sure. She clutched her tea cup with both hands and sipped slowly, deep in thought.

"So come on then, what happened at the meeting?" He

asked, nudging her with his knee.

"Look at the DNA results for yourself," Catherine replied, opening her bag and handing him the report. "They had to assure us several times they hadn't made a mistake or mixed the sample up."

"This seems impossible," Thomas declared as he skimmed through the report. "Pretty much every species of cat in Europe and Asia is listed in one context or another. It can't possibly share genetic markers with so many different animals."

"It at least confirms some of your theories. Its mother was almost certainly a melanistic jaguar. That solves half of the mystery at least," Catherine offered.

~

Meg slowly raised her head, distracted from hunting the voles and mice in the long grass. She pricked her ears and lifted her nose into the air. She stood motionless, listening to the sound of the wind moving through the trees. She glanced at the door at the back of the research centre. She was about to go back to her hunt, when she heard the creak of the rowan tree. Her eyes darted to it and she noticed a single shake as it shuddered under unseen strain. She took a few steps and then froze, glancing again at the back door. The rowan tree was between her and it. She waited in silence, knowing not to bark or give away the quarry until it had been identified. It was second nature to her now, but all her senses were focused on the tree.

~

As Catherine leaned over to get something out of the bag, Thomas saw the pictures that the school children had drawn for her poking out of the top. They were slightly crumpled but he reached over and pulled them out, flattening them out on the desk as best he could.

"How is the boy doing?" Thomas asked without looking up.

"He's recovering, but still in shock. He hasn't made much sense so far. He keeps talking about monsters. They wanted him to identify the cat, but he started screaming as soon as they started showing him pictures."

"Poor kid," Thomas exclaimed. "But have a look at these drawings those girls did for you." He passed them over to Catherine. "I know even the best witnesses, let alone children, are prone to exaggerate and refer to monsters, but what do you see?"

"I see exactly that, a big black monster cat."

"Yes," agreed Thomas, "but look at those teeth especially. They've drawn them extending past the jaw-line, deliberately it would seem."

"It's a drawing of a monster Tom, all teeth and claws. I don't think it can be used as exhibit A when it comes to identification. They've just seen something they don't understand."

"It's just frustrating. They got a real look at this thing and yet we're no closer to understanding what it is," Thomas shrugged.

"That's hardly their fault Tom. What do the blood results suggest to you?" Catherine asked, the tiredness in her voice becoming obvious.

Thomas looked through the report again. "Remember

what I was saying about ligers?" He asked.

"Sort of," Catherine sighed. "You talk a lot. Remind me."

Thomas shot her a sarcastic but playful glance. "They're a hybrid cross between a male lion and a female tiger. They tend to be effected by gigantism as well as a few other odd genetic mutations. They can grow up to twelve feet and weigh up to 1,200lbs. They're truly enormous animals. What if our cat suffers from something similar?"

"We certainly know it's a hybrid, so it would make sense. And we know it's much larger than anything normal." She picked up the drawings again and looked at them closely. "It is strange how they've drawn those teeth isn't it?" She admitted, reclining back into her chair. "It looks like a sabre-tooth tiger."

"Sabre-toothed cat," Thomas corrected. "Or a dirk-toothed cat, there were several species with similar dentistry," he explained. He was about to say something else, when he turned his head sharply. Meg was outside, barking frantically. A low and thunderous growl rumbled along the confines of the research centre. It seemed to pass right through them. Catherine froze and her eyes were fixed on Thomas, filled with fear. Thomas had to shake himself free of his own fright before he stumbled into a run towards the back door.

~

The creature dropped from the tree, already almost on top of the dog, which stood its ground and continued to bark. It snarled threateningly, but knew it no longer had the element of surprise. It turned its head towards the forest again and licked its muzzle. With an almost lazy cuff of its paw it sent the dog flying backwards. The dog crashed into the wall of the dwelling and crumpled to the ground. The creature hesitated only momentarily before turning and leaping over the boundary wall. It let out a savage roar as it slipped back into the trees. New prey lay within their darkness.

CHAPTER TWENTY-FOUR

Catherine was trembling as she stepped up to the window. She gasped as she caught a glimpse of a long, thick, black tail as it disappeared over the wall. The ear-splitting roars were already growing fainter as the cat sought the refuge of the forest. She suddenly realised just how close things had come for them. The daunting realisation that the creature had indeed been behind her on the road just as she'd feared, and that it had then followed her, caused her to sink back towards her chair in shock. Thomas came into view on the other side of the window. They both looked down towards Meg's limp body.

~

The creature accelerated through the forest, the trees becoming thicker and denser as it went. It had become silent now, slipping along hollows and shadowy gullies towards the baying dogs. A thin mist was spreading through the glen and it paused as it reached the well-worn path of a game trail. The wind was in its favour and it scented the air. Sensitive pressure points in the pads of its paws picked up the tiny vibrations rippling over the ground. It recognised the fast gallop of the four dogs racing towards it from the west, and the heavy slog of the men to the south. The creature panted for a second or two as it filled its lungs with air. It turned and sprayed the path liberally with urine, using its back paws to scrape at the sweaty slush it had left on the ground. With a final glance behind, it trotted at a gentle pace away from its pursuers.

~

Catherine carried Meg into the examination room, and was almost pleased to hear the soft whimper the dog let out as she put her down onto the table. She began to feel and stretch each leg, looking for breaks and injuries. As she extended her front left leg, Meg jumped with pain, yelping shamelessly. Thomas leaned in and stroked her head lovingly, letting his hand slip down to the ruff of her neck. The touch of the hot, wet, matted fur surprised him, and he moved round to the other side of the table to get a better look. The blood seeped from four deep slashes, trickling into a stream that ran down her neck and began to drip onto the floor. Catherine took Thomas's shaking hand and applied pressure to the wound as she turned to a cabinet for a sterile pack of catgut and dressings.

~

The creature stopped and glanced behind it, again scenting the air and listening to the baying dogs as they began to close in. It stepped off the trail and began to loop back, stealthily moving through the dense gorse, box and hawthorn bushes that kept it hidden. Each calculated step brought it back onto an intercept course with its pursuers. It found a hollow a few yards from where it planned to meet the path again and hunkered down into it. It hunched its shoulders ready for the spring and became still amongst the brush as the mist swirling around it steadily thickened.

The large black and tan coonhound galloped along the fresh trail it was now on, baying eagerly as the lurid scent filled its sensitive nostrils. It didn't feel the impact of the unseen force that lifted it into the air, and barely had time to let out a yelp of pain as slicing teeth severed its spine and cut through its torso. The dog hung limp between the creature's jaws. It enjoyed the taste of the flesh but let the canine fall to the floor in a bloody ruin. It trotted along the trail at a faster pace this time, skilfully gauging the approach of the second dog before it disappeared into the thick gorse and brush for a second time.

Lobo trotted along the trail. No longer able to hear Boomer ahead, the big dog immediately became more cautious and let out a low, warning growl. At Boomer's sudden silence the men had started calling to the dogs more earnestly, but they were too far behind now for their commands to be heard clearly. The bloodhound in Lobo made him follow any trail to the end determinedly, and the mastiff in him made that unfortunate for anything he found there. The brindle coloured dog came to a halt over the mangled remains of Boomer and let out a menacing growl. Lobo nosed the dead dog and barked a warning to the big cane corso that was approaching him from behind. Arturo came up alongside Lobo and also nosed Boomer's body. Working as one, both dogs wheeled around to face the gorse, entering the brush to flush out the animal whose spore lay so thickly upon the trail.

~

Thomas stroked Meg's head gently. He occasionally looked

up at Catherine as she worked. She had used bandages to create a tourniquet around the dog's shoulder and was starting on another further down the leg. Meg whimpered, but licked both his and Catherine's hand when they were offered. He watched as Catherine prepared injections and cleaned the wounds. She cut away the matted fur and busied herself with dressing the slashes. Her veterinary skills were far superior to his.

"You little fighter," he whispered kindly and softly to Meg. "I'll call the vet too," he indicated to Catherine.

Catherine sighed as a dark red jet of arterial blood found a hole to vent through. She turned quickly for another pack of catgut to prepare more stitches.

"That would be a good idea," she whispered as he left the room.

Thomas knew the cat hadn't given Meg a killing blow. It had been a frustrated swipe, probably for giving its position away as she had, just like a lioness would cuff a straying cub. But the size of the animal had put Meg in serious risk from the start. He gathered his thoughts and steadied his hands before lifting the phone receiver from the wall and dialling the veterinary surgery in the village.

~

The creature was agitated by the dogs following it into the difficult bush and scrub of the forest. It heard them split and begin to flank it from either side. It hesitated, realising that taking on one of the dogs would mean exposing its back to the other. It turned quickly and began to head down a slope. It hurried its pace, stretching the distance between itself and the two pursuers. As it passed by a babbling stream hidden in a small gully below, it heard the third and smaller dog approaching from the ridge, cutting through the brush to join the others. It leapt down into the gully and spun back to face the opening above it, rippling to the ground in silence. It watched eagerly in anticipation as it listened to the dogs get closer and closer, their loud and careless barking giving them away every few seconds. The creature licked its muzzle, satisfied it was downwind and hidden by the natural channel.

The men reached Boomer's body and paused to listen to the fading barks of the dogs as they began to drive the cat downhill. Logan now realised that following the cat on foot had been a mistake. He had misjudged the speed of the animal and the eagerness of the dogs to follow the trail.

"Well," he sighed, "He's heading in the right direction, back towards the lake and the clearing. Brandon, you take Boomer back there and put him in his crate. We'll get the critter."

"Just bring the bastard to me," Brandon grunted.

The men all nodded, still slightly out of breath from their fast pursuit along the trail. Brandon scooped Boomer's bloody remains into his giant arms and walked back the way they had come. Logan, Ryan and Ethan checked their guns and set off in the opposite direction.

The creature heard the small yellow dog before it saw it. The yapping, slim built Cody was the first to arrive at the gully, and skidded out of the brush onto the loose gravel. He began to sniff at the opening between the rocks that gave way to the stream below. Just as the dog caught its scent, the creature rose up to meet it. It snapped its jaws round the head of the dog, crushing its skull as it hauled itself back onto the rocks. It let the body fall to the ground and then instinctively began to follow the brook downstream. It stopped, registering the barks of the bigger dogs behind and the sounds of the men coming down from the ridge. It growled both in warning and in anticipation, then roared defiantly towards the mountain. It turned back to its path, and purred softly as it went.

Logan and the others stopped in their tracks.

"That didn't sound like no mountain lion," Ethan whispered in alarm, his eyes wide in fear as they searched the night sky and trees around them.

"I think we're all aware it ain't a damn mountain lion," spat Ryan angrily.

"We keep going," commanded Logan quietly. "The dogs are doing their job. The plan's simple. We push it towards the traps and blow the bejesus out of it." He cradled his shotgun and stepped past Ethan and Ryan back onto the trail. The discussion was over.

The creature stood on the sandy beach of the loch, looking straight up the trail as the two dogs approached. The mist was thicker here, but it could still sense movement within the shadows. Where its vision failed, its hearing filled the gaps. It waded into the water and lay there in the shallows, the cool water refreshing it and softening its hot, hard muscles. The fog was heavier over the loch and its ears and whiskers flicked forward to pinpoint the dogs as they approached.

The big cane corso sniffed at the paw prints in the sand and growled, but trotted on along the shore past the black lapping water. Lobo paused though, and growled more menacingly at the mist laced ripples lapping the shore. Arturo gave a gruff bark and looked back. Lobo dropped his head and growled again. The folds of skin round his eyes made it difficult for him to see in the dark and fog, but his nose was filled with the heavy musk of his prey. He turned his head to bark another warning to Arturo.

The creature exploded out of the water, fuelled by its rage and the close presence of the dog. It tried to catch the canine under the throat, but Lobo also went on the attack, and flew in low towards the creature. He fastened his teeth on the fleshy skin below the creature's jaws and hung on, growling through his vice like grip. The creature yowled with pain and panic, unaccustomed to the strength and ferocity of the dog. It dashed from side to side and swung its head high. As it did so, Lobo was flung violently upwards, helpless as the creature vented its anguish. The creature spotted the cane corso racing back over the sand towards it, and twisted its head round to meet Lobo's flailing hind quarters. It bit down savagely, cracking the dog's hips and slicing through its flesh. Lobo cried out in pain and went limp in the creature's jaws, only to be dumped onto the sand as the creature wheeled to meet the gaining cane corso.

Arturo thundered along the shoreline, his heavy body adding momentum to his speed. He bayed loudly as he approached the creature, and launched into a leap towards its rear legs. His jaws clamped onto their target, and he began to pull and worry at the flesh between his teeth. The creature bucked and slashed out with its free hind paw, catching the dog across the face. Arturo growled at the pain but still would not let go, planting his feet into the sand and pulling back hard. As the creature swung round to try and reach its aggressor, Arturo matched its movement like a prize fighter, keeping out of reach of the teeth and jaws. A second slash from the kick of the rear paw opened up his shoulder, and the big dog winced but bit down harder. He could now taste blood in his mouth and he growled with fading triumph as the first wave of weakness and shock swept over him. The creature whirled again and Arturo lost his footing for a moment. It was all that the creature needed. The blow from its front paw sent Arturo crashing into the sand. The creature stood over the big dog, trembling with rage. It opened its jaws in a snarl set to end the dog's life, only to hear the sudden sounds approaching from the trail. Its growl was low and guttural, but it backed away towards the trees and away from the water. Arturo watched it go and shifted his eyes to Logan, Ethan and Ryan as they appeared out of the mist. A soft, pleading whimper found its way into his throat.

At the sound of Arturo's muffled mewing, Ryan ran forward and fell to his knees in the sand beside the big dog. He hadn't made a sound like that since he'd been a pup. Ryan petted him and checked the wounds, which were deep. Logan stood over Lobo's bloody body. The big dog's face and muzzle had been flattened and crushed, distorted into a gargoyle-like grimace of death. Logan shook his head in bewildered anger.

"Ryan, you'd best get Arturo back to the truck. The critter's still heading where we want him to go," Logan declared. "I'll come back for Lobo once we've dealt out a little payback. Otherwise we're all gonna be carrying our dogs back at this rate."

"Why don't we all go back to the truck anyway?" Ethan

asked. The fear in his voice was all too plain for the others to hear.

"Now's not the time to break kid," Logan scolded. "We're headed there anyways, might as well do the job we've been paid to do at the same time."

Ryan watched Ethan and Logan disappear into the mist along the beach. He knelt down next to Arturo and rubbed his ears to comfort him. The dog whimpered a little and licked at his shoulder, the only wound he could reach without moving too much. It was then that Arturo stiffened and growled, pawing at the sand in an attempt to drag himself forward. Ryan didn't hesitate to whip round, just as the hairs on the back of his neck began to stand on end. There was something moving beyond the mist but he couldn't make it out, although he had no doubt as to what it was. Ryan listened intently as his eyes tried in vain to pierce the darkness. Other than the sound of the lapping waves behind him, the shore was eerily quiet. He raised the Browning shotgun, pointing it slightly towards the fog-embanked tree line. He sucked in a breath and held it.

The creature emerged out of the mist in a silent charge. It had flanked the man using the fog bank to its advantage. It leapt just as Ryan caught the movement to his right, but it was too late. He was hit full on by a steaming locomotive of fur and fangs. The air was knocked from his lungs as he was sent flying backwards. His head spun, his body trapped beneath a writhing mass of muscle. He expelled a sharp breath of shock as he felt the cold embrace of the loch, the dark water instantly finding his open mouth and pouring down his throat. He felt the thud of the sandy bottom on his back and he tried to rise upwards in a fit of panic. The dark mass above pinned him beneath the surface. A cry of rage gurgled in his throat as he clawed and raked at the animal's sides. The creature dipped its muzzle into the water and sent its fangs through the man's skull and neck, ceasing his struggles instantly. Keeping a firm hold of the flesh between its teeth, the creature waded out of the loch and carried Ryan along the beach. Arturo cowered in unblinking, silent terror as the creature passed. Only when it had fully disappeared from view did he let a soft whimper escape into the night.

~

Thomas sighed, suddenly releasing the tension that had built up inside him. Catherine had given Meg a sedative and it was beginning to take effect. The vet was on his way and Catherine had also phoned for two dog handlers, whose charges would act as blood donors if necessary. He stroked Meg's head as she passed into a laboured doze.

"What if those blood results aren't from random crossings of hybrid after hybrid?" Thomas asked, almost to himself.

"What do you mean?" Catherine replied. The tiredness and strain showed in her voice.

"What if those kids drew what they saw and not what they imagined?"

Catherine eyed him quietly. Her green irises were backed with a fire he knew was only seconds away from being vented. She was just waiting for him to say it.

"All the remaining genetic markers were carried over from one parent. We know the mother was a jaguar, so it wasn't her. What if the other parent had the genetic footprints of so many other big cats because it was simply related to them? What if it was their predecessor, something that came before them?"

"Just stop!" Catherine snapped, raising her voice. "Just listen to yourself. You're now talking about extinct big cats, most of which were only ever found in the Americas. It's ridiculous. I know you're upset about Meg, but get a grip. I mean it." She glowered at him in warning.

"It's not just a crack-pot theory, there's evidence now," Thomas explained, slowly and calmly. "Remember what I was saying about the Dangerous Animals Act and that being when it all started?"

"Exactly!" Catherine exclaimed, exasperated. "No big cats before 1976, ergo no prehistoric relics running around either."

"But that's just it. The sightings go back for centuries before that, maybe even further."

Catherine sighed. "The Romans collected exotic animals, the Victorians did too. Zoos, circuses, escapes, NOT whatever you think it is!" She shook her head in angry bewilderment.

Thomas raised his hands in frustrated surrender. "You know, there's at least one manuscript where a Roman general describes the ferocity of Britannica's 'cave lions'. There are three of the damn things on the Royal arms of England. We are also one of the richest sources in Europe for fossils of many ancient cat species. It's not so much to suggest they've always been here."

Catherine shook her head, her eyes wet with tears. They had never raised their voices at each other like this before and it didn't feel right.

"It's too much," she said tiredly. "I can't believe it, I just can't."

"What you believe almost doesn't matter right now," Thomas exclaimed, snapping to attention in realisation. "Logan and the others are out there right now and have no idea what they're up against. You think it's them against it? It's the other way round. I've got to warn them."

He turned and made for the door, but Catherine shot across the room and grabbed him, slamming him against the wall.

"I can't," she whispered. "I can't let you go out again. I'm not going to lose you."

Before he knew it, her lips were brushing his as salty tears washed down her cheeks. He felt their cold sting on his skin as he took her into his arms and held her for a moment.

She broke away from him with a girlish smile, one he now realised he had always loved. They were both a little in shock. Catherine wiped her tears away still grinning as Thomas raised his fingers to his lips, as if to check it had really just happened. Neither of them expected the sudden sound of the doorbell.

~

Logan and Ethan reached the clearing and found Brandon waiting for them. He stepped forward as they approached. He froze mid-stride, his face draining of colour as he went for the tomahawk tucked into his belt, glancing only momentarily at the shotgun resting against a tree a few yards away. Logan and Ethan heard the guttural snarl lift into the air from behind them. Ethan only had a moment to let out a strained gasp of realisation before he was lifted into the air and thrown to the side. Logan too was knocked to the ground as something passed him with violent force. He tumbled across the path, his flailing left foot falling heavily onto the pressure pad of a hidden spring trap. It snapped shut with a metallic ping and the steel jaws sank deep into his leg. He grunted at the sharp, agonising pain and began to try and prise the trap open. His gun lay where it had fallen in a puddle of disturbed mud and ice beside him.

The momentary distraction was all that the creature needed to spring towards the biggest of the men. Brandon saw it coming and didn't hesitate to send the tomahawk flying. It hit the creature in the shoulder and it yowled in pain, halting its charge. But only momentarily. It wheeled around with a vicious snarl and leapt again for Brandon. The large man was dwarfed by the creature as it brought him down to the ground. Brandon reached up for the tomahawk, still wedged into the fur and flesh of the cat's shoulder. It came free too easily and Brandon knew it hadn't struck bone. It was the last thing he thought as the creature drove its teeth through his skull and its bunched rear legs and extended claws gutted him, using the frozen ground his body was pinned against like a butcher's table.

Logan ceased his struggle and picked up his gun, his hands only trembling a little from the pain caused by the biting clamp of the trap. The cat was no more than thirty feet away and had its back to him, its muzzle deep in Brandon's chest cavity. He took careful aim along the sights of the black barrel of the browning and pressed the trigger, waiting for the following explosion from its tip that would blow out the animal's lungs. Instead, the chilling and cold metallic tapping sound of metal on metal that signified a misfire was all he heard. He glanced down at the puddle and felt the bite of the freezing fog. The sudden emergence in water and the air temperature had been a little too much to ask for the gun. He dropped it without a second thought and reached for the S&W500 revolver tucked into his shoulder holster. He had already loaded it with 700 grain bullets known as T-Rex Thumpers. The animal in front of him was larger than the biggest grizzly he'd ever faced, but he didn't doubt they would still be enough to take the cat down.

The creature looked up as it heard a metallic ping from behind it. It growled as it noticed the man sitting on the ground. It sank its head a little lower and gazed at the man in silence. As his hand moved slowly down to his side, the creature let out another warning growl, stepping over Brandon's body to face Logan as it did so. When his hand moved again, the creature shot forward, covering the ground between them in one easy bound. It swiped at Logan when the man was at the furthest reach of its claws. Logan gasped as he was knocked to the ground and he felt his bowels spill through his torn stomach. He cried out in pain and shock as he gazed at his own innards steaming in the cold air. The gun went off in his hand, the force and pain of the impact ricocheting along his wrist. The formidable bullet's flight was thrown off by the tremble in his arm and the weakening of his grip, but the thunderous noise was enough to drive the cat away from him, if only momentarily. As it rushed back in, Logan used the last of his strength to rip the bowie knife free from its sheath. As the cat towered over him and his world went black, Logan's arm fell back towards the ground and the blade slashed neatly through the toe of the creature's front left paw. It let out an aggravated hiss that turned into a savage growl as a wave of pain shot up its leg from the blow. The creature's face was set in a silent grimace as it edged a little backwards. Only when it was sure the man was definitely dead did it flip the body over with its good paw and take a few careful bites from the legs and buttocks. Then it lifted its head and pricked its ears up, gazing back into the fog towards the loch. It trotted off back down the trail, with only a trace of a limp on its left side as it went.

Ethan staggered up the steps of the impressive dam that sat at the eastern end of the loch. He felt dizzy and sick, and his head was spinning. He didn't know where he was headed, only that it was away from the scenes of horror in the clearing. He could barely breathe and the thickening fog was making him feel disorientated. His mind and body were firmly in the grip of shock as he dragged his feet over the cold, hard concrete along the dam.

The creature paused at the lapping water. It could scent the human, and as it gazed out across the water and up to the bank of stone, it was able to pick out the movement against the shadow and mist. It slipped into the water, enjoying the cooling caress on its wounds. It cut straight across the loch in a diagonal line, where it knew it would meet the bank at a junction, as it turned at an angle towards the northern shore. It had ambushed deer on both sides of the loch before using the same shortcut. It slipped out of the water and propelled itself up the steep, smooth slope with a few powerful strides. It hunkered down directly in the path of the man, listening to the echo of hurried footsteps coming nearer and nearer. It flicked its tail in anticipation.

Ethan came to a sudden halt. The mist was thicker here, almost half way across the loch as he was. He could no longer see the shore on either side. But through the mist he did see something. A stream of moonlight had rippled through the fog just for a moment, revealing what had looked like a pair of softly glowing green eyes ahead of him. Then he heard it. The purr-like growl reverberated off the concrete walls on either side of him and he backed away in terror. The sound seemed to pass straight through him. He felt weak and sick, and wasn't surprised when his legs gave way. He sat on the ground panting, confused and trembling with the cold. He closed his eyes as a wave of warmth washed over him. He could hear water and he suddenly felt safe and comforted, unaware he was curling up on the ground.

As the creature drew closer, its whiskers moved forwards to guide it towards its prey. At such close range its vision was slightly blurred, and it relied on the impulses and signals from its sensitive face to guide it the last few inches. It rolled Ethan over onto his back and stepped onto his chest. Reality flooded back to Ethan, and he cried out in pain as his ribs and sternum cracked under the pressure. He didn't know he was already dying. The surges of pain that rippled through his body were being caused by the crushing weight on his chest, which now had no support. His lungs were collapsing and his heart cavity was beginning to fill with excess blood. The great cat peered at him through glowing green eyes, the soft purr emanating from its throat now the most terrifying sound he had ever heard. Ethan could taste blood in his mouth as he shut his eyes. His final scream was drowned out by a thundering roar that rolled out across the water and along the mountain walls of the glen.

CHAPTER TWENTY-FIVE

Kelly Keelson waited in her van as she watched the local vet leave. She hadn't been late on purpose, but she had been thrilled to discover such a scene of apparent panic and mayhem. She knew by instinct something had happened. There was a story here. This time, she was literally on the doorstep of breaking news. She smiled, reassuring herself that at least some of her instinct was still intact. She opened the door of the van and walked towards the entrance of the research centre. One side swung open before she was even half way across the gravel. Thomas Walker loomed in the doorway, watching her walk over.

"And to think I thought you might miss all the excitement Ms Keelson," Thomas exclaimed. He paused, as if making his mind up whether to let her inside or not. "Come in," he motioned eventually. "The office is first on the right."

She followed his guiding arm as he swung the door open to let her through. As she entered, she could hear Catherine's muffled voice coming from the room opposite, the door of which was firmly closed. She seemed to be agitated and on the phone to somebody. Kelly loitered only for a second as she expertly hid her attempt to overhear the conversation. She took a seat opposite Thomas on the sofas in the corner the office, discreetly switching on the dictation machine in her pocket as she did so.

"Why was the vet here Mr. Walker?" She let her arms fall into her lap, suggesting the question was open and innocent.

"My dog was attacked by the cat," Thomas replied stiffly.

"The wounds were quite severe and we've had to sedate her." For a second his thoughts drifted across the hall to the limp dog lying on the examination table, drips and drugs pumping through her, maybe to no avail as far as he knew at this stage.

Kelly leant forward, unable to hide her intrigue and excitement.

"Mr. Walker, I'm looking to put this story together and air it by tomorrow morning, maybe even tonight. But first, I want to ask you about David Fairbanks accusing you of being scared of this animal. Is that true?"

"I'm terrified by it, and even more so by what it has shown us it can do," Thomas replied sourly. "And you should worry about any person who isn't."

Kelly eyed him coolly. "And what about you having gotten so close, yet having never fired a shot or come into harm's way?"

Thomas took a breath and steadied himself. He thought carefully before answering. "On both of the occasions where I've been able to track the animal, it has been straight after a kill. It was moving slower and more obviously, which helped. At the same time, I've never set eyes on it through a riflescope or otherwise. If I did, not much in this world would stop me pulling the trigger."

Kelly reflected on his answer for a second, but seemed satisfied. She continued her questions as they discussed the blood results, the size of the animal, the recovery of the schoolboy and the decision to bring in the American team. She then turned tack, probing the many reported previous sightings across the UK and the involvement of DEFRA. After over an hour, Thomas felt tired and Kelly brought the interview to a close, but they both felt very satisfied with the ground they had covered.

As Thomas showed Kelly Keelson out, Catherine opened the door to the examination room and walked up behind him. He turned to face her.

"There hasn't been any radio contact with Logan and the team," she explained. She was calm and quiet, trying her best to reassure him. "It's probably the weather, but we're going to give them until first light, then we're sending an Army unit up after them."

Thomas slammed his fist into the wall, the plasterboard easily giving way instantly under the assault. Dust and fibres floated gently to the ground. They stared at each other in silence. Catherine had been slightly startled by the sudden flare of rage he had shown, but now smiled, unable to hide her amusement. Thomas looked sheepish as he withdrew his hand from the hole he had just made in the wall.

"I'm going to take you home and then come back here to keep an eye on Meg. You need to rest. Unless there are any other walls you don't like?" Catherine smirked.

"Sorry," Thomas grumbled, shaking his head.

"I'll pick you up in time for us to both go up with the Army unit, and mountain rescue if needs be. From now on, we're doing everything together, okay?"

Thomas nodded, smiling for a brief moment. Then before he knew it, he was being guided out of the door and towards the car. Catherine switched the lights off and closed the door behind them.

As they drove, Thomas kept looking out of the window. He scanned the thick fog bank and the shadows of the trees and fields beyond as they went. Catherine glanced over to him occasionally, worried by his silence.

"Tom, you're way too weak to do anything stupid like go out and look for them, so don't even think about it," she warned.

He looked back round to her and smiled. She could see he was guilty as charged.

"When all this started, I just wanted to find it and study it, prove it was there," he exclaimed with a sigh. "Now...?" He trailed off with his thoughts, looking back to the window. "I've hunted man-eaters all over the world. I've nearly been killed several times by one species or another. I lost my wife. But I've never actually hated an animal before. I have to kill it."

"That just shows how unwell you are," Catherine replied. "You wouldn't normally talk like that, you need to rest."

She stopped the car in front of Sàsadh, letting the engine run. Thomas undid his seatbelt and reached for the door handle. He stopped and turned towards her.

"I wasn't so unwell to have imagined the kiss was I?"

"No, that was real," she smiled. "I was also ready to do anything to stop you going out again." The playfulness in her voice definitely got his attention. Her eyes flashed mischievously in the green glow of the dashboard lights.

"Anything?" he asked, raising his eyebrows in surprise.

"Well that's for me to know and you to find out isn't it?" she smirked. "But tonight you really do need to rest. It's only a few hours until dawn. Try to sleep."

She leaned over and kissed him gently on the lips, then her head slid past his and she wrapped her arms around him. The embrace seemed to last forever, and Thomas felt he was in a warm and comfortable dream that was somehow coming true. The same warmth guided him as he took the few steps towards the farmhouse. It was an incredible sensation, as if he'd been cured of an illness he never knew he had. He turned, waving as the car headed back down the track. He closed the front door behind him and began climbing the stairs, still smiling as he went.

~

He woke a few hours later, rather dizzily at first. He was surprised to find Catherine beside him, her back snuggled firmly against his chest. It was still dark outside and he definitely didn't want to move. Catherine's warmth and closeness was very comforting.

"Did I drool?" Catherine murmured, stirring beside him. She stretched her left arm up and her fingers found his hair, pulling at a few stray sprigs gently.

"No, but I think I might start if you stay there too long," he smiled.

"I put the coffee on when I came in, but I was so tired I couldn't resist curling up for a minute or two," she mused. "I thought you might like to see the papers though."

She sat up, and handed him a copy of The Guardian newspaper from her bag on the floor. A picture of David Fairbanks was on the front page, showing him hastily getting into a car. It was the kind of photo that the press always used to suggest subversion and that trouble was a foot. It certainly wasn't a publicity shot. The headline read 'Fairbanks not so fair after all: How the cat became catastrophe for DEFRA'.

It appeared Keelson had done her homework and

worked as fast as she had promised. Along with the rumours that Thomas had helped confirm, she had also managed to find two senior police chiefs from different constabularies willing to come forward. They confirmed independent reports of road accidents in Gloucestershire and Dorset involving big cats in recent years. Their stories were too similar to dismiss, both mentioning DEFRA trackers and disposal teams specifically employed to deal with these things. It appeared that not only did DEFRA know about the animals, but that they had also been widespread and present for a number of years. Suddenly things weren't looking very good for Fairbanks.

"I see you left out the bit about it being some kind of giant prehistoric relic," Catherine smirked.

"Well my boss didn't completely back me on that one," Thomas replied dryly.

"Smart woman," she retorted back, but with a smile. "But you come out of it very well I think. Your story has never wavered. You've clearly been made the scapegoat, and I already know the Major-General and Chief Inspector won't hesitate to back your version of events now the balance of power has shifted."

Catherine hurried Thomas, peeling back the duvet. The draft of cold air was all the motivation he needed, and he quickly washed and dressed. The seriousness of what lay ahead began to eat away at the pleasant thoughts and feelings they both had started the day with. He could smell the fresh coffee bubbling in the pot as he made his way downstairs. She handed him a Thermos mug and they walked out together in silence.

They both climbed into the Overfinch. He felt well

enough to drive and he suspected they would need its superior off-road capability at some point, especially if they were to be involved in the search. It also didn't pass him by that it meant Catherine might consider coming back to the house later, if they didn't go back to the centre as planned.

The allegations against DEFRA and especially against Fairbanks were being discussed on the radio as they cruised through the lanes. The sun was still low in the sky, bathing the glen in a gentle ghostly light. Mist still clung to the valley and hillsides, not yet ready to be banished and burnt away by the golden glow above. Kelly Keelson's report had been broadcast on the late news and again in the morning, as well as making most of the papers as Thomas had already seen. Catherine's mobile beeped in her pocket. She took it out to read the text message and couldn't help smiling.

"Looks like Fairbanks flew down to London last night. He won't be around this morning, or much longer after I'm guessing. I'll have to remember to stay on your good side," she quipped, smiling teasingly at him.

"That shouldn't be too hard," he replied warmly. "At least it means we won't have to worry about him whilst we get on with the search," his voice more solemn.

After nearly half an hour's drive, they found the track they were looking for. It was overgrown, potholed and heavily banked on both sides. He slipped the four-wheel drive system into a low range, and then flipped a switch near the gear lever to fix the suspension at its highest setting. *We're going to need it* he thought.

He gently made his way up the track, sometimes precariously balanced on the banks, at other times revving the engine hard to power through the water and mud. As he entered a standing pool of water, the bonnet of the Overfinch dove violently for a moment as they hit a hidden dip. The water crept up past the wheels, and he was suddenly thankful for the snorkel exhaust that prevented the engine from flooding and allowed him to power through without hindrance. Then, as they came round a bend in the track, they saw the black American pick-up truck ahead of them.

"I didn't think they'd be able to make it much further after that," Thomas exclaimed.

He parked next to the big Ford and they both got out of the car.

The forest smelled fresh and ozone-like. The green pine boughs seemed to glisten in the early morning light, the effect magnified by the clinging sheen of dew that laced them. Thomas tested the ground with his boot and found it soft and giving. If the same conditions had been in place the night before, he knew the tracking would be much easier. He guessed though it would have been a little firmer, and there had almost certainly been a frost. That meant that the tracks might have been caught in the freeze, or had turned to slush in the dew and thaw. But they wouldn't have disappeared altogether. He would just have to make sure he didn't miss them. He opened up the tailgate of the car and took out the rifle from the lock box. He had cleaned it meticulously and checked the firing mechanism. He wasn't going to take any chances today. He snapped the bolt back and fed in the H&H .465 Magnum round and slipped a 5-cartridge magazine into his pocket just in case.

Thomas picked up the trail of Logan and the others within a few feet. The quick succession of heavy boots surrounded by the numerous paw prints of the dogs weren't difficult to find. In some places, the imprints were so well formed in the mud and ice he could pick out the individual treads and boot size of each wearer. Thomas led the way to the clearing in silence, only stopping to dismantle the barriers the team had put in place to try and channel the cat where they wanted it to go. Thomas already had a feeling things hadn't gone to plan.

"Watch your step," Thomas indicated, exposing a wire snare with a gentle swipe of his boot. "This one's not too well hidden but the others will be."

Catherine nodded.

As Thomas stepped into the clearing, he froze. His eyes met those of the large black bird that was tearing at something it was sitting on. The raven turned its head to the side, exposing the shred of pink, half-frozen flesh it held in its beak. Thomas's gaze lowered and he let out a gasp as he recognised the ragged shirt and shooting vest at the raven's feet. It was perched on Logan's chest. He took a few careful steps towards him, scaring the large bird off with a furious shout. Logan was lying on his side with his back to Thomas. As he got nearer, Thomas saw the spring trap and Logan's crushed and tattered skull. No eyes remained for him to shut or worse, to stare back at him in death. The ground around Logan had been stained a deep red with his blood, and his hands lay frozen across the slash to his abdomen. The sight of Logan's eviscerated body caused a glob of vomit to rise into Thomas's throat, and he knew his hand was trembling almost uncontrollably. He took his finger off the trigger of the rifle, realising he had brought it up to his shoulder instinctively. He slowly lowered it again. Everything here was already dead.

"Oh God," Catherine exclaimed.

Thomas turned back, noticing her gaze was centred on the left of the clearing. He followed her stare with a cold dread until he saw Brandon's body. It was bloody and battered, but less so than Logan's. Thomas spat to get rid of the taste of acid in his mouth.

"Where are the others?" Catherine murmured.

Thomas heard the strain in her voice but didn't answer. His gaze was fixed on a thawing paw print in the mud. He spread his fingers out to check its size, although he had little need to. It was the cat, and it had walked away from the clearing. He walked a few feet, finding a mushy imprint this time. This one though was laced with a few drops of blood. His gaze lingered as he studied it closer. By the time he looked up, Catherine was at his side.

"I don't think he got away clean this time," Thomas explained, pointing at the muddy mush. He walked on, his eyes searching the trail from side to side as he went. The cat had been brazen, perhaps out of necessity. Its trail was obvious, almost casual, and it was definitely favouring its right side where the prints were heavy and deeper than usual. It was clear it was headed towards the loch. He froze when he realised why. The relatively small but clear boot prints also led in that direction, and the cat's own trail fell in behind them.

"When will the Army and mountain rescue ambulance get here?" Thomas demanded, his wits returning.

"They should be on their way already. I'll let them know what to expect," Catherine answered, a little shocked by his sharp tone.

"Sorry," he murmured, touching her arm, and softening immediately when he saw the hurt in her eyes. "I think Ethan ran off this way and the cat followed. I just can't believe it got Logan." Thomas shook his head in disbelief, but she could see the anger bubbling and building within. He took a few more steps down the trail then looked back at her. His stare was cold and distant now. It sent a shiver down her spine.

"You'd better warn them about the traps and what to expect. You wait here whilst I look ahead."

"No way," Catherine yelped. "I'm going with you and your gun, even with that murderous look on your face."

Thomas softened again and smiled. "Okay. I'll wait whilst you make the call. But hurry."

It didn't take them long to walk the trail down to the shore of the loch. Thomas paused, confused by the tracks left in the silt. He walked back and forth in silence with a puzzled look on his face. He paused and looked back along the beach.

"What is it?" Catherine asked.

"Two lots of tracks," Thomas sighed. "It came from the west then approached the clearing along the trail. It used the same path to follow Ethan back, but went off towards the dam," he explained, pointing towards the east end of the loch.

"How do you know it's Ethan?"

"Small boot, light step. He was also running here and there. The others are heavier and I don't think they'd run from anything."

"Why do you think Ethan did," she asked, confused.

"It's hard to say, but if he wasn't just plain scared, it

could be something called infrasound. It's a pressurised sound wave emitted by some animals like tigers and elephants. People in close proximity have sometimes complained about feeling disorientated or sick. Others have felt hot, stripping their clothes even in the coldest of conditions. It can be euphoric, or it can paralyse. It can also be used to communicate, but it's thought predators might use it to subdue their prey."

"So, which way do we go first? Her eyes were drawn to the west, along the curving shore.

"Let's see if we can find anything along the beach first," Thomas offered kindly. He could see she was having a hard time keeping calm.

They walked along the beach in silence. There were numerous prints in the mud and silt, and following each took time. Catherine's eyes darted to the tree line nervously every time they approached it. Thomas's gaze followed the trail down the loch shore, coming to rest on the lifeless body of Lobo. As he started towards the dead dog, Catherine's hand reached out for his shoulder and pointed him back towards the trees. He spotted the small movement at the base of a large pine and instantly raised the rifle to his shoulder. He held his breath and moved his finger towards the trigger. His eye rested a little way from the scope, all senses directed at the movement in the brush. As he slowly exhaled, he lowered the rifle, a slight shake evident in his arms. Then he was running towards the tree before Catherine could call out. He dropped to his knees beside the trembling Arturo. The big dog licked his hand timidly, letting out a soft whine as it did. As Catherine walked closer, Thomas jumped up and went to meet her before she got to him.

"I don't want to upset you," he explained, slightly breathless. "Arturo is guarding the tree for a reason."

"What do you..." her voice trailed off as her gaze drifted up towards the branches. Thomas cringed as the scream echoed across the loch. They both looked up at Ryan's torn and bloody body that hung lifeless from a forked branch twenty feet above.

~

The Army and mountain rescue team co-ordinated a full search of the clearing and surrounding area. The three bodies they found were taken away, and Thomas helped clear some of the traps and equipment. Ethan's body remained missing, but they had found the point on the dam where he had been ambushed and attacked. Thomas had split from Catherine to set up a trail camera at the pine where they'd found Ryan. It was part of the equipment the squad had brought with them, and he hoped the cat would return to its food stash, as it no doubt intended. Catherine had used the Army and mountain rescue medical kits to dress Arturo's wounds. They had been deep and dirty, but the mastiff seemed as resilient as the tales of his breed depicted. Thomas and Catherine sat in silence as they drove back to the research centre.

Thomas carried Arturo through to the examination room where Catherine began to run a bath to help clean the dog off.

"I'm so sorry," Catherine murmured finally.

Thomas smiled weakly, his eyes glistening. He couldn't

quite bring himself to say anything.

"There was nothing you could have done, if you'd gone out..."

"Then I'd probably be dead too, especially in the condition I was in last night. I know. It doesn't help," Thomas replied softly. He went back to washing the dog. "So what are we going to do with you Mr?" He ruffled the dog's head and smiled. But his voice was shaky and broken.

"I've always had a soft spot for mastiffs," Catherine cooed, smiling affectionately. "Why don't you get him some food," she suggested.

Thomas nodded and went to the kitchen. He poured some of the organic lamb and rice dog food he kept for Meg into a large metal bowl. Then he remembered Arturo's size and poured in a little more. As he walked back into the examination room, Catherine met him with a smile.

"I think you need another bowl. Someone wants to see you," she quipped.

Meg raised her head out of the comfortable basket Catherine had placed her in. She thumped her tail slowly and gently against it as he approached, trying to rise up to meet him as he knelt down to fuss her. They finished checking over and feeding the dogs then took them though to the office. Thomas lit a fire and let them get comfortable in front of it. He smiled as they lay down together and occasionally raised their heads to lick each other's dressed and healing wounds.

Thomas sat back down at his desk. He took out an ordnance survey map of the area from a drawer and grabbed a marker pen. He crossed off where they had found the stag's body. He marked the farm that had lost the sheep, as well as the other missing livestock and pets he could remember from the first briefing. He picked up a red marker and then began to plot the human attacks. He marked the part of the forest where they had found Archie Campbell, and then the school. The small gully where the soldiers had been attacked was next, then Palaeo Park, the campsite and quarry. Finally he crossed off the clearing and the Mullardoch dam itself. Just like before, a pattern began to emerge from the map. He stared at what the black and red crosses seemed to encircle.

"What's bothering you?" Catherine enquired, curious. "You're not normally this quiet."

Thomas smiled. "I think I've found something," he exclaimed. "Everything comes back to one point, the mountain. I think our cat lives on Càrn Eige, not in the forest."

"What makes you think that?" She asked, peering over his shoulder. She butted his shoulder gently with hers to nudge past him and slid onto his lap, a little awkwardly. His hands naturally swept round her slim, tight waist, holding her close as she studied the map.

"It's the one place you can get to each attack site from. It's also where he always seems headed afterwards. When I tracked him from the park and the quarry, it's the direction he was going. I bet if I track him back from the clearing, it will lead me there too," he whispered into her right ear, resisting the temptation to kiss her neck.

The sound of the doorbell sounded out along the hall.

"I think I'm going to disconnect that bloody thing," Thomas laughed as she got up to get the door.

He walked through to the hall behind her. They both

stood in silent shock for a few moments. David Fairbanks was the last person they were expecting to see on the doorstep.

CHAPTER TWENTY-SIX

The creature carried the man's body through the gorse and heather as it climbed the mountainside. It had already fed a little from the large man it had stashed in a favourite tree, casually selecting the tastiest parts for immediate consumption in the cool comfort of the darkness. The ascent through the forest was making it more aware of its injuries. Its front paw throbbed and was still painful. The gash to its shoulder was deep and had torn through muscle, making its stride stiff and exaggerated. The dog on the beach had also ripped at the tendons in its rear right ankle. Worse still had been the grazing touch of Logan's bullet. It had nicked a bloody piece of flesh from the top of the creature's pelvis, and left a small impact fracture in its wake. It dropped the corpse it was carrying in order to rest, panting hard as it fought the muscular spasms shooting up its hind leg.

The creature licked its wounds carefully and meticulously. Its saliva was laced with natural antitoxins, anaesthetics and antibiotic agents that would ease the pain momentarily, only for it to return each time it moved off. The cool chill of the morning air soothed it a little, and its tail swished and twitched in the cold. It shuddered involuntarily as it rose to its feet again, a frustrated yowl accompanying the ripple of pain along its hind leg.

It could see the familiar path that led to the cave, its entrance hidden by two small rowan saplings and a dense patch of brown and gold dead bracken. The creature took the body in its jaws again and padded slowly up hill. Its silhouette disappeared into the shadows of the dense brush.

It paused only momentarily to liberally mark the cave's entrance. Everything that lived on the mountain usually kept a wide berth, but it had been a few days since it had last passed this part of its territory, and the scent had faded. Ever since it had fled its father's rich hunting grounds it had never come across an adversary to defend its own against, but it still diligently marked and patrolled the glen, and its favoured spots such as the cave.

It padded down the small slope, letting the body fall to the floor. It walked stiffly over to a pool of water that collected at the bottom of one of the stony walls of the cave. It licked at the stream of salty liquid that seeped from the rock, savouring the taste before it lowered its head to drink from the purer water below. The coolness was refreshing. It lay down in the shallow but wide pool, lying on its injured right side so that its hot muscles and wounds were covered by the foot or so of water. It let out a satisfied growl as it rolled a little onto its back, the temperature numbing the pain. It was not so tired to miss the movement just within its peripheral vision. It instinctively rolled and brought its paw down to pin the mountain hare as it tried to bolt for the mouth of the cave. It had chosen the wrong place to shelter from the overnight storm. The creature lifted its paw, and let the terrified animal dash forward, only to trap it again with ease with the other. The hare let out one fitful scream before the creature took it between its jaws. It rolled onto its back again and tugged the flesh from the bones, finishing it in a few mouthfuls. Reminded now of its hunger it stood up and stepped out of the pool, making its way over to where it had dropped Ethan's body.

~

Thomas sat back down on one of the sofas. Fairbanks sat opposite and Catherine squeezed in next to Thomas as she joined them. *He looks a mess* Thomas thought. Fairbanks' thin hair looked scraggly and out of place, and his tie was loose around his neck. Thomas got the impression he hadn't slept or had slept in his clothes, and not for very long if so. Fairbanks' eyes moved slowly from Thomas to Catherine. He didn't hide his tiredness.

"So, to what do we owe the pleasure?" Thomas asked stiffly, a tone of quiet distrust and menace all too audible.

Catherine's hurried glance warned him to back off, but he was in no mood to play games, no matter how curious she might be to the purpose of the visit.

"I've come to sort this out," Fairbanks offered, with none of his usual pomp. "I've spoken with the PM. Unfortunately our knowledge of certain animals at large in the UK can no longer be denied, but I think even you would agree this is no ordinary big cat."

"Yes, that would seem somewhat obvious now," Thomas sighed with a lack of patience. "If only somebody had been telling you that from the start," he added dryly.

"Naturally the public need their scapegoat. It's almost ironic that amidst all these killings there is still a cry for more blood," Fairbanks sighed, poignantly.

"It's not your blood they want David, just your resignation," Thomas quipped with a satisfied smile.

"And they'll get it dear boy," replied Fairbanks. "I don't suppose I could trouble you for a drink could I? It seems to have been a very long night."

Thomas couldn't help but soften a little. Although he had been happy to clear his own name, Fairbanks probably didn't deserve all of the blame either.

"I've been promising Cath a glass of Scotch for the last three days now," Thomas offered.

"That sounds just the ticket," Fairbanks replied, a glimmer of the shiny official self showing through for a moment.

Thomas went through to the kitchen and uncorked the bottle of Lagavulin single malt whisky. He wasn't feeling generous enough to have offered Fairbanks anything older than a stock dram, but even a mere sixteen years in the oak barrels left a more than satisfactory impression. He poured three short measures into some glasses. At least being in Scotland he didn't have to ask if anyone wanted ice. This wasn't a London bar, and ice took away the warmth and flavour of the spirit. If you took away those things, he and most Scots didn't see the point of drinking it. He walked back through and handed out the drinks.

"As I was saying", Fairbanks continued "the public will get my resignation, but not straight away. I've been given a further twenty-four hours to try and sort this out." He paused, savouring the taste of the whisky for a moment. "I think if we work together, all of us can come out of this much better than we expected."

"By us, you mean you," Thomas replied bluntly.

"That's a little short-sighted Mr. Walker," snapped Fairbanks, not letting the retort break his stride. "I'm sure Ms. Tyler will appreciate the publicity of a successful outcome, and let us not forget that even with me out of the picture this centre will be able to benefit, or not, from

DEFRA contracts in the future."

Thomas bristled, but Fairbanks jumped to his own defence pre-emptively.

"I'm not threatening you, I'm trying to bribe you if anything," he yelped. "Just think if you were our prime source for wildlife research projects."

"Well at least your data would be right for once," Catherine quipped. "But we're thinking of reducing our government work as it is."

"Universities and the private sector pay more," Thomas shrugged. He enjoyed how naturally he and Catherine had deflected the threat as an idle one at best.

"Look, when this animal is found and taken care of, people will still want to know what's being done about the other sightings around the country," scoffed Fairbanks. "There isn't anybody else better qualified to lead that kind of investigation. Wouldn't you want to be involved?"

Damn right thought Thomas. "Let's hope your successor thinks the same way," he replied adamantly.

Meg suddenly raised her head and whined. She strained her head towards the door and Catherine smiled as Arturo barked an encouragement.

"I think she needs to go outside," she exclaimed.

Thomas realised she was right. Meg was probably nervous about going outdoors again, and he realised there was a chance she could still pick up traces of the cat's lingering scent.

"Come on," he said, relieved to have a reason to leave the room. "If you'll excuse me for a moment or two," he nodded to Catherine.

As he walked out, Meg and Arturo trotted behind him.

Thomas couldn't help smiling at the thought of Meg having a new bodyguard in Arturo. A moment later, Catherine and Fairbanks heard the back door swing open. Fairbanks stood up and beamed awkwardly at Catherine. He slowed himself. Even though his mind had begun to race as soon as Thomas left the room, he was too well practised at concealing his thoughts. He shot a glance at Thomas's desk and was immediately intrigued by the map. He casually walked over for a closer look.

"Tom was mapping all the known attacks, trying to establish the territory of the cat," Catherine explained, seeing no reason to hide anything from Fairbanks. "We've only found small pieces of evidence so far. The hunting area gives us the best clue yet."

"Very clever," admitted Fairbanks. His eyes darted over the map from top to bottom. He had to suppress the grin he felt forming. This had been exactly what he had been looking for. Twenty four hours to sort things out, or to turn the tables once more. The latter was his preference. He drew his finger across the map, north of Glen Cannich and Mullardoch altogether. The plan he was forming was simple, but would serve his purposes.

"Walker thinks the cat is on the mountain does he?" Fairbanks enquired.

"Yes," replied Catherine hesitantly. She was suddenly weary. Fairbanks whole demeanour had changed in the last few seconds and she hadn't failed to notice it.

Thomas walked back into the room, accompanied by the two dogs. He slipped them a couple of treats each and fussed them as they made themselves comfortable. He glanced accusingly at Fairbanks, who was still standing over the map at his desk.

"I'm trying to narrow down where on the mountain it might be," explained Thomas. "Unfortunately, it could be one of a hundred places. A male patrolling a territory will typically use several shelters, travelling through his area over the course of a number of days. They'll also make use of new ones they find. They do this to make sure they don't exhaust prey or resources in any one area. The main problem we have is the simple size of his territory. There are numerous water sources, including the loch, and prey is readily available. He has at least three deer herds of three different species to choose from, as well as an abundance of game and livestock. I think it's also safe to say he well and truly counts us as prey now, so he's probably expanded his territory to include the village. That gives us an area of about 40 square miles to consider."

"I see," murmured Fairbanks deep in thought, still looking at the map. "Unfortunately, I have to add to that. One of the reasons I'm here is because there has been a reported livestock attack near Loch...erm." His eyes shot down to the map to check the name again, "Monar. Unfortunately, I'll...need Ms. Tyler back at the town hall," he added, flashing his most charming smile. "But I thought if we split up...err, we might cover the ground better anyway, wouldn't you say? We might even be able to offer the press something a little more conclusive by working different ends of the case."

"What are the details of the livestock killing," Thomas asked, a little surprised.

"There is a police station at Monar," Fairbanks blurted, almost triumphantly. He remembered seeing it on a report when he had drafted in extra men. "There will be an Inspector waiting to escort you. He's...um...expecting me, but I'm sure he'll recognise you dear boy."

"I know the station," Thomas nodded. "I can't believe it's related though, it's nearly thirty miles away." He knew it wasn't impossible though. He had once tracked a leopard over thirty miles in one night through India's Golis mountain range. *And anything a normal cat can do, this one can do better* he reminded himself.

"Still, best to check," Fairbanks scolded mockingly. "No time like the present eh?"

Thomas looked at Catherine and shrugged. She smiled reassuringly and nodded.

"Okay Fairbanks," he agreed with a nod of his own.

Thomas took the dogs into the kitchen and put down a large litter tray just in case, as well as slipping them a few more treats each. As he walked back through, Catherine handed him his coat. He smiled and touched her elbow gently. He wasn't looking forward to driving thirty miles through Highland lanes without her, and he knew they would probably be back before him.

"Don't be too long," she whispered, "there's something I want to go over with you," she smiled mischievously, glancing sultrily at the rug beside the fire for just a moment.

He smiled, half considering throwing Fairbanks out there and then. With a sigh and a quick pinch to her ribs, he closed the door behind them. He climbed into the Overfinch and waved through the windscreen as he headed off down the drive.

"Let's take your car shall we Ms. Tyler," Fairbanks suggested. "I imagine it will be a little more practical than mine."

Catherine climbed into the Barbarian and opened the passenger door for Fairbanks. He slipped into the seat and fussed for a moment in order to accommodate his long coat. He slipped his hand into its pocket as he made himself comfortable. He watched carefully as the Overfinch disappeared out of sight.

"Now Ms. Tyler, you know the area much better than I do. Take me to the best road for us to get onto the mountain," he commanded.

Catherine stared at him, confused. "But you said we were going to the town hall. You had new information?"

"I did. It was that map our dear Mr. Walker went to the trouble of making," he replied coldly and casually.

Catherine stared at him, her gut twisting as the truth slowly dawned on her. "There was no livestock killing was there?" She couldn't help feeling nervous.

"None that I know of," laughed Fairbanks. "I imagine Americans probably provide more calories than us Englishmen, I doubt it needed to feed again quite so soon," he scoffed.

As Catherine went to undo her seatbelt, her face glowing with rage, Fairbanks drew the pistol he had been readying with anticipation in his pocket. He held the Glock 17 at waist height, angled upwards towards Catherine's head. It hadn't been too hard for him to distract his bodyguard and procure the backup weapon. He hoped the girl he had provided would keep the special branch officer busy for at least the next few hours. It had been hard to find a suitable escort so quickly in the Highlands, but she had certainly been attractive enough.

"I can do this with or without your help Ms. Tyler," he threatened. "Without is a mere inconvenience, but don't make the mistake of thinking you're an essential part of the plan."

Catherine recoiled at the sight of the gun, but stopped herself from making for the door handle as had been her first instinct.

"Now, if you don't mind, we need to get going," Fairbanks continued, "and I don't expect to be heading anywhere near the village or stopping for any friendly little chats with anyone either. Just to the mountain, do you understand?"

Catherine nodded, frightened by the sincere menace behind his words. She could see in his eyes he meant to kill her. She moved her trembling hands to the ignition and started the car. Fairbanks kept the gun pointed at her as they drove. He wasn't going to let her know that she was indeed an essential part of the plan. In order to fully win back the trust and respect of the public, he intended to discover the creature's den alone. And Thomas Walker needed to be taken down in the process. The newly redeemed great white hunter would be implicated again in a careless death of a woman he was close to and worked with. People would want to know why she was alone and where Thomas had been. Fairbanks knew all he had to do was deny anything about sending Thomas to Monar, backed-up by the sworn statement of his security detail, and that would be that. The press would quickly turn on Walker again. He also hoped the cat would kill Catherine outright, but he was prepared to help out with a bullet if necessary. Either way, Fairbanks knew he was coming back from the mountain alone.

They drove in silence, Catherine occasionally glancing nervously down at the gun and over to Fairbanks. He watched out of the window, carefully scrutinising the roads she chose. As far as he could tell she was following his instructions. They appeared to be getting closer to the mountain, and although still in sight, the village was gradually getting lower and more distant in the valley as they gained height. Eventually Catherine began to slow and turned onto a gravel track, taking them off road completely.

"The truck might not get to the top of the track. We'll have to walk a little way. I hope you didn't bring the appropriate footwear," she stated icily.

"Oh, and there I was hoping we could still be friends," Fairbanks mocked. "Just take us up as far as you can."

The truck bucked and slid its way up the track. Catherine pressed the accelerator hard, pushing the engine in the hope that someone would hear their noisy ascent. Fairbanks didn't seem to care and sternly beckoned her on. The further they made it from the main road the better. He didn't want the car to be found prematurely. As she came off the top of the track and onto an expansive slope, Catherine gunned the truck into a rut of mud and thawing snow. For a moment it jolted upwards and it seemed the momentum would carry them through. But then they slipped back, the wheels bogged down and spinning deeper and deeper into the sticky quagmire beneath.

"It seems we must walk from here Ms. Tyler," declared Fairbanks with a grin, "or more to the point, you do. Get out."

He waved the gun at her. She wasn't sure if the tears forming were from rage or fear, but either way she wasn't going to give him the satisfaction. She swung the door open and stepped out. The mud squelched around and over the top of her boots as she walked forwards. She looked behind and found Fairbanks training the gun on her as she went.

"Round to the front of the car please Ms. Tyler, where I can keep an eye on you," he barked, sliding the window down. Then he slowly leaned over and began to sound the horn of the car. "Here kitty-kitty, dinner's ready," he smiled.

~

The creature woke with a start. It growled, unsure of its sudden wakefulness, its senses on full alert. It was in less pain now and it could move a little more freely, although still with an uncomfortable stiffness. It jumped to its feet as the alien sound that had woken it resonated again through the cave. It padded forward, jumping to the small ledge that led to the entrance. It let out a small yowl of pain as it landed, but carried its momentum forward as it brushed past the saplings and out into the open air. It pricked its ears as the sound came again, instantly turning its head in the direction from which it came. It wasn't far away. It hunched and slunk through a boulder field as it descended the steepest part of the slope, approaching the cover of a ridgeline where the noise seemed to be coming from.

~

Catherine stood trembling as Fairbanks continued to sound the horn. She ignored the first shrill ring of her mobile phone, but grabbed it from her coat in panic when she realised what it was. Thomas was calling, but strangely it was the number for Sàsadh that showed in the caller ID. Fairbanks didn't hesitate in letting a shot off, the bullet ricocheting off a boulder to her left. She let out an involuntary scream as she stumbled and ducked behind a dense patch of gorse and alder buckthorn bushes. She crawled on her hands and knees into their intertwined darkness until she found a boulder at their centre. Through the dark and compact branches where she lay, she could just make out where she had dropped the phone in front of the car. It continued to ring.

Fairbanks swore under his breath, striking the wheel in frustration. He hadn't meant to miss. He tore off his seatbelt and opened the passenger door. He took a few hurried steps over to the ringing phone and brought his foot down hard, breaking it and burying it in the mud with a heavy strike of his heel. Satisfied, he then pointed the gun towards the thick bushes in front of him. He cradled the pistol with both hands, his eyes darting over the dense cluster of shrubs for any sign of the slightest movement. He knew he didn't have much time and would have to flush her out of hiding. He stepped forward.

Catherine watched as Fairbanks drew closer. As Thomas had taught her when they watched wildlife together, she became absolutely still and sucked in a silent breath and held it. Fairbanks cut to his left, beginning to look where she had originally dived towards cover. Her eyes flickered back towards the car. He'd left the door open. Very carefully she moved an inch at a time on her belly and edged round the boulder. Fairbanks wasn't in sight, but she could hear him thrashing the bushes and branches behind her. She looked towards the car again. It was nearer now, nearer to her than Fairbanks was in fact.

Fairbanks fired a shot off into the bushes in front of him. Catherine threw her hand up to cover her mouth to stop the scream escaping. He fired again, letting off a volley of vented frustration. The boulders around the base of the bushes acted as her shields, but the explosive rapport of the pistol and the noise of the bullets pinging against stone as they sliced through the brush towards her was all the motivation she needed. It was now or never. She burst from cover, running harder than she had ever run in her life. Her heart pounded in her chest, but her gasps of breath and the impact of her feet seemed slow and heavy, as if gravity had suddenly increased. She heard no sound except the heavy thud in her chest and her scraggly, sharp intakes of breath. As she jumped through the open door and swung up into the seat, a crescendo of noise returned to her world as she caught her breath. She slammed the door shut and locked it with her elbow. She panted, taking comfort in the automatic click she heard as the other doors locked in unison. Spent and exhausted, her eyes drifted upwards and she peered through the windscreen. Then she screamed.

~

The creature grimaced a silent snarl at the sound of the gunfire. It paused motionless just below the ridge. It was watching the man. As he turned his back, the creature dropped low to the ground and advanced several steps. This was the opportunity it had been waiting for. It made a short and silent leap forward before sinking again to the ground.

Its hunched shoulder muscles rippled as they began to pump and power the creature forward with incredible speed. All its senses honed in on its prey.

~

Fairbanks was pointing the gun straight at Catherine, his face twisted in fury. She ducked below the dashboard and covered her face with her hands as a hail of bullets smashed their way through the windscreen. They punctured and penetrated the seats and cabin around her, but then there was silence. She snapped out of her terror and raised her head slightly above the dashboard. She froze as her eyes met those of Fairbanks. He was much closer now and he smiled evilly as he pointed the gun straight at her head.

As Fairbanks went to pull the trigger one last time, he paused, confused as he watched Catherine's face twist in terror, her eyes drawn not to him but directly behind. For a split second he was aware of a blur of movement, then he was flung forward over the bonnet of the truck, his head and arms flailing against the windscreen. His mouth contorted into a final smile as his eyes met hers, comforted by knowing she was next. The thought was severed by an ivory coloured tooth smashing its way through his skull.

Catherine watched in horror as the creature dragged Fairbanks off the truck back onto the ground. Where its paws had rested momentarily on the bonnet were two large welts. She knew her options were bleak, but she also knew she wouldn't live long if she stayed in the car. She couldn't stop the tears flowing as she flung open the door and ran. She sped up the slope, conscious of the cat still feeding

345

behind her. She sprinted towards the ridge and didn't dare look behind as she weaved through boulders and brush on either side. She saw what seemed to be an opening between the rocks ahead of her and she scrambled over them, until she slipped between two saplings and into darkness. As she fumbled forwards, her eyes began to grow accustomed to the poor light. She heard the crunch of something brittle beneath her feet as she made her way forward. The realisation came at the same time as she heard the heavy thunder of padded feet as they approached the entrance to the cave. She was in the lair.

CHAPTER TWENTY-SEVEN

Thomas began to make his way up the glen towards the next valley. As he drove, he began to go over the best route to take to Monar. He still had doubts about the livestock killing being the work of the cat. *Why would it leave an established and productive territory to wander thirty miles away?* he thought. He couldn't think of one reason that made sense. There were more than enough sources of prey on the mountain and it had already killed during the night. It wasn't in search of food and it had already fulfilled its other primal urge, the only other reason it might leave its territory for. As soon as the attacks had begun, Thomas had correlated the data and eye witness reports to look for similarities and anomalies. He knew of every alleged sighting going back years, and as far as he was aware, Monar was a significantly cat-free zone. He saw no reason why it still wouldn't be, and it began to irritate him.

As he rounded a bend, he realised he was on a familiar road. A few hundred yards further along would be the track that led to Sàsadh. As he thought again about the long trip to Monar and the inconsistencies of the reported attack, he made his decision quickly and pulled onto the track. *No harm in checking*, he thought as he headed towards the house. The mountains surrounding the valley often made it difficult to have a long conversation on a mobile phone, but he would be able to call the Monar police station from the house easily enough.

He slipped into the house and crossed the hallway to the side table, on which sat a Panasonic digital smart-phone style unit and answering machine. He used its search facility to quickly find the number at Monar and hit dial. It connected and began to ring. Monar was small and probably unmanned so he let it continue to ring, occasionally glancing back out the door to the car. Just as he was about to hang up, it was answered by a man with a deep Scottish accent.

"Monar Police, how can I help?"

"Hello," Thomas said with some relief. "Look, this may seem a little odd but my name is Thomas Walker. I'm part of the investigation dealing with the recent animal attacks in Glen Cannich and I..."

"I can't give you anymore men I'm afraid, we're down to a skeleton crew here as it is," interrupted the gruff voice in an unappreciative tone.

Thomas was taken back for a second, but then continued. "No, sorry, we don't need any more men. I was told that you had a recent livestock killing that may have been the work of our cat. I was also told there was an inspector waiting for me?"

"My name is Inspector Graham and I'm the only one assigned to Monar laddie. I do 'née know what y' talking about."

"Are you quite sure?" Thomas asked, exasperated. "I was told quite specifically there had been an incident at Monar."

"I've been on duty all night and there's nothing out of the ordinary here. It sounds like someone's pulling yer leg lad. I know nothing about it."

"Thank you for your help anyway," Thomas replied, unable to hide his confusion and frustration completely.

He ended the call and brought up the number for the village hall. He was quickly put through to Major-General

Fitzwilliam.

"Hello Walker, what can I do for you?"

"I was just wondering if you'd seen Fairbanks or Catherine," Thomas explained. "They were meant to be heading down there."

"To be honest, I didn't even know Fairbanks was back from London," replied the Major-General.

"That's odd. He was up at the centre a little while ago and said that he needed Catherine to look at some new evidence."

"Unlikely," sighed the Major-General. "Officially, Fairbanks should now be running everything through me now his authority has been revoked."

"This just doesn't sound right," exclaimed Thomas shaking his head. "Can you let me know if anyone sees them?"

"Of course," replied the Major-General, a little startled. "Is everything alright?"

"No," Thomas sighed, "I don't think it is." He put the phone down, deep in thought.

He began to feel slightly panicked. If Fairbanks had intended to go to the town hall as he had said, they would have arrived ages ago. He picked up the phone and dialled Catherine's number. As he held it to his ear he thought he heard the crackle of an answer for a few seconds and the sound of wind, but then it broke off suddenly into electrical silence. He dialled the number again, but this time there was no connection, just a dead line. He told himself that she was in the valley, where reception was at its poorest. But then he realised there was no way Catherine would have failed to call him once she had realised they weren't going to the village hall as planned. He could now only think of one thing. Fairbanks had must have somehow forced her to go with him.

It was then that he remembered Fairbanks' interest in the map. The pieces of the puzzle were beginning to fall in place now. This was no official mission. Fairbanks was trying to save his own skin. *How?* Thomas thought. Then it dawned on him. *He's trying to find the lair.* If Fairbanks could claim he had found a pivotal piece of evidence like that, he could take credit for bringing it down. *Or even try to kill it himself, damn idiot.* But he slowly realised it was worse than that. Fairbanks wasn't alone and he must have a purpose for Catherine. He couldn't waste any more time.

Thomas ran through to his study where a large antique map of the area hung on the wall. His eyes darted over it as his mind raced. There were a number of tracks that led to the mountain, all from different directions. If he chose the wrong one, he could end up being miles out of position. Catherine's truck was capable of making most of the climbs, so that didn't help him narrow things down. He decided there was only one sure way, and that was to track the animal itself. That way he would at least know where the cat was, even if he couldn't find Catherine. He didn't know what kind of a threat Fairbanks was, but the cat was undoubtedly worse. And he knew that the longer he left it, the colder the trail would be. He could only hope he might also be able to track Catherine once he was on the mountain.

He hurried round the house grabbing supplies. He threw a large Maglite torch into his canvas pack. Not only did it have a powerful beam but it was also encased in steel, making it an adequate weapon if needed. He hesitated as his line of thought made him contemplate a problem that had bothered him for some time now. His rifle was in the car, but it would be almost useless at close-quarters. If he did encounter the cat there would only be time for one shot. He wouldn't be given the opportunity of a second by a cornered animal, and if he missed or failed to kill it, it wouldn't hesitate to try and even the score. He needed something that he could use to keep the cat off him and still kill it with, if he could.

He went back through to the study, where his eyes came to rest on the long wooden shaft of the zagaya spear. He walked over and carefully picked it up from its mountings. In the Xarayes marshes of Brazil's Mato Grosso, the tropical grasses and dense undergrowth grew so thick that local hunters had called it the green hell. The dense foliage made it almost impossible to effectively hunt something like a jaguar with a rifle. It was one of the reasons why there had only ever been, and only ever would be, a small number of professional tigreros. The learning curve was often a literal killer. If you made a mistake, you rarely had the luxury of living to learn by it.

The spear was the perfect weapon for close quarters. It was almost equal to Thomas in height, and it was finished with a double-edged blade that was separated from the rest of the shaft by a solid cross-bar a foot down from the spearhead. It was made for thrusting, not throwing. He knew that being close enough to deliver a blow from the spear wasn't an ideal situation with this cat, but he had been on enough hunts to know it was likely to happen.

He ran out of the house and threw the spear and bag into the Overfinch. He decided to head back to the clearing where Logan had been attacked. It was where he was most likely to find a fresh trail. If it had been wounded, as he had suspected from its gait and the blood in its spore, he knew it might be more inclined to return to safety and shelter to recover, especially after a successful hunt. He gripped the steering wheel, feeling slightly sick to think of it that way, struggling with the cold logic and his shifting emotions. He ignored the guilt he felt at the excitement of the hunt. He shivered as he thought of the terrible teeth in the child's drawing and then finally he let his anger cloud over everything else. It gave him vicious focus as he slammed the door shut and roared off towards the clearing.

~

Catherine backed away from the entrance of the cave. Her whole body trembled and her breath seemed as loud as thunder, even though she was trying her hardest to make no sound at all. Her heart pounded dangerously fast in her chest. She could see the glistening surface of a pool below and she dropped from the ledge she was on as she began to edge her way past. She pushed her back against the far wall of the cave and made her way along it. Her eyes were trained on the rays of sunlight that filtered through from the mouth of the cave. A large shadow fell across the wall of rock and then passed. The creature had entered the cave. She heard what sounded like a cough as she fumbled her way further back into the darkness. Her fingers became lost in a cold draft of air as she reached out from the rock into nothing. There was another opening, even bigger than the first one. Even in the poor light, she could tell it was vast. As she edged further in, she couldn't help the uncontrollable trembling that accompanied every step.

The creature paced back and forth at the entrance to the cave. The female human's scent lingered heavily in its nostrils and it was unable to stifle the snarl the hot, familiar odour enticed. It half-coughed, half-sneezed its displeasure. The scent of this live prey was quite different from the staid perfume of the corpses it had surrounded itself with and was therefore more used to. It made it more cautious and uneasy. It cocked its head as it picked up the sounds of movement from inside the cave and it hesitated no longer, roaring defiantly as it swept inside. It emitted a low and savage growl as its gaze pierced the darkness in search of its fleeing meal.

~

Thomas flew along the lanes at breakneck speed, gunning the engine through the bends and roaring along the straights with reckless determination. He turned the wheel hard, barely slowing as he skidded across the tarmac and thundered onto the track that would lead him to the clearing. He could feel the strain he was putting on the engine as it tried to pull the slipping tyres through the thickening mud. He pressed the accelerator down harder, hoping the power would be enough to pull him up the track. For a moment it seemed to be working, but then the car bucked and jolted as it came to a standstill, and Thomas realised how foolish he had been. He tried a few more times, but each spin of the wheels simply sank the car further into the mud. Thomas struck the steering wheel in frustration and then flung open the door.

He took the spear and unscrewed the ebony shaft, splitting it in two so that he could attach it to his bag, which he slung over his shoulder with his rifle. He hiked quickly to the top of the track until he found himself standing in the clearing once again. He sank to one knee and crouched there, closing his eyes as he took in the scents and sounds that came to him from the forest and further up the mountain. He could just hear the lapping waves of the loch, somewhere beyond the trees. He opened his eyes and studied the flattened grass around him. He could see where big, heavy boots had run from the trail to the loch, and where they had stopped abruptly close to the centre of the clearing. There were disturbances to the earth, made by an impact. In his mind he visualised the men being ambushed and being thrown to the ground. He swivelled his head in the direction the footprints seemed to face.

He knew by the blood stain that this was where Logan had fallen. He lay close to the ground, noticing a strange streak against the long grass. It was the scorch from a burn, perhaps from a hot barrel. Logan might have gotten a shot off after all. Not far from there, a few flecks of blood marked where he had found the spore of the cat leading back towards the loch. Thomas paced back and forth across the clearing, putting together what had happened piece by piece. It didn't take long, especially as he was able to fill in the gaps with what he already knew. Satisfied he had gleaned what he could from the clearing, he decided to head back down to the loch and pick up the trail at the tree where they had found Ryan and Arturo. He found new blood-laced prints as he went, confirming the cat had indeed been hurt.

The thought only made him hurry more though. Confronting an injured man-eater was the worst possible scenario he could imagine.

He didn't have any trouble picking up the trail from where the cat had back-tracked along the shore. Its exaggerated gait and the occasional drag mark from what it carried left behind a more obvious signature. Some of the prints had been destroyed by the frost and weather, but enough remained for Thomas to soon realise that it could only be Ethan's body that the cat was carrying, the only member of the team they hadn't been able to find. As he followed the trail past the tree where they'd found Ryan's stashed body, he realised the man with such hidden strength had been killed before Ethan and the others. Thomas decided to pull his rifle from his shoulder and slowed his pace, knowing he was finally on the track of the cat as it had retreated.

He followed the thinning trail back up through the forest. Where the heavy prints disappeared, the wake of the cat was still evident in broken brush. He scrambled over a rocky outcrop and came to a halt. The torn remains of Cody, the yellow coloured Carolina dog, were strewn over a ledge that led to a stream. He scoured the rocks for any sign of the cat, but they gave no indication which direction it had gone. He had no choice but to start out along any possible trail he could find. A little searching gave him three choices. After finding no further signs after a hundred yards along the first two, he raced back to the third. He paused, knowing this was his last option. He guessed the trail skirted the mountain and led further up its north-western side. If he lost his nerve now, it meant Catherine's death. The dice had rolled and there was simply nowhere else to go. There was no way to be sure, so he checked the other two trails again. They were as empty as before. All that was left was his gut instinct, and that told him to keep moving up.

Nearly thirty yards along, he let out a deep sigh and sank down onto one knee. The print was pristine and unmistakable. His gut had been right and he had re-found the trail. He followed it upwards again, checking his pace and orientation as he went. The forest was becoming less dense and the trail was thinning with the elevation. He couldn't afford to lose it again. The hike had eaten away at the daylight and his shadow now lay longer and more distorted against the ground. The sun was setting. He guessed he had another hour before dark at best.

He eventually broke from the tree-line altogether, the mountain still stretching out ahead of him. The soft green slope before him was naturally smooth thanks to the caressing blast of the Highland winds over thousands of years. Higher up, he could make out small clusters of boulders and the exposed rock face of a lofty crag. In the distance, the peak itself was hidden in swirls of mist that had begun to descend from the grey expanse of cloud overhead. A distant rumble of thunder echoed above him and along the corridor of peaks of Glen Cannich. He lingered no more and began to traverse the slope.

~

Catherine scrambled over the slippery rocks. She could just make out the overhanging stalactites that were sending a constant drip of mineral-laden liquid down onto the cave floor. The roar had echoed around the pitch interior, sending her into a panic as she had tried to run in the darkness. She knew the cat was inside, closing in on her even now as she caught her breath. She lowered herself from a large boulder and stepped onto the floor of the cave, once more hearing the crunch of something brittle beneath. Ivory coloured shapes gleamed in the half-light and littered the ground. She tried to smother her sound as she moved, but she couldn't help the sharp intake of breath she took as she recognised the shape of a human skull at her feet. It was missing its jaw, and as she sought out a path forward, she slowly realised she was stepping on the littered carcases of the cat's past victims, animal and human alike. She had run from the clutches of one would-be murderer straight into the lair of another, but this one had been a natural-born killer all along.

She felt the fear begin to overtake her, her body shuddering violently as cold sweat covered her skin. As she stepped forward, she imagined the eyes of the cat upon her, watching her in the dark. She stumbled, panicked by the thought of joining the collection of bones at her feet, never to be found. It was then that she noticed a thin ray of light, piercing the cave from a small opening above. She could make out small pieces of rotten wood jutting out from the hole and heard the unmistakable sound of water dripping down from it. She rushed forward, peering up to glimpse the spec of sun as its failing rays melted over her. *A mineshaft* she realised, her excitement breaking through her fear and giving her focus again. The area had once been a rich source of iron and copper ore, and she could see this was a test hole, barely a yard across. The company apparently had better luck elsewhere, as the rest of the cave looked natural enough.

She explored the opening above her with her fingers, finally finding handholds on both sides she was happy with. She began to haul herself upwards, slipping back down on her first attempt. She had been so relieved to find the mineshaft that she had almost forgotten she wasn't alone in the cave. As she sensed the movement behind her and heard the echo of exhaled breath, she couldn't stifle the scream that escaped her throat. She threw herself upwards, her legs kicking violently as they dangled momentarily in the void below. Her arms frantically scrabbled at the column walls as she fought against the leaden feeling in them, telling her to give up and fall back. She tore her nails and fingertips as she bored upwards, and it was that pain she felt, not the reaching claws that cut like daggers through her jeans and sliced even more easily through the soft flesh of her calf muscle. She slipped on her own blood and her head slammed against the rock wall.

Wedged in the hole, barely able to move, she braced herself against the cold granite, only now all too aware of the pain. She looked down. Something gleamed in the darkness below. A pair of bright, green eyes stared up at her and drew nearer. A gnarled muzzle was thrust up towards her and a menacing growl reverberated into the stone column. She screamed as its pink tongue parted its lips and whipped over the long curved fangs waiting for her. Then it vanished from sight. She screamed again as a searching paw and unsheathed claws reached up for her, but she fought desperately upwards, just managing to pull herself out of the cat's reach. She took deep breaths, fighting the shock that was now beginning to creep over her. She knew she was losing blood too quickly and was already beginning to feel faint and weak. She glanced upwards again at the dying light and knew in an instant she didn't have the strength to make it. The shaft rose at least another sixty feet she guessed. She would either fall and be killed by the cat below, or slowly drift into unconsciousness as she bled to death in the darkness of the mineshaft. She looked up again and realised this was the last sunlight she would see. She began to weep.

~

As Thomas neared the top of a scree slope he was scrambling up, he spotted Catherine's truck. He pulled himself clear, taking a moment to catch his breath before he stumbled forward. He took in the bullet peppered windscreen and noticed the bashed and dented bonnet as he carefully edged round the vehicle, bringing his rifle up as he went. A few feet from the car he saw Fairbanks mauled body lying in the grass. He approached carefully, kicking over the pistol that lay a few inches from Fairbanks' outstretched hand. Thomas began to grasp just how far Fairbanks was prepared to go and the ghoulish nature of what he had hoped to achieve. *You're lucky the cat got to you first* Thomas thought. He felt nothing as he glanced over the corpse, noting the slashes that had ripped through the man's back and where the flesh had been stripped from one leg. He turned away, a slight tremor building in his right hand as he tried to control the swells of anger and fear that threatened to overtake him.

He had no difficulty following the trail of both Catherine

and the cat. He half ran, half stumbled up the slope as his desperation momentarily overwhelmed him. The wind was picking up now, stinging his face like lashes from an unseen whip. A bolt of lightning streaked across the sky above, touching the rod on a weather station closer to the peak. The resultant thunder brought him to his senses as it boomed and crackled over the rocky mountainside. He gasped, taking deep breaths to steady himself. His eyes had settled on a dark opening between two saplings. A second bolt of lightning flashed overhead, revealing it to be a cave as he had suspected. Then, almost lost in the roll of thunder, he thought he heard a scream. He bolted forward, hurling himself into the dark opening.

He stopped as soon as he was inside, quickly drawing the Maglite from his bag. He flicked on the torch and allowed its beam to slowly sweep over the cave's interior ahead of him. He saw the pool and the still-wet pugmarks on the stone floor. He let the beam wander further and spotted the ledge that led to a second, deeper opening. As the light shone back onto the wall nearest to him, he stopped. It was covered in what looked like drawings. He peered closer, beginning to recognise the depicted animals such as elk and bison. They were drawn beautifully in charcoal outline and coloured with red chalk and clay. His eyes rose to the highest part of the scene, where a huge and maneless lion stood at the entrance to a cave. As he stood back from the wall he realised that they weren't individual pictures, but one large painting.

The lion in the picture surveyed the herds of animals below him, even watching the band of hunters that were stalking the bison in the far right of the panel. It held the highest position, seemingly commanding the most respect. It was depicted almost god-like in its dominance of its domain. It could only represent a cave lion, an ancient species almost identical to its modern namesake, despite being larger and heavier set. It was assumed to have had no mane, based on studies of early cave paintings found in France. The same seemed to be here, where clearly a lion had once lorded over this landscape too.

Thomas knew the rifle would be useless in the poor light. He rested it against the wall of the cave and put down his pack, pulling out the two sections of the zagaya spear. As he put it together, his eyes never left the darkness of the second opening at the back of the cave. He took a final breath to steady himself and lowered himself from the ledge into the cavern beyond, holding the spear out in front of him. As he did so, a stone loosened by the touch of his boot tumbled nosily over the edge and dropped to the floor below, landing amongst what he recognised as a sheep's rib cage. A monstrous shape moved in the darkness and rippled to the floor. He saw the flash of a pair of green eyes in the revealing light that seeped from the shaft. He heard a murmured whisper above him and had to fight every urge he felt to rush forward. His heart told him it was Catherine. The penetrating and brutally guttural growl that followed was from something else.

The creature spun on its heels has the man entered the cave behind it. It recognised the scent instantly. It had watched this man from the trees when it had killed the female human after stalking the younglings. It had abandoned its kills on his approach. It had found him again in the snow, but been unable to reach him. His taint had even been at the place on the edge of the forest where a dog had given its ambush away. It would tolerate his invasions no longer, and it snarled angrily, shaking its head and opening its jaws wide to expose its deadly fangs.

Thomas froze at the sound of the growl. It felt like the sound had moved right through him. The darkness ahead of him seemed to encroach and take form. He shuddered fearfully as it stepped closer. The cat was monstrous. It dwarfed even the liger he had compared it to. A mere twenty yards separated him from the hulking, bear-like form of the cat spitting angry snarls at him. He realised there could have been no contemplating the fight he was about to take on. No cat he had ever faced compared in size or ferocity to what was edging towards him through the darkness.

Thomas gripped the spear firmly in his right hand and held it out in front of him, poised at waist height and braced in position under his arm. He let his left arm float out to the side in order to balance. The great cat and the man measured each other cautiously, the creature pacing back and forth and uttering chilling snarls to vent its anger. Every one of Thomas's senses were locked onto the cat as he began to edge closer, beads of sweat forming on his brow. He knew he had to provoke the cat into a charge.

The creature searched for an opening, its eyes fixed on the man in a constant gaze that sought the slightest opportunity. It came as Catherine slipped inside the shaft, letting out an involuntary scream. Thomas only took his eyes off the cat for a second, as he glanced up at the hole towards the noise that confirmed to him that Catherine was still alive, but it was all that the creature needed. It launched itself at Thomas with a terrible roar. The thunderous noise rippled through the cave and out into the open. The tumultuous echo travelled miles through the glen, throwing startled birds into flight and stampeding deer herds down the mountainside.

Thomas knew he was off balance, but he was quick enough to pivot round, just landing a glancing blow to the cat's neck with one side of the spearhead. A paw the size of a dinner plate reached out and swatted him to the ground, but he rolled and sprang upwards immediately, finding his feet quickly enough to see the monster shaking its head in pain. The tremor of agony that worked its way down his left arm from his shoulder took him by surprise. He felt a flash of dizziness as his fingers quickly found the hot sticky liquid on his skin. Both he and the cat were now bleeding freely from wounds to their necks. It was now just a question which of them had the strength to finish the fight. A renewed malice seemed to glow in the eyes of the cat, and Thomas didn't care for his odds as they began to circle one another again.

Thomas didn't break his gaze with the cat as he slowly raised his arm, ready to throw the heavy Maglite torch. Its beam fell across the creature's face, giving Thomas an up close glimpse of his would be assassin. The curved fangs were larger than he'd imagined, and unmistakable. There was nothing else to call it. The sabre-tooth wrinkled its nose into a threatening snarl at the touch of the unwelcome beam of light. The irises of its shot-glass sized eyes contracted as the beam passed across them. Thomas was frozen with awe and fear at the sight of the animal rippling with fury in front of him. Experts had always predicted that the legendary teeth of the sabres were fragile and rarely used in combat. He decided to put the theory to the test, throwing the heavy metal torch with all his might towards the cat's open maw.

As if responding to his challenge, the cat snapped its jaws shut over the torch, splintering the metal casing and spitting the strange tasting shards back out onto the ground. Thomas reeled back in horror. He knew the pressure in the jaws and the strength of the teeth had been something left unrecorded by the fossil record, but this was something new. Its very size suggested it was a hybrid like he had predicted, but somehow its shape and movement seemed natural and familiar.

The two combatants began to circle each other again. Thomas raised the tip of the spear slightly in warning, letting the cat know its sting was still within reach. The cat replied with a guttural growl. Thomas felt the blood begin to soak into the collar of his shirt, the smell drifting up from directly below his nostrils. His stamina began to ebb away as steadily as the stream of blood flowed from the gash to his neck. Thomas repositioned the spear, its tip pointing upwards and the shaft pointing down towards the ground at an angle. His strength wasn't going to last, he had to force the cat to charge now. He let the spearhead drop again slightly, as if letting his guard slip.

Without warning the great cat exploded at Thomas with a terrible roar, its outstretched claws looming over him as if to take him in a final and terrible embrace. The charge was over so short a distance that he almost didn't have time to raise the spearhead, angling it up towards the chest of the beast. With the last of his draining strength he pushed upwards, bracing his foot against the shaft as it met the back wall of the cavern. He heard the penetrating pop as the spearhead was thrust through the cat's chest by its own falling weight, then he was engulfed and smashed against the stone floor beneath. The air was crushed from his lungs and he heard a crack from his side that told him of his broken ribs.

The cat rolled, screaming with pain. Unable to withstand the monstrous pressures being put upon it, the shaft of the spear gave in and snapped as the cat writhed in agony and rolled again onto its back. Thomas watched in horror as the creature tried to right itself. He didn't wait to see if it would. He threw himself forward, picking up the largest rock his strength allowed and brought it down with a hammer blow onto the broken end of the shaft. He gasped as he felt the spearhead plunge further into the creature's chest. For a moment, both their eyes met and in them Thomas saw a flame of venomous fury which suddenly flickered and became more distant, as a final shudder rippled through the monstrous body. In that moment he saw the pure, intelligent and sentient soul of the creature. Then the gleam in the giant green iris he stared into faded and disappeared altogether, as its eyelids rolled shut in acceptance of death. Thomas didn't know why he wept so sorrowfully as he leant against the broken shaft of the spear, or how long he knelt there against the chest of the great cat. He knew nothing more than that it was dead and he was alive.

Thomas lowered his hands to the soft pelt of the animal, his fingers exploring the soft bristles in deluded silence. It was like running his hands across thick velvet, and his soft touch left a wake in the dense black fur. Along its back and on its chest, the animal was jet black in colour, but down towards its stomach he could now see the deep rosette markings underneath. The obsidian coloured claws matched the fur and seemed in sharp contrast to the pale nine inch fangs that protruded from either side of its jaw. The paws were so thick and heavy that Thomas couldn't lift them. As he took in the heavyset, muscle laden form of the creature, he knew why the old poacher had thought it was a bear. The elegant, feline tail that stretched six feet behind the body seemed almost out of place on the animal.

As he was freed momentarily from the grip of shock and blood loss, he stood up and staggered towards the opening above where he had heard Catherine's whimper. He looked up into the light, his eyes meeting hers as she shivered, still wedged in the narrow column and too scared to move. He managed a weak smile as he reached up for her, mildly amused that with the fading light above her, she seemed to be descending in an angelic haze. She lowered herself carefully, but still almost fell into his waiting arms.

They stumbled their way out of the cave, Thomas eventually losing the last of his strength as they tried to scramble back down the rocks. Catherine took out his mobile phone from the bag and dialled the number for the village hall. On her third attempt, she made a crackled connection. She kept the line open, waiting for them to trace the location, eventually smiling as she heard the Major-General confirm a helicopter was on its way. Thomas lay down, his eyes barely open as Catherine cradled his head in her lap. His hands were trembling, and now outside in the light she could see how deep the slashes to the back of his neck and left shoulder were. She knew he always had a first aid kit with him and she began to hunt around inside his pack. She tore off the sleeve of his jacket, twisting it into a rope and using it to plug the wounds as best she could. She opened the first aid kit and took out the dressings and antiseptic.

"How bad is it, doc?" Thomas whispered with a croak.

"Terrible. Unfortunately your face is perfectly intact," she smiled.

She tried to dress his wounds and her own, but she soon felt her own strength sapping. She lay down beside him and held him close. By the time she heard the helicopter sweep over the mountain towards them, she could barely still stroke Thomas's hair with her fingers. The rhythmical thump of the rotors made him open his eyes again and she smiled and leaned in close.

"Okay, I do believe it's a sabre-tooth," she whispered with a last smile, before they both drifted into unconsciousness.

CHAPTER TWENTY-EIGHT

Thomas glanced at the calendar on the wall. The picture of the Border collie pup poking its head out of a very pink basket of flowers was a definite sign that the house was no longer just his. He stared at the date. It was just four days off from being a whole year since he had confronted and killed the giant cat inside its mountain lair. Even now, after all the publicity and the research that had begun with the discovery of a sabre-tooth ancestor in Britain, he had no intention of being in Scotland on the anniversary of his own near death. In his pocket were two British Airways tickets for business class passage to Rome. No first class was available on such short flights these days, but he had remedied that by reserving one of the three Via Veneto suites at the Westin Excelsior. Nervously, he felt the other thing inside his pocket, still wrapped in its exquisite little blue bag from Tiffany's. *If you're going to ask, there are worse places than Rome* he reminded himself. It was a somewhat expensive risk to take, but he figured it would be bad manners for her to say no by the time he surprised her with the question, after a few days of well-planned romance.

He took the two large leather bags out to the car and loaded them into the back. The sun was just beginning to set behind the mountain. He let out a deep sigh. Scotland was once again beautiful to him. He had spent the last few weeks lecturing at various zoology departments in universities up and down the country. *Panthera onca Rex*, the self-fashioned, half-joking name of 'jaguar king' he had given the creature was proving a big hit. When it had been removed from the cave, it had weighed in at 1,587 lbs. Studies had suggested its insatiable killing spree had been brought on by its formidable metabolism due to its size, and in the end both his theories regarding the origin of the animal had been right. Various genetic traits associated with gigantism had been identified in the cat as a result of its mixed ancestry. But undoubtedly, the cat was also in essence a sabre-tooth.

The conical and serrated teeth were attributed to just one ancient species, *Xenosmilus hodsonae*. It had once roamed northern Asia and Russia, being one of the first species to cross the land bridge that allowed it to populate the Americas, and now it seemed it had once spread west too. Like all sabre-tooth cats, it had long been suspected that the fearsome teeth were actually extraordinarily fragile, often breaking in fights with other cats, or if used directly to attack prey. But from its jaguar mother, the creature had gained her much newer, strengthened teeth, helping it become the incredible and unique predator that had ravaged Glen Cannich. The number of other genotypes that had been identified in the cat's DNA suggested it wasn't a first generation animal, although that could never be proved without finding a living, breathing example. To all who gazed upon the ferocious animal, now posed and on display at the Natural History Museum in London, it was clear that somewhere in its ancestry, the long-dormant sabre-tooth had been part of the creature's unique family make-up.

Thomas had never been able to bring himself to visit the museum since, despite it being one of his favourite places in the entire world. He was still scared of it, but it was more than that, he respected the animal. He knew he wouldn't be able to stand in front of the exhibit whilst the smallest of children passed by, probably making faces at the man-eater. It deserved a greater respect than it would ever gain. Thomas had secretly vowed to never add to its humiliation, always stressing in his lectures the raw power, strength and majesty of the animal. He always finished with a slide of the god-like depiction of the lion in the cave painting.

Shortly after the death of the creature, the nation had become fixated with big cat sightings, and there had been a massive call to sweep the countryside for what the public had come to know as mystery big cats. A number of animals had been found and either captured or killed. Most had been the widely reported pumas and black leopards, but other species such as caracals and jaguars had also appeared. Customs and excise authorities strictly enforced new animal control legislation to stop a boom in underground imports of exotic pets in the wake of the discoveries, but as Thomas and most of the general public were beginning to suspect, the cats were already at large and probably had been for far longer than anyone had ever known.

~

How many were really out there was something Hugh Chisholm pondered as he stood in front of the holding cage within the converted barn. As soon as he had realised that his female puma Doris was pregnant, he had removed all other staff from her care and transferred them across to the main building. The four cubs were now nearly nine months old, and were already larger than their mother. He had become a regular visitor to them recently, noticing their restless behaviour in the close confines of the holding pen.

He had been preparing to unveil the cubs to the public, but he didn't want to risk it if they were sick or somehow subject to disease. He knew that a deficient immune system was a common legacy in crossbreeds, as were blood infections passed from one generation to another.

The four cubs were enormous. There were three females and a single male, who was jet black just like his father. He had named him Thor in respect to his size and strength. The three females were all different in colour too. Ellen was a dark, rusty red. Tama was a rich, golden caramel, and Powder was pale silver and his favourite of the four. She had soft blue eyes and her fur was thick and bushy compared to the others. On her underbelly were the soft rosette markings she had inherited from the sabre-tooth cross, and they were a contrasting dappled dark-grey against her silver hair. All of the cubs had the formidable teeth that made their parentage so obvious.

Hugh watched with pride as Doris rolled onto her back as the big male approached her. She batted a playful paw at her son, catching him off guard. He roared his displeasure, jumping on her instantly and sinking his fangs into her leg. Hugh jumped forward, striking the bars with an iron rod in an attempt to distract the male. Thor's size and strength meant that he could possibly kill Doris even in play. Hugh panicked, unwilling to let the mother of the cubs die. She was an essential part of the merchandise he had devised and put into production. He stepped forward, unlocking the door to the cage and stepping inside, brandishing the rod. In his mind, the monstrous cats were still cubs. He didn't realise the danger until it was far too late.

Thor ripped round to face Hugh, roaring angrily at the

intrusion into his cage. But the attack didn't come from him. Ellen flew at him in fear and sank her teeth through his shoulder. Hugh screamed in agony as he was knocked to the ground. Powder sprung forwards and took his flailing arm in her jaws. She bit down through the elbow joint, and tore it free from his body before scuttling to a corner of the cage to eat her prize away from the others. Thor approached confidently now, shaking his head as he opened his jaws wide and brought his fangs down into Hugh's skull with shattering force. The family began to feed on their first natural kill, the wounded mother joining them with submissive mewing.

The four cubs cautiously took their first steps into the world outside their cage through its open door. From the entrance at the back of the building, the mountain called to them. Thor thundered out without a look back, covering the ground with long, agile bounds. Powder was next, only looking back for a brief moment when Doris called to her anxiously. Ellen and Tama, who resembled each other the closest both stayed in the barn. It was only when a keeper started walking towards the building, shouting for Hugh that they scampered off after their siblings. The keeper opened the door to find Hugh's mauled remains and the wounded Doris beside his corpse. He locked her back in her cage and returned moments later with a shotgun. As far as he could see, it was Doris who had killed and devoured Hugh. He knew nothing of the cubs as he raised the gun and took careful aim. He braced the weapon against his shoulder and pulled the trigger.

~

Kelly Keelson ran through the video again. Her new source at DEFRA, a man called Pettigrew, had finally come through for her. On the anniversary of the death of the Scottish sabre, she would be able to give the world the only known footage of the animal in all its terrifying glory whilst it had been alive. She had also prepared a glowing tribute to Danny Reeves, the cameraman whose last act had been to capture the images of his killer. She finished her review and clicked on "send", knowing her editor was going to be very pleased.

~

Thomas smiled as he looked over at Catherine. He was still fairly certain she had no idea they were going on anything more than a romantic break, one they had both earned and the first they had been able to take. She was so beautiful and he knew in his heart he had wanted to be with her since the day he'd met her. As he stared into her green eyes and caught her mischievous smile, he couldn't help be reminded for a moment of the cat he'd faced and killed. He let out a deep, satisfied sigh as he looked out of the plane's window. As the mountains and forests slipped further and further away beneath them, he was blissfully unaware that as he left Scotland and his memories behind him, a sabre-tooth roared once more in the green and pleasant land.

EPILOGUE

The four cubs didn't stay together long. Thor would not tolerate the company of his sisters and they separated soon after they escaped from Palaeo Park. Only Ellen and Tama had affectionately rubbed heads before they turned tail and disappeared into the shadows in opposite directions. They had the curiosity of any young animal, and had wandered far from each other before they began to miss the familiar surroundings of the cage or the warmth of their mother and siblings.

Ellen was the first to be discovered. Three months after the escape, a farmer whose sheep she had begun to kill had shot her. She was suffering from malnutrition and was close to starvation. She had never acquired the skills of stalking and hunting prey, her meek and timid character denying her natural instinct. She had turned to livestock out of desperation, having always kept her distance and shunning the farms and villages of people before.

Thor's fate was sealed when he scared a family on a camping trip. His green eyes had loomed out of the darkness at them as they sat round a campfire. He had stalked into the camp after and sniffed at the tents, alerting them to his presence. In the wake of a hunt organised by DEFRA agents, he was hit and killed by a train two days later. He had defiantly charged the locomotive as it had bore down on him. DEFRA never released details of his killing and let his identity remain a secret, even from Thomas and Catherine, who were still officially running investigations into big cat activity in the UK.

At the bequest of a black-market trader, Tama was tracked and captured alive by a hired specialist who smuggled her out of the country to the United States. The undisclosed bidder for her recognised the majesty of her ancestry, and waited for his opportunity to unleash her upon the world.

Powder wandered far from Glen Cannich, forever called northwards by instinct and curiosity. She finally found herself standing on a wind-beaten cliff face, jagged rocks below her and black storm clouds above. Her keen eyesight could make out the islands further out to sea. She stood statue-like, braced against the wind as the waves continued to thrash and thunder against the rocky shore. She felt the ocean spray against her fur and smelt the salty air deep in her nostrils. As a bolt of lightning flashed across the sky, she roared with triumph as she leapt from the cliff, hitting the water with an enormous crash and an explosion of surf. Her head bobbed in the froth as she began to swim, her huge paws acting as paddles as she headed into deeper water.

The End

THOMAS WALKER

WILL RETURN

IN

THE DAUGHTERS OF THE DARKNESS

ABOUT THE AUTHOR

Luke Phillips has always been a keen student of the natural world. During his studies of zoology at Liverpool John Moores University, he was surprised to find the Loch Ness Monster referenced in the first lecture he attended. But even before then, having spent time on the shores of that famous Scottish landmark as a young boy, and with a keen imagination fuelled by horror films glimpsed through his childhood fingers, his interest in myths and monsters was evident from an early age.

He lives in the west Kent town of Sevenoaks in the UK. Despite having always been encouraged to write by teachers and readers alike, Shadow Beast is his first novel.